AFTE... DEATH...

"What happens when we die? The answers come in the form of 34 stories that explore diverse notions . . . Though the majority of the pieces come from the darker side of the genre, a solid minority are playful, clever, or full of wonder. This strong and well-themed anthology is sure to make readers contemplative even while it creates nightmares."
—**Publishers Weekly**

"*AFTER DEATH* raises the eerie voices of many of today's top horror writers in a ghostly chorus of wonder, magic, and tragedy. Highly recommended."
—**Jonathan Maberry**, New York Times *bestselling author of* Extinction Machine *and* Fire & Ash

"I don't want to die, and the stories in *AFTER DEATH* offer numerous examples why. This terrifying collection presents stories that are unsettling, disturbing, frightening, heart-breaking and, in the end, guaranteed to chill your bones and make your blood run cold."
—**Rick Hautala**, *Author of* Indian Summer *and* Chills

"With stellar contributions by some of speculative fiction's most talented writers, *AFTER DEATH* offers a deliriously diverse array of imaginative hereafters. By turns chilling, poignant, funny, hallucinatory, and awe-inspiring, these stories fascinate in a manner worthy of the ultimate mystery they explore."
—**Stephen Woodworth**, *author of the* New York Times *Bestsellers* Through Violet Eyes *and* With Red Hands

AFTER DEATH...

EDITED BY ERIC J. GUIGNARD
ILLUSTRATED BY AUDRA PHILLIPS

dark moon

LARGO, FLORIDA

DARK MOON BOOKS
an imprint of Stony Meadow Publishing
Largo, Florida

www.StonyMeadowPublishing.com
www.DarkMoonBooks.com

After Death . . .
Copyright © Eric J. Guignard 2012-2013

Editing by Eric J. Guignard
Cover design by Eric J. Guignard
www.ericjguignard.com
E-mail: eric.guignard@gmail.com

Cover art by Kevin Scott Sutay
www.halonacc.deviantart.com

Interior illustrations by Audra Phillips
www.audraphillips.com

First edition published in April, 2013
Library of Congress Control Number: 2013930612
ISBN-13: 978-0-9885569-2-8
ISBN-10: 0-9885569-2-8

Made in the United States of America

dark moon

This anthology is dedicated to all
who wonder at the mysteries of the great beyond
and who, perhaps, may find a bit of illumination
or fascination within these pages.

And, of course, this is for my beautiful wife, Jeannette,
and extraordinary son, Julian.

May we all live forever, in this world and beyond.

CONTENTS

Introduction	Eric J. Guignard	ix
Someone to Remember	Andrew S. Williams	1
Boy, 7	Alvaro Rodriguez	10
Sea of Trees	Edward M. Erdelac	14
The Last Moments Before Bed	Steve Rasnic Tem	27
The Resurrection Policy	Lisa Morton	33
High Places	John M. Floyd	44
Circling the Stones at Fulcrum's Low	Kelda Crich	49
I Will Remain	David Steffen	54
Tree of Life	Aaron J. French	64
The Reckless Alternative	Sanford Allen & Josh Rountree	70
The Thousandth Hell	Brad C. Hodson	84
Mall Rats	James S. Dorr	94
Afterword	Ray Cluley	102
Like a Bat out of Hell	Jonathan Shipley	108
The Overlander	Jacob Edwards	121
Forever	John Palisano	125
My Father Knew Douglas MacArthur	Bentley Little	130
Robot Heaven	Jamie Lackey	140
Beyond the Veil	Robert B. Marcus, Jr.	145
Prisoner of Peace	David Tallerman	153
A Feast of Meat and Mead	Christine Morgan	160
Be Quiet At The Back	William Meikle	175
Cages	Peter Giglio	184
Hammerhead	Simon Clark	191
Marvel at the Face of Forever	Kelly Dunn	200
The Unfinished Lunch	Trevor Denyer	216
I Was The Walrus	Steve Cameron	223
The Devil's Backbone	Larry Hodges	231
The Death of E. Coli	Benjamin Kane Ethridge	247
Final Testament of a Weapons Engineer	Emily C. Skaftun	256
Acclimation Package	Joe McKinney	263
Hellevator	Josh Strnad	282
In and Out the Window	Allan Izen	287
With Max Barry in the Nearer Precincts	John Langan	295

INTRODUCTION

ERIC J. GUIGNARD

Death.

Who has not considered their own mortality and wondered at what awaits, once our frail human shell expires? What occurs after the heart stops beating, after the last breath is drawn, after life as we know it terminates?

Humans have asked this grand existential question ever since we comprehended life is finite. In fact, I would argue there is no greater mystery than that which occurs after we die. What exactly *is* the destination of our journey?

Essentially, we can start by agreeing there are two possibilities: In the broadest sense of definition, either death is final or it's not. If it's final, then life is ultimately for nothing, each of us a grain of salt washed away into the ocean of nothingness. If it's not final . . . well, pull up a seat. It's going to be a long night.

Does our spirit remain on Earth while the mortal body rots? Do remnants of our soul transcend to a celestial Heaven or sink to Hell's torment? Are we offered choices in an individualized afterlife? Can we die again in the hereafter? Are we given the opportunity to reincarnate and perpetually maintain the life cycle? Can we find ways to cheat death and maintain a semblance of living even after the mortician declares 'D.O.A.'? Is life merely a cosmic joke, or is it an experiment for something greater?

Throughout the tomes of history, countless philosophies offering countless solutions have been suggested, though most are riddled with outlooks entirely contradictory to each other. This poses a baffling dilemma: The desire to know resides in us all but, simply put, *nobody has the answers*. After awhile, it becomes mere intellectual exercise. Consider the small wrapped package under your Christmas tree. You can look at, shake it, take a guess, and convince yourself you know what's inside. But you can't really be certain until that day arrives to open the package and behold its mysteries.

For example, the Christian faith believes Jesus Christ rose from the dead, proving that the soul is not destroyed after death. Further, that soul will be judged by God according to conduct while alive and blessed or punished accordingly. Over two billion people accept this core doctrine. However, the Buddhist faith states there is no supreme ruler. A being's essence will be born over and over through the process of reincarnation until, through self-enlightenment, all desires are released and the attainment of *nirvana*, or freedom from suffering, is attained. Though not quite as numerically prevalent, Buddhism still counts an impressive half billion followers.

And so we have two of the largest and most fervently believed religions in the world that are completely and diametrically opposed as to what occurs after death. Personal faith aside, trying to logically prove one is "right" and the other "wrong" is a troublesome argument.

And those are just two systems of belief. It's estimated there have been over 75,000 additional religions communicated throughout the history of the world that include unique opinions of continuance after death. Or, look at it another way: Over 102 billion people have lived on Earth. Like personalities, everyone's idea of god or religion is different. What you and I may consider aberrant is the social norm for someone else.

Most of us are familiar with certain alternative views of after-death possibilities. For instance, as children we learned the ancient Greeks believed that those traveling to Hades must be ferried across the river Styx by Charon at the cost of a coin. But were you aware that the Jivaro Indians shrink the heads of their enemies so that the souls are trapped and cannot escape to take revenge? The Karni Mata Temple in India is overrun with tens of thousands of rats, each believed to be the reincarnation of a dead human who is waiting to be reborn into a higher life form. Some forms of orthodox Christianity believe bodies which defy normal decomposition are symbols of divinity. The Yaohnanen tribe in Vanuatu swears Prince Philip, consort to Queen Elizabeth II, to be a god and worships him accordingly. Some traditional denominations of Judaism transfer their sins into a chicken and then slaughter it for the pre-Yom Kippur feast. Mormonism allows the dead to be baptized through the proxy of living members, regardless of the deceased's own belief. Shamanism allows practitioners to astral project, control the weather, and gain control over spirits. The Aghori, a breakaway sect of Hinduism, believes that to abandon *anything* is sacrilege and thus eat the corpse of the deceased.

Again, what this all means is (and not to put too fine a point on it) what occurs after we leave this mortal form will never be known with absolute certainty until our time comes. Until then, it's okay for each person to reach their own conclusion—formulate their own belief—according to science, religion, or perhaps dark, personal experimentation.

The reason I'm playing up this rumination is because most of us simply believe in whatever religion and great-beyond was taught us by our parents. We question little our inherited beliefs. For most, once a matter of faith is formulated, it becomes an unshakable matter. Personally, I'm one of these. I'm a religious man, but I also realize there is no certainty in what awaits. So I defer again to the theme of this message: *Just keep an open mind.*

Which leads us to the enclosed thirty-four authors.

The point of this anthology is not to deliver affirmations, but to offer suggestions. Anything *is* possible when the mysteries of the afterlife are concerned, and have I got a gold-standard collection of speculations to share with you. Do other life forms besides humans experience an after-death phenomenon? Can curses transcend the life-death boundary? Are there different hereafters to accommodate multiple religions? Do we all share a common singularity?

Included within this book are answers to these queries alongside tales and suppositions relating from traditional ghosts to the afterlife of e-coli. Explore the afterworld of an Australian cowboy. Discover what the "white light" really means to the recently departed. Consider the impact of modern, or future, technology on the dead. Follow the karmic path of reincarnation. Travel from the cruelest levels of Hell's torments to the celestial realms of eternal paradise.

These authors wonder, like you and I, what ultimately awaits after we die. Whether their words seem brilliant, absurd, cruel, or impossible, just remember that anything is possible.

Remember, too, we'll all learn the truth soon enough.

—Eric J. Guignard
Chino Hills, California
December 7, 2012
Memento Mori

SOMEONE TO REMEMBER

ANDREW S. WILLIAMS

Though not the only, Andrew S. Williams was the first author I accepted into this book who also contributed to my first anthology, Dark Tales of Lost Civilizations. *As then, I read his newest story and knew immediately he had gifted me a brilliant gem.* Someone to Remember *explores one of the truest fears I can imagine after death: beyond merely the loss of loved ones is the loss of ever having* known *those loved ones. A haunting emptiness, if any form of consciousness exists at all, in the back of your thoughts wondering at what is missing, what once* was. *Or are we completely stripped down—purged—on our way to the lands beyond death? If there is any way to retain the memory of what it is that we lived for, this author may have found it . . .*

Every day Charon asks me, in that thick accent of his, if I'm going to board the ferry. And today, like every day, I watch the hordes of people stream soundlessly onto the boat, and I tell him, "No, my friend. Not today."

"Still waiting, then," he says. "For your girl."

I smile. "Of course."

The Ferryman leans against the pier and takes a long drag on his cigarette. It glows red, lighting up the lines of his face. Under his curly black bangs lie a pair of sharp blue eyes that look out of place on his grizzled visage. "One day everyone boards the boat," he says. "It'll be easier if you get it over with. What's the point in staying here and pining?"

I look up at him. I'm a tall man, but Charon towers over me by a head. "How many times have you asked me that now?"

He shrugs. "Can't rightly say. I ain't one to keep track of the days."

When the ferry is full, a whistle blows a long, mournful note and the gates on the boat swing shut. There's still plenty of folks waiting to board, but they'll have to wait for the next run. It's an injustice they suffer without complaint.

Charon drops the cigarette, and stubs it out under the heel of his boot. "Days, weeks, years—don't mean nothing to me. Just gotta make sure the ferry leaves on time." He turns to leave.

"Do you ever miss the rowboat?" I ask him.

"What?"

"The rowboat." I gesture to the mighty gray ferry, sitting tall in the black waters of the Lethe. "It's true, isn't it? That you used to row the dead across the river?"

The Ferryman chuckles. "Aye, it's true. And hells no, I don't miss it. Diesel power is the best thing to come to the underworld since fire." Then he cocks his head at me. "Tell you what. You ever decide to take the ride, you won't have to stand with the horde. I'll let you up in the wheelhouse." He turns away. "It's the only thing I miss from the rowboat days."

"What's that?" I ask.

I watch his broad back as he walks toward the boat. "Company."

I watch as the Ferry disappears into the gloom. It reminds me a lot of the boats I used to pilot when I was alive—perhaps that's why I've befriended Charon. He'd blend right in with the folks I used to work with. What would the Ferryman of the Dead say if he knew I thought of him as a tangible link to the living? There are so few things here that remind me of life, I'll take what I can.

Around me mill the ranks of the dead, driven to the water's edge by an innate desire to cross the river. I can feel it, too, the yearning to cross to the far side, to continue the journey, to escape this strange place that is little more than a way-station along the path of souls. People are not meant to stay on this side of the bank. It's a barren place, wreathed in a gray eternal twilight, so dim that I can't even see a hint of the far bank. Or perhaps the river is just that wide.

Most of the dead stand waiting for the ferry's return. Others wander about, confused. There are men and women, old and young. None of them speak. I wander through the crowd, as I always do, looking for a familiar face—a face with a pert nose and green eyes, framed by long auburn hair. Would she have aged by now? Would her hair be speckled with gray, would lines crease her perfect cheeks? I don't know. Charon is not the only one who cannot track the years in this place. But I will recognize her when I see her.

Someone grips my arm, and I stumble. I turn and stare into the wild eyes of a young man, a man who was perhaps a few years younger than me when he died. "Where are we?" he asks me, shouting, his voice echoing loud in the oppressive silence of this place. "Why won't anybody speak to me?"

I've already stumbled and stared at him; it's too late to pretend I'm just one of the crowd. I yank my arm away. "Quiet down, you idiot. You want to get thrown into the river?"

His eyes widen. "You talk! You understand me! Please," his grip tightens, "tell me what's going on!"

I grimace and look around. Along the path, not far away, is a small rundown building, and in the window I see the orange of a flickering neon sign: *OPEN*. Lethe's tavern is always open.

"I was walking with my daughter," the man says, "when a car jumped the sidewalk, and next thing I know I'm here! Where is she? Where am I?" Folks are glancing this way now—we need to get away from the riverbank. "Please," he grasps at me, his voice growing even shriller. "I just want to go home!"

I ball up a fist and punch him in the face, and he falls to the ground. I brush off and straighten my tattered shirt, then kneel next to the man.

"You talk here," I tell him, "you'll draw attention. Do it enough and you'll find yourself thrown into the river. Keep screaming at me, I'll throw you in myself." I glance up at the placid black waters. A few people wade along the shore, but no one tries to swim.

"Look. If your daughter isn't here, then she's still alive." I hold out my hand. "Get up. What's your name?"

He takes my hand, and furrows his brow. "Alex. I think. Or was that *her* name? Shit." I pull him up, and he stumbles to his feet. He touches his lip where I punched him, but there's no blood, of course. "Why'd you hit me?"

"You were making a fuss," I say. "It's dangerous to disturb the dead. Come on. Let's get out of this crowd."

Half-dragging the man, I push him through the door and up to the decaying wooden bar. Low murmured voices fill the room—this is the only place I ever hear voices, other than Charon's. Clustered around the table, people hunch over their drinks, and behind the bar, elbows resting on the countertop, the second most beautiful woman I've ever met raises an eyebrow.

I let go of the man as he bumps into the bar. He grips it with his hands, supporting himself on unsteady legs.

The bartender smiles, her perfect teeth framed by the curve of red lips, and pours two mugs of the House Special. "Aren't you going to introduce me to your friend?"

"Alex," I say, "this is Lethe. Lethe, Alex."

The man clambers onto a rickety barstool and looks up. "Jesus Christ," he whispers, "you're beautiful."

She laughs. "I knew that man, but he and I did not get along. Drink," she places a mug in front of him, "and you will know the bliss of the gods." She places the other mug in front of me. "And you, my friend. Are you at last going to partake?"

"Do I ever?"

She smiles at me, and for a moment I feel like I could forget why I'm here. "You bring me so many customers, yet you never drink yourself," Lethe says. She gestures to Alex, and winks at him. "This man, I can tell, appreciates the finer things in death. Go on."

Alex sips from his cup uncertainly, and then she turns to me. "This fellow misses his daughter. You miss your Beloved. What makes him so different from you, that you would have him drink while you do not? Why shall he forget his life, and pass without pain or grief into the lands beyond, while you stay here and hold onto the misery of what is lost?"

I grit my teeth and push my mug away. "Because I made a promise."

There is a mocking edge to Lethe's smile, but she is no less beautiful for that. "What promise? *Until death do you part?*" She gestured to the room, then leaned in close. "I do not know if you have noticed, but death has happened, and it has parted you."

"No!" I slam my fist down on the table and immediately regret it.

What little conversation there was vanishes, and the bar is as quiet as outside. A shiver goes up my spine, and I lean in close to Lethe's ear. "She will come here one day, and we will ride the ferry together. But until then, I will not drink."

Lethe pushes the mug closer to me, and stares me in the eye. "You gain nothing by staying here. Even if your Beloved joins you, you will still not be able to cross into the afterlife." There is no smile on her face any more, only a fierce determination. "None who remember life can set foot on the far bank of my river."

"On the far bank," I tell her, "is Hell."

"No," she whispers through gritted teeth. "Hell is right here, spending eternity yearning for a life and a Beloved you will never see again. You want to know eternal bliss?" She lifts my cup. "Then drink. Or bathe in my river. Either will cleanse your soul."

I look around. The bar, like the land outside, is dim and bare. No color, except for the flickering sign in the window, which draws in the few of us who remember. The recently dead come here for comfort, for solace, for answers, and find all but the last.

There is a tap on my shoulder, and I turn to see my companion smiling, all hints of his former depression vanished. He raises his half-empty cup to me. "Care for a toast, stranger?"

Lethe holds out my mug. "Take it." Her eyes gleam with an energy I've never seen. She's never been this insistent; I guess she's finally tired of my stalling.

I take the cup from her, and stare at the water inside for a long moment. "A toast, then. To Alex." I raise my mug to his with a wooden click.

"Who's Alex?" he asks.

"Someone to remember." I raise my mug to my lips and take some of the water into my mouth. It's cool and refreshing, and where it touches my lips and tongue it leaves behind a numbing sensation, as though I were rinsing my mouth with liquid painkiller. The numbness works its way through my skull, leaving me lightheaded. Without even swallowing, I could soon forget my Beloved, and the wait would be over. I could board Charon's ferry and find out what lies beyond the river.

I barely have enough strength to spit the water back into the mug. With a quivering hand, I place it back on the bar top, and meet Lethe's stare. There is anger in her face now, and I realize the room has fallen silent again. "No, Lethe. You will not claim me."

"Oh, but I will," she hisses, a fierce, inhuman edge to her voice. Then she turns to my companion, her face and words once again filled with beauty, and smiles. "Do me a favor, dear. Take this man to the river, and cleanse his soul."

I turn to her in shock and watch as Alex rises from his seat. He shrugs his shoulders, an apology in his eyes, but then he grabs me by my shoulders. I punch him again, sending him sprawling, and turn to leave, but Alex is not the only man who has risen from his seat. Every person in the bar stares at me.

I try to run, but that only seems to animate them. Rough hands grab me, and I am carried, struggling, out the door. I fight, screaming and cursing, but that only draws more. The dead don't like to be disturbed, but it's too late to worry about that—all I can do is fight.

I curse every god and demon I can name, I cry for my Beloved, I struggle with every muscle. Through the crowd, I see Lethe standing by the door, watching as the mob pushes me toward the river. I try to push back, but the crowd is too strong. They drag me out onto the rickety wooden dock, and the last thing I see is Alex, as he gives me one final shove.

A moment of free-fall, then the shock of the water. The river is cold and deep, so cold it freezes my muscles, and I struggle to keep moving, to reach the surface again. Already I feel the numbness in my limbs, a paralysis that creeps along my arms and legs, crawling relentlessly toward my head and my heart. I cannot drown here, but that does not lessen my panic, and I struggle toward the surface.

Looking up, I see the wooden dock shimmering in the water and faces staring down at me. But for all I push my arms, the surface gets no closer.

I'm sorry, Beloved. I tried to wait for you, here on the banks of the Lethe. But your face is slipping from my mind already, and the cold water is fading into a bliss that envelops me. I could hang here, suspended forever—perhaps that is my fate, to be held for eternity in Lethe's grasp.

Something hard hits me, and I slip even deeper. The dock is invisible now—all around me is cold blackness, but it feels as though I am being wrapped in an embrace by pure bliss. Lethe is everywhere, gripping my legs, my torso, my hands—my left hand.

Then the water rushes past and suddenly I am pulled upward again, dripping wet. Charon is kneeling on the dock, holding me easily with one strong arm. He pulls me close to his face. "I told you, and I know damn well I've told her. Everyone rides the ferry in the end."

Then, as if he were tossing a rag doll, he flips me over the railing and onto the deck.

The wheelhouse of the ferry is sparse—it's the only part of the ferry that sits on the upper deck, separated by a stair and two locked gates from the masses below.

There are no chairs. I sit against the wall, still trying to clear my head, staring up at Charon's back as he pilots the ferry. It feels reassuring to be here—the floor is uncomfortable, and the smell of diesel is everywhere—but it also feels familiar, in a way I can't place. The waters of the river may have been heaven, but this is home.

"Tell me about this woman you waited for."

I cross my eyes, trying to remember. "Who?"

"Every day you spoke to me of love, of life, of waiting for the woman you called *Beloved*." He turns back to look at me, disgust in his expression. "A little dip in the Lethe rid you of all that? You're weaker than I thought."

I brace myself against the wall and struggle to my feet. "I'm not weak." I stumble forward to put my hands on the window, looking out across the river. A reddish glow pierces the far gloom, and I can see the outline of the far bank. "What's over there?"

Charon's expression doesn't change. "Eternity. Rebirth. Hell. Maybe you get what you always wanted. Maybe you get what you never wanted, or what you didn't know you wanted. Or what you don't want."

"You mean," I ask him, "you don't know?"

"When we dock," said Charon, "you'll be as far into the underworld as I've ever been. I'm just the ferryman. Ain't my place to know what's beyond the banks."

In the distance I can make out the edge of the water and an empty dock. Only a single pathway leads away, looking much like the pathway on the other bank. It's as if the path runs under the river and just keeps on going.

Charon swings the wheel and throttles back the engine—the wheel is solid oak, the nicest thing I've seen since I got into the underworld. I reach out my hand and touch it—it's solid, and real . . . and memories come back to me. I look up at the ferryman's face. "Mind if I guide her in?"

He looks at me like I've grown a second head.

"Please," I say. "I remember how. I'm sure. And I need to do this."

He stares at me for a moment, then steps aside. "All right. I'll go down and throw the ropes. But," he stabs a finger in my face, "you hurt my boat, and I'll find a special Hell just for you."

I can't help but smile. "Yes, sir." Then I wrap my fingers around the wheel and watch as the dock approaches, pressing the engine into reverse as we glide in. I remember it all now, guiding ferries across the sound where I lived, back and forth for years. On one trip, I happened to meet a girl with a pert nose and auburn hair framing a beautiful face with the most perfect green eyes . . .

"Katherine!"

The memories flow like the dam of a river has broken, and now I remember everything about her, the fog of the Lethe fading like mist under the noonday sun. The sound of her laugh, the feel of her hand in mine, the conversations we had over coffees and dinners and early morning breakfasts, and the way she looked on a sunny Spring day when we promised each other everything.

The memories are so bright and vivid that I almost forget to cut the engine before we sail back out into the current. The boat taps lightly against the wooden dock, and when I walk out of the wheelhouse to find Charon, I'm grinning ear-to-ear. He's already off the boat, standing on the dock as he takes a long drag off a cigarette and watches the dead make their way to . . . well . . . wherever it is they're going.

He nods gruffly. "Welcome back."

"Thank you." Then I realize where I am: the far side of the bank. And no one sails the opposite direction—the ferry is a one way trip. If I stay here, I will never find Katherine before she joins the ranks of the dead, claimed by Lethe. I look at Charon, panic filling my mind. The Ferryman nods slightly, as if affirming my thoughts.

"I'll give you this," he says. "You know what you're doing with a boat. That was a mighty smooth pull-in." Then he stubs out his cigarette and beckons with a rough hand. "Follow me. I want to show you something."

Mounted on the back wall of the wheelhouse is a wooden oar, rough and worn from centuries of use. Charon reaches out and takes it.

"This here is all I have from the old days." He handles it like a priceless artifact, touching it softly, running his hand along the grain of the wood. "When you asked me if I missed the rowboat, well, I have to admit, my words weren't all truthful." He didn't take his eyes off the oar. "For a long time now, I've guided a ferry. Before that I had a steam-powered riverboat, and before that I had a longboat. But I was always a rower, first and foremost." He laughs. "Times change, even here."

He looks at me. "And these days, one ferry's not enough. You've seen the crowds we're leaving behind on the docks. They're getting bigger every day."

"So you need a bigger boat?"

Charon's expression is impossible to read. "A bigger boat, or two ferries."

"But you can't pilot two ferries."

"No," said Charon. "I can't. Someone else'd have to pilot the other one." He pauses. "You don't want to leave the river, but now that you've set foot on the far bank, Lethe will never let you off her dock on the side of the living. People just don't go that way."

"But—"

"You keep an eye out for your Beloved on your ferry, and I'll keep an eye out for her on mine. Either that, or you get off the ferry on this side, go wherever you're supposed to go, and the powers that be send me someone else."

The second ferry is already waiting for us on the close side of the river. Charon shakes my hand, and then the hordes of the dead board his boat. I look for my Beloved but, as usual, I do not see her. I've told Charon everything I could—maybe one day he'll find her, maybe he won't. But if she remembers me, then she'll be looking, just like I'm looking for her. All she needs to do is wait long enough for the second ferry. And we'll find each other.

Then, together, we will guide the dead across the waters of the Lethe.

Andrew S. Williams lives in Seattle, where he tries to write stories worth remembering. His work has appeared in various anthologies, including Dark Tales of Lost Civilizations *and* Flush Fiction. *You can find him online at* www.offthewrittenpath.com.

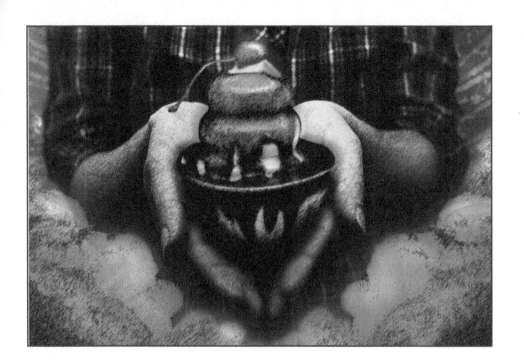

BOY, 7

ALVARO RODRIGUEZ

Boy, 7. *It's a simple, telling title that leads us into this next story by famed noir writer, Alvaro Rodriguez. Grim and stark, the author presents a nightmarish scene for anyone to envision: the thoughts of a kidnapped child. Like the young protagonist, we all wish we could change the circumstances of our lives sometimes, wish we could take away the pain and tragedy, wish we could "have everything we ever wanted." Can our wishes come true after we die? I like to think so . . .*

Someone would open the trunk.

That's what the boy thought. Someone would come along and open the trunk, and he would be safe. The bad man would be gone—dead—if he could have everything he ever wanted. If he could have everything he ever wanted, the man would be dead from a gunshot to the face, and then he'd fall to the ground and be eaten by dogs. If he could have everything he ever wanted, the man would be torn apart, his arms and his legs pulled so hard they would come off his body like a plastic doll.

But for now, he was in the trunk. Tied up. Tied up good. His mouth, too. His head was wrapped in something that stank. Maybe it was the bad man's shirt. It smelled bad, like the bad man smelled. Like sweat. And fear. Maybe the fear was his. *Yes*, the boy thought, *it was his own.*

The car moved fast. It had swerved many times but was steady now. That meant the bad man still drove, but maybe if it swerved again that would mean policemen or someone else chased after him. He prayed for the car to swerve again.

It did.

His body, cinched up like it was, bounced inside the trunk. Bounced against the spare tire. Bounced against something else, something hard. Bounced as the car swerved, two things in motion, moving around.

Everything was black inside the bad man's shirt. It covered his mouth and his eyes. Tight. But even in the darkness of the trunk, he saw light. He didn't know where it came from. Maybe from God. Maybe from his own head. He prayed for the light to go away. It bothered him, the *not-knowing*. The light bothered him, too. It appeared spangled, like stars, and it wasn't bright. Instead, it was dull, and sometimes colored, but not brightly, and still it was light . . . but it was the wrong kind of light.

The bad man made the car swerve again, harder this time, and this time he didn't bounce, he didn't bump. He went airborne. Nothing touched him for a full second or two—not the floor of the trunk, not the side. Nothing.

The car came down hard, and so did he. He bled from somewhere, but with his eyes shut tight, and the ropes around him, and the bad man's shirt sleeves crisscrossed over his head, he couldn't tell where the bleeding was, but he knew. He knew he leaked blood.

Bam!

Something hit the car, or the car hit something, or both, and he was airborne again. He didn't like the feeling. It made him sick inside and even his stomach felt like it was airborne in the car trunk of his body, this thing inside another thing, weightless for a full second or two, touching nothing.

The car swerved. The bad man was still driving. The boy prayed he would stop and give up, or stop and get shot by the policemen who followed him. Maybe he could hear sirens, or maybe, like the lights, the sound they made came from God. Or inside his head. He prayed the sirens were real.

Then came the biggest *bam* of all . . .

Bam!

And he felt himself being crushed. His lungs, like his stomach, weightless a moment, then his body was a sandwich around them, his front and back the bread, his lungs the meat.

And a sound, a horrible metal sound, like the big thing in the junkyard that eats cars and spits out boxes.

And then, nothing. No light, no sound. Nothing any more.

He leaked a lot.

He heard a scratching sound. Not a mouse, but something else, like a key trying to find its way into a lock. It was close—real close—and he almost let himself believe it was someone trying to open the trunk and he hoped, he prayed, it wasn't the bad man who had put him there in the first place.

All the sounds that came before gave the boy hope it wouldn't be *him*. It would be someone else. The fire department with the jaws of life opening the smashed car like a tin can while the policemen emptied their guns into the bad man. That's who it would be. The fire department.

But the key wouldn't go in the lock. He heard someone trying, trying really hard. Maybe it was the wrong key.

If he could have everything he ever wanted, it would be the right key, and it would be his mother holding it. She would pop the trunk just like she did when they had a flat tire, and she checked for the jack and the spare. If he could have everything he ever wanted, she would be the one to open the trunk, and she would be surprised and happy to find him there. She would take the bad man's shirt off his head and pepper him with kisses and wipe his face. She would untie the ropes and find the place he was leaking blood, and she would stop it. She would make a call, and the ambulance would come and take him to the hospital, and the doctors would make him well.

If he could have everything he ever wanted, his mother would give him an ice cream sundae with caramel—not hot fudge—because caramel was better. He would be in the newspapers, and on TV, and on the internet, because people would want to know what happened to him, and how the bad man had taken him, and how he had bounced in the trunk and gone airborne, and how the man's shirt wrapped around his head had smelled, and the lights, and the sirens. He would tell them everything because everybody loved a good story, and it would make good television, and a link to the clip would be passed around through email, and his grandparents would call because they got the email, and they clicked on the link, and they would be so glad he was safe and alive, and they would never let anything like this happen to him or anyone else again.

But he still had the feeling he was a sandwich. Except now it felt like there wasn't room for the meat. It was peanut butter and jelly, crunchy peanut butter because there were still bones inside him, and jelly, and the pieces of bread were smushed together, and the jelly was coming out the sides, and he couldn't breathe. Couldn't breathe . . . couldn't breathe.

And then the key went in.

And the lock turned.

And the trunk sprang open.

And there was light.

Dim light, getting dimmer, like with the round switch on the wall that wasn't really a switch, but a thing you clicked and turned . . .

Clicked and turned.

He felt warm and cold all at once, like the time he had a high fever and his mother was scared. She would be scared now.

He felt hands on him.

He felt the ropes coming loose.

He felt the shirt come off his head, but it still felt like it was on. Still smelled like it was on.

He opened his eyes, and he saw the bad man. It was the bad man's body standing there, his neck and his torso, his arms and his legs, but his face was gone. It been blown away by a gunshot. Up close.

The man was there, but he was falling, falling, down to the ground. The boy watched as dogs came and pulled the bad man apart, tearing away his arms, his legs, like a plastic doll. And then he saw his mother. She held a caramel sundae, and she wore a nice dress.

He took the spoon out of the plastic wrap and ate the sundae, sitting there in the trunk of the bad man's car, until it was all done.

Alvaro Rodriguez has worked as a reporter, editor, and screen-writer. His credits include From Dusk Till Dawn 3: The Hangman's Daughter *for Dimension Films and* Machete *for 20th Century Fox. He lives in Texas with his beautiful wife and three amazing children.*

SEA OF TREES

EDWARD M. ERDELAC

Suicide. Intentionally causing one's own death is viewed differently throughout cultural and historic perspectives. Influences such as honor, religion, or health lead some people to believe that it is celebrated to end life on one's own terms while, for others, it is the ultimate desecration and a guarantee of eternal condemnation. For many, however, it is simply an escape from despairs that seem to have no solution. An escape that, in reasoning, must lead only to better things. But does it? Edward M. Erdelac explores the taboo through one man's eyes who feels overwhelmed by burdens that we all face. Compelling and relatable, Manabu must decide between life and death as he searches for relief in the Sea of Trees.

Manabu stepped out of his car and let the door close. He did not take the keys. The car was a rental and the *Tocoo!* agency in Fujiyoshida would want it back.

He took the hiking trail out of the parking lot and walked for an hour into the woods before he came to the *No Hiking Beyond This Point* sign. He stepped over the rope to pick his way among the tangled roots.

His mother had told him as a boy never to play in Aokigahara Forest, the *Sea of Trees*, because it was haunted by the miserable ghosts of those that every year wandered in here to die. The practice had been going on since the old days of the daimyos when the destitute families around Mount Fuji used the woods for *ubasute*, abandoning their elderly infirm to the elements in times of famine, to spare the remainder of the household.

Manabu's mother once told him the Ubasuteyama story.

This wasn't in Aokigahara, but in Nagano somewhere. There was a famine, and a boy chose to carry his crippled old mother up to the mountain to leave her in the woods. He carried her very deep into the forest, perhaps thinking to lose his conscience too.

When at last he set her down, he saw that he might become lost himself on the way back down.

"Don't worry, son," croaked the old woman. "As you carried me, I spread out my hands and broke off the twigs of the trees. There is a trail of the broken ends behind you now to follow home."

Manabu's mother had ended this story by clasping both sides of his pudgy face in her hands and promising him that she loved him as much as the old woman in the story had loved her son.

Manabu's mother was two years dead now.

She died in Fujiyoshida, and he hadn't even been able to attend the funeral. No money to travel from Tokyo. He couldn't even afford to take the time off from his job.

Always it was money.

Without money there could be no love, no shelter, no life. He had pondered these things on the walk home from his last day at the accounting job he had held for five years. The twelve, sometimes fifteen, hour days he worked had hungrily sucked all passion from him, chaining him with paper links of yen to a cubicle desk, where he squinted at figures on a computer screen until his eyes grew weak and his shoulders drooped, spine permanently bent both from hunching over his desk and from the immeasurable, unendurable burden of subsistence. He was paid well enough, but his rent and various debts and bills were exorbitant. It was impossible to save, impossible to afford even the most meager amenity. He lived like a hermit.

The company he served had reached the end of the fiscal year and decided he was a redundant expenditure.

So he had walked the streets of Tokyo, hopeless in the deceptive glow of neon lights which gave no warmth, unwelcome by the laughter and smiles that drifted from the bars and clubs, with not even enough in his bank account to cover next month's rent on his disheveled, tiny apartment.

He withdrew the very last of it and bought a bus ticket home to Fujiyoshida and a rental car. He had visited his mother's grave and told her of his intent to go into the Sea of Trees.

Now, walking through the trees, he came upon a large sign nailed to one of the gnarled trees.

Your life is a gift to you from your parents. Please think about your parents, your siblings, and children. Don't keep it to yourself. Talk about your troubles. Contact the Suicide Prevention Association.

A telephone number punctuated the message.

But Manabu's mother was dead. He would see her again, he reasoned, after today. He had no siblings, no love (and therefore no children), no one to talk to. Not even a phone with which to call the Suicide Prevention Association.

So he walked on.

A half hour later, picking his way randomly over the thick roots, he began to see other signs nailed to the trees.

One small placard, written in red lipstick read:

I loved you. How could you forget me? I hope this will make you remember.

And another:

Do not look for me. You will not find me.

And another:

I am sorry, mother and father, and little brother. This life is too hard. Please try to forgive me.

There were more. Epitaphs and valedictions scrawled in unsteady hands, driven into the oblivious wood.

There were other signs of those who had passed into the Sea of Trees. Discarded compacts, shoes, keys, empty wallets, clothing.

There was tape, too, and bright ribbon winding around the tree trunks, littering the place. It didn't seem to follow any real pattern. It didn't mark anything special. It just went out in every direction, like gaily-colored spider webbing.

He had no idea where he was going, so he picked a long yellow strip of ribbon and followed its meandering path through the trees, peering at the various articles buried among the dry leaves.

The forest was silent. No animals crashed through, no birds chattered in the branches. The only sound was of his own feet rustling through the leaves and kicking the volcanic black earth beneath.

He still wore his work shoes, black, the heels worn down, the aglets cracked, the laces bursting from them, frayed. The cuffs of his dark slacks suffered the torment of the undergrowth. He felt cold, having left his jacket in the car with his ID. He had only his white collared shirt and tie between his pimpling skin and the chilly mountain air.

He saw frayed ropes dangling from the tree limbs now, triple-braided twine most of them, and unbuckled belts, their grisly burdens taken down no doubt by one of the forest rangers or the army of volunteers who every April trudged through these woods to recover the bodies for burial, sometimes as many as a hundred at a time.

That was why Manabu knew there were no ghosts, no pale, legless *yūrei* floating among the trees like in the stories.

His mother had told him that when a body died, the spirit sat in purgatory until its funeral was held. Then it moved on, and could return to visit the living during the Obon Festival, a joyous celebration culminating in a brilliant parade of colorful paper lanterns, each inscribed with the name of the departed and set bobbing upon the river. The river, his mother had told him as she held his small hand in the darkness, carried the departed souls back to the land of the dead.

So he knew, because it was the end of the fiscal year, that he would only have a month to spend in purgatory before his body was found by the volunteers and buried. He had prepared a note and tucked it into his breast pocket, a note asking that he be given a modest funeral and buried, so he might rejoin his mother, the only human being who had ever seen worth in him without looking at him through a yen.

He wondered what purgatory would be like. Surely being bodiless was no worse than blearily watching money pass between the rich on a dim computer monitor. At least he would have no responsibilities. He would not be enslaved to money.

And then his heart pounded in his chest, for he heard a noise, a rustling up ahead.

He feared it was one of the forest rangers who he knew sometimes patrolled the woods independently. The father of a childhood friend had been a ranger in Aokigahra, and his friend, Aki, had related second-hand many of his father's stories about rousting suicidal campers from the forest, or discovering black-faced bodies buzzing with flies.

He froze, and a deep, blustery voice called out:

"There's no point in standing there, I can see you. Come on up here!"

Manabu had never been an assertive person, and he felt compelled to answer the authoritative summons.

He walked around a tree and along to where the voice originated, at the end of the yellow ribbon path.

A woman sat with her back to the base of a thick tree. She had been dead for days, a blue-black patina about her bloated face and hands. Her swollen limbs stretched the sleeves of her blouse. The yellow ribbon was tight around one puffy hand. Ants flowed up and down her, and flies clustered in her eyelids and ears, packing her half-open mouth.

At her side, neatly arranged, lay an open compact mirror and a makeup kit.

The smell was horrendous. Manabu put the back of his hand to his face and looked away.

His forehead broke out in sweat.

"Yeah, she's been here a while," said the voice. "Sleeping pills. The women usually go for the pills. I read somewhere that they think they leave a nice looking corpse behind that way. She tried to pretty herself up. What do you think? Would you kick her out of bed?"

The voice chuckled, and Manabu looked back to see a man, younger than him, in a black leather vest and ripped jeans, his hair roostered and streaked with red and green dye. He wore a surgical mask and thick work gloves, a plastic bag sagging with items in one hand. A tattoo of a striking snake showed on his thin arm.

"Relax, man," said the young man. "I'm not a ranger. Name's Orochi."

Manabu clasped his hand over his nose and mouth to shut out the reek of the body.

Orochi came up to him.

"Come on, walk over here, away from the smell."

They left the rotting woman behind.

"Why did she carry along all that ribbon?" Manabu asked. "So she would be found?"

"Sometimes they get indecisive. They leave string or ribbon so they can find their way back if they change their mind."

Manabu tested the air gingerly and took his hand away from his mouth.

"So how are you gonna do it?" Orochi asked, swinging his rustling plastic bag.

"What?"

"Did you bring pills too?"

"I'm just . . . walking."

"Come on. Nobody Japanese just goes *walking* in the Aokigahara. Especially not dressed like you. What happened, salaryman? You lose your job?"

Manabu looked at Orochi as he took out a pack of cigarettes and slapped it. He slipped his surgical mask down around his neck. He had a stubbly beard and a gold hoop in his bottom lip.

When Manabu said nothing, Orochi shrugged and lit a cigarette.

"Wanna smoke?"

"I never tried."

"This could be the chance of a lifetime then."

Manabu took a cigarette from the pack, held it to Orochi's, put his lips to the filter, and drew. He didn't like it. The smoke roiled and burned in his lungs. He choked and coughed. By the time he stopped, Orochi had finished his own cigarette. He took Manabu's from his fingers and began to smoke it too.

"What about you?" Manabu wheezed. "What are you doing here?"

"Best job in Fujiyoshida," he said, holding up the bag and twirling it. "I always come around this time, right before the volunteers. People come in here with their wallets, their purses, jewelry, sometimes car keys . . ."

"You're a thief?"

"I don't think of it that way. I don't rob anyone. What I take, the owners don't need anymore. What about you? You wanna give me your wallet and save me the trouble?"

"What kind of a person are you?"

"I'm going to walk back out of these woods and get some *sake*, maybe get laid. That's what kind of person I am."

"You sicken me," Manabu spat, trying to exorcise the foul taste of the cigarette. "I want to be rid of this shitty existence."

"You sure about that?" Orochi said, taking a long drag on his cigarette.

"Of course! I want nothing more to do with this pathetic world." He wiped his lips with the back of his hand violently.

When he finished, Manabu found his hand was shaking, and he made a fist to quell it.

"How do you know the next one's any better?" Orochi asked.

"It must be!"

Orochi shrugged, then asked, "You know what a fardel is?"

"What?"

"A fardel. Have you ever read William Shakespeare?"

"No."

"And you want to die?" Orochi said, squinting at him, the bag of wallets and jewelry over his shoulder. "Never having read it?" He shook his head and cleared his throat impressively, spat, and stuck the cigarette in the corner of his mouth. It bobbed as he recited.

> "Who would Fardels bear,
> To grunt and sweat under a weary life,
> But that the dread of something after death,
> The undiscovered Country, from whose bourn
> No Traveller returns, Puzzles the will,
> And makes us rather bear those ills we have,
> Than fly to others that we know not of."

Satisfied, he moved the cigarette back to the front of his mouth and took a long drag, blowing it from his nostrils like a dragon.

"I don't care about William Shakespeare," Manabu hissed. "Fuck William Shakespeare! Why don't you just leave me alone?"

Orochi shrugged. "Alright, salaryman. I'll leave you to your fardels. Do what you want. See you later."

Orochi walked off, swinging the bag of loot and trailing smoke.

Manabu watched him go. For a moment his heart ached, and he wanted to call the strange young man back, or to yell for him to wait, so he could go with him, drink *sake*. Maybe meet a young woman.

But then what would he do? Walk these gloomy woods with Orochi? Haunt them like a real demon, looting bodies for a living and quoting Shakespeare to the trees?

He shook his head, deciding.

No, he would do what he came here to do. Orochi was a parasite. Obviously he had never tried to make anything of himself. Was that the sort of person that would make Manabu lose his resolve? A vagrant and a corpse looter?

He looked around and found a tree that had fallen against another.

He walked over to it. It looked like an easy climb and there was a branch, a good thick one.

He took off his belt. It was a cheap thing. He hoped it wouldn't break.

Manabu started to climb with the belt in his teeth. He had to keep reaching down to hitch up his pants. He wondered if his pants would fall down when he died, and he decided to turn the lip of the waist over once to prevent this.

What sort of a world was this where the best someone who worked as hard as Manabu could hope for was to live like a rat in a cage, while freewheeling vagrants like Orochi prospered and were content? Where fat-stomached old men could dictate the lives of the young, flogging them into submission with chains of currency?

Who would fardels bear?

Those words kept going over and over in his mind.

No, this world was diseased. It was sinking in a sea of misery and he was getting off. He wanted the peace of the afterworld.

Now.

He took the belt from his teeth and put it around his neck. It was difficult to keep his balance as he threw the other end up around the branch and fumbled with the buckle to cinch it.

He glanced down at the forest floor; it wasn't a big jump. He had jumped farther as a child. How happy he had been to run and play then, imagining the life he would live, a grand life of fulfillment and adventure. There had been no fear in him.

Now, he was struck through with it. Fear clogged the vessels of his body, mired his blood, made his heart thunder as he looked down at this nothing little jump. He had always been afraid to live. Afraid to speak to the girl at the lunch counter. Afraid to demand of his boss that he be allowed to attend his mother's funeral. Afraid to splurge and travel and *be.*

Must he now be afraid to die as well?

No!

He must step out of this life, leave all his crushing burdens behind, and plunge into the afterworld like a boy diving into a pool of water.

He could hear an insistent pounding in his ears, his body demanding to live, pleading. But what was life if it could not be lived on one's own terms?

He stepped from the branch into eternity.

As he did, a panicked thought entered his brain. He forgot to turn over the lip of his trousers.

But it was no matter. After a brief sharp pain there was a loud snap and a rush of wind and he landed soundly on the forest floor, lucky not to have broken his ankles.

That damned cheap belt! The only one he had, the only one he could afford, five years old, bought only for that lousy job, the thin leather cracked and worn, new holes punched through it, one for every year he'd wasted away on desiccated noodle packets and bad food. It had snapped!

He snickered. He no longer heard his blood in his ears, as if his entire body had collapsed in relief.

He scowled and then giggled nervously.

Perhaps it was a sign. Maybe his mother's spirit had reached out and severed the old belt. Maybe fate had something else in store for him. He thought about Orochi's words. He never had any real inclination to read William Shakespeare, but he found that the passage

Orochi recited did resonate with him somehow. Something about fear of the 'undiscovered country' making men 'bear what ills we have.'

What of the ills he had? Money. Lack of it. But there were people who lived perfectly happy without it, weren't there? Could he be one of those people? Could he go to Australia and learn to surf? Live on a beach and grow his hair long? Fall in love? Have children?

Was it possible he could seize such things from this world? He was back in his hometown, in the cool mountain air, away from the stink of Tokyo. Perhaps the heavy air there, the closeness, had cluttered his soul, his mind. Perhaps in Fujiyoshida he could start again. Sure! Why not? He could look up old friends who remained. Perhaps they could help him somehow. Perhaps Aki's father still worked for the forest service. Perhaps he could be a ranger here until he saved enough to travel.

He thought about the burial note in his shirt pocket. What a silly thing! He reached up to take it out and tear it up, leave it here among the possessions of the successful suicides, for some curious volunteer to piece together and wonder who he was. How many of these placards nailed to the trees had been placed there by actual suicides, he wondered. How many of them, like Manabu, had been spared by a trick of fate, or had a change of heart and followed their strings and their breadcrumbs back into life, back into a new day?

But he couldn't reach into his pocket. He had no pocket, and his hands dangled limply from his wrists, flopping weirdly about as if all muscle control were gone from them. Indeed, he couldn't move or feel his fingers.

He looked down, and saw he was dressed in a white kimono, the sleeves long like in a *Noh* play. And he was not standing on the ground, but floating just a little above it, for he lacked proper legs and feet. Below his waist, he faded into nothingness, like an illustration partly erased.

Then he heard the wailing. It seemed to come from all around, from every direction, from dozens, hundreds of voices. The previously quiet, empty forest was suddenly crowded with sounds and movement.

He saw pale shapes drifting like fog among the trees, white, wispy shapes, and legless. Yet they had heads and bodies, for their cacophonous, disordered lamentations were terrible to hear, like the ravings of the mad. They passed close and far, wandering without any apparent destination in mind.

Manabu was terrified these ghosts were coming for him, but they took no more notice of him than they did of each other.

He saw that some were pale and black-eyed, with long black hair, and some looked like rotting corpses, the flesh dripping from their brown bones. He even saw the woman at the end of the yellow ribbon, her limp hands slapping in a frenzy like a chimpanzee's against the sides of her own swollen head, as if she tried to shut out the terrible sounds all around. Her shriveled lips were parted and she shrieked in short, shrill blasts, a terrible, hair-raising sound.

Manabu hugged himself with his useless hands and grimaced at the noise.

Then a tall, thin figure dressed in black came out of their midst. He appeared calm and obviously not one of their number, but he was terrible to behold, obscenely long-necked and fish belly-pale, with teeth like a piranha, clawed hands that brushed his ankles as he walked, and large, luminous blue eyes like wavering pilot lights.

Something scuttled along beside him, trying its best to keep up with his long strides, an impish little thing in a loincloth with a great hairy belly and face like a boar, his head encircled by a wreath of spiraling ram horns.

The pilot-eyed thing stopped before Manabu and looked down on him.

"Manabu Nakamura!" It proclaimed, in a dreadful, gravelly voice that was loud enough to be heard even above the screaming.

Then it waited, observing him with a look of patient disinterest.

"Yes?" Manabu ventured sheepishly.

The thing sniffed and looked to its stout, many-horned companion expectantly.

The horned thing held a clipboard. It paused to set a pair of ridiculously out of place black-rimmed spectacles over its eyes, which had previously dangled from a beaded chain around its brushy neck.

"Manabu Nakamura," it said at last, in a squeaky voice, "aged thirty-two. Accountant."

"Accountant, eh?" rumbled the tall blue-eyed thing. "You'll fit in well. We'll situate you at a desk just like the one you had in life, and you can get set up for the next one hundred fifty years."

"I don't understand," Manabu stammered. "Am I dead?"

"As dead as dreams. You killed yourself only a minute ago." It raised its hairless brow. "Have you forgotten already?"

Manabu's shoulders hunched and he felt a coldness spread through him. He did not want to look back at the tree. He did not want to see himself hanging there, ripening and blackening like an unpicked fruit.

But slowly, he did turn around.

There was his own body, the belt tight beneath his chin, his neck purple, and his head so far to the left that his ear nearly touched his sagging shoulder. The tip of his tongue protruded from between his lips and his eyes bulged. A tear slipped down Manabu's paling cheek.

His despair was compounded when he saw that his pants were around his ankles. His knobby pale knees were ugly to behold but, thankfully, his underwear was hidden by his shirt. One shoe lay in the mud.

He had done it . . . he had truly done it.

"Oh," said Manabu, more than a little disappointed, turning back to the two figures. "No."

"Alright then, Manabu, let's get you to your desk."

"Wait. What desk?" Manabu said. "Who are you?"

"I'm your *shinigami*, Manabu. Our job is to get you situated in your new work environment."

"Work environment?"

"What do you think? That there is no order to the universe? There are millions of stacks of etheric ledgers kilometers high that need going through. They won't balance themselves. Come now."

"What are you talking about? What ledgers?"

"The karmic records, where the deeds of every man, woman, and child are recorded and reviewed. We cannot be expected to determine the placement of souls correctly unless balance sheets are kept in proper order. And you have the qualifications."

"I don't want to be an accountant!"

"You don't?" The *shinigami* looked querulously at his diminutive assistant, who thumbed through some papers and shrugged, shaking his grotesque head.

"It says here you were an accountant your entire adult life," said the horned thing. "If you did not want to be an accountant, why spend your life that way?"

"Well, I'm not going to be an accountant anymore," said Manabu. "I refuse to accept I'm expected to spend eternity doing that."

"Not eternity," corrected the horned thing. "Only until you earn enough karma to move on."

"What? You mean to say I have to work in the afterlife for karma?"

"Yours is a special case, Manabu," said the *shinigami*. "When you take your own life you enter into debt. Any positive karma you may have accumulated during your lifetime is of course applied against the balance of that debt, but there are penalties for suicides and, unfortunately according to our records, you didn't have much to begin with." The *shinigami* chuckled, his eye-flames dancing.

"I . . . I didn't have enough time. I worked twelve hour days . . . "

"You had the entirety of your life. Plenty of time for most. But you cut it short. Backed out of the deal, so to speak, with your account in arrears. It says here you didn't even attend your own mother's funeral."

The assistant demon sucked its teeth.

Manabu and the *shinigami* looked at it, and it shrugged apologetically.

"Sorry."

"My mother . . . will I see my mother?"

"Oh . . . we're not really permitted to divulge client information, you know. Confidentiality."

"Non-disclosure," the hairy thing added.

Manabu sighed.

"*How* long must I work?"

"As I said, by our calculations, only about a hundred fifty years."

"What? I had no idea it would be so much! How was I to know?"

"Well, we do our best to educate the mortal world against suicide. No one reads the pamphlets, I'm afraid. To be fair though, this forest at least is clearly marked even in the mortal world, so . . . " he shrugged, letting his voice trail off meaningfully.

Manabu shuddered, and then remembered the screaming ghosts all around them.

"What about them?"

"Ah, the *yurei*," the *shinigami* said. "Of course, you *do* have that option."

"What? What option?"

"You are legally allowed the right to enter into a ghostly state to repay your karma, but I must warn you, the exchange rate is not favorable."

"Not favorable," the assistant demon echoed, shaking its head.

"Quietus, what is the rate currently?" the *shinigami* prompted.

"Fifty to one," Quietus answered automatically.

"Fifty to one," the *shinigami* repeated. "There, you see?"

"Then," Manabu whispered, "my choice . . . is one hundred fifty years as an accountant, or seven thousand five hundred years as a ghost?"

"Yes," the *shinigami* said. "You voluntarily enter a fugue state for the duration. Most of your memory is gone, and what you do remember torments you. As you can see, madness usually takes hold within the first few years."

Manabu felt like weeping as he watched the confused ghosts chattering and wailing about the forest.

"But . . . it's not like I thought it would be."

"Things rarely are," Quietus said.

"I thought . . . there would be peace at last. My mother said . . . purgatory . . . "

"Ah, purgatory," said the *shinigami*. "Well, that's reserved for those who live out their natural span, you see. So there you have it."

The *shinigami* must have seen his downcast expression.

"There, there," said the *shinigami*. "There is an old poem I've heard the dead sometimes repeat. A poem by . . . William Shakespeare. An Englishman. It goes (and Manabu felt ill as soon as the creature began):

> "Who would fardels bear,
> To grunt and swcat under a weary life—"

"Do you know what a fardel is?" Quietus interrupted, to his superior's obvious consternation. The little demon smiled a snaggletoothed smile at Manabu, very pleased with himself. "It's all right. I had to look it up. It's an Arabic word for burdens. Like a bindle."

"Yes, I knew," Manabu muttered.

"Ah," said Quietus, somewhat deflated. He took his spectacles from his snout and folded them.

"Yes," said the *shinigami*, frowning, the soliloquy forgotten now. "And so, what is your decision, Manabu Nakamura?"

Manabu watched the wandering, raving dead and wished the belt had broke.

Edward M. Erdelac *is the author of the acclaimed weird western series* Merkabah Rider *and* Dubaku *from Damnation Books,* Buff Tea *from Texas Review Press, and* Terovolas *from JournalStone. He has contributed fiction to various anthologies and magazines, including most recently,* Deadcore *(Comet Press),* Slices of Flesh *(Dark Moon Books), and* Welcome to Hell *(E-Volve Books). He has also written for Lucasfilm's* Starwars.com.

THE LAST MOMENTS BEFORE BED

STEVE RASNIC TEM

A despondent man prepares for death each night, hoping the dreams he has will be his release. Or has he died already? The shroud separating what is, and what was, and what is to be, is truly thin—permeable even—and we slip through its folds sometimes without even knowing. A master of expressive and supernatural prose, Steve Rasnic Tem is a writing inspiration to many, myself included, and a legend in the world of fiction. He brings us the next selection, The Last Moments Before Bed, *a beautiful reflection on the temperament of life and our fleeting place in it.*

"Time for bed, monkey," he whispers to himself. His wife used to say that, as did he, when the kids were small. He has not heard that phrase spoken aloud in years.

He examines the six or seven pillows, places them so they will provide support for him in some areas and softness in others. He finds the pillow he will hold tonight, the one meant for his arm, the one he can pretend is close to what he once felt, when she was still alive and this room smelled mostly of her.

If he were more settled, if there were a calmness here, he would have a more exacting routine. Each night the pillows would go into the same positions. It would be the same pillow he would hold. But there is no calm. Each night he must start over, rediscover the geometry that will bring him sleep.

The dog in the corner rises to its feet and looks at him. He cannot see the dog right now, but he can hear it, and this is what it does every night at about this time. He has never been able to see the intelligence in animals that others seem able to see. And he has always been skeptical of testimonies regarding their remarkable sympathy, their unwavering loyalty. But his dog clearly senses something each night at this time. Each night at this time his dog waits as he feels his way through his ritual of arranging comfort, waits until he has turned out the light and laid himself into the hopeful pattern he has made. The last thing he hears each night is the dog dropping its head onto its paws as it finally gives in to its own sleep.

The dog belonged to his wife. He himself has always been terrible with pets. Unfairly, before she died she made him promise he would take good care of this creature. And every day that is exactly what he does.

He always envies the dog because sleep has never come so easily for him. He knows that before this night is over he will have rearranged himself a dozen times in his rehearsals for oblivion, and his bed in the morning will resemble a battlefield.

Years ago he would have spent some moments picturing the locations of his children. He would see them in their beds. He would notice what their little mouths and fingers were doing. As they got older, he would think about them somewhere at the movies, out on a date, and more often than not sleep would have to wait until they came home.

Where were they tonight? Miami, Albuquerque, somewhere in Oregon. Watching over their own children in their beds, wondering about what their own children might be dreaming. Rehearsing, perhaps. Practicing for a life without her, without them. Trying out for the end.

How do you get ready? Can you possibly ever be ready?

One of the last things she ever said to him was, "I'm worried about what you're going to do without me. Your heart breaks so easily, sweetheart."

One of the last things he ever said to her was, "I'll be okay. I have all that scar tissue holding me together."

He reaches for the clock to set the alarm. And stops there, slightly confused. Since his retirement he's never sure what time to choose. He's always tempted to set it later and later, but he worries that late sleeping is a slippery slope—eventually you reach the point that getting up at all appears futile. But shouldn't he be allowed to sleep when it pleases him?

Of course, sleeping has rarely pleased him.

He sets the alarm for ten. He's rarely been able to sleep that late, but it would hardly be a disaster if he gets an earlier start on the day. And if he does manage to sleep until ten he will have just that much more rest, and still be up and alert for lunch.

The final bit of his nightly ritual is to review for himself a mental list of things not done, things not seen, things not said. Did he perform some unasked-for favors this week? He has always believed that life is hard enough—much harder than absolutely necessary—and so we have no business making it harder for each other. He's never thought of himself as a particularly good man, or in any way noble, and the doing of small favors could hardly be called an ambitious undertaking, but at least it is something he knows he can do.

Every week he sends each of his children a letter whose main purpose is to remind them that he loves them. He does not know if this means anything to them now, or if it will mean anything to them later, but at least it is something he can do.

Unable to delay the moment any longer, he lays himself carefully into the arrangement of pillows, pulling on top sheets and blankets as he goes, covering certain areas, leaving other areas uncovered—the same ones each night. When he was a boy he always covered himself completely, cowering there as an aural landscape he dared not picture unfolded around him. Each night he held his breath until he thought his heart would burst and the knowledge that it had not burst the night before still failed to reassure him. Sleep finally came only when he was exhausted and no longer cared whether death decided to take him or not. The next morning was always both bonus and escape.

During the first years of their marriage he could not wait to go to bed. He worked hard at his job, but still found time to socialize, so by the time bedtime arrived he was eager, at times even enthusiastic, for sleep. It was his reward for reaching the end of the day.

As he grew older, digestive problems sometimes made sleep problematic, and during a three year span he slept propped up in bed, fearful that he might drown during the night in his own stomach acid.

These years sleep comes easier again, except for the questions that arrive as soon as his head hits the pillow: *How do you get ready? Can you possibly ever be ready? Will you wake up in the morning? What, after all, have you done?*

He could stay up all night fruitlessly trying to answer these questions, and indeed, sometimes he has, but most nights he is too tired, simply from the prolonged daily struggle with gravity, and so must lie down, must close his eyes, must give himself over to the body's slowing rhythm, to sleep.

Where he goes when the tides of unconsciousness are high enough to cover him is largely undocumented, for he has never been good at remembering dreams, if dreams are what they are. He rarely remembers specifics, but he is often left with a sense the next morning that he had been in the place he should have always been, being the person he was always meant to be. But when he wakes, all he has to show for it is a bitter taste on the tongue.

Tonight his body feels unusually heavy, even though in recent months he has lost weight. When he begins his descent through the surface of the mattress into its interior he isn't in the least surprised, but he is interested. In any case there is no apparent way to reverse the process: the springs grab his fingers, robbing him of leverage.

Out the bottom and through the dust under the bed, then through the floor boards into a maze of pipe and wire, and he closes his already closed eyes because he is suddenly afraid there may be monsters here, in the dark and under where he has slept his entire adult life. Grown men aren't supposed to be afraid of monsters, but if he has ever been grown he cannot remember exactly when and precisely where it was. He is simply a boy in a bigger size.

This cannot be a dream because he never remembers his dreams, but perhaps the rules are different because this is his last dream.

This fancy makes him afraid again, but he reminds himself he cannot know if this is true. He cannot know if he is alive or dead, sleeping and dreaming or making some final shift out of the stream of memory and time.

He exits the floor into the wall of the house, then through the brick and then into dark, cold air. Here he sees others much like himself: grown men and women, a few children, flattened thin as paper, floating like leaves, their hands clutching desperately the corners of their new geometry.

Even the birds flying tonight are narrow, and have only one eye. He is sure there will be a number of serious collisions, but they avoid each other without even thinking, though instead of reassuring, this makes him sad. He floats along peacefully and solo, left and right sides rocking gently with the rhythm of his heart.

Far below him a rabbit chases a fox, having a very fine evening.

He thinks about his late wife, and wants to share with her how wonderful it was when that great day came, when all the people at last revealed how they felt about one another, and it was for the first time possible to really see the person speaking inside, without that distracting mask of bruised and twisted flesh they'd all called "body."

But that day hasn't yet occurred . . . Or has it?

He so wants to do a good job. He wants to be ready, but how can you possibly ever be ready for such a thing?

The trees floating by are full of babies, their eyes shining the color of new. He tries to touch one, but navigation is not under his control.

The air is so full of damp only his tears are dry. They make a series of negative spaces on his cheeks, shiny like gems.

How could you ever be ready? The love of his life, had she been ready? Only once did she tell him she was frightened, and it was the worst thing he'd ever heard his whole life. After that she'd told him nothing about what she was going through, just her hopes for the children and her worries for him, and a slow recounting of memories, savoring each one before she allowed it to drop to the floor.

Later (and he had been so shocked by this he could not now remember if it had been three days before her death or three weeks), she had looked up at him and said, "Honey, you know it's not the end of the world."

Just below, barely out of his reach, the world turns over without him. Cows return to the barn, the farmer walking alongside with lantern in hand. A child closes his book, the best he's ever read. A young girl cries herself to sleep, convinced she will never love again. People are dancing. People are making music. People are making love. Their rising voices lift him sideways, almost out of control.

But he knows the world has always moved without him, so how can he complain?

The edges of the sky fray, the clouds grow dirty, and he thinks of a poor woman's dress, and how at the end of a long day of begging she prepares to remove it.

He coughs. He coughs again. A startled head flies out of his mouth. It is his own.

He raises his head and blinks. The numbers on the clock blaze red in the dim landscape of his bedroom, but he cannot quite decipher them. 3 or 4 or 7. Most people die, what do they say, between 2 and 3 a.m.? But still, he cannot read the clock. Zeroes abound. In any case it does not matter. He is alone in his bedroom, the middle of the night, numbers flashing before his eyes, isolated and lost in the dark. As he has always been. Did she feel this? Was *this* what it was like? He lies down inside the safety of pillows, which can be mountains, which can be clouds, which can be anything he wants them to be. These are the last moments before bedtime, and beyond these walls an eternity waits.

Steve Rasnic Tem *was born in Lee County, Virginia in the heart of Appalachia. He is the author of over 350 published short stories and is a past winner of the Bram Stoker, International Horror Guild, British Fantasy, and World Fantasy Awards. His story collections include* City Fishing, The Far Side of the Lake, *and* In Concert *(with wife, Melanie Tem). Forthcoming collections include* Ugly Behavior *(crime) and* Celestial Inventories *(contemporary fantasy). An audio collection,* Invisible, *is also available. His novels include* Excavation, The Book of Days, Daughters, The Man In The Ceiling *(with Melanie Tem), and the recent* Deadfall Hotel. *In this Edward Gorey-esque, Mervyn Peak-esque novel, a widower takes the job of manager at a remote hotel where the guests are not quite like you and me, accompanied by his daughter and the ghost of his wife—"a literary exploration of the roots of horror in the collective unconscious."*

You may visit the Tem home on the web at www.m-s-tem.com.

THE RESURRECTION POLICY

LISA MORTON

Our lives are filled with the effects of burgeoning technology, from enhanced safety and education to revolutionized entertainment and healthcare. Industrialization is intertwined so much into our existence that life is difficult to imagine without it, so much so that even the great slumber, death, seems to no longer be the end-all. Consider Cryogenics, the study of freezing people in order to resuscitate at a later time. Consider even the real possibility of gene cloning our descendants. Consider, as in the following story, the insurance and sales packages associated with these advancements. Lisa Morton—one of the hardest working and most respected writers in the horror industry—brings us a wicked tale of business, treachery, and resurrection. Note to self: Don't ever miss a payment on The Resurrection Policy.

100101100110001
Wlfj
Whe
Where am I? What hap—
I can't feel anything. Or see, or hear, or smell, or taste. Nothing.
Did I . . . have a stroke? Am I paralyzed?
Thoughts are unconnected, loose, randomly ordered. Must try to remember.
Good. Finding connections now. Money—something about money. A lot of it. I . . . yes, I lost a great deal of money. Market crash. No gas. Food riots. Specialists saying the global economy was going belly-up. IRS took my houses. Locked out of offshore accounts. Tasha filed for divorce and took the last of our assets. And then . . . and then . . .
Was in my office, arguing with my CFO, that bastard idiot, Gerard. I remember a pain in my chest. Gallons, miles, a million volts of pain, exploding. Couldn't breathe. Falling. Vision failing. Distant sirens. They didn't make it. Neither did I.
I think I . . . I died.
Yes, that's right. I died. I'm dead now.
Dead.
Jesus. Well, that explains why I have no sensations. But I—
I'm not supposed to die. I paid for a top-of-the-line resurrection policy for both Tasha and I. We had the recording chips installed in our heads and our clone bodies prepared, fully grown and waiting in the vats. I was supposed to wake up in the new, fresh, younger version of myself, good as gold and ready to rock. That'd serve the Queen Bitch Tasha right, wouldn't it? I'd look twenty again and she'd still be forty-six.
That's how it should've gone. My money wasn't supposed to evaporate, and Tasha wasn't supposed to divorce me, and I wasn't supposed to die, and I wasn't supposed to wake up in—well, wherever this is.
My thoughts are settling into lines and patterns now, and I become aware that I am definitely *somewhere*. I sense energy, fluctuating and billowing around me. I sense something in that energy—numbers. A gush of numbers, endless ones and zeros. I imagine reaching out and plucking numbers from a void . . . but of course I'd need arms and fingers for that, and I—
I miss sensation. This is like being trapped in a soundproofed, lightproofed cage. This could drive anyone crazy, and drive them there *fast*. This is no fucking good. This—

"Hello, Mr. Lavelle."

Some of the numbers form and tumble around me and transmute into letters, then words. They take shape in my thoughts, interrupting the stream of *me*. It's not exactly that I see the letters, but . . . well, it's like remembering something seen in a dream, something insubstantial but witnessed nonetheless.

"You're probably wondering where you are."

"Goddamn right I am," I want to say, but I don't know how.

"My name is Lindsey Rockwell, and I work in Claims Resolution at Bentford-Griffin, specializing in Resurrection Policies."

Great, I try to think loudly (if that's even possible), *then put me back in my brand new body and get me the hell out of here.*

"Mr. Lavelle, sir, are you aware that you missed the last two payments on your policy?"

Everything stops. I don't like where this is leading.

"We were about to send you a notice that your policy would be cancelled in ten days if we didn't receive payment, but unfortunately you died before we could. Oh, excuse me, sir, I apologize if you hadn't yet grasped that fact, but . . . well, I'm sorry to inform you that you died. Heart attack at only forty-eight. We try to caution our clients that owning a resurrection policy shouldn't be taken as a license to indulge in unhealthy life practices, but apparently smoking, overeating, and stress were factors in your demise."

I don't believe this dipshit (Man? Woman? Lindsey? What the fuck is a Lindsey?) is lecturing me on my lifestyle. I make a mental note to have this fucking grub fired when I'm back on my feet.

"Because your premium was past due and technically expired, but we hadn't notified you yet—as we are required by law to do—we are willing to offer you what we believe is a very fair settlement."

A settlement?! No, no, no—I paid into that policy for fifteen years, ever since the technology first became available. So I had two bad months when everything went to shit—they can't offer me a "settlement" and expect me to take that.

"Mr. Lavelle, we're not required to offer that."

Can you—actually hear me?

"Yes, sir. You—or, more accurately, your consciousness, stored in digital form—is currently residing in a folder on one of our servers. We've given your folder access to our special patented communication software and we can read your responses on a screen."

Oh, great. No privacy, huh? Aren't there laws against that?

"Sir, there are, but we think you'll agree that the urgency of this situation negates the need for privacy. Now, If you'll permit me to continue: Bentford-Griffin, without any legal obligation to do so, is willing

to offer you a body for purposes of resurrection; however, please be advised that your waiting clone has already been recycled for parts, due to failure to make required payments."

So I'm getting . . . what?

"We have a body that had been prepared for another client, but encountered difficulty in the cloning vats and has been ruled unsatisfactory. We will allow you to resurrect in this body, if you so choose."

Choose? What's my other choice?

"You can continue to reside within our servers in your current digitized state."

You're kidding, right? I can be—whatever the fuck *this* is, forever? Uh, no thanks. I'll take the body.

"Very good, sir. We'll make arrangements immediately. Thank you for your understanding."

Wait—just how 'unsatisfactory' was this other—

I wake up.

My eyes open and I see lights. They hurt, and I blink and look aside. There are faces bending over me. "The patient's awake," says one of them, behind his surgical mask.

I flex fingers. Everything seems to be working, but . . . well, I can tell this isn't my old body. Something feels . . . strange. Parts of me hurt.

"Can you hear me?"

I turn to look up at the man who's just spoken. "Yes, I can hear you," I try to say, but my tongue feels thick, and it comes out slurred.

"Good. I'm pleased to tell you that your chip has been transplanted and you've been resurrected, but this body is probably going to feel a bit . . . uh . . . strange, just at first . . . "

One of the nurses snickers. Jesus, what've they put me into?

I try to sit up, but everything spins and the doctor pushes me back down. "Not yet. Soon."

It takes a night for the anesthesia to wear off. For some reason I'm slow coming out of it. As I begin to regain full awareness, I notice a few things:

I feel heavy.

My thoughts are sluggish.

I ache, mainly in my abdomen.

I'm in a room with another patient, an old woman in the bed next to mine who wheezes and drools. The paint on the wall is peeling near the ceiling, and I can tell without even trying to use it that the television mounted above my bed is broken. What the hell kind of cheap hack joint is this, anyway? *This* is what I paid for?

I tug all the needles and tubes out and stand up. I make a *thud* when I hit the floor. I reach out to grasp onto the bed, and when my vision clears I see that my fingers are chubby, and . . . feminine.

What the fuck . . . ?

I plod to a mirror in the bathroom—and nearly vomit.

I'm a woman. The bastards stuck me in a female body. And not just any female body—one that's got a shitload of problems. I'm doughy, as if the muscles didn't grow as fast as the skin in the cloning vat. My fingers are as short as a child's. I've got just a few wisps of stringy hair growing from my lumpy pate. One leg is longer than the other, making me walk with a clumsy side-to-side waddle. Christ, even the eyes don't match—one's blue, the other green.

I storm out of the bathroom, nearly toppling over because of the leg problem. "You fucks!" I scream, and I hate the voice—I have a severe speech impediment, thanks to some kind of problem with my tongue. "Get in here!"

A nurse rushes in. She's wearing ridiculous pink scrubs with little cartoon bears printed on the fabric, and she has a thick accent I can't even place. "What seems to be the problem?"

"What the fuck is this?" I gesture at the absurd lump of flesh I've been saddled with. "This is some kind of mistake, or a joke, or—"

The nurse looks at my chart, and frowns at something. "Uhh . . . Mrs. Lavelle . . . " She pulls out a pen to make a correction.

"No, don't change that 'Mr.'—*that* is why I need to see somebody—a doctor, or the administrator here, or whoever—just get them in here *now*. Tell them Martin Lavelle needs to speak with them."

The nurse gives me an angry pout, then leaves. A few seconds later a man walks in; he looks harried, hair is askew, face covered in dark stubble. "No, no, I need to see a *doctor*—"

"I *am* a doctor, Mr. Lavelle. Or, more properly, a surgeon. I performed your resurrection today."

Lindsey. Lindsey Rockwell from Bentford-Griffin has decided to fuck with me. He/she obviously didn't like it when I made a note to fire his/her little ass, and this is payback—stick the annoying client in the cheapest, dirtiest clinic you can find, and give them a body that's so defective it was on its way to being cut up for organ transplants.

"Look, some mistake's been made. This can't be the right body—"

The little haggard-looking fuck actually smiles, and if I had my old body I'd punch that expression right off his ugly face. "Oh, I'm sorry, but it absolutely *is* the right body. I understand there was a problem with your premium payments . . . ?"

"But . . . this isn't even the right gender."

He offers me the most insincere sympathy I've ever seen. "I believe it's all that was available. You know, the clones don't often come out . . . well, this badly."

He starts to turn away. I yell after him, "You're not leaving! Not until we get this straightened out."

"I suggest you talk to your insurance company about that. Now, if you'll excuse me, I've got four more surgeries scheduled for this afternoon."

He leaves. I stand there, letting the fury build, then squelching it back down. Who do I call first?

Before I decide, two nurses show up and tell me I have a 3 p.m. release time, and it's 2:30 now. One of them hands me a bag full of shapeless clothes. They offer to help me dress; I tell them I can manage. I pull on the clothes, struggling to fit the cheap, stretchy fabric over my flabby legs and torso, then they bring a wheelchair to ferry me out. They hand me a phone, and I'm somewhat amazed to see it's my old unit. Amazed and relieved—it's got all my personal data stored in it, so I'll at least have access to money and help.

I'm not surprised when the doors open and I see I'm in the worst part of downtown; the clinic is surrounded by rundown medical buildings and shelters. A drunk is passed out on a nearby bus bench. Garbage fills the gutters. It's a hundred degrees out, and the smells are so thick you can practically bite off a chunk and gag on it. The sky overhead is orange with smog.

Think . . . who to call first . . . thinking's hard, and I realize that on top of everything else this body's brain isn't up to speed. Who can help me right away? Get me money? Get me medical care? Get me revenge on fucking Bentford-Griffin and Lindsey Rockwell?

I need money before anything else. I use the phone to bring up one of the accounts I know is still open. It asks me to supply a voice password. I talk into the phone—and freeze at the high-pitched squeak that comes out of my throat.

Of course the security program isn't going to recognize this.

I'm fucked. My face doesn't match, my eyes don't match, my fingerprints don't match, my voice doesn't match. All the standard forms of security will tell my accounts I'm not me. How the fuck am I supposed to operate in this shitbag?

I consider calling Tasha, but realize she'd be less than inclined to help me even if she believed me. Ex-wives aren't typically willing to help their ex-husbands . . . especially when the husbands are suddenly women.

Gerard. Of course. The bastard saw me die, and as CFO of Lavelle Industries, he'll be able to get me money. So I tap the icon for his private number on the phone. After a few seconds, the screen fills with his face, and I can tell from the background that he's in my old office in the penthouse at Gates Tower. Rat bastard.

"Martin . . . ?" His face goes from astonishment to perplexity as he sees me. "Who are you? What are you doing with Martin Lavelle's phone?"

"Gerard, it's me—Martin. Those bastards at Bentford-Griffin resurrected me into this body. Check with them if you don't believe me."

He frowns, thinking, then something flickers across his expression—was that cunning? Or caution?

"I'll do just that. Let me call you back. If you're *not* Martin Lavelle, you're in very deep shit."

"Fine—" But he cuts me off by hanging up before I even finish.

Something's wrong here. I suspected Gerard of moving funds before I died. Now I wonder why he's already taken my office, less than a week after my death. And what was that look?

Five minutes pass with no return call. Meanwhile, I'm feeling less and less good about standing out in the open like this, sweat pooling on me from the heat, junkies and winos staring at *me*, like I'm the freak.

Then I remember: I *am* the freak now.

I'm trying to decide where to go—I'm too weak and heavy to walk far, but every second I stand out here, anxiety eats away a little more of me—when I see a patrol car round the corner. At first I feel relief, then the car stops in front of me and two cops get out. Coming for me. My gut feels like ice.

Gerard tracked my phone and sent them for me, I'm sure of it. I don't have a prayer of outrunning them. As they tell me I'm under arrest, I try threatening them—"You'll regret this when you find out who I am!"—but that just makes them shove me into their car harder.

Three hours later, it's been straightened out. The cops talked to Bentford-Griffin, who've at least had the decency of confirming that I am the proper owner of Martin Lavelle's phone. Embarrassed and nervous about the lawsuit I've threatened to launch, they release me and ask where I'd like to be dropped off.

"Gates Tower," I answer without hesitation.

I look out of the back of the patrol car as we cross the city, passing the thirty percent who are unemployed, lined up at food kitchens for handouts (instead of working, the useless leeches), passing the ones who have jobs but will die for good because they can't afford resurrection, passing the buildings that are crumbling and abandoned because no one wants to live in this city anymore, and then I see Gates Tower standing high above it all like a stern father. My office is at the top of that tower. I used to look down on this city and imagine that I owned it. I will again.

We arrive at the tower, and I can tell the cops are glad to be rid of me. They drop me at the curb and then speed away without a word.

I enter the lobby—and stop. I don't know the security guard on duty at the front desk. He'll have to issue me a pass. Still, I have to figure out some way past this ant . . .

I try to remember the name of the usual guard; it takes a moment, then I come up with it. I approach; he doesn't smile at me as he looks up. "Yes?"

"Is Antonio around?"

"Antonio?"

"The usual guard."

"Oh, right—sorry, ma'am, he doesn't work here anymore."

I'm fucked. And I'm *ma'am*.

I've got to try Gerard. "Can you call Gerard Chew at extension 7612 and tell him that . . . Ms. Lavelle is here to see him?"

The guard peers at me, skeptical, but finally picks up the phone. He speaks into it softly.

I glance around the lobby as I wait. The doors on the express elevator up to the seventy-sixth floor open, and Gerard steps out.

With Tasha on his arm. They laugh and smile. They walk in perfect synch with each other.

Suddenly it all makes sense: He *was* moving funds, moving them into places where only he and my bitch wife could access them, leaving me no money to survive on. Talk about trickle-down economics—my money all trickled down to *him*, and I was stupid enough to let it.

"Gerard, you fucking pig," escapes my mouth before I can stop it.

Gerard and my ex-wife stop and look at me, uncomprehending. Everything freezes, except me. I maneuver my fleshy, lumbering body toward them. "You rotten, deceitful fucking traitor," I try to say, although my malformed tongue mangles the syllables.

But it's enough. Gerard goes three shades of pale. "Christ—" he mutters, and I know he knows.

A voice sounds behind me. "Ma'am, stop!"

It's the guard. I ignore him. I reach my intended victims, who just stare, wide-eyed. My ridiculous cow of an ex-wife has no idea. "The money won't last, you know," I tell them. "You can't even access the biggest accounts—"

Gerard suddenly steps back, feigning panic. "I think she's got a gun!" he shrieks.

The guard behind me yells again. "Ma'am, step away from Mr. Chew *now!*"

I look back. The guard's got a sidearm drawn, pointed at me. This is too much. "You imbecile, who do you think pays your goddamn salary?" I sneer at him.

Confusion flickers across his face, but a glance at Gerard reaffirms his resolution. "Ma'am, I'm gonna ask you one more time: Step away from Mr. Chew and Ms. Lavelle."

I consider briefly, and realize it's entirely possible that Gerard could have me shot, right here, and I'd be dead for good—no more resurrection. No more second chances. Gerard would get away with everything, for however long it would last him. Hard to say which will run out first—the money or Tasha.

I raise my stubby fingers and back away. "Okay. Okay, I'm going."

"Mr. Chew," the guard says, never taking his eyes off me, "do you want to press charges? I can call the police . . . "

"No. Just get this—this *woman* out of here," Gerard says, putting a little extra spin on the gender just to piss me off.

I reach the door leading out of the tower, but turn and look back one last time. The guard holstered his gun, but is still watching. And Gerard is smiling at me.

I smile back. Then I walk out.

I need to find somewhere to spend the night. I remember that maybe my credit is still good. I'm standing on the sidewalk, trying to check, when a voice interrupts me.

"Mr. Lavelle . . . "

I look up to see an icy beauty in an expensive suit, flanked by two rent-a-cops. If I was in my old body, I'd probably be hard after just one glance. As it is, I just feel dread because even though I've never really heard her voice, I know instantly: This is Lindsey Rockwell, Claims Resolution specialist at Bentford-Griffin.

"I'm afraid I'm going to have to ask you to come with us." She gestures at a large silver van parked at the curb.

"Why? What's this about?"

"I'm afraid you've violated the terms of your policy, sir."

The gorillas drag me to the van and I have no strength to resist. "What terms?"

"Paragraph Forty-Eight, Section C, Sub-section Three: 'The client will not engage in any life-threatening activities after achieving resurrection.' Paragraph Fifty-Three, Section F, Sub-Section One: 'Insurer may, at its own discretion, revoke this policy at any time should . . . '"

There's more, but I'm not hearing, because we've reached the back of the van, the doors have opened—and inside a stretcher and two men in surgical masks wait for me.

"This is wrong—I haven't engaged in any 'life-threatening activities'—"

"Did you not just threaten Mr. Chew until a guard had to draw his weapon? Oh, by the way—threatening another client is also a violation of the policy—Paragraph Sixty-Two, Section B, Sub-section Two."

Now I know why Gerard didn't press charges after our encounter in the tower lobby. He had something better in mind. Something more permanent.

"This is murder," I scream at Lindsey, as I feel a needle enter my arm and the sedative begin to work through my system.

"Oh, we're not going to kill you, Mr. Lavelle," Lindsey says, before stepping back as the doors to the van close.

The last thing I feel is the steel of the stretcher beneath me as I'm laid back.

What a shitty final sensation.

I

Wha

Nothingness. Again. Of course.

They couldn't kill me, because that would be murder . . . but they *could* take away the body they gave me and send me back here, to my digital hell.

Here's what they didn't count on: *Me.* I may not have sensations, but I can think better here than I could in that malfunctioning mess of a clone, and as long as I can think, I can figure things out. That's how I made a fortune—sure, I inherited plenty, but then I figured out how to make more. And I'll get it back. I'll escape this folder and this computer, expand to the net, make Gerard Chew and Lindsey Rockwell sorry they were ever born.

I'll use the information flow to . . .

Wait. Something's wrong. The information flow . . .

It's not there anymore. The numbers, the energy. There's nothing to latch onto, there's no . . .

Am I . . . really dead? Is this . . . But I never believed. There's nothing after we die. Unless we paid for resurrection.

The power's off. That's got to be it. The other possibility . . . No, it's just the power.

It'll come back on. It has to. It always does. I won't be here forever. That's not possible.

The power will come back. And when it does . . .

I'll be ready.

Lisa Morton *is a screenwriter, horror author, four-time winner of the Bram Stoker Award, and Halloween expert. Recent short fiction appearances include* Blood Lite III, Danse Macabre, *and* Dark Discoveries Magazine, *and books include* Witch Hunts: A Graphic History of the Burning Times *(with Rocky Wood, illustrated by Greg Chapman),* Trick or Treat?: A History of Halloween, *and the novella* Hell Manor. *She lives in North Hollywood, California, and can be found online at* www.lisamorton.com.

HIGH PLACES

JOHN M. FLOYD

Dante Alighieri wrote that there are nine spheres of angelic hierarchy within Paradise, whereas each sphere further inwards is home to the increasingly revered and closer to God. One can imagine though, that even those at the furthest plane—the outskirts—of Paradise, should be pretty relieved to have at least "made it," and not been sent elsewhere. For those who are the marginal performers, consider the following selection by John M. Floyd. Reminiscent of O. Henry, High Places *is quick, funny, and clever; For even in the social tiers of the righteous, there's always someone on the bottom rung.*

Jack Hollister woke up in a room he'd never seen before: Two doors, three windows, bare walls, no furniture. It contained, besides Jack, one man in a blue robe and three people with red X's marked on their foreheads. The man in the robe held a clipboard and pencil, and looked at Jack with a bright smile. Since Jack felt he'd just awakened from a deep sleep, the fact that everyone was standing, including him, seemed a bit strange.

That was only the beginning.

"Good morning," the man said.

Jack blinked. "Do I know you?"

"You did. I was Bob Wilson."

Jack's eyes widened. He remembered now. He and Bob and several others had been on a tour bus in the mountains north of Anchorage. They'd been looking down into the icy gorges and joking about Jack's lifelong fear of heights. It seemed only a short while ago.

And then he remembered the grinding of brakes, the skid, the sickening lurch as the bus went over the cliff—

Jack swallowed. It *had* been only a short while ago.

"Where am I?" he asked.

The man who had been Bob Wilson smiled again. "Your new home. Mine too, for that matter." He pointed, and through one of the open doors Jack saw a green and flowery meadow. People dressed in robes of every color strolled along grassy paths. In the distance he saw what looked like a waterfall and a rainbow. The breeze through the windows smelled of gardenia blossoms.

"We got here ahead of you," Bob added. "You lived just long enough to get carried to a hospital."

Jack's mind was spinning. "So this room . . . this is—"

"A reception area," Bob said. "One of many." His face grew solemn. "And for some, a temporary stop."

Bob Wilson tipped his head toward the three people marked with red X's. Jack turned to look at them: Two men and a woman, dressed in coveralls. They stood together in a corner, their faces blank and eyes vacant.

"Those were the others on the bus?" Jack whispered.

"A sad thing," Bob said. "I'm afraid they weren't ready for all this."

Jack blinked again. "You mean . . . "

Bob nodded, and pointed to the other doorway. Beyond it, at the base of a sloping lawn, the world fell away into a vast, rocky chasm. It looked like pictures Jack had seen of the Grand Canyon. He could barely see, in a bend of the canyon wall, a steep, narrow path that snaked downward, hugging the cliff face until it vanished from sight. A dull roar rose from the depths, and Jack caught the odor of smoke and gases.

"They'll be sent down there soon," Bob said.

Jack swallowed. "I can't believe it. They're just . . . thrown in?"

"Not thrown. Everything's very civilized here. They're escorted down, when the time comes."

He felt sick. Just the thought of that narrow ledge along the wall reminded him of his fear of heights and made him dizzy.

"Looks like the one in Arizona, doesn't it?" Bob added.

Jack barely heard the comment; his mind was still on the fate awaiting the others. Then he had an even more disturbing thought. "What about me?" he asked.

Bob grinned again. "Don't worry, no X on your forehead. They've already logged you in—you're based up here, like me. We have jobs to do, now."

"Jobs?"

"Assignments," Bob said. "You missed the briefing, but the gist of it is, all of us who weren't—" he shot an uncomfortable glance at the three others, who didn't seem to be listening "—most of us, that is . . . were given positions to fill."

Jack stared at him. "You mean, like, from now on?"

"Yes, from now on. It's called eternity." Bob held up the clipboard and pencil. "They gave me these, and my robe, and told me to make a note of any new arrivals—at least those from the area we left. Apparently a patient from a Juneau hospital's due shortly and a couple of fishermen from the Gulf of Alaska."

"But—how do they decide who does what?" Jack asked.

"What position, you mean? Depends on what you did in your previous life."

"Like your area of expertise?"

"No, your track record." Bob paused a moment. "You know—your good deeds."

Jack gave that some thought. He couldn't recall many good deeds. Neither, probably, could Bob Wilson. After all, they had both been lawyers.

But at least they hadn't been selected to make the trip into the canyon.

Jack felt a shiver ripple down his spine.

"It's sort of like Santa Claus," Bob said. "If you've been good, you get a bicycle, or a chemistry set. Bad, you get switches and ashes."

"Ashes?"

"Poor choice of words. But you get my drift. For humans, robe color indicates rank—the lighter-colored ones go to those with the best records."

For humans? But before Jack could ask what that meant, he had another thought. Bob's robe was blue; what color was Jack's? He almost checked, then decided not to. So far he had carefully avoided looking down at all in case he bore some kind of visible injury from the accident. Since he was already stressed out, maybe he should just wait, take one thing at a time. He kept his eyes level.

"Bottom line is, you passed their tests," Bob said. "Someone'll be along soon to go over the details." He licked the point of his pencil and made some notes on his clipboard.

Jack sighed. His mind boiling with unasked questions, he turned his attention again to the two open doorways. Except for the ominous presence of the canyon, everything outside seemed peaceful and pleasant. Happy, even. A more populated Garden of Eden minus the snake.

He began to relax. He had made it. In fact, Paradise looked pretty darn good. Despite Bob's words about rank and status, everyone Jack had seen through the doorway looked content and fairly well off. Maybe this was an all-or-nothing deal. Maybe it didn't much matter how good you'd been in your earthly life, so long as you hadn't been bad enough to get the axe.

To Jack, who had been a marginal performer at best, that system sounded just fine.

Adrift in his thoughts, he turned to look through one of the windows. To his surprise, he saw a furry white dog dozing in the sun with its head resting on its paws. Jack smiled. Even the pets here looked satisfied. In a second window a big-eared, squinty-eyed mule stared back at him. A third window revealed an eagle sitting in the branches of a live oak.

The eagle seemed to be studying a group of people in the distance. As Jack watched, the huge bird floated down to light on the shoulder of a white-robed man playing—incredibly—a golden harp. The eagle seemed to speak into the man's ear. Then it rose lazily to its perch once more and resumed its vigil.

Jack remembered Bob's comment about humans. "So there are animals here, too?" he asked.

Bob looked up. "Yep. Just like home. Except they used to be people."

"They what?"

Bob chuckled. "They were people, like we were. It's not a demotion or anything—they can still talk and reason." He pointed to the window. "That eagle you're watching was John McFinney, I'm told."

"The senator?"

"That's what the orientation guy said. McFinney was squeaky clean, you know, a model citizen. His job here is to monitor and report to the main guys. An important position." Bob scratched his head with the pencil and continued. "Animal assignments are based on rank also. Lions and eagles are the highest."

Jack felt another twinge of concern. "When will they assign me something, you think?"

"They already have. I meant to tell you—they even dropped off your stuff." Bob bent over and picked up a sack. It looked heavy and clanked when it was moved.

Sounds bigger than a clipboard, Jack thought.

Bob reached inside and took out a small saddle and four horseshoes.

Horseshoes?

"Maybe I'll be in charge of recreation," Jack said, brightening. "You know, games and such."

But then Jack remembered the second window—the closest to him—and the mule looking back at him. A mule with squinty eyes.

That's when the truth hit him. Jack whirled, and stared. The second window wasn't a window at all.

It was a mirror.

Jack gulped. He looked down at his hooves. "You mean—"

"It's not bad duty, I've heard," Bob said.

"What? Pulling a *plow*?"

"Running the shuttle."

"The shuttle?"

"Well," Bob said, nodding toward the three condemned souls, "they can't get down there by themselves . . . "

John M. Floyd's *short stories and features have appeared in more than 200 different publications, including* The Strand Magazine, Woman's World, Alfred Hitchcock's Mystery Magazine, *and* Ellery Queen's Mystery Magazine. *A former Air Force captain and IBM systems engineer, he won a 2007 Derringer Award and has been nominated three times for the Pushcart Prize. John is also the author of three collections of short fiction:* Rainbow's End *(2006),* Midnight *(2008), and* Clockwork *(2010).*

CIRCLING THE STONES AT FULCRUM'S LOW

KELDA CRICH

Life is difficult enough, if not downright cruel, to be victimized by others based solely on your appearance or beliefs, to be betrayed and condemned due to circumstances beyond your control. It's even more difficult when those circumstances continue to haunt you after you die . . . and die . . . and die again. Kelda Crich bears the tragic story of a young woman who is pursued mercilessly by those she is forced to live amongst. Someday, Esmar Tanner will find her escape, if not her revenge. For now, she is trapped, Circling the Stones at Fulcrum's Low.

The night wind unwinds over the stones at Fulcrum's Low. Once the stones stood upright, touching the face of the sky. Now, they are fallen altars, grown over with the runes of lichen. But it matters not, their power is the same.

It is always the same.

On this night of the October Hunter's moon, Esmar is woken by the sound of men's voices. She throws a shawl over her nightshift and looks out her bedroom window. She sees the weave of their lit torches, glimmering in the night, a path of stars fallen to the ground.

Eomar Tanner is only twenty years old. It seems as if her time is getting shorter. She wonders what she had done to betray herself . . . this time. It's so difficult to keep the small details correct, when your mind is overfull, a dish of water trembling with too much knowledge and too many memories. Sooner or later, she always sees them: the righteous men wanting to murder her.

The men are at the front of her home. Esmar hears the noise of smashing glass, but she knows that the windows are too small for them to squeeze through, and it will take them some time to break down her solid oak door.

She walks quickly and noiselessly down the stairs and slips out though the kitchen door. A high brick wall stands between Esmar and her would-be killers. She listens to their murmuring voices and recognizes them all. Gabriel, her dog, barks furiously. She hopes they will not kill him as her familiar.

She runs through her herb garden, wondering who will take care of it now. She slips through a hidden door covered with ivy and runs across the fallow field adjacent to her cottage. The severed barley stalks slice into her naked feet. Esmar heads to the river. In the distance she sees the mound of Fulcrum's Low rising high above the surrounding countryside. Fulcrum's Low where once, so many years ago, she was taken.

Angry shouts in the distance tell her that her absence has been discovered. She winces as the sound of Gabriel is abruptly silenced. He was a good dog.

Now she has reached the river. She's tired of running but she's not without other resources. Under the Hunter's moonlight, Esmar slows her breathing, slipping into the dark waters of her flesh. Slower, slower now, floating within the blood of her body. Her breath becomes mere whispers drawn along the long road. Her heartbeat becomes a quiet stone. She slips into the River Trent that runs alongside this Fulcrum town. She waits in the silt, her breath almost nothing, extending onwards, a silent fish in the deep waters.

Time passes in the soothing, cold darkness, until Esmar sees the burning of the torches and hears the men's voices above her.

"She won't go this way. They can't cross water." The voice of Aaron Bletchley. Esmar set his broken arm, two months past.

"Aye, and they say that they're crones too. But look at her. She's no crone. Besides, I've seen her cross water many times." The voice of Mitchell Cross. Last spring, she helped his wife birth twins.

Esmar sees a shape bending over the water. "She's in here. I think she's dead."

Esmar thinks the trick might fool them. Then she might have longer in this body, longer to study. She could, perhaps, add to the incremental accumulation of knowledge that, surely one day, if the gods have any pity, will lead to her release.

A hand reaches into the water, touching her cold flesh. She is motionless, praying that they will leave her be, until her staring-blind, open eyes recognize the face bent over her. That sudden recognition causes her to move. The man bending over her is William, her love. It's William who's betrayed her.

"She's alive. Get her out of there." William pulls her out of the river waters. She falls, cold and wet into his embrace. William drags her onto the river's mudded bank that intrudes into the mouth of the river like a greasy, black tongue.

She lies on the ground, gasping as the breath returns to her body. The men circle around her. They watch her. Their hatred is palpable, expelled from their bodies and forming wreathes of mists in the cold air.

The priest steps forwards. Esmar never liked him, a no-nothing outsider from Nottingham. He doesn't understand the ways of Fulcrum. He raises a trembling hand and points at her. In his other hand he clutches the bible to his chest, "You are a witch, indeed, Esmar Tanner."

"What do you want with me?" Esmar finds her voice. "Just let me be."

"You know what we want, witch. It is the Lord's work," the priest says.

Esmar knows what will happen next. Her body is limp and unresistant at the memory of death. She turns her face into the mud and moans. Her actions scare them. They're expecting venom. They want something more. They want some irrefutable sign to justify their actions.

"Are you sure?" Aaron Bletchley asks.

The priest gestures to William who grabs Esmar and turns her around. His pushes his contorted face close to hers. "You bewitched me. You made me do things."

"Are you sure, William?" Aaron asks again. "Did you actually see her magicks?"

"I told you already," William says. "She was a ghost, when we was . . . when we was fornicating. Her body was under me, but I saw her ghost wandering the room. And she tempted me. She made me betrayal my wife."

The men nod. A witch can leave her body, that was well-known. And it was also well-known that a witch can tempt a man off the path of righteousness.

Esmar is not surprised. She's usually betrayed by the ones she loves most. She will endeavor to be more careful—the next time. She must guard her wandering spirit.

"She is a witch," the priest says. "I've long been suspicious of her medicines. We've all seen her magick." He stares at each man in turn. "No natural woman could live under the water like she has done tonight. It is proved. We will not suffer a witch to live. It is God's work we do." He nods to Samuel and Parkin Woods. They grab Esmar and pull her to her feet. William loops a rope over the branch of an ash tree, and Samuel pushes Esmar's head into the noose. All the men take hold of the rope, for this is to be a joint action. They pull, dragging her upwards. Esmar is subject to the long moments of struggle. She claws desperately at the necklace of rope around her throat. She endures the endless moments of frantic violence, until her spirit is freed from her clay. It is a nasty death, strangulation, but better than burning.

Esmar drifts, walking the wind. She leaves her murderers. She sees the old stones that are drawn on Fulcrum's Low. They are her incessant anchor to this village. How she would dearly love to be released. Her spirit walks to the village. She re-enters the flesh, nesting within the cells forming in a woman. She floats in the warmth, remembering her small time of freedom. Esmar reads the world through the eyes of her new mother. After a time the door of the cottage opens.

"It's done." The man walks in and sits at the table.

"She's dead?" the mother asks.

"Yes. She was a witch. I told you."

The mother insists he tell her tell her all the details. The mother is glad that Esmar has been killed, yet she's afraid.

"It's a bad thing, to be linked with this business," she says. "Are you sure it's all over? She bewitched you, right, William? It was because she was a witch that you betrayed me."

William sits with his face buried into his hands, his voice, when it comes, is weary. "I told you what happened, and now she's dead. Let that be the end of it."

The mother takes Esmar away from him. She goes to her bed where she washes her face with almost noiseless grief.

Esmar swims within that body, nested within the body of his wife. She begins her period of waiting. A new life beckons. She's pleased that she will be with William, again.

Esmar wonders if this is the same for everyone. Do all spirits circle in this endless dance? No one she's ever met has remembered as she does. Many times, many lives, Esmar has tried to gather knowledge. She has been called by many names: witch, wise woman, seer, hag, cunning woman, figure flinger, weird sister. Many names they have called her, many names as they cut her, stoned her, burnt, drowned, or strangled her. Many lives Esmar has had, and many deaths, all to be returned to the flesh again, returned within sight of the stone boundaries of Fulcrum's Low. The stones where she met her first death four thousand years ago. She remembers that first death, bound as sacrifice to the Stone Walkers: *Those who flit along the edge of the world.*

Esmar, the unending sacrifice, returned, once more, to the flesh, dreams of those precious few moments of freedoms, walking the wind. She wonders if her next life will bring the key which might unlock her eternal prison of this sequential flesh.

Kelda Crich is a new born entity. She's been lurking in her creator's mind for a few years. Now, she's out in the open. Find her in London looking at strange things in medical museums. Her work has appeared in Lovecraft Ezine *and in the* Future Lovecraft *anthology.*

I WILL REMAIN

DAVID STEFFEN

Perhaps upon death our consciousness never leaves the confines of this biological world. Like water, the soul may simply convert into other measures, solidifying or melting under shifting circumstances or absorbing through a gaseous state into the carbon or the consciousness of other living things. We are composed with the memories of life-before-us ingrained into our DNA and, perhaps, some of those memories may struggle more than others to dictate our lives. Do we remember the fears of others that now whisper in our atoms? Their pains, their ambitions, their desires? Why exactly do we make decisions that would otherwise seem irrational? The talented David Steffen suggests that reincarnation may influence our choices more than we could imagine. I Will Remain is a touching tale of mystery, love, and the struggle to carry on.

I am not insane. I wondered, at first, whether I was simply a dog dreaming he was a man, but if that were true I wouldn't understand English or recall the sights of London. These things are too real to be mere fancies. I know many things a dog shouldn't. Fragmented memories of life as a man mingle with recollections of my canine existence.

Emily rolls in her sleep and her arm flops off the bed to dangle by my face. She tosses and turns too much. Something troubles her.

She is my everything. She pats me behind the ears and calls me a *Good Boy*, but I would love her even if she ignored me. I will be her Good Boy for the rest of my life. I wish I could be more.

I see a hint of movement on the floor, a mouse, barely illuminated by the moonlight. I lift my nose ever so slightly and sniff. The creature pays me no mind, walking in a straight line for the bed.

It smells of the ocean, of salty sand and rotting fish. A strange scent for a land animal. The only other that I've smelled like this was the fox on the day of my last hunt, the hunt that precipitated my current lucid state. Before that hunt I had been an ordinary dog in every respect. I begin to drool. That fox tasted like nothing else I've ever eaten.

The mouse darts for Emily's bed, but I am quicker. I crush it in my jaws and swallow it in one gulp. My mind effervesces like a glass of freshly poured champagne. Memories burst into my consciousness, memories of a life with Emily: a chance meeting at the opera, falling in love, picnics in a glade not far from her home. Our courting was the happiest time of my life.

My name was Ian.

The tingle is what I'd imagine opium would feel like, but I feel more lucid with each dose. If I can find others like the mouse and fox, then perhaps I can remember why I am here. If there are two, there must be more.

"Emily, dear, haven't you grieved long enough?" Mrs. Wilkinson's voice is level.

Emily's hand pauses in its traversal of my back. "Eternity isn't long enough, Mother."

"You need to move on. Do you really think Ian would have wanted you to be unhappy the rest of your life?"

Emily's hand runs across my back again. "I can put on a smile if it will soothe you, but I won't be happy again until he and I are together in Heaven."

"Two years is long enough. I don't want you to end up a spinster."

"Better a lonely spinster than a loveless marriage."

Mrs. Wilkinson raises her voice. "Do you think your love for each other was so unique? The two of you were no different from any others!" Her voice lowers to a whisper. "Your father and I were like that once. Your life is not over. You will love again."

"Our love *is* different." She doesn't say this in anger, only as a simple statement of fact.

Mrs. Wilkinson sighs. "At the least, you should have *people* for company instead of spending every waking moment cooped up with that dog. I will arrange outings for you, and you will attend. If you meet men there, you will give them a chance. Be civil, at the very least. Is that clear?"

"Of course, Mother."

Mrs. Wilkinson bustles from the room, leaving me alone with Emily. She grunts in a very unladylike manner. "Why can't she leave me be? Ian was perfect for me. There can be no replacement."

I feel relief at her words and guilt at my relief. It is wrong to be happy at her unhappiness, but I can't help it. If I were gone from this world like I should be, I would want her to move on, to find a new man. But I cannot stand the thought of her courting if I am bound here to watch. I crave a confessional, but it would do me no good in my current form. I lay my head in her lap and she scratches me behind the ears, my favorite spot.

A gunshot rings out, startling me. I jump to my feet, almost knocking Emily off her chair. The Master and his wife rise from the table.

"What in the world was that?" Mrs. Wilkinson says.

"I'd best find out." The Master steps toward the door.

Emily rises.

"No, Emily, this is man's business. Stay here. Finish eating."

Emily sits down, a little too hard.

The Master steps out and I follow him quietly. He enters the parlor just long enough to grab his rifle off the wall. His eyes meet mine when he comes back out, but he waves me along.

Morning dew dampens my paws as I trot along behind him around the perimeter of the house. The first thing I see is a man dressed in working clothes, chest bare. His blood-soaked shirt is bundled around one hand, held in place by the other. A shotgun lies at his feet. He sobs deeply.

The air smells of blood and gunpowder and something else. Something out of place. I take another few steps before I discern it as the same rotten scent I'd found on the mouse. I've come to think of it as the *Bad Smell.*

I begin to drool, remembering the impossibly compelling flavor. The odor isn't coming from the worker. By the outer wall of the house is a dead body lying face down, a man in a suit. His back is a bloody mess from a shotgun blast. His clothes are torn and the skin underneath is covered in scratches.

The Master runs to the worker's side. "What happened, man? Are you badly injured?"

"He wouldn't stop. I tried to stop him but he wouldn't—"

"All will be well. Tell me what happened from the beginning."

As they talk, I inch closer to the dead body. The smell tickles my nose, and I lick the air.

"I was out working the western fields when I saw this man walking straight toward the house. I shouted after him to stop, but he didn't listen. I followed after him, shouting some more. I tried to talk to him, but he wouldn't even look at me."

I sniff the body. A china doll lies pinned under its arm, an unlikely accessory for an intruder.

"I didn't know who he was or what he was doing. He's dressed awfully nice for a criminal, but he wouldn't listen. I was afraid of what he might do to the women, sir."

The Master turns away from me now, looking at the young man. I lick the open wound, and my brain tingles. I grab a mouthful of meat, and pull slowly, tearing it free as quietly as I can. The Master is too enrapt in the story to notice.

"I grabbed his shoulder and tried to hold him back, but he just kept on going, digging in his feet and pulling me along. I didn't know what else to do so I struck him square in the face. That knocked him down, right enough, but the bugger got right back up and started walking again. He didn't even seem to notice his broken nose."

I resist the urge to grab another mouthful. The Master will notice if I eat too much. I don't want him to know I'm a Bad Boy.

"I stepped in front of him, and this time he finally looked at me, and his eyes looked like he'd gone feral. I tried to strike him again, but he caught my hand. He grabbed it and bit my damned finger off!" The man pauses. "Excuse my language, sir. Well, after that, I wasn't taking no chances. I knew you kept a gun out in the stables so I grabbed that and I used it, sir."

The Master pats him on the shoulder. "You've done nothing wrong. Go, wash your hand. I'll have someone take you to the doctor."

The young man nods and walks off. The Master turns and I face away to hide the bloodstains on my face. I hear him step over to the body and stop for a few minutes. Then he walks away around the edge of the house.

I dart a glance. I am alone. I tear another chunk of meat from the corpse. The part of me that is dog screams that I am a Bad Boy, and the part of me that is human cries in despair for the terrible sin I am committing. But my hunger drives me on. I take another bite, then another, and another. Buckshot lodges in my gums and scraps of cloth catch in my teeth, but I pay them no heed.

I remember. Emily and I were married. Her father gave us a wonderful wedding gift, a trip to America, the adventure of a lifetime.

I remember. We'd waited, like the good Christians we were, until our wedding night to know each other in the Biblical sense. The night was embarrassing and awkward, but wonderful. I have never felt clumsier.

I remember. I was so proud of my new wife. I brought her everywhere with me, introduced her to everyone. She was so beautiful, so smart, so willful. She was as comfortable on a picnic in the glade, sitting on a blanket and shooing the squirrels away, as she was at the opera in her intricate dresses and with her elaborate hair styles. Nothing else mattered as long as I was by her side.

The sound of voices travels around the corner, breaking my reverie. I hadn't realized I'd eaten so much; the man's body is a mangled ruin. I struggle to run, but my distended stomach undulates beneath me. I settle for a fast waddle, and I escape out of sight before they turn the corner.

I force myself to keep moving until I reach the solitude of the grove, where I stretch out in the glade. Flopping to my side, I lay there a long while, maybe days, getting up only to defecate. Finally, the pain subsides and my belly shrinks from its grotesque size. I feel able to walk again, but I am still plastered in dried blood. I need to wash or they may think I'm a mad dog and shoot me.

I've never believed in reincarnation, but maybe my belief doesn't matter. Maybe it's something that just happens, like a bodily function, and your belief doesn't matter one bit.

I thank God for every moment I spend with her. My time was up, yet here I am with her again. But I do wonder: why a dog? Perhaps He put me here as her guardian angel to protect her in her time of need.

There is the pond, waiting for me. When my feet touch the cold water, panic grips me. Fear freezes my joints in place, and I struggle to breathe. With a supreme effort I jump out into the water.

I cut through the deceptively smooth surface and the water closes over my head like the lid of a tomb. Half-remembered memories flash through my mind: mountains of ice rushing by on either side, impact, screams, the world teetering on edge, and then the cold void going on forever and ever.

My muscles convulse and I thrash to the surface. In that moment, my mind is empty of everything but the desperate need to get out of the water. Nothing has ever felt so good as the ground beneath my feet at this moment.

A few rolls in the grass wipe the remaining blood away, and then I run from the cold, dead eye of the pond.

"If God exists, then he's powerless or apathetic. No just God could let people fall in love and then tear them away from each other."

She is talking to no one but me, thinking that I don't understand. I am happy to play the role of confessor, though I don't like to hear Emily talk this way. In the darkness of her bedroom, her words seem to become tangible things, bogeymen lurking in corners. I shiver, despite the night's warmth. Please, God, don't hold her words against her.

"The church talks about His master plan, but it's all rubbish. They don't know anything. They're just babes in the woods, looking for reassurances."

If only I could speak, so I could tell her I'm by her side through thick and thin. I lick her hand and she strokes my ears until her breathing slows and a tiny snore escapes her lips.

Something thumps against the window and flaps and flutters against the glass. A bird or a bat trying to gain access to Emily's room. More and more animals have been acting strangely.

I suspect that Emily is the reason for all of this. All of the strange animals and the strange man are coming straight for her with unflagging determination. I cannot fathom the reason for their strange behavior, but whatever the cause, I know my course. God put me here to protect her. I will not fail.

A second thump sounds at the window, followed by the sounds of birds fighting, terrible squawks and shrieks. Then silence. Whatever drives these creatures to seek her does not cause them to cooperate. If two of them cross paths they fight to the death, but no matter how many lie dead, there are always more.

I eat the bodies when I can and regain more and more of my lost life.

I stand guard in her room every night and patrol the grounds restlessly when she is away on her social engagements. I would go insane if I did nothing but wait in her room, never knowing if she will return to tell me of newfound love.

So I patrol. I find the Bad Smell wherever I go. The lines of scent radiate out from the house in a lopsided sunburst. Most extend to the west, so I rove to that side of the house, watching for fresh trails. If it carries the Bad Smell, I kill it and eat it.

Over several weeks I find more humans that carry the Bad Smell: three men and two women, each carrying a china doll. Killing them is easy. They pay no attention to me until I jump at them, knocking them flat on their backs. I tear out their throats and gorge myself on their meat. My obligation to Emily is the only thing that allows me to stop eating before I am immobilized by my greed. I will do Emily no good if I'm killed by a beast as I lay bloated and helpless. I bury the china dolls in the glade. When I go back to check the body a few hours later, there is nothing left but bones.

Every night Emily calls me up onto the bed. She tells me about her day, and the men who have come to call on her. Some are crass, or pompous, or just boring. She tells it all in a level tone; there isn't a hint of attraction in her voice that I can detect.

She confides in me. I know there's nothing personal about it, that she's using me like a diary. But I can't help feeling there's more significance to it than that.

One night she returns, and something has changed. The Bad Smell trails behind her, but weakly. She is not the source, but she has been touching something that smells of it. Frustration and anger at this betrayal well up inside me. How can I protect her from those things if she seeks them out while she's away?

She walks past me without the customary head pat and undresses as if in a trance before lying down. When I jump up to join her, she looks up in mild surprise. After a moment she pats the bed to tell me to sit.

"Do you believe in Heaven? I don't. Not anymore. How do we know it's really there? What if life on Earth is your only chance at happiness? You owe it to yourself to make *this* life the best it can be. Otherwise you've just wasted it."

I wag my tail uneasily.

"I met a man today. His name is Walter. He's different from the others. He is polite, kind, thoughtful. His nose is too large, but he's handsome despite it."

My stomach lurches. She's going to move on, and I'll be helpless to do anything. I want to lie down and die.

"He reminds me of Ian. The two of them could have been friends in a different life, a different world. I can't wait for you to meet him. He loves dogs."

She pets me a while longer before speaking again. "If there is a Heaven, will Ian be waiting there for me? What if I marry Walter? Who would I be with in Heaven? Both? Neither? Either answer seems ludicrous. Perhaps my soul will be split in two and each half will live happily with just one man."

After she falls asleep, I slip off the bed and pace the room. What can I do? The answer is simple. I can do nothing. They will marry or they won't, and I can't do a damned thing. I will stay to protect her either way, but if they marry then my presence here will turn from blessing to curse.

Walter is one of them. A dense cloud of Bad Smell surrounds him like a cloud. When he bends to pet me, I must clench my teeth to keep from biting. I would be doing Emily a favor to kill him, but she wouldn't like it. She might even have me killed.

"Scratch him behind his ears," she says. "He'll be your friend for life."

I suffer him to scratch behind my ears for just a moment. That's my favorite spot. Only Emily touches me there. I tilt my head away from him to get away from his hand. He reaches with the other hand and I snap at him, teeth clicking shut mere inches from his extended digits. If Emily weren't there, I would relieve him of a finger, maybe two.

"Bad boy!" she says. "We don't bite."

I slink away, tail between my legs.

"I'm going for a walk," Walter says. I've spent the afternoon hiding behind the sofa, where I can listen without being subjected to his petting.

"I'll go with you!" she replies, and the fondness in her tone sickens me.

"No, I'm sorry, dear, but I wish to be alone with my thoughts."

This is my chance! I wait until he has been gone for several minutes before slipping out of the house and following his trail.

Instead of traveling along the road like I'd expected, he walks north, straight as an arrow to the very same grove that holds the glade where Emily and I used to picnic. He passes through the trees into the quiet space beyond. Out here there are no witnesses. My mouth waters in anticipation.

I peer at him from behind the cover of a tree. He stands in the glade, facing away from me. Why is he here? I wonder, but I can't afford to waste this God-given opportunity. I leave the tree cover and tense to pounce. I will knock him down and tear his neck open.

As I jump, he spins, revolver in hand. He's a half-second too slow. I knock him to the ground and the gun fires. The bullet misses, though I can feel its heat brush my ribs. My teeth close around his esophagus and tear it away, strings of flesh stretching and snapping.

As I gulp down the chunk of meat, an explosion rings out in the clearing, and a stabbing pain tears through my gut. The man's body convulses as he chokes on his own blood and then his body goes limp.

My own blood pours out of the wound in my side. I am not dead yet, but I won't live much longer. Already I feel weak, but the Bad Smell draws me even in my final minutes. I grip his shirt and pull, opening it in a spray of popped buttons. My teeth dig into the soft meat of his belly and I feast.

Sparks and flashes of light fill my vision. This meat is worlds richer than any of the others I've eaten. His memories fill my brain as his blood fills my stomach.

I remember. The china doll I bought Emily after our wedding, a promise of the children we would have.

I remember. Our last goodbyes as she boarded the life boat. I promised her I would follow on a later boat, a promise we both knew I couldn't keep. I kissed her one last time and pried her white-knuckled hand off my arm.

I remember. My death. I jumped ship as the great vessel went under and I crashed into the freezing water. My last words were a murmured prayer to see Emily again. I wore a life preserver, but the water was cold and I had always been a thin man. My body succumbed very quickly to hypothermia.

I remember. What came after. There was no glowing tunnel of light, no choirs of angels, but neither was there fire and brimstone. Apart from the ceasing of my bodily functions, nothing changed. I remained aware as my body bobbed along like a piece of driftwood. I saw the others around me scooped out of the water, first the living, and then the dead. They missed me.

Time passed. My body rotted and fish picked at my legs. With each bite, they carried away a bit of my body, and also a bit of my mind. My consciousness fragmented into hundreds of tiny pieces, each holding a fraction of my memories, but every single one of them held my love for Emily, my need to see her again, to hold her in my arms.

These creatures began a mass migration toward England, to Emily's home. The fragments of my mind were too stupid to understand their shared goals, only aware of their own drives, their new set of instincts. Along the way, many died, but when their bodies were eaten by other animals, those animals each became one of me as well.

The man and dog are one and the same, merely the two largest pieces of the same puzzle. Together, I am nearly complete again. With each bite, he and I become we, become me.

We . . . no, *I* have made a terrible mistake. If man or dog had proved victorious, then we both would have lived on in the remaining body, more complete than either of us had been alone. With the man dead and the dog dying, we have no body to inhabit.

I will survive this, after a fashion, as I have before, but what of Emily? The greatest loss will be hers. Another lover dead in the prime of his life, and her favorite pet gone with him. Our bones will be picked clean of every scrap of meat by the time they find us, but they may recognize the man by scraps of his clothes.

My belly bloated with the man's meat, I collapse and do not rise again. My breathing stops, but I am still aware.

One day, Emily will die and pass on to Heaven. Will I? Or will I simply pass from body to body, an eternal parasite? I whisper a prayer that I may one day reach Heaven. No one answers. The carrion and the scavengers come in droves and fight each other for the right to eat. Each of the victors takes a bit of me with it, and I am scattered once more.

David Steffen *hails from the land of glaciers and mosquitoes, where he resides with his pack of dogs and humans. More than a dozen of his stories have been published or are pending in more than a dozen venues, including* Escape Pod, Daily Science Fiction, Pseudopod, *and* Uncle John's Bathroom Reader. *He has written several other stories about wild speculations on the afterlife, this being one of his favorite topics. You can find out more about him at his website:* www.diabolicalplots.com.

TREE OF LIFE

AARON J. FRENCH

There are many cultural and religious beliefs examining how to reach a representation of heaven. Blending parts of Christianity, Judaism, and New Age philosophies, Kabbalah symbolizes one method by explaining the pathways taken to ascend the great Tree of Life. *There are ten, and through them the nature of the universe is defined with its treetop, Keter, being the equivalent of God. Frank and tender, Aaron J. French guides us up this great Tree, as he shares the pain and triumph and transition from our mortal life.*

. . . light.

That's the first thing I see. And a tree. A crooked assortment of branches sprouting from roots toward the sky, where the light is, where clouds tear apart like shrouds of mist. I'm reminded of my mother, Judith, and her soft brown eyes, which once nurtured me through the trials of my youth.

Where are those eyes now?

The delicate blanket of light covers the crowning of leaves. The light is beautiful to look at. I feel heavy warmth falling over me like an angel's wing. My mother isn't with me anymore; there is only this heavenly light.

And then I'm amongst the roots in the earth. But I'm not alone. There are many—hundreds of us—small colorful bodies like translucent fetuses with vaguely humanoid appendages, orbiting half-visible in the underground streams. We dance around the roots, in places of pooling water, in notches carved out of sediment.

The root matrix spirals over my head. When I look up I see it coiling and untwining. It is only one tree—a Great Tree. A glorious pillar of bark and branches, with millions of wide glittering leaves. Its crown seems to reach to the heavens, to penetrate the sky with its luxuriant bloom.

Others begin to climb, and I climb too. Our upward momentum is like a storm, a blustering wind of thought and emotion. I see heartache in their gestures as, monkeylike, they ascend the roots. For the Great Tree is isolated in this Spirit Country. But together we are willing ourselves out of the darkness. And at the crown, light spills over the golden leafage, probing the cloudy heights. At the apex, the last circle is a portal leading out of this strange world up to something much greater.

The air breathes to me: *Keter.*

I kneel. I feel love in my knees, which is strange. I've never felt love *in* my body. I've only felt it in my mind, yet there it is in my limbs. How odd that it should be alive, sensations like homey comfort in my bones and blood.

Love rises, as we too rise, along the surface of the roots, which swell to the size of mountains over the spectral landscape. I'm drawn up off my knees. Soon this feeling will pass through my stomach, into my heart. And afterwards up my throat to my head. Can I stand it? Can I experience love outside my mind?

What is this? a mystic vision? a hallucinatory dream?

I don't know. Something must be wrong. My family should be here with me. They *were* standing beside my hospital bed. Until the light swallowed them . . .

Now phasing through transparent soil, the mighty trunk rears its lofty mass. My fellow travelers come with me, ringing around the gnarled bole, which rises before us like a medieval tower. Maybe *they* are my family. They may not look like Sarah and the girls, but they certainly *feel* like family. So confusing.

I hear music. A whispering sound, like a choir of wind. The voices are so sweet, so resonant.

Keter
Chokhmah
Binah
Chesed
Gevurah
Tiferet
Netzach
Hod
Yesod
Malkuth

Words that make no sense, which are almost incomprehensible, sounds like something a baby would make. And yet they are vaguely familiar.

I realize they are Hebrew.

Mother had been Jewish. And her sister, Aunt Carmela, spoke words like these when she got upset while babysitting me, back when Mom waitressed tables and dropped me off at Aunt Carmela's on her way to work. Long before Dad had been laid in the ground in his army uniform.

Aunt Carmela had been a practicing Kabbalist and she tried to explain her spiritual philosophy to me when I was older: what the Hebrew words meant and where the true Jewish faith was supposed to culminate.

I believe these are the same words now being sung. And I believe they are inscribed upon the trunk of the Great Tree, leading up to its crown, for I see several blooming rings of color which bear the sacred letters.

I suddenly remember that the Hebrew words denote different pathways to God, each signifying a distinctive "emanation" of the Divine. *Keter* is the sphere closest to God, and it is the ultimate destination for some Kabbalists, who believe they can rejoin this state by overcoming and connecting the other spheres of desires, emotions, virtues, and constructs of divine creative force.

By connecting the pathways—*Keter, Chokhmah, Binah, Chesed, Gevurah, Tiferet, Netzach, Hod, Yesod, Malkuth*—a veracious aspirant can ascend to the realm of the Divine, starting with *Malkuth* and working backwards through the creative process until ending at *Keter*, merging finally with the godhead and becoming one with the *'I Am.'*

But I never embraced my Jewish heritage, though I enjoyed listening to Aunt Carmela speak, and I never fully grasped what she tried to tell me. I couldn't decide one way or the other if Moses, HaShem, Jesus Christ, Buddha, Allah, or any of the others actually existed. How could I put my faith into something for which there was no proof? And yet science offered me no absolutions, either.

Was it any wonder I felt so lost?

Could Sarah and the girls *blame* me for what I did?

The ten Hebrew words continue cycling in the air again and again, sung by my fellow travelers, all of whom grow to become like little children. I can barely make them out. Their squat, ghostly forms move swiftly as they twirl, dance, and leap. Sometimes they move so quickly that all I can discern is the colorful trail streaming behind each.

Watching them reminds me of something: *I was a child once.*

But now that memory, like those playful spirits, is ghostly. I only recall the images of childhood in a kind of foggy veil. I feel somehow cheated by this as if I've lost something precious that was vouchsafed to me. I know the world seemed different all those years ago. It seemed more like this world, with its roots and streams, its auric clouds and towering ancient tree.

That world was magic, and then it died. And I died, too. Would Sarah forgive me? I do miss her. I miss my little girls. I could never live in a world of weekend visitations, one bedroom apartments, and no loving wife to come home to, and so I did it: I took myself out of a godless unfair world. And I find myself with the spirits now, traveling through this Spirit Country, and things are looking up—literally.

But I still miss my family.

As the tornado of capering child-ghosts ascends the trunk, the clouds poised over the crown part further. It happens symmetrically—a perfect circle opens in the sky. The gold of the sun spills through and reflects off the leaves. Glaring spears of hot light ray outward.

And then I see faces, giant androgynous faces gazing down from the cloud opening. They look so kind, so soft and gentle and noble. The faces of angels. I recognize some, recalled from some existence I must have lived long ago, which was like a dream—which *was* a dream. A dream of flipping through pages of the Hebrew Bible, then closing the covers and telling my mother: "*No.*"

We lift ourselves up, all of us children, scaling the ancient bark of the tree, rising toward the soft faces in the sky. The loving feeling has spread from my arms and legs and has entered my stomach and simmers there. Next it's in my lungs, journeying through my throat to my head, and when it twines its fingers into my skull I become conscious of a low reverberating hum, which rattles my teeth and vibrates the backs of my eyes.

The cavorting children around me start to grow until they reach the height of adults. But I still hear their wondrous laughter, ghostly giggles, and devotional recitation of the Hebrew words. They dance and bend into each other, streaming all as a unit like the colors of a rainbow.

I, too, have grown. I keep up with them. My strongest thought is that I don't want to be left behind. Where they are going, I also want to go. We approach the crown of the tree, where the last circle opens, and my body is humming, fully enlivened by the love coursing through it. I wonder if this is something new or if I have always felt this way. I wonder if the others moving up the trunk feel as I do.

We enter the leafy bloom and disperse, firing out in all directions to take our manifold positions among the branches. The Great Tree is gorgeous. Clouds continue to part, forming the circle. I gaze up through foliage, a burning intense stare, a neophyte posed in devotional worship and peering up at old Egyptian gods.

The giant angelic beings now bend their faces out of the sky. I realize the voices of the spirits have begun chanting a single word again and again—*Keter, Keter, Keter.* Vast arms unfurl like colorful tongues, reaching down to the abundant beings dispersed among the leaves and branches. These etheric feelers collect us, gather us into the center of the crown, where I notice my fellow travelers have become elderly—and yet serene, resigned, as I too have grown elderly and resigned. Together, we have released our struggle.

I am reminded of my childhood again, of those years I remember distantly, like a half-forgotten dream, and I want to cry. I want to hug my poor mother in that old folks' home, where she'd lived with the other forgotten souls waiting to die. I want to dig up my father and stand him upright, salute him as his men saluted him during their military tour of Vietnam. I imagine having Sarah back, living in our house on Madison Lane, with the girls coming home from elementary school in the afternoon and me coming in later after a hard day at the office. I kiss her, and I kiss them too, then we sit on the sofa to eat popcorn and watch TV.

I remember that.

I can remember it all, actually.

But suddenly the images fade, and I'm being borne up with my fellow travelers, funneled into a splendiferous column at the center of the crown of the tree, a tempestuous tornado, a storm, a beacon of living, vibrating souls.

The colossal arms reel us in, siphon us up. I may look elderly but I feel so young. And when I look into the angelic faces dominating the sky, toward whose bosoms we stream with single purpose, I forget about the small child I once was. I forget about my poor parents. I forget about the divorce and Sarah's new husband, Paul; about the girls calling him "Daddy," even though I asked them not to. I forget about that night I was drunk in the one-bedroom apartment with the loaded 9mm handgun. I forget about this Spirit Country, and I forget about *Keter*, the clouds, the angels, and even the Great Tree.

I can forget about all of it, if I really try. And I feel one thing and one thing only. And I know only one true experience . . .

. . . *peace.*

Aaron J. French (a.k.a. A. J. French) is a member of the Horror Writers Association. He recently edited Monk Punk, *an anthology of monk-themed speculative fiction with an introduction by D. Harlan Wilson, as well as* The Shadow of the Unknown, *an anthology of nü-Lovecraftian fiction with stories from Gary A. Braunbeck and Gene O'Neill. Aaron's fiction has appeared in many publications: Magazines include* Dark Discoveries, *D. Harlan Wilson's* The Dream People, Black Ink Horror, Something Wicked, *and* The Lovecraft eZine; *anthologies include* Potter's Field 4, M is for Monster, Chiral Mad, Zippered Flesh: Tales of Body Enhancements Gone Wrong, *and* Dark Tales of Lost Civilizations. *Aaron's recent article on Thomas Ligotti appeared in issue #20 of* Dark Discoveries Magazine, *where he is also an associate editor.*

THE RECKLESS ALTERNATIVE

SANFORD ALLEN & JOSH ROUNTREE

Whatever the afterlife may be, I don't think it will be the same for all people. It may be a culmination of our life's experiences, a spiritual design derived from our knowledge and choices. If we do have a consciousness in another plane of existence, I suspect that we'll still encounter challenging dilemmas. We'll still ponder our being, still have hopes and dreams and fears . . . still have an awareness of identity. Sanford Allen and Josh Rountree explore this very idea in the following story that depicts what eternity awaits for a certain rock star. Even the innovative— the daring—in life must face difficult decisions when confronted with The Reckless Alternative.

West. *Always* west.

The Cadillac thundered along an unending stretch of afterlife asphalt, headed nowhere because there was nowhere really to go. But Joe was patient, with the wheel in one hand, and smoking a fat spliff in the other. Visions from his life played amongst mirages that rose from the endless desert: Joe the diplomat's kid, shuffled from continent to continent. Joe the art school dropout with his hippie hair and ramshackle *Notting Hill* squat. Joe the punk rock icon at the height of his furious powers. It was an interesting life to be sure, but Joe took it all in with a comfortable level of detachment.

Nostalgia wasn't his thing.

One of the mirages shimmered, and a girl separated from the rising waves of heat, signaling for a ride. She hopped in the car and introduced herself as *Coma Girl*. That wasn't her name really. It was Jen or Julie or something like that, but inside the Caddy it was Joe's world, and in Joe's world nobody used their real name for long. She was young, late teens probably, and death hadn't erased her scars.

"Oh shit," she said. "You look like—"

"I am," Joe said, offering her the spliff. "Smoke?"

"I guess," she replied, looking uncertain. She took a drag, choked up half a lung, and handed it back. "I'm a . . . I *was* a huge fan of yours. I think I was listening to *London Calling* when I . . . I guess, when I died?"

"What side?"

"It was a CD. No sides."

"Fucking CDs."

"So I'm dead? I mean, I know *you're* dead. So . . . " She scratched at her wrists, smearing a bit of fresh blood away on the leg of her jeans.

"You know, I had a brother," Joe said. "Killed himself when he was hardly older than you. Worst thing that ever happened to me. Pissed me the fuck off, too. Way I saw it, he chose death, so I was going to choose life. Live like your time on Earth is worth something, you know?"

"I don't know if I really wanted to," Coma Girl said.

"Live?"

"No, kill myself."

"Shouldn't of done it then."

"You see your brother here?" Coma Girl was half a ghost, nightmare black hair and near-translucent skin. Her wrists kept up a slow bleed, and she gave up trying to clean them.

"Haven't seen *anyone* here. Except you."

"There have to be other dead people."

Joe shot her a sideways grin. "I've been in this car for . . . well, not sure how long. But for a long time. Nothing but road and desert and more road."

"It's a road," she said. "It must go somewhere."

"Yeah," Joe said. "Most likely straight to Hell."

Nothing. More nothing. And then a town.

Or close enough.

The highway split the tiny town in two, a few dilapidated buildings clinging to one side, a few more crumbling away on the other. Busted cars with no tires, sidewalks assaulted by graying weeds, and probably enough rattlesnakes lazing in the scrub brush to fill a bathtub. But there was a sign hanging askew from the nearest building, a red neon thing that read *BEER*.

"Our fortunes are looking up, kid," Joe said. "Looks like a pub."

Music drifted from the clapboard building, the determined lope of roots-reggae. A few more steps and Joe placed it. *Police and Thieves*, by Junior Murvin. He'd recorded that once. Done a good job of it too.

He stepped onto the bar's rickety porch and poured sand from his boot while Coma Girl caught up.

"After you, love." He pushed open the door, and she looked inside, reluctant to step in. An old rope fishing net stretched across the ceiling, and a Jamaican flag hung behind the bar.

"Well, come on then, Elvis," boomed a voice basted in Jamaican patois. "Don't let the whole desert blow in through the front door."

Joe and Coma Girl stepped inside and let the door slam. A heavy Jamaican man sat on a stool behind the bar. Dreadlocks snaked from under his green-and-yellow tam.

"*Elvis?*" Joe said. "Who's that make you? Peter-fucking-Tosh then?"

The man grinned wide and slapped his knee. "Him's a funny one. No, no, not Peter Tosh. Name's Tommy. You here for a drink, I imagine."

Coma Girl walked to the bar and examined the dusty bottles shelved behind it. Empty to the last one.

"Well then, *Tommy Gun,* that thing pour a pint?" Joe nodded to the single tap behind the bar. Someone had duct-taped a police truncheon onto it as a makeshift handle.

"One pint or two?"

"You alright to drink?" Joe nodded to Coma Girl's dripping wrists. "I mean, in your condition?"

"I already smoked your pot. I don't think a beer's going to hurt."

"Make it two, Tommy Gun."

The man yanked back the truncheon and filled a pint glass with foamy stout. He handed the first to Coma Girl. She took a swig and coughed.

"Used to American beer, eh?" Joe asked, smiling. "Poor kid."

"My stepdad drinks Schlitz. Blame him."

Tommy slid a pint to Joe. "Enjoy it, *mon.*"

"Think I will." Joe savored the bittersweet and cool stout. He looked out the window, watching his life play out amid the dunes.

He saw himself beside a hospital gurney. A man in a white coat pulled back a sheet, and Joe watched himself look down into the face of his brother, dead long enough that his skin was the gray-green of sculptor's clay.

He turned his back to the window and took another pull from the pint.

"What are you looking for out there?" Coma Girl asked. She found a napkin on the bar top and wound it around one of her wrists.

"Just watching. This place constantly replays your life for you, like a movie. You see the good and the bad."

Tommy pointed out the window. "You been here long enough, you learn to control it. Out this window, most days, I see Kingston Harbour. Reminds me of growing up. I can even see the man selling meat patties out of his cart right there."

Coma Girl leaned forward. "I don't see Kingston Harbour."

"Of course not," Joe said, turning back around. "You don't see what he sees. I don't see what you see. The way it works, you just see your own life out there."

"I don't see anything but sand."

"Nothing?" Tommy asked.

She shook her head.

The big man frowned and shook his dreads. "If you don't see nothing, girl, you don't belong here."

"Great, so I can't even die right."

The door banged open, and they all turned to see a mismatched pair of men step in from the heat. One looked liked he'd ordered his getup from the *Punks-R-Us* catalog; obligatory red mohawk, busted gray teeth, and a second skin of torn cotton, spray paint, and safety pins. The guy was obviously trying way too hard to fit in on the punk scene. The second newcomer was a clean cut man entering early middle age, decked out in a brown bow tie and a tan linen suit that defied wrinkles. Not a hair out of place, with eyes kind but intense. Joe recognized this man—he'd seen photos.

"Now it's a party," Joe said. "Lorca! I was hoping to run into you somewhere."

"I'm not Lorca," he said, smiling. The two men took seats at the bar on either side of Joe and Coma Girl.

"Two more then," Joe said to the bartender. "Looks like they're staying." He turned to the man who mimicked the dead poet, Federico Lorca. "Tell it straight. I've been to your grave, mate. You were killed by the fucking fascists in Spain. You look well enough now, though."

"I'm not Federico Lorca," the man said, refusing the pint that Tommy set in front of him. His faux punk companion quickly snagged the glass and set it behind his own.

"Then it's a damn good disguise, mate."

"I look this way because of you. You can relate to this image. It's like this bar. Do you think everyone who comes to the way station sees it the same? No. You're in the early stages of death. You can still shape it to your whim, like sculptor's clay. You see me as Lorca because of what he represents to you. Your higher self. Your ideals."

"Oh yeah?" Joe asked. "Then what does this comic book anarchist over here represent?"

"Just that, mate!" the punk said. "I've come to help you tear down the pillars of the afterlife." He shed his leather jacket and, when he leaned across Coma Girl to offer his hand, Joe could read the man's misery in the track marks scarring his arm.

"Name's Bernie," he said.

"Of course it is. My band's manager." Joe tipped back the rest of his pint and called for another. "Don't look like him, but you've damn sure captured his vibe. Listen, no offense, but anarchy's not really my thing. It's kind of juvenile, *innit*? When you give it some thought, I mean."

"If you aren't an anarchist, what are you?" Tommy asked.

"A little socialist on my mum's side, but mostly I just like to pick fights with fascist wankers. Me and Lorca here, we would have been brothers in another time. I cried at your grave, mate," he said, raising his glass to Lorca. "It's about principles, yeah?"

"I'm not Lorca," he said. "As I explained, I'm just this way because of you. We are as the dead see us."

"Yeah?" Joe asked. "So what about this young lady here? How come you don't change to her whim?"

"Julie isn't dead." Lorca said.

"The fuck's *Julie*?"

"Coma Girl."

"Right."

"Wait," Coma Girl said. "What do you mean I'm not dead? All this blood would seem to indicate otherwise." She raised her hands above her head, and fresh crimson poured down her forearms. "Not to mention the fact that, you know, I'm here. Wherever here is."

"You're a halfie," Bernie said. "A fucking veg."

"There are more diplomatic ways of putting that," Lorca said.

Bernie ignored him. "Your brain is dead, but your body's still kicking. It's why your arms are making all that mess. Not too many open wounds after you die, love."

"Oh God," she said. "That sounds worse than being dead."

"You shouldn't let it concern you," Lorca said. "You'll be dead soon enough, and then we'll come back for you."

"Come back?" Joe said. "You going somewhere already?"

"*We* are, John."

"That's not my name anymore."

Lorca sighed. "Fine, *Joe*. Regardless, we must go soon."

"Go where you like," Joe said. "This place suits."

"For now, but you can't stay here forever," Lorca said. "The only question is whether you will choose the path I offer or that of my companion."

"My rule is to not make any important decision unless I'm well pissed," Joe said. "Another round for everyone, Tommy Gun."

Joe turned to face the bar, but it was gone. The walls had faded into a tangle of knotted trees, and a crescent moon shone silver light through the branches. Joe felt someone grab his hand and realized that Coma Girl and Lorca had made the trip too.

"What's going on?" Joe asked. "Where are we?"

"You're about to meet the Spanish Republicans," Lorca said. "Marxists, anarchists, landless farmers, Hemmingway, Orwell. Your people, yes? All of them fighting the fascists."

Leaves crunched underfoot. A short woman in a tattered brown overcoat stepped through the trees, flanked by men carrying rifles. She nodded to Lorca. The black handle of a pistol poked from the waistband of her trousers.

"Who are these people?" she asked.

"Friends, Alma," Lorca said. "Reinforcements, if you like."

"Ever fired a gun?" The woman narrowed dark, penetrating eyes at Joe.

"Only on a movie set," he said. "But I'm right with you. Got no use for fascists, and this man's a hero of mine." He clapped Lorca on the shoulder.

Alma snorted derisively. More armed men and women stepped into the clearing. They leveled their weapons. Apparently, knowing Lorca—or almost-Lorca, or whoever he was—didn't guarantee a warm reception.

"And you?" Alma turned her eyes on Coma Girl. "Ever fired a gun?"

"No. But I can play guitar." She nodded to the bearded man who held a rifle on her. The neck of an acoustic guitar poked from his backpack. "Does that help?"

"You want to join the Republicans, *guitarrista*?" Alma laughed. "Then play *Ay Carmela!* for us."

"I don't know it. What are the chords?"

"Carlos, show her."

The man with the guitar set his rifle against a tree and pulled the instrument from his pack. His right hand strummed in a choppy pattern as he sang through a verse:

> *The army of the Ebro*
> *Rumba la, rumba la, rumba la*
> *The army of the Ebro*
> *Rumba la, rumba la, rumba la*
> *Crossed the river one night*
> *Ay, Carmela! Ay, Carmela!*

Joe knew the song. He'd sung it drunk over Lorca's grave. He joined in.

"Quiet," Alma said, jabbing a finger into his chest. "You're no singer. You sound like a braying sheep. I want to hear *her*."

"Can I try it?" Coma Girl reached for the guitar. "I saw what chords he played, and I think I can remember the lyrics."

The bearded man handed her the instrument. She gave it a few tentative plucks then perfectly mimicked his strumming pattern. Blood trickled down her hand as it chopped the strings. More glinted red on her left forearm as her fingers formed chords.

The man sang, and Coma Girl joined in a quavering voice that seemed too large for her small body.

By the middle of the verse, the man dropped out, and Coma Girl continued alone, her voice more confident with every note. The guitar was sticky with blood, but she seemed oblivious to her wounds.

The Republicans clapped and whistled.

"You know the song, sister," Alma said. "And you showed us you will bleed for the cause. Tomorrow, you and the braying sheep learn to fire a gun."

When dawn came, they gave Joe a rifle.

His blood thundered with the cause. How many times had he imagined himself in the thick of something so real? He'd lamented the deaths of a thousand sons of Spain, celebrated them in song, but it took his own death to finally become one of them.

Alma roused him with the announcement that they were moving, staying ahead of the Nationalist Army. He asked after Lorca, but the man had vanished.

"How come you didn't tell me you could play and sing?" Joe asked Coma Girl as she shoved her bedroll into a canvas bag.

"You never asked." She threw the bag over her shoulder and picked up the guitar. Apparently it had become hers during the night. Joe remembered her playing it around the campfire, but things got hazy after the Spaniards passed a bottle.

"I even know some of your songs. Learned *London's Burning* right after I figured out *Loudmouth,* by the Ramones, and *Born to Lose,* by the Heartbreakers."

Good taste. Poor kid was born too late.

"So, you can play and sing. Talented and pretty smart. Why'd you do that to yourself?" Joe asked and lifted up one of her newly bandaged wrists.

She pulled it away.

"Because life's one disappointment after another. Maybe not when you're a rock star, but for most of us it is."

Joe wasn't in the mood to argue. Something, though—maybe the vision he'd had of his brother—wouldn't let him drop it.

"Maybe it is. I've had my share. But I don't think you've lived long enough to make that call."

"No, but I see what it does to other people, like my mom. She used be creative. She was a painter. But after my dad left, she gave up. Moved back to the little shit town she came from, dragged me along, and married an asshole who walks all over her. She's broken and helpless now. If that's how life works, no thanks."

The pair fell in line behind the Spaniards as they left the woods and trudged toward a dirt road that cut between wheat fields.

"Just because your mum's afraid to leave doesn't mean you can't," Joe said. "Great big world out there, you know."

"How am I gonna do that? I've never held down a job for more than a week."

Joe shrugged. "You can play and sing. Better than me, if you believe the Spaniards."

"Yeah, yeah. I should have just gotten a band together and hit the road." She walked faster, pulling ahead. "Tons of people in my hick town would just kill to join a punk band."

Joe let it drop. Why was he debating suicide? It was all past tense for her now, wasn't it?

A sharp crack sounded somewhere to the right, and one of the Republicans fell, dead before he could cry out. The party scrambled.

Coma Girl ran into the field, the dead Spaniard's blood splashed across her face and shirt. Joe raised his rifle and pointed in the direction of the enemy, scanning his surroundings for someone to shoot back at. But the Nationalists were like wraiths. Terrified, he tossed the rifle and ran after Coma Girl.

Joe stumbled a few yards and almost tripped over her. She huddled in a ball, hands over her head.

"I wasn't ready to die the first time," he said, tugging her to her feet. "And I don't think you're ready to die either."

"Tell me again why people are shooting at us?" she said as Joe drug her through the hissing wheat field.

"Short version? We're fighting against a military coup. They want to run the country and we don't want them to. So they shoot at us."

"So we're the good guys?"

"Of course we are. We're the free people of Spain, and they're goddamned fascists. This was a glorious fight for freedom."

"Was? So this already happened?"

"Oh yeah. Long ago."

"So who wins?"

"Ah . . . the bad guys."

"Not very comforting."

They emerged from the wheat field onto another unpaved road. Gunfire sounded in the distance but there was no sign of their companions or their attackers. Joe hustled Coma Girl along, eager to put more distance between them and those flying bullets. He tried to tell himself he was just looking after the kid, that he'd have stayed behind to fight if he'd been alone. But he knew his own heart. It was a glorious fight, sure, but it was also fucking dangerous. Fighting for a cause and dying for a cause were two entirely different things.

"Can we slow down?" Coma Girl asked. "I mean, you're already dead and I'm . . . whatever I am. It's not like you can die twice, right?"

Fresh gunfire brought them up short. A bullet punched through Coma Girl's chest and she fell backwards.

"Oh . . . this is not . . . "

Joe dove for her, tried to heave her up and drag her to the relative safety of the high wheat stalks, but the stalks parted before him to reveal Coma Girl's killer. He wasn't the monster Joe had expected. He was little more than a kid, Coma Girl's age. His uniform was dingy and ill-fitting, filthy from days of marching. His dark eyes were wide with terror, and the rifle in his hand shook.

"Don't shoot," Joe said, holding out a hand. "*Por favor*, mate! This is crazy!"

The young man wavered in his resolve. Then his comrades spilled from the wheat into the road and the solider remembered why he was there, what was required of him. He raised his rifle and took aim.

"*Lo siento*," he said.

He put a bullet through Joe's skull.

"Thanks for the fucking headache," Joe said, tipping back another pint.

They were back in the pub, Tommy laughing at his discomfort. One second Joe was catching a bullet with his brain and the next Tommy was passing out another round. Bernie sat on one side of him, grinning like a maniac while Lorca crouched stiffly on the opposite stool. Coma Girl had a death grip on Joe's arm, and her blood soaked his shirt.

"That seemed . . . real," she said.

"What's all that about?" Joe asked.

"One option for your afterlife," Lorca said.

"What do you mean by that?"

"We're both here to tempt you, if you care to look at it that way. I'm here to offer you a meaningful eternity, and he would have you chose an afterlife of a baser sort."

"You're stuck up is what you are," Bernie said. "I'm here to offer him an afterlife of not having to care about all the bullshit."

"So you're like God and the devil?" Coma Girl asked.

"Nothing so quaint, love," Bernie said. "If anything, we're both devils."

"Is there a God then?"

"Hell if I know. I'm just doing a job. Speaking of, let's move this along."

Without so much as a groan of preamble, the pub ceiling collapsed and crushed them all.

Joe took Coma Girl's hand, heaving her up from the rubble, and dove into the middle of a pogoing crowd of sweaty punks. The pub was gone but stray chunks of ceiling continued to fall.

"This is more like it," he said.

"Is that you?" she asked.

"Hell yes."

Joe was onstage—a young Joe. A screaming, spitting, flailing Joe on the verge of tumbling into the tidal wave of kids crashing into the stage. The other Joe—the old Joe—bobbed through the chaos, disconnected from the spectacle. His mates were onstage too, furious in their youth. They were sloppy, those kids, but they had bite. Bernie put a hand on Joe's shoulder, steering him deeper into the madness.

"That's you, mate," he said. "Pure animal, right?"

"That's part of me."

"This is incredible!" Coma Girl said, pulling away from Joe and shoving toward the stage.

"See, that girl only thought she knew rock and roll," Bernie said. "We know better, don't we?"

"We do."

"This can be *forever* for you."

Bits of the ceiling continued to fall as the bass rattled the rafters, but the crowd seemed unconcerned. Coma Girl was gone now, lost to the mercies of the crowd.

Bernie clapped Joe on the back, and suddenly he felt as if he'd smoked the mother of all spliffs and chased it with a few bottles of rum. The room revolved, and he was pretty sure he wasn't standing on the ground anymore, but he let the sensation take him. Joe blinked, and then he was inside his younger self, commanding the stage, and there was Coma Girl in the front row, screaming and laughing and living in a memory she'd always coveted.

The song ended and Joe charged the band into *London's Burning* and the room nearly exploded. The ceiling fell in earnest now, but Joe didn't care. He was young and angry and *fuck* how he'd missed this. He looked for Coma Girl, but she'd been shoved back into the crowd, still grinning, and as he cast his eyes over the mass, he saw Bernie, the costume store punk, light up a Molotov cocktail and hurl it at the nearest wall. The club burned fluorescent orange as the flames advanced up the wall and across the ramshackle ceiling with unnatural speed. None of the kids stopped slamming into each other, even as the flames fell like napalm and took hold of their grinning faces, their screaming throats.

Somewhere out there, Coma Girl was dancing and dying with them and, in spite of this, Joe found he couldn't stop playing, couldn't stop choking out his fury. Nothing mattered but the message and the music and fuck all else.

By the time the song ended, everyone was dead.

"You didn't have the burn the place down, did you?" Joe said.

"Naw," Bernie said. "But it was fun, wasn't it?"

"Not that much fun," Coma Girl said, dusting ash from her hair. They were back at Tommy's place but remnants of their travels had followed them home. Joe's head spun pleasantly.

"Better than being chased around by blokes with guns," Bernie said.

"Apart from the burning and the melting, I guess." Coma Girl said.

"Choice is obvious, *innit*?" Bernie ignored her and threw a brotherly arm around Joe's neck. "Tell the poet here to piss off, and we'll head back to the party."

"He's not going with you," Lorca said.

"The hell he's not," Bernie said.

"Maybe I won't go with either of you," Joe said.

"It doesn't work that way," Lorca said. "You can't just wander the afterlife with no direction."

"Well that's a kick in the rude bits, *innit*?" Joe said. "Figured when I was dead, at least there'd be no one trying to force feed me their ideology. Fucking figures."

"We're force feeding you your own ideologies," Bernie said.

"What about the girl?" Joe asked. "What's your plan for her?"

"I'm right here," Coma Girl said. "I can talk for myself."

"She's a different case," Lorca said. "First she must decide whether she wants to stay here or go back to her life. If she decides to stay, then she'll be visited by manifestations of her own personality. She shouldn't even be here with you now. Her soul hasn't really followed procedure."

"Hello!" Coma Girl snatched a grimy rag from the bar and tossed it at Lorca's head. "Talk to me like I'm a grown-up and not some kid who can't make her own decisions. I'm making the choices for me."

"Fine," Tommy said, visibly impressed by her spunk. "What's it you want to do then?"

She considered for a few seconds. "I'm not sure."

"You want to go on living," Joe said. "I ain't seen anything here that would make me want to stay, apart from maybe this pub."

"I'm not exactly crazy about the real world either," she said. "Staying here is maybe easier."

"Listen up," Joe said. "When I was a lad, I loved Indians. I don't mean from India, but the American ones. Apache, Navajo, and all that, right?"

"Hello left field."

"Hang on. I read somewhere that anytime a Cherokee had a tough decision to make, he'd always choose the most reckless alternative available. That's not a safe thing maybe, but it's a hell of a way to live life. It's how I lived my goddamn life, every second of it. I ain't gonna tell you what to do. But that's the best advice I can give. It's worked for me."

"The reckless alternative," she said.

"Always."

Coma Girl turned to Tommy. "How do I leave here? You know, don't you?"

"Car's still out front," the Jamaican said. "Drive west until you run out of road."

"You can leave," Bernie said, then pointed to Joe. "But this one can't."

"The hell I can't," Joe said. "Listen, mate, I choose neither of you. Not right now, at least."

"It doesn't work that way," Lorca replied.

"It works however he wants it to," Coma Girl said, grinning. "He walked that razor line right down the middle his whole life. Why change that just because he's dead?"

"You heard the girl," Joe said. "I'll finish up this pint and we'll—"

Coma Girl pulled Joe from his stool, spilling the last of his beer across the bar top.

"Let's go now," she said. "Before I stop feeling so reckless."

West. All the way west.

"What do we do now?" Coma Girl asked.

The end of the road was a chasm so wide they couldn't see across. Roiling dust obscured whatever might be at the bottom. In that dust, Joe could see a life play out. Not his, but Coma Girl's. Not her life to date, but what lay ahead.

He saw her wailing at a battered Fender Telecaster on a club's stage, and planting roses in front of a white wood-frame house, and pushing a child in a swing. *Her child?*

"What are you smiling at?" she asked.

"I think you're supposed to jump," he said. "To wake up. Trust me, you want to do this. You've got a hell of a life ahead of you."

"I think maybe you're right," she said, wind whipping her to the edge of the precipice. "You coming too?"

"Not sure if I should. Might come back from the dead. Might be a goddamn zombie, yeah? That'd be about my luck."

"You never believe in laying back, saying how bad your luck is."

"Huh?"

"It's from one of your songs."

"Right. Throwing my own words back at me?"

"And whatever you find down there has got to be better than hanging around here. If this is death, it's kind of a drag."

"Except for the pints."

"You coming, Joe?"

"I suppose I am, Coma Girl."

"It's Julie."

"Right. Julie."

She reached out and took Joe's hand. The wind pulled them, and they pulled each other. Over the edge. Into the world. And, as it turned out, Joe was right.

Julie lived a hell of a life.

Sanford Allen is a musician and former newspaper reporter from San Antonio, Texas, who has way more fun writing lies than he ever did uncovering the truth. His short fiction and prose poems have appeared in Innsmouth Magazine, Big Pulp, and Necrotic Tissue, among other anthologies and publications. His band, Boxcar Satan, has both served as backing band for Brooklyn-based gospel singer, Rev. Vince Anderson, and performed a benefit at the Church of Satan in San Francisco. Visit him on the Web at: www.sanfordallen.com.

Josh Rountree is a street walking cheetah with a heart full of napalm. He wishes he could write novels like Larry McMurtry and songs like Paul Westerberg, but everything he makes falls somewhere in between. His short stories have been published in some very cool places like Realms of Fantasy, Happily Ever After, and Polyphony 6, and received honorable mention in both The Year's Best Science Fiction and The Year's Best Fantasy and Horror. His first short fiction collection, Can't Buy Me Faded Love, is available from Wheatland Press. Visit him on the Web at: www.joshrountree.com.

THE THOUSANDTH HELL

BRAD C. HODSON

Every culture has a different view on what eternal punishment awaits for those who live their lives contrary to that culture's laws and beliefs. The Greeks feared Hades, and the Norse dreaded Hel. Islamic sinners slip from the bridge of afterlife into Jahannam, while the Mayan dead are sent to live in the terrifying house of Xibalba. Taoist Chinese teach one of the most gruesome visions, that of the multiple Hells of Fengdu. Here, every person suffers a personalized torture and, once that is completed, they are then moved to the next level of personalized torture. Brad C. Hodson's The Thousandth Hell is the culmination of one man's journey of punishment, followed by those who always judge the harshest—family.

"You should have been aborted," my old man said and smacked me hard enough to grind the broken glass into my gums. "It wouldn't have been an ordeal. You had an older brother I ended with a coat hanger when I was fifteen. I heard that girl could never have children again. But two years later when I met your mother I could have made *dong quai* strong enough to turn you into little more than harsh cramps and a messy three days."

He grabbed a stick from the fire burning next to us and crouched against a pole. The orange light cast dancing shadows across his face and illuminated a charred hand, little larger than an infant's, that still wriggled as it smoked on the end of the stick. Moans echoed in the darkness and when I squinted I thought I could make out taller poles deep in the black, shapes squirming on them as they slid down.

My father took a wet bite from the hand, blood and black ash staining his mouth. As he smacked his jaws together, tiny bits of gristle dripped down his chin.

"The food here isn't as bad as you'd think." He laughed. "I've been wanting to ask you . . . "

I spit a fistful of blood and glass onto the ground. The cracked earth drank it in. "Ask me what?"

"What's been the worst for you? So far, I mean."

"Other than having to see you again?"

He tugged on the chain piercing my bowels and my insides threatened to unravel.

"The maggots," I said when the pain eased and I caught my breath.

He laughed again. "Not the boiling oil? For me it was the boiling oil."

I shrugged. The Hell of Boiling Oil had been a lifetime ago. The burning tickle in my organs from the Hell of Burrowing Maggots was much fresher.

He thrust a thumb behind him. "Wait until you get to the Hell of Upside Down Sinners. Those people are not happy."

Some say Fengdu consists of Eighteen Hells. Others, Nine Hundred Ninety-Nine. Buddhist, Taoist, and Confucian teachings about the afterlife all seemed to be true, even where they contradicted each other. Even the Maoists and Christians had gotten a few things right. And, of course, there were surprises for even the most theologically minded. The result was a never-ending panoply of torments with no clear path on how to rise above it.

"What do you want?" My gums still ached when I spoke.

He wiped the mess from his mouth with his forearm. "I wanted to see you."

"To gloat?"

"It's part of my punishment," he said.

Seeing as I was the one on a leash, I couldn't help but laugh. "Part of *your* punishment? How so?"

"Knowing what I did to you." He stared at his shoes. "Our ancestors are not pleased at how our line ended."

"Not pleased with *me*, you mean." Here I was, dead for God knows how long, and I still felt like a disappointment.

"They blame me," he said. "You were my responsibility. I went wrong somewhere."

"You can say that again."

He yanked on the chain and I passed out.

When I came to he was crouched low, hands moving in and out, breathing deeply.

"Buddha breathing hands?"

"It helps to focus," he said.

I climbed to my knees. The chain was wrapped around my waist. Aside from the festering knot of pus-filled flesh it poked out from, it could have been a belt.

"You should try it," he said.

"I don't know how."

"That's a lie. I taught you. When you were young we'd do it together. Those are some of my favorite memories."

"It's some of my worst." I stood and stretched. "That's why I don't remember."

"You try hard to make your words like knives, Fei-chu."

"Yeah, *Ba*. I don't know why I would do that. You've always been so good to me."

"Chan Pou-soi," a voice rumbled like a rockslide.

"Ox-Head," my father said and stood.

The guard snorted. He glared at us, yellow eyes narrowing inside thick black fur. He slammed the end of his *kwan do* into the ground. The thick blade at its top caught the light of the fire and cast it back onto Ox-Head's red armor. "His Imperial Highness, Majestic Overseer of Divine Cruelty and Keeper of the Ten Thousand Pains, Master of the Earth Prison and Judge of the Thirty-Six Courts of Hell, Yan Luo the Yama King requests your presence."

"And his too?" My father motioned to me.

"Bring the whelp."

My father unwrapped the chain and dragged me along like an obedient dog.

We stepped along a path of scuffed human skulls, the air thick with the suffering around us. Tiny bursts of flame lit up the sky here and there followed by the fluttering of paper as Hell Money rained down from the Middle Kingdom above. Souls were released from their suffering long enough to snatch up the bills meant for them and hide them away. There was no use for the money here, but the act of burning it offered respite to the dead for the few blissful seconds it took them away from their torments. These small kindnesses were the only thing that kept some people going.

No one had ever burned money for me.

"*Ba?*" I asked.

"What?"

"Did you burn Hell Money for your father?"

"Yes."

"How often?"

"As much as I could."

"Did it help him?"

"I don't know. He was gone long before you sent me here." He shrugged. "But he was a good man."

We walked in silence for a long while.

"Fei-chu," he said as we neared the Hall of Butchered Hearts, "was I as bad of a father as Devil Kwan said?"

"Yes." I didn't even pause.

The chain gained some slack.

Devil Kwan was the closest thing I ever had to a friend. He was also a pimp, a butcher, and psychotic in a way that frightened even the police. Yet he was one of the funniest and most vibrant people I ever met. Strange how that works.

We'd sit around Devil Kwan's apartment, getting high and contemplating our futures. He would go on and on about how one day he would be famous, a movie star or a politician. He was confident that he had an important purpose in the universe.

I never had that confidence. I knew I would never amount to anything. Even then, I felt leashed to my father. My biggest fear had always been that my destiny was tied to his.

Walking through Hell, my chain in his hand almost felt natural.

We passed through the Hall of Butchered Hearts, the fleshy walls pulsing as blood raced through a million arteries threaded along the length of it.

In the Upper Kingdom are the Courts of the Celestial Bureaucracy where, so I've heard, statues of the Eight Immortals rise so tall it's impossible to see their faces. Crystal clear water pours from the bottom in magnificent fountains and any who drink from them can instantly relive the best moments from their life.

In contrast, here there are the only the Faceless in Hell, horrendous creatures whose limbs bend in unnatural directions and cover their shapeless skulls with smiling Buddha masks. One of them scurried to us and ripped its mask away.

Its blank canvass rippled and shifted. My mother's tear-streaked face appeared, screaming at me. "Why did you let it all happen, Fei-chu? You've disgraced my memory and damned me to this place. Do you know what they do to me here?"

The tears came too fast and she leaned forward and licked them from my jaw.

The Buddha mask slid back into place and the Faceless scampered back to share my suffering with its pack mates.

Ox-Head sat us on long steel benches. A fire burned deep in the earth beneath them and it seared the skin of my thighs to sit. Yan Luo's court was dark, the stench of stale urine, feces, and burnt flesh filling the hall. The sounds of crying and vomiting echoed around us.

"I tried with you, Fei-chu."

I was quiet.

"Fei-chu?"

I ground my teeth together. My name had always been one of the primary reasons I hated my father. Who names their son *Fat Pig*?

"You should have obeyed me."

"You're a miserable old shit," I said.

"You heard your mother."

"That damned thing wasn't my mother."

He shrugged. "She'd still be ashamed of you."

I punched him in the jaw. He fell from the bench onto the floor, the chain pulled taut between us.

Someone cleared his throat. A small man stood at the end of the bench, long Imperial robes stretching to the ground, and clacked eighteen-inch fingernails together in front of him. "Please forgive my intrusion. Chan Pou-soi and Chan Fei-chu?"

"That's us," my father said. He stood and dusted himself off.

"This way, please."

We followed him deep into the black. I didn't know why the King of Hell had requested us and I didn't care. I suppose I should have been afraid, but I was too angry. Even with all the tortures I'd been submitted to, having to subjugate myself once more to my father, in any fashion, was the worst of all. If there was mercy in Hell, as the *arhats* claimed, then our time together would be over soon.

The temperature dropped in chunks as we made our way down into the black. The darkness was absolute, the way I imagine the depths of space to be, and all I had to go on was the direction my chain was pulled.

When I was young, my father forced us to walk behind him no matter where we went. My mother would shuffle along, head low, holding my hand and deferring to him in all things. The village they were from was a small one outside of Chongqing and they lived a life far beyond what most people considered "traditional." Growing up, my father was downright medieval in his mindset. The factory he worked for moved us to Hong Kong when it reverted to Chinese control and even there, on that bustling modern island, he forced the old ways on us while he spent his evenings drinking and gambling *mah jong* with the Tonka boat people. I think he took to them more than anyone else because they lived such simple lives—backwards in my opinion—but pious and true to my old man. It was the will of Heaven to him and his new friends if a man neglected his family unless he was beating them.

"Did you get off on it?" I asked.

He snorted. "What are you babbling about?"

"Beating the shit out of us. Did that get you off?"

"You shouldn't speak to your father that way, Fei-chu. I never spoke to *my* father that way."

"The difference is that you were scared of your father. I just hated mine."

"I did what I had to do."

"Right."

"And what should I have done, O Wise One? Should I have sat by while the Western cesspool around us corrupted you and your mother?"

"It's not corruption, *Ba*. It's progress."

"That's what they called the occupation of Shanghai and the Rape of Nanking. *Progress*."

"There's no talking to you, is there? There's just nothing rational going on in that hollow skull of yours."

The slap rang my head and left my cheek stinging and raw. "You will show me respect for once, Fei-chu. You never gave it to me in life and I'll be damned if you don't give it to me now." He turned and stepped away.

I grabbed my chain and jerked it back until I could feel my father's face in front of mine. "I respected you, you pathetic pig. I spent half my life respecting you. I only stopped when you proved that you didn't deserve it."

"It was those friends of yours. Devil Kwan and his cronies. They ruined you."

"*You killed my mother.*" If I could have murdered him again, I would have done so right there.

The small man stepped beside us. "A thousand pardons, gentlemen, but we do not have time for this. Yan Luo does not like to be kept waiting."

We kept on through the black. The cold grew unbearable, my ears and the tip of my nose threatening to shatter to the floor.

One winter, my mother convinced the old man to let her and I go back to Chongqing and visit her family. He didn't like the idea, but her own father was ill and *Ba* at least paid lip-service to filial piety. The train ride west was one of my favorite memories. As soon as we left Hong Kong, a personality blossomed inside my mother. I had only known her up to that point as a slave to my father and a housekeeper to me, her mouth kept shut unless there was a lesson that needed to be taught to me or a question of my father's to answer. She showed me love and tenderness but always in a quiet way, with a hug or a bowl of soup and a pat on the head.

But on that train, shaking our way through the snow-dusted countryside, my mother sang to me. She had the most beautiful voice and I was shocked I had never heard it before. Being away from my father, I felt that I was seeing my mother for the first time. She told jokes that made me double over in laughter and taught me how to play Western card games. We spent a month with her family high in the mountains and, while I had always loved my mother as a son should, I fell in love with her the way best friends do. When it came time to head home, I hoped a transformation had come over her that she would carry back to Hong Kong.

When we were close to home, she grew quiet and stared out the window. The woman she was fled like a ghost that only haunted the countryside, exorcised by the threat of my father's presence. There were glimpses of her true self, winks at me over dinner, a game of cards quickly played while *Ba* was out drinking, but she hid that side of her away like the money that the old man won from the boat people was tucked inside a shoe box in the closet. She was a secret even to herself, a beautiful secret only whispered about when there was absolutely no chance anyone could overhear.

As I loved my mother more and more, I learned to hate my old man.

We were led into an opulent parlor of jade and ivory, red silk draped in long banners from column to column. Lanterns were lit inside paper balls around the room. Our guide sat us on a gold sofa upholstered in red leather.

"Please wait," he said and backed from the room.

Jasmine and incense accented the scent of untold wealth in the room. A bowl of oranges sat on a cherry-wood table next to us, and I took one. It was velvety sweet and juicy and, for the first time since I died, I didn't feel like I was in Hell.

My father yawned beside me and I was reminded that the torture was far from over.

Footsteps shuffled into the room. We turned as a small group of men made their way in. Their dress ranged from the tattered rags of a farmer to the brown robes and wooden armor of a Han Dynasty soldier.

My old man fell to his knees and kowtowed.

Our ancestors eyed me as I remained seated, savoring the orange.

"Hey, Fei-chu." Devil Kwan plopped down beside me. "How you been?" His smile was as wide and inviting as it had always been and his dark, thick hair meticulously styled like he had just rolled out of bed.

I embraced him while my father stayed face down on the floor. "Kwan. What are you doing here?"

"I'm the new King of Hell."

"What?"

He laughed.

"What about Yan Luo?"

"Funny thing about that. Seems Yan Luo is a title instead of a name. Who knew?" He smacked my back. "Good to see you."

My head swam. This was all too much for me. "How did you . . . ?"

"Turns out my cruelty is boundless. I always suspected it in life, but here in Hell? Man, once I was unleashed there was no stopping me. For a thousand years, my tortures were legendary. So I was rewarded."

"Have we been here that long?"

He shrugged and picked a shred of pork from between his teeth. He sniffed it and sucked it down. "Who knows? Time doesn't mean much here. I've been here that long. You may have only been here a few days." He motioned to our ancestors. "Anyway, these guys are why I called you here."

"My ancestors, right?"

"Yeah. They're not much fun. They came down from the Celestial Courts to complain."

"Complain?"

A Maoist soldier stepped forward. I think he was my grandfather, but I'd never met the man. "You two have ruined our line. Your impiety and resentment have dragged us all down."

"See?" Devil Kwan stood. He patted my father on the head like he was a mutt.

My old man creaked to his feet, eyes wide. "Father," he said to the soldier, confirming my suspicion.

My grandfather smacked him across the mouth. "You will not address me. You have disgraced me."

The Han soldier nodded. "Disgraced us all."

My father slumped onto the sofa next to me.

Devil Kwan grabbed an orange and leaned against the wall. He peeled it with one sharp fingernail. "These are good, huh?"

"What do we do now? How can we make amends?" My father looked to our ancestors, to Devil Kwan, to me. His jaw quivered and a tear leaked from his eye. It made me hate the man even more.

"That's the interesting part," Devil Kwan said. "Your souls must be scrubbed clean of all the baggage you carry. Weird, huh? It's like a buffet of beliefs down here." He laughed. "What do you hate the most, Chan Pou-soi?"

He looked at me and lowered his head. "My failure."

"And you, Chan Fei-chu?"

I stared at my old man and saw the night he beat my mother to death in a drunken rage. I saw the bribes he pulled from the shoe box when the police came. I saw the night I spent snorting lines with Devil Kwan, bitching about the old man, complaining about how we had no money, telling Kwan how much my father kept hidden in the house. I saw the old man rushing in and hitting me across the back with an iron bar, cash flying from the shoe box and across the floor, my knife catching the light as I plunged it into his gut over and over, his eyes wide, spittle flying from my jaw and onto his face, his blood soaking my hand. He clutched at me as the life fled from him and I laughed. Even when the firing squad cocked their rifles and readied to end me, the memory of that look in his eye made me laugh.

He had that same look now and I couldn't hide the chuckle.

"Him," I said. "I hate him."

Devil Kwan squeezed onto the sofa between us. He grabbed my chain and gently pulled it from under his ass. He took my hand, and then my father's, and smiled. "It's time for both of you to lose this weight you carry. It's time to be reborn." My father exhaled and tears leaked down his face. "Thank you, oh thank you."

Devil Kwan winked at me.

His cruelty deserves its reputation. I never thought it possible, but arcane texts speak of rare individuals born with two souls. Two souls trapped together in one body, never able to escape one another.

As we prepare ourselves for being reborn, my father is optimistic. But I know that the suffering we've endured until now has only been a prelude.

Tomorrow, we begin our true punishment.

Brad C. Hodson *is a writer living in Los Angeles. His short fiction has appeared all over the place and his first novel,* Darling, *is being published by Bad Moon Books. He also co-wrote the screenplay to the award-winning cult comedy* George: A Zombie Intervention. *When not writing, he likes to drink mead and lay siege to neighboring villages. For more information, please visit* www.brad-hodson.com.

MALL RATS

JAMES S. DORR

Malls are a cornerstone of modern society, a symbol of commercial success and entrepreneurial capitalism. And, if you're a young teenager, they're a means to escape from life's troubles; the perfect place to hang out with friends, eat junk food, shop, and have fun. Sometimes, when you're having such a good time at the mall, you don't want it to end and, sometimes, you don't know that it's already ended long ago. An impressively prolific author, James S. Dorr brings us the next tale, Mall Rats, *in which three adolescents enjoy a break from school that seems never to end . . .*

They were the mall rats, John, Mark, and Wendy, the kids you don't see. The children whose parents did not supervise them, who just seemed to blend in with the shadows. Who mixed with the crowds when the mall was crowded, who shrank into corners and just disappeared when the mall was empty—if it could be said *ever* to be empty—who seemed to live there. To have no other life.

John thought, sometimes, that they were dead.

But Mark was the skeptic: "How could we be dead, man? We wouldn't be here then. We'd be in heaven or someplace like that."

"Or maybe in hell," Wendy sometimes added, a knowing smile crinkling on her lips. She was a year older than Mark or John.

"But shouldn't we be in school or something?" John might persist.

"It's summer, silly," Wendy would say, dismissing the whole idea. "Anyway, did you guys see the paper? They're having a sale at the new department store. Dresses and things—and underwear too. I might try some on."

John and Mark would follow her, John not so interested in things like that yet, but nonetheless curious. Or perhaps Mark would have seen a display of new hunting rifles at the sporting goods store and he and John would go off to inspect them, that being something that *did* interest him, he recalling a time when his father once used to take him hunting.

"Do you think it's fall?" John might ask then. "You know, hunting season?"

"You heard what Wendy said. If it were fall yet, we'd be back in school."

Sometimes John went into the parking lot out by the back entrance to the mall, when he could find it. The mall, as malls will, was ever expanding, ever changing, adding new stores, papering over others' display windows until, one day, they would once more reopen as something entirely different than before. But, when he *could* find the mall's back entrance, he liked to go out and talk to the old man who sat on the sidewalk next to the dumpsters.

Sometimes he would steal a pint of whiskey or vodka to take to the old man who seemed to like it. The old man would unscrew the top very slowly, then purse his lips, licking them with his tongue, then finally tip up the bottle of whiskey, or whatever else, and swig half of it down before he recapped and tucked it under the old coat he always wore, even if Wendy said it *was* summer.

He asked the old man once: "Do you think we're dead?"

The old man looked puzzled.

"I mean *you* can see me. You even talk to me. And Mark and Wendy do. But the others, the ones in the mall, they just ignore us. Mark says it's because they're too busy shopping, but even the guards at night ignore us. Except some kid maybe, once in a long while, might join us for a night, but then, the next day, we never can find them again. And as for the others, it's like we weren't there either."

The old man nodded. "And what does Wendy say? I mean about the guards? The night watchmen?"

"She says it's because we're too clever. Or too small or something. We're able to hide when we hear them coming—behind display counters, things like that—and that's why they don't see us. Even though, sometimes, they're looking right *at* us."

The old man reached into his ragged coat and pulled out a bottle, one different from the one John had brought him. He looked at it thoughtfully. "Maybe the real question is," he said, "if *you* can see you."

Some nights the mall was nearly deserted, but never entirely. There were always the guards and the cleaning crews, if no one else, and some of the big stores were open all night too. It hadn't been like that always though, John thought. He seemed to remember one time at least . . .

But then Wendy called to him. "The ice cream place," she said. "They must have had trouble with their freezer. They left a whole tub of Rocky Ripple out in the service hall in back, most of it melted, but some of it's okay. Quick, before the janitors see it!"

Some nights they scrounged like that, finding new clothes too— Wendy especially liked to find new clothes—irregulars that had been left out for pick-up. Things that were going to be thrown away anyway. And, afterwards, they each had their own places for sleeping.

John slept in the basement, the four-foot utility corridor under the mall's oldest section, where the furnace that heated the mall was located. He curled himself among the insulated ducts that led from its top to the various stores, back in a shadowy part where the people who came to check it from time to time were not able to spot him. Mostly there was only the soft hiss of furnace gas lulling him in his dreams.

Wendy, on the other hand, had built a home in the sky, beneath the mall's roof but above its false ceilings. She found a spot where two blackened steel beams crossed, making a true floor where she could set furniture—pre-teen-sized beds and dressers and mattresses, clothes and cosmetics for her to try on each day—where there was no danger of them falling through the tiles beneath them. There she dreamed *her* dreams, whatever they might be.

Sometimes Wendy invited them up to join her for parties, with child-sized tea sets. With half-stale cookies he found in the dumpsters out in the parking lot when he visited the old man.

While, in his own nest, he sometimes dreamed of cemeteries.

"Maybe you were in one once," the old man said, cackling. "Just a joke, kid, but you know what I mean. We'll all be there someday. But me"—then he held up the bottle he just finished draining—"they say *this*'ll kill you. Like someone like me's more'n half dead already."

Then John remembered that sometimes the old man did *not* seem to see him. At least not until he'd brought him a new bottle.

And there were times, too, when John could not find the parking lot outside the mall, even when he found the back exit. He wondered sometimes then about his parents—if he *had* parents or if he had always been an orphan, like Wendy and Mark. Those times, outside, all he could see was a kind of gray swirling, like fog in a graveyard or in the old movies they sometimes watched in the video store, after it closed for the night.

At those times John remembered, however faintly, a time when the mall had been filled with people, police in uniforms, and then a time when it had been empty—when there didn't even seem to *be* a mall— and then more people, with tools and hammers. But the mall was *always* expanding . . .

He asked Wendy once and she said, "It's winter. That's all it is. You just saw a snowstorm—that's why you couldn't see the cars and stuff. As for the cops, well, maybe someone held up one of the stores. It happens all the time. Maybe someone got shot."

"But if it's winter, how come we're not in school?"

Wendy shrugged, then smiled that smile of hers. "It's Christmas, silly!"

Then Mark called to them: "Hey, guys, look at this! They've got a big tree set up in the rotunda. They're giving stuff away!"

And sure enough it *was* Christmas at the mall, and they saw Santa although, somehow, when Wendy went up to sit on his lap, suddenly she was back standing with him and Mark. "What did you ask for?" he asked her, while they filled their pockets with free candy.

She smiled and shrugged—but a puzzled smile this time. "I don't remember."

And then it was Halloween. Kids in costume. He was a soldier while Mark was a scarecrow and Wendy dressed as a ballerina. But other kids were there too, dressed as ghosts and witches and skeletons, vampires and Frankensteins. There was one kid they even talked to, dressed like a pirate, but bloody and dirty like he had been in a real pirate battle, and all he could do was babble something about a car skidding in a rain puddle out in the parking lot.

And then, again, the mall seemed to close down, but only for one night. That night they took cider up to Wendy's house.

The next morning, the kid in the pirate suit was no longer there. But there were newspapers on the kiosk at the mall's front entrance, one—a local one—with a headline about a car crashing into a school bus. Something about a Halloween party.

He asked the old man the next time he managed to steal a bottle from the liquor aisle in the drugstore. "Was there an accident a few days ago?" he asked.

"Lots of stuff happens around here," the old man said. "Don't bother me much." He took a long drink, but then looked thoughtful for a long time. He reached in his coat. "The mall changes and the world changes. I've lost track of how long I've been out here."

"There was one thing once I seem to remember," the old man said, "about how I was some kind of a hero." He pulled out a yellowed, faded newspaper. "But that was a time back."

John looked at the newspaper, reading its headline, seeing the picture on the front page. Policemen and bodies.

"Some psycho guy," the old man said. "Started shooting the place up. Kids and their parents—it was the end of summer, I guess, with those big 'back to school' sales. Anyhow, this guy came up with a rifle, just started shooting and shooting and shooting. I got scared, panicked with the others, blood all over everything, spurting around us from guys he killed while he's just sticking a new ammunition clip into his gun, then shooting more people. 'Cept when I tried to run with the others, I slipped and fell. Slid right into his legs, knocking him down with me . . ."

John looked again at the faded headline: *HOMELESS MAN HERO. DISAPPEARS AFTER TAKING OUT GUNMAN. POLICE ARE SEARCHING.*

"That was *you?*" John asked. He seemed to remember—*something about an evening after his parents were home from work. Something about a gun and shooting, and then his mom and dad, and Mark's and Wendy's too, lying, unmoving*—and even as he did, the memory slipped away from him.

The old man nodded.

"They give you a medal or something then?" John asked.

"No," the old man said. "Because, like I say, I was panicked too. Once the cops came, in all the confusion I did what I started to—just kept on running." He paused and stuck the paper back in his coat, then took another pull from his bottle. "And cops and me, kid, we just don't get along . . . "

John remembered—*trying* to hold on. *Mark and Wendy pulling him back with them, panicked and running too. Huddling later in the mall basement, where he slept nights now, hearing the furnace hiss . . .*

Then the old man's voice, pulling him back as well: "Course that wasn't all that's happened here. Not by a long mile . . . "

John heard the wind whistle over the old man's voice, blowing papers like leaves across the parking lot's asphalt. More recent newspapers than the old man's, yesterday's, last week's, but some of them ancient, too. And, he remembered, in the basement where he had his sleeping nest, there were bundles of newspapers, too, dirty ones, crumbly-edged, like they had been stacked for recycling, but then forgotten.

"What do you mean?" he asked.

The old man snorted. "Psychos everywhere," he said. "Copycats, some call 'em. But each one's got to do better than the last. *Escalating*, that's what they said it was back in the war, when I was in Vietnam." Then he pointed a finger toward his own head. "Some of us didn't get out entirely whole, know what I mean, kid?"

Leaves and newspapers, and psychos everywhere. John understood then, or at least *thought* he did. His morbid dreams of cemeteries. Of stones with his parents' names—sometimes *his* name as well. How the whole mall even sometimes seemed to fade, almost as if it was *it* that had disappeared, and not just some of the kids he remembered. Like the one that was dressed like a pirate, but others from time to time as well.

And his own thoughts that he was dead—what had the old man said? That the real question was if you could see *yourself*?

There was his hand, though. Stretched out in front of him. His knee. His elbow. His feet. His stomach. He even felt hungry, which dead kids did *not* feel as far as he knew. Except maybe in those *Living Dead* movies they watched in the video store at night sometimes. And all around him were stacks of newspapers, as solid as himself.

And all around them the mall was expanding, parts being rebuilt, other parts torn down. New stores opened every day that even he and Mark and Wendy could drift in and out of with the other shoppers, even if *he* had become a psycho. Because of that evening, that memory he could never quite wholly grasp—'shell shock' is what the old man would have called it—that slipped away from him whenever he tried to remember what came *next*.

"Hey, John!"

He heard Wendy's voice. But in his hand he held a newspaper and, as he looked at it, he heard other voices too. *"John, come to us instead,"* they seemed to whisper.

But he shook them from him.

He would be no psycho. Not some kind of nutcase who heard voices calling. Telling him maybe to take a gun someday . . .

Or else a bomb. When the mall reopened. Underneath in a utility tunnel, planted next to a leaky furnace.

He looked at the headline clutched in his hand, in the newspaper *he* carried tucked in his shirt, dated just one day after the old man's.

EXPLOSION TEARS MALL APART. MANAGEMENT PROMISES TO REBUILD.

And he and Mark and Wendy huddled not ten feet away, lulled to sleep by the furnace's hiss. Then Wendy awoke: "Do you hear something ticking?"

Psychos everywhere.

But he and Wendy and Mark were okay. He remembered *good* memories, of getting his first bike. Of him and Mark discovering the mall, riding to it one afternoon after school. Finding that it was a good place to hang out until their parents got home from work and it was time to go home to dinner.

A year later they met Wendy there at the mall and the three palled together. Until . . .

He heard voices. Distant at first, but now coming nearer and, as he watched, the corridor that he stood in became flooded with white light. "John, please come with us. It's time to join us." He saw his parents, approaching where he stood, his grandparents with them as well, though they had died when he was little. Beckoning to him. "Please, John, let us guide you . . . "

He saw them smile and he smiled at them in return, reaching his hand out to let them take it . . .

"John!" Wendy's voice screamed, drowning the others' out. "John, quick! Mark's found a new pizza place. He says they're giving out free slices, but they'll be all gone if we don't hurry!"

He turned. The mall was their life!

And he *was* hungry—

dead kids did not feel hunger, he thought

—as he dashed with them, noticing in the corner of his eye that, as they passed the polished store windows, they had no reflections.

And later, when he and Mark and Wendy had wolfed down their pizza, he wondered if he was wrong. That maybe the real question was whether kids like them could ever feel full.

James Dorr*'s newest collection,* The Tears of Isis*, is due out from Perpetual Motion Machine Publishing in May 2013, when it will join* Strange Mistresses: Tales of Wonder and Romance *and* Darker Loves: Tales of Mystery and Regret *from Dark Regions Press and his all-poetry* Vamps (A Retrospective) *from Sam's Dot Publishing. An active member of SFWA and HWA with nearly four hundred individual appearances from* Alfred Hitchcock's Mystery Magazine *to* Xenophilia, *Dorr invites readers to visit his site at* http://jamesdorrwriter.wordpress.com.

AFTERWORD

RAY CLULEY

Do we create our own afterlife? Is the final sanctuary of our essence crafted unwittingly by the choices of our everyday life, or are we all just constructs made in the image of another? Existence, perhaps, is much more planned and orderly then we expect. The accomplished Ray Cluley presents our next selection, in which one man's immortality is a fitting tribute to the lives he affected. Afterword is the tale of Jim, Fred, Mary, and many others living in a ghost town where every day is a sunny Sunday.

It isn't a ghost town in the traditional sense. The houses are not rundown empty shells with their windows and doorways boarded over. Dust doesn't swirl down empty streets, nor do tumbleweeds roll erratically with the wind. And there are people here, lots of them. But it's a ghost town nevertheless.

It's a small town even by small town standards. A collection of cul-de-sacs branch out from a central hub that is the town square: dead ends for new beginnings. From the sky it looks like a fully-opened book, cover touching cover with the pages spread like a fan between them. Birds sing. Bicycle bells ring. Neighbors speak over garden fences and children yell as they play, bouncing a ball safely in the road or hop-scotching on the pavement. A lawnmower whirrs, and more than one lazy sprinkler adds its soft *swish-swish-swish* to the peaceful sound of continuous everyday life.

Jim is one of the early settlers. He lives in a house that is an exact replica of the one he had before he died. He's washing his car in the driveway, even though driving is something he doesn't do anymore. Not because of the accident, but because nobody in town needs to drive. Cars are for washing. The sole purpose of the town drains is to gurgle with foamy streams of soapsuds, for it rarely ever rains. Every day is a sunny Sunday.

"Hi, Jim."

"Hello, Fred. Glorious day."

"It is that."

Jim soaks his sponge full in a bucket of warm water and splashes it across the windscreen. "Off to help with the decorations, I see."

Fred stands at the bottom of the driveway with a big box of streamers and balloons cradled in his arms. "Yep. Just doing my bit to make the big guy welcome."

Jim lowers the windshield wipers back into place, throws the sponge into the bucket, and wipes his hands dry on the back of his jeans. He looks at Fred for a moment and asks, "Think it'll be soon?"

Fred gives a happy sigh. "I hope so." And with that, he hefts the box up close to his chest and sets off toward the square. "I'll see you there. Later, Jim."

"Later, Fred."

Jim admires his car for a moment. It had once been crushed to the size of a suitcase, himself the folded luggage inside, but now it gleams, sparkling clean with a wet sheen, looking brand new. He decides to let the sun dry it, as he always does, and shoves the drying rag he never uses into a back pocket.

He goes next door to call on Mary.

Mary kneels in her garden, turning the soil with a trowel. Her lawn is a neat rectangle of green that stretches out behind her, continuing right up to the house where it splashes against the wall and turns into climbing ivy. Borders of glorious flowers shine in the sun like fallen rainbows.

It's a town of clean cars and beautiful gardens.

"Lovely roses, Mary," Jim says.

Mary blushes as if he's made a rude joke, turning the same color as the flowers he's complimented. "Jim, thank you." She smiles. "Are you going to the party already?"

"No, not yet. Doesn't feel like time to me."

"Nearly. Will you help me take some things down when it *is* time? I made some food."

"Of course. Just let me change and I'll come over."

When Jim emerges from his house, freshly dressed, most of his neighbors are also closing their front doors behind them, making their way to the square. Jim knew them all very well before they died but now he knows them better. He calls hello and words of excitement to those who can hear him, and waves to those who cannot, as he crosses the yard to Mary's.

Claire is there, chatting with her over the front gate.

"I was just asking, how old do you think he'll be?"

"Hello Claire," Jim replies. "I'm sure I've no idea." There's no need to ask *who*.

"Do you think he'll be handsome?"

Jim and Mary laugh, but before they can answer, Claire disappears.

She's gone for nearly half a minute before reappearing. Even so, she remains only long enough to blink and open her mouth to speak, barely a flicker, and then she disappears again.

"I hope she's not long," Mary says.

They wait patiently. Jim is about to suggest they make their way without her when she returns.

"Sorry," she says. "Flashback." She pats at her hair, as if the process might have disheveled it. "Been a lot of them around town today. Poor Tom's popped off five, six, times so far."

The three of them walk to the square together, Jim laden with containers of food and a cooler of soft drinks. Others are walking the same way, chatting, excited, each carrying their own contribution for the celebration; food, drink, decorations. The McCally boys struggle with a stereo between them. Where the roads lead into the square, colored streamers dangle from telephone wires. Bright posters adorn windows and the sides of buildings. Huge banners hang across from the lampposts: *Welcome!*

Crowds have gathered here, and everyone's in conversation. There are people from every title, and from the Back Storeys apartment complex, too. They're grouped around tables that bow under so many refreshments.

"Jim, good to see ya."

"Jim, my man."

"Hello Jim, long time no see."

Jim greets them all, adding his voice to the nervous noise, an increasing volume of competing chatter. The short walk to the square had been one of quiet excitement, but at the square itself these collected voices create a secondary sound, a singing vibration underneath the words, an anticipation every one of them can feel.

When the silence comes, it is sudden: someone new has appeared.

He's an old man, with a white smile and blue eyes watered down by his years. He wears red shorts, an open shirt, and his skin is tanned.

Everybody stares.

"Are you him?" someone eventually asks. Jim thinks it might have been George.

"No," the new one says. He looks around in wonder at the faces surrounding him. "I'm Gerald. He'll be here soon, though."

Suddenly everyone greets him at once. Some realize they had known him and greet him with new familiarity.

"How did it happen for you?" Mary asks. Someone always asks.

"On the beach, as the sun went down."

"Oh, how lovely."

"I suppose some sentimentality is to be expected at this stage in his life," Gerald says. Then, thinking it may have sounded ungrateful, adds, "It was a beautiful way to go."

The second hush comes when young Billy cycles into the square, blasting the horn on his handlebars, *hyonk! hyonk! hyonk!* He circles the townsfolk, wobbling as he tries to point behind and steer at the same time.

"New people!" he calls. "New people coming!"

Everybody surges in an eager wave to meet them. They know where the new ones are coming from, even without Billy's directions, because there's now a new edition to the roads. The crowd rushes as one to find them, welcome them, and lead them home.

Jim decides he'll wait—there will be plenty of opportunity to meet them all—and Mary lingers with him. She brings him a party hat. He puts it on at a jaunty angle.

"Thanks."

"Very handsome."

He bows, offers his arm, and the two of them walk a slow and comfortable pace around the square. They've shared more than a few pages together, Jim and Mary, have many memories in common, and it's a good day for reminiscing. They talk about the various chapters of their brief but very full lives.

It's Mary who eventually brings them back into the present. "I wonder if we should thank him."

"Doesn't seem enough, does it?"

She smiles, squeezes his arm. "No."

Jim will say thanks anyway. He's about to tell Mary as much when he notices the man at one of the tables.

He looks lost—they all do at first—yet he also seems strangely at home. Confused and curious, yet he somehow seems to know where he is. He picks up a bottle of beer. Looks at it. Smiles. Puts it down. He looks up at the decorations, the welcoming banners, and chuckles quietly. Then he sees Jim and Mary.

"Hello."

"Hello," they reply.

He looks at them unafraid. "Are you ghosts?"

Mary blushes, as she often does. "Sort of."

"We always were, really," adds Jim.

"It's Mary, isn't it?" the man says.

She nods.

"Wow. It really is. And Jim too, right? Hey, I'm sorry about the car accident. It was never my intention. It just happened. No hard feelings I hope?"

"None at all. If it wasn't for you . . . " Jim holds his arms out to encompass the surroundings.

The newcomer uses the gesture as an excuse to look around the square some more.

"We've been expecting you," Mary explains. The words feel well-used.

"So I see." Then, "Is this heaven?"

"It is to all of us."

Jim gestures for the newcomer to turn around.

The rest of the town have returned, bringing with them twenty or so new faces. They stand at the edge of the square, wide-eyed. They're young and old, male and female, a multitude of colors, creeds, and cultures, and every one of them an ink-relative.

The man recognizes them all. "I hope I'm not very late," he says. "I had a couple more pages to write."

Their reply is hesitant quiet laughter. Gerald says that he, for one, is glad, and people laugh some more. They begin stepping forward to offer shy greetings and thank-yous, and somehow it all escalates into a cheer. Food is unwrapped. Drinks are poured. Somebody, probably one of the McCally boys, turns on the music. When an elderly lady called Jessica May pushes her way to the front of the crowd, a knife in her hand, Fred calls out, "Watch out, she's lost the plot!" and people laugh more than the joke deserves because it's just such a joyous day.

"Hush now," says Jessica May. "We have something to say." She's been redrafted so many times that she always refers to herself in the plural; once Jessica and then May, she's now forever both. She clears her throat and puts a hand to her breast in ceremony. "The pen may be mightier," she declares in a clearly rehearsed tone, "but not when it comes to cutting cake."

There's applause as she hands the knife over to their creator.

People ready themselves with plates and Jim lights the candles of a magnificent cake. It's typewriter-shaped, and on each of its keys sits a candle. A sheet of marzipan curls in sugar-dusted splendor, curved to look like a page emerging from the cake's chocolate glaze, iced with the two words that have brought them all here together:

The End.

Ray Cluley is a writer living in Hampshire, England. His work has been published in Black Static, Interzone, *and* Shadows & Tall Trees, *amongst other places. His stories have also been republished in* Ellen Datlow's Best Horror of the Year *and translated into French for the* Ténèbres 2011 *anthology. He writes non-fiction occasionally but generally prefers to make stuff up. You can find out more at his blog* probablymonsters.wordpress.com.

LIKE A BAT OUT OF HELL

JONATHAN SHIPLEY

If creatures of mythology are born from belief systems, what occurs after their deaths? Perhaps they simply fade away from irrelevance or, perhaps, they meet death and experience afterlife the same as those mortals who once revered them. Jonathan Shipley explores this idea through one eternal youth who suffers in Hell due more to political misaligning than to any reprehensible behavior. After all, how "bad" can someone be if the purpose of their existence is merely to sing, dance, and drink wine? Consider Like a Bat out of Hell, *in which we learn the fate not only of one individual, but of an entire mythos.*

The gray gloom of Hell was shattered by the heavy beat of drums, joined by wild singing from a hundred throats of the bacchanalian horde. Grapevines burst from the parched, rocky ground to blossom into luscious grapes that were already fermented into wine on the vine. The wine-children gulped down the potent grapes, then joined hands and began a great circle dance. With all three—song and wine and dance—this qualified as revelry as defined by the god, Bacchus, whom they all served . . . or used to serve. And, regardless of their reduced circumstances, revelry still brought them power.

Beyond the edge of the dancing circle, one pouting youth sat apart, dwarfed by the hulking form of the three-headed dog beside him. Like most of the youths, he was dressed in plastic garbage bags, which were easy to find in the Circle of Gluttony. It seemed as if all the world's rotting garbage, bagged and unbagged, ended up here in the thick slurry of sewage that covered so much of the ground area. The ambient stench was a frontal assault to the nose.

"Attend to Cerberus," the youth, Revel, mimicked bitterly, catching just the right inflection of his older brothers and sisters who had set him to this task because he was the least and youngest of the horde. "You do it so well."

He grazed his palm on one of the sharp stones that littered the empty field, letting drops of blood drip onto the earth. Immediately a grapevine sprang up. Revel harvested three of the juicy grapes and tossed them—one, two, three—at Cerberus. The heads snapped them up and waited for more. After several rounds of grapes, the dog's six eyes lost some their savage intensity and the whole body sagged to the earth, half dozing, half watching.

It was true, Revel knew, that he *was* good with Cerberus. One of the heads actually liked him. The monstrous dog was set there to guard and harass the damned of the Third Circle of Gluttony, but there was always backdoor accommodation between fellow creatures of the Old Ways. And the status of the wine-children was ill-defined to start with. They were hardly mortals damned by their own excess since the very nature of Bacchus's children *was* one of excess. Yet, unlike many creatures of the Old Ways now consigned to Hell, they hadn't been drafted into the service of Lucifer to torment the souls of the damned. After all, how much of a torment would drunken youths be? Not much by Hell's standards. So here they were, confined to the Third Circle of Gluttony because it seemed fitting in someone's mind, though they were neither demon nor damned.

The children had a degree of freedom. They could wander to the Second Circle of Lust, but the storms were too violent there, and in the Fourth Circle of Greed on the other side, the damned were too obnoxious. So for the most part they stayed in the Third Circle where they had been assigned and avoided the numerous sewage pits as best they could. There was a sentry post near the center, where Cerberus stood guard on a pinnacle of rock that the foul garbage-rains seemed to avoid. It was the favorite gathering place of the wine-children; not a lot of space but relatively dry. A dozen high-proof grapes for Cerberus and he became as good a host as they were likely to find anywhere in Hell. It was here that they danced tonight.

Personally, Revel thought it was pushing things to bring all of them together at one time. Too conspicuous. A few dancers might be overlooked, but dozens of them raising full revelry was just asking for it. True, they were hemi-demi-semi-gods, descended from Bacchus himself, but hemi-demi-semi wouldn't be enough if they roused the powers of Hell against them. In his opinion, they would be better off finding a way out of the nightmare entirely. He saw no reason why they had to be banished from the World of Men just because they weren't mortal. That was senseless. And the centuries were long down here in this part of the Underworld. Where were the Elysian Fields? Did they still exist? The Underworld had never been the same since the world had changed and Hades morphed into Christian Hell. Old Hades had been dismal, but this place was unrelentingly miserable.

Cerberus raised a head suddenly, then another, and a third. They all looked toward the distant City of Dis, then the heads tilted up to the dark cavernous space overhead. One head—the friendly one—shot Revel a warning glance. *Not good*, Revel thought, scuttling closer to Cerberus. Offering a few more grapes, he pushed between the great paws, pressing himself against the furred body where he could still see but not be easily seen. They'd really done it this time, daring a full revelry. The Fallen had finally taken notice.

For a few minutes nothing seemed to happen. Then great winged figures dropped from the darkness. Their feathered wings were black, but their skin was the dead-white of marble and their eyes blazed red. One by one they alighted, then unfurled whips of flame. *Punishment*, Revel thought with a shudder. He'd never felt the bite of those lashes, but he'd seen Fallen Angels punish the damned often enough.

Amazingly, the revelry went on unheeding. His brothers and sisters were too far gone into the wine and music to care that danger was dropping out of the sky around them. Then the whips fell, and the song turned to screams of pain. But what was that? Revel stuck his head out a little farther to be sure he was seeing right. The horde was fighting back, sending their own whips of writhing grapevines to attack the Fallen!

This will not end well, Revel realized with a grimace. No one ever fought back against the Fallen Angels who ruled the Infernal Realm. Now there would be consequences beyond punishment. He buried himself deep in Cerberus's fur and tried not to watch as more and more Fallen from Dis joined the fight. There was never any doubt of the outcome—there were too few wine-children and too many dark angels. In the end, all the revelers were dragged shrieking and fighting up into the air and off toward the Lower Circles of Hell beyond the walls of Dis.

Finally, the oasis of rock became silent and empty. Revel emerged from his hiding place and walked slowly through the residue. Withered grapevines and crushed grapes were everywhere, interspersed with dark feathers torn off in the fight. He stared at the scene a long time. He had been part of the bacchanalian horde since birth. Being alone was a new and strange experience. And dangerous. He would have to move quietly, remain unseen, or be dragged off to the lower regions like his brothers and sisters.

He looked at Cerberus, who stared back dolefully with six eyes. "What do I do now?" he asked the beast.

He wasn't expecting an answer, but the friendly head gave him a wink that promised one later. Revel knew how that worked and settled into his perch on the rock for the long haul. Eventually Cerberus curled up and dozed off, head by head. But then the last head lifted and gave Revel a nod. The youth scuttled over.

"Can't stay here," the dog-head growled. "Fallen will be watching. Bad situation for lone wine-child. Need to get out of Hell."

"Wouldn't I love to," Revel said. He started to say more but paused as another of the dog-heads whuffled and almost woke. Waiting until the head dozed again, he whispered softly. "Is there a way out? I thought being here meant I was dead."

The friendly head was silent a long time. "Then maybe not being here means not dead anymore," it finally rumbled. "Don't know. Takes better heads to answer that."

At first Revel thought it meant his companion-heads, but then it added, "Halfway around the Circle is another rock, another guardian. She knows secrets. Careful, though—she likes tearing apart soft flesh."

Revel wanted to argue that his flesh wasn't particularly soft, then considered it from an alternative perspective. Dancing, drinking, lolling about—he wasn't exactly a Hercules. He could see a predator regarding him as easy prey.

"Use my name," Cerberus suggested after moment. "Now go. Find the sphinx."

"Cerberus?" the woman-headed lion creature repeated suspiciously. "Why would Old Three Heads even care?"

Revel, filthy and reeking of sewage after his long trek, gave a sigh. He actually didn't know why Head Number Three was so helpful when One and Two didn't care. And now faced with the sphinx, he saw more lion and less woman than he expected . . . and a lot more claw. It reminded him that sphinxes tore unwary travelers apart for sport. But he was here, and that was something. He had slogged halfway around the Circle of Gluttony on this quest, and none of it was easy going. The distances felt immense and the time seemed like centuries . . . and, for all he knew, it might well have been centuries since the Fallen captured the horde. Time was funny in Hell.

"He cares because I feed him the grapes of Bacchus," Revel finally answered. "And because there is still honor among us Old Ones," he added pointedly.

"I'm a half-woman, half-lion demon," the sphinx corrected. "By decree of Lucifer there are no more *Old Ones*, just demons."

"Lucifer wouldn't be so full of himself if Lord Pluto were still around," Revel shot back.

The sphinx gave a sudden bound that brought her face within inches of Revel's. "Quiet, fool," she growled. "That's the last name you want to bandy about so freely. No regime likes to be reminded of its immediate predecessor. The world has changed and we are now demons—accept it."

"I refuse. I want to be quit of this place entirely. I'm not a demon and I'm not damned, so I don't belong here. I need to find a way out."

The sphinx sat back with a snort. "In Hell, what hope of escape is there for those constantly trodden underfoot?"

Revel blinked at the shift in inflection. Then he grinned. "You just phrased that as a riddle. From a sphinx, that means you're hiding obscure knowledge. But I'll trade you—grapes of Bacchus for the answer to your own riddle?" To tempt her, he quickly cut his hand on a sharp rock and let the blood drip down. A grapevine bearing plump, red fruit sprouted up in answer. He popped a grape into the sphinx's mouth and let her savor the heady juice. "Deal?"

"I can't just give you information," she insisted. "But I'll give you another riddle: When does vengeance fly on six wings?"

The six-winged seraphim? Revel wondered, then quickly dismissed that. Those high denizens of the celestial realm would never degrade themselves by visiting the Underworld. The answer must be someone or something more hellish. Then he thought about the word "vengeance" and realized he knew this answer. "When vengeance is the three Furies," he said.

"And of the Furies, Tisiphone always enjoys a good joke. There, I've riddled you all you need to know. If you have the wit to put it together, you're better than most of your brood."

From anyone else, that would have been a most unsatisfactory exchange, but this was a sphinx. Sphinxes never told you anything important directly; you had to guess. It was strange, but it was a start.

Time trudged by. Revel mulled over the riddles as he wandered back to Cerberus's side of the Circle of Gluttony. *I've riddled you all you need to know.* Presumably that meant all he needed to know to escape. Except all he knew right now was he should talk to the Fury, Tisiphone, who enjoyed a good joke. There had to be something more he wasn't seeing.

When he reached the guardian rock, he kept low and crawled up the side farthest away from Dis, in case the Fallen were still watching. As he reached the pinnacle, he saw Cerberus looking off in three directions. Fortunately, the head pointing his direction was the friendly one. But it gave him a sharp look and slowly shook from side to side. Warning.

Revel backed down the rock to wait. There might not be day or night here, but Cerberus had a regular sleep cycle divided into shifts between the heads. All he had to do was catch the right head awake.

He waited an hour or so, crawled up the rock, saw it was Number Two on watch, and crawled back down. After another couple of hours, he tried again. Yes, Number Three this time.

"Careful," the head growled as he approached. "Fallen looking for you. Other wine-lings told that you were missing. Fallen came back and gave orders to report if we see you. Number One will do that."

Revel gave a shudder. He assumed his brothers and sisters had not reported his absence voluntarily. Glancing at the first head, he saw it slept soundly. But if it was now an enemy, he needed to be gone before it awoke. This might be his only opportunity to get Number Three's take on the sphinx.

He came closer. "The sphinx said to talk to the Furies—Tisiphone, specifically, because she likes jokes. Then the sphinx said she had riddled me all I needed to know if I had the wit to put it together. I'm not sure I have that much wit."

The head leaned closer. "What did sphinx say and what did sphinx riddle? That's important. If she *said* to talk to Furies—"

"No, she riddled me that, and I guessed it correctly."

"Then talking to Tisiphone is important. Were there other riddles?"

Revel thought back. "Yes, one other. Something like—"

"Exact words."

That took more thinking. Finally, Revel remembered. "Here it is. In Hell, what hope of escape is there for those constantly trodden underfoot?"

"Ah, Type Six riddle," the head nodded. "Talk to sphinxes for a couple centuries and you'll see that all riddles fall into categories. Type Six is when inverse of riddle is answer. In Hell, hope of escape for those crushed underfoot is from those elevated overhead."

"So the Furies again," Revel shrugged.

"But not specifically the Furies. Those overhead can also be griffins and Geryon and even Fallen. What do those have in common?"

"Wings . . . they fly."

"So that's the escape."

"Hitching a ride on Geryon—I don't see it."

"But sphinx did, so is possible. And second riddle about Furies adds in something else you need to—"

A loud yawn erupted from one of the other heads. Number Three frowned and said quickly, "Tisiphone likes darkish Fury jokes. Use those to get on good side. Now go before others wake up."

"Grape?" Revel asked. It was the only tangible thanks he could offer.

"Can't—they'd smell it on breath. Go."

Revel skittered off as more sounds came from the two waking heads. Down a level, he passed through the plateau where the Fallen had wrecked the bacchanalian revelry. The scene looked strangely fresh, as though the fight happened yesterday, not weeks or months ago. Withered grapevines snaked across the area, tendrils still clutching bunches of feathers. He paused, staring at that image. He never claimed to be smart, but even a wine-child could spot an answer when it was right in front of his nose.

Finally Revel was ready . . . or thought he was. The problem with sphinx plans was that they all depended on guesswork. But he was more or less ready for Tisiphone. He'd wracked his brain for everything he'd ever heard about the Furies, looking for material for "darkish Fury jokes." He'd actually come up with a couple. And he was getting used to making jokes or puns out of unlikely subject matter.

He found an almost dry place with a good line of sight across Greed and the River Styx to the distant, shattered gate of Dis where the Fallen congregated. The Fallen and the Furies. He was still dressed in garbage bags, and beside him another garbage bag quivered and rustled ceaselessly. Revel took a deep breath and drew blood from a finger. As the droplets fell, he whispered, "Tisiphone," three times. It wasn't the usual bacchanalian magic, but anyone of divine descent knew how to summon with blood. He reached over and placed a possessive hand on the quivering garbage bag beside him and waited.

A movement caught his eye, something dropping from the sky, but different from the fluttering wings of the Fallen. A moment later, an armored woman landed beside him, furling black bat wings as she alighted. Her face was ringed in curls of serpents and her eyes dripped blood.

Revel gave a nervous smile. "Hullo, Tisiphone."

"What are you?" the Fury demanded, then shook her serpent curls impatiently. "No, I see now you're one of Bacchus's multitudinous bastards. I could smell the hint of god-blood all the way across the river. The real question is what sort of idiot summons *me* of all creatures."

"Someone looking for you maybe?" he suggested.

Her serpent curls hissed in irritation. "No one comes looking for the Furies," she snapped. "People flee our retribution."

"*Used* to flee," Revel corrected carefully. "If I'm not mistaken, it's been a while since you and your sisters were actually at large in the World of Men."

Tisiphone gave him a narrow look. "What are you saying, you wine-sodden child?"

"Nothing, really," he said quickly. "Just wondering if the change from Fury of Hades to demon of Hell was all that great. I know for someone like me who lives for wine and music, this place is a nightmare."

"It's what happens every time the world changes," Tisiphone snapped. "My sisters and I are old enough to remember the times before Mount Olympus, before what's-his-name set up his kingdom of Hades. Now that it's changed into the Christian Hell, it's all different again, and all the inconvenient creatures of the Old Ways have been swept in here because they no longer fit in the remolded world. The only question is why one of Bacchus's wine children is hanging on to Old Ways that have now vanished."

"What happened to our world? What happened to Lord Pluto?"

"The gods can take care of themselves, even when the world changes. That's why they're gods. And you'd be smart not to mention him anymore. The Fallen are dour, humorless masters who see things only one way. They wouldn't take kindly to a wine child contradicting the way they have re-ordered Hell."

"They don't take kindly to much of anything," Revel muttered. Then he looked up slyly. "But this wine-child isn't sticking around to experience their vision of Hell. I've figured it out."

"Figured *what* out?" Tisiphone asked suspiciously.

"Why some have a better deal with this re-ordering than others. The satyrs are savaged, but the griffins have free rein to hunt as they choose. The wine-children are tormented, but the Furies are elevated to guardians and gate-keepers. For centuries it made no sense, but then I saw the reason. It's the winged creatures that fare the best . . . those that can fly like the Fallen."

The Fury's expression remained wooden and unreadable.

"You don't have to confirm any of this," Revel continued. "That's what I've seen, so I know it's true. There's not much power in being a minor godling, but we are hard to deceive. I'm guessing there was an accord between the Fallen and all other winged creatures."

"And why would there be?"

Revel's grin grew wider. He knew he was on the right track. "Because I've watched the skies and seen what no one else seems to notice . . . the Fallen never fly and fight at the same time. Those whips of fire are quite effective on the ground, but I'm guessing airborne, they get tangled in the moving wings. So the first order of business for the Fallen was an alliance with anyone else that might attack them in the air."

The serpent curls hissed ominously as Tisiphone brought her face close to his. "This side of Dis is a walk in the park compared with the lower Circles on the other side of the wall. And that kind of talk, wine-child, will get you thrown in some very disagreeable pit in the lowest Circle of Hell. The Fallen do not tolerate dissent."

"Yes, yes—I'm not blind. I see what they do. But I have a plan to escape Hell altogether."

"To escape Hell," the Fury snorted. "As if. There's an entrance at the First Circle and an exit from the Ninth Circle, but the likes of you can't pass either of those."

Revel gave a careless shrug. "No, I can't." Then he pointed a finger straight upward to the darkness overhead. "But you're forgetting the *other* exit from Hell . . . the one that you Furies used in the old days to bring quick retribution to oath-breakers in the World of Men. Somewhere up there, isn't it? I'm guessing the Fallen don't know about *that* one."

"That's deadly talk," Tisiphone murmured dangerously. "If there were an exit in the high vaults of this cavern that the Fallen were ignorant of, it would be a secret easily worth the disemboweling of an overly mouthy wine-child."

Revel swallowed hard. A Fury's clawed fingers were not just for show. He was close to his goal, but he had to tread carefully. "All the more reason to want an overly mouthy wine-child gone entirely," he suggested carefully. "If I escape, the secret's safe. All I need to know is how to find that exit and I'll be out of your hair." *Unfortunate choice of words*, he thought as the curls hissed at him again.

"And then you'll do what?" she scoffed. "Thumb a ride on the next griffin to fly you up there?"

Considering griffins were highly carnivorous with a penchant for fresh livers in particular, that wasn't much of an option. "Oh, I have my ways," he said breezily. "Among the magical detritus that was chucked in here over the centuries, I came across a wishing ring. Not much power and not much range, but it's still got one good wish left in it. If I give it an exact course, it should be able to levitate me out of here."

Tisiphone considered that and sat back with a frown. That was the problem with Hell being the garbage dump of all older belief systems—nobody knew what was in the mix. Nobody . . . not the Fallen and certainly not the Furies.

"Let's see it," she demanded suddenly.

Revel shook his head. *There was no ring, of course. But he didn't want to give away his actual plan, and a magic ring was a believable cover.* "No, you'll try to take it from me, but it wouldn't do you any good anyway."

"Eh?"

"You'd want to become beautiful, and I already told you it's not all that powerful."

A moment of tense silence, then Tisiphone erupted into raucous laughter. As the cacophony faded, she gave him a hideous grin. "How I've missed jokes! Our former lord's irreverent humor kept us all in stitches, but it's been sour times with the Fallen. I'm halfway tempted to help you just for the sake of the joke."

"If you're only halfway tempted, then let me give you another for the other half," Revel said quickly. "It's in the form of a riddle and, moreover, a riddle about our very topic of discussion. Why do the Furies not escape Hell themselves?"

The mood grew suddenly colder. Yes, this was risky, but that was the nature of Fury humor.

"So tell me, wine-child. Why do we Furies not escape Hell ourselves?"

Revel took a deep breath, at the same time gathering his legs under him in case this was ill-received. "Because it would prove all the humans right who keep saying, *Hell hath no Fury . . .* "

Again the moment of dead silence. Then another round of raucous laughter. Revel let himself relax a little. This might actually work after all. "So are you now more tempted to help me?" he cautiously asked.

Tisiphone let the question hang a while before giving a disdainful shrug. "I have no loyalty to the Fallen or their master. And it's certainly not a matter of fear. The Furies are ancient avatars of vengeance and not much afraid of anything. But there is this . . . alliance, as you call it. Is it worth jeopardizing that?"

Revel realized the question wasn't addressed to him, and he had the good sense to keep silent. There was too much at stake. If Tisiphone turned against him at this point, it wouldn't be good. If she didn't rip him apart herself, she would surely turn him over to the Fallen. He had revealed himself as too dangerous to wander Hell freely.

As the silence stretched into minutes, he resorted to his old fallback. Stabbing his palm with his trusty shard, he let the blood drip to the ground and willed the grapes to come forth. He had no idea if a Fury could be tempted with fruit of the vine, but it was worth trying. The grapes of Bacchus were pretty tempting to a whole range of creatures.

As the grapevine pushed its way through the rocky soil, he stooped and casually popped the first grape into his mouth. Then as more fruit appeared, he left the bounty on the vine and stepped back, letting the offer be inherent in his actions.

"You forget how the Furies were birthed," Tisiphone said, her voice low and dangerous.

Revel remembered they were born from the blood of Uranus when the Titans overthrew his rule a generation before the gods of Olympus. Blood-magic must take on a different slant for those who were creatures of blood themselves.

"No disrespect intended," he said quickly. "The grapes are the only hospitality I have to offer in an inhospitable environment." A bit of inspiration struck, the product of many nights of forcing jokes out of nothing. "But I should have realized that my fruit of the vine and a creature of vengeance would produce a potent cocktail indeed. The mortals even have a phrase for it."

The Fury cocked her head. "Which is?"

"Grapes of wrath."

It produced only a snort, but her eyes lost their dangerous glint. "I'll pass along a rumor," she said. "What you do with it is your business, but it's been long rumored that an exit from the Underworld does exist far overhead. If someone were to follow the course of the River Styx to its junction with the River Cocytus, the exit lies directly above. And that," she added, "is the last I want to see of an overly mouthy wine-child." With that, she spread her bat wings and shot upward into the gloom.

Revel gave a great exhalation and sagged to the ground as the tension of that encounter oozed out of him. For interaction with a Fury, that had gone exceedingly well, but he didn't deceive himself that Tisiphone was any sort of friend. He had caught her in a good mood and amused her—that was all. He could easily imagine a darker encounter if her mood turned and she decided a certain wine-child knew too much. There was value in haste.

He gathered the other grapes from the vine and munched them, one after the other. He would need the liquid courage in a moment. He could have one chance at this. The moment the Fallen realized there was an unauthorized flier in Hell, they would be all over him.

He thrust his arms toward the denuded grapevine and willed it to come. Like a leafy green snake, it slithered up his arms and around his shoulders, squeezing him so tightly he could barely breathe. But it had to be tight.

Reaching over, he pulled open the other garbage bag with its constantly rustling contents. A pile of quivering, dark feathers spilled onto the ground, gathered from the last revelry's short-lived attempt to fight off the Fallen. Revel had no idea how many feathers it would take to hold him aloft; he had gathered all there were and only hoped it was enough. At least the feathers were still feisty and ready to fly. He had fed them on wine and blood and that seemed to energize them.

At his thought, the encircling grapevine exploded with more writhing tendrils. He lay down in the pile of feathers and concentrated on pulling the two elements together. Icarus had famously managed this with wax and feathers, so surely a grapevine of Bacchus could do what inanimate wax had once achieved.

He couldn't see what was happening at his back, but he sensed when the questing tendrils finished twining themselves around feathers. Cautiously, he climbed to his feet, feeling oddly back-heavy. When he looked back at where he had lain, the pile of feathers was gone. He gave a tentative flap of his new appendages and felt an upward lift.

This was it: Fly or die. He stood for a moment, tempted out of habit to invoke the blessing of the gods on this venture, but who of Olympus was left to hear him? With a shrug, Revel gave up that thought and concentrated on flapping his wings again, this time faster. The uplift pulled him off his feet.

As the sodden ground of the Third Circle of Gluttony fell away beneath him, he reviewed his flight plan—find the juncture of the Rivers Styx and Cocytus, then straight up. *It has to work, it has to work*, he thought in time with the flapping at his back. He kept a watchful eye on the wall of Dis, fearing to see Fallen rising to meet him, but so far nothing. Then something, a fluttering. Some of the Fallen sensed something gone wrong. As soon as they caught his scent—

Suddenly a great baying sounded below. Cerberus. Had Number One spotted him? Then he saw a flutter of movement from Dis head through the air in the direction of the Circle of Gluttony. Had to be Number Three, he realized suddenly. His favorite friendly head was providing a distraction.

Revel shot upward, abandoning secrecy for speed in this moment of opportunity. Up and up above the junction of the two rivers until he saw a crack of light. Closer. Closer. Then abruptly he exploded into sunlight that he hadn't seen for over a thousand years.

For a moment, fear of the unknown paralyzed him. How would a lone wine-child survive in the mostly hostile World of Men? Then his brain kicked in, reminding him that anything would be better than his former accommodations where the stench alone could knock over a Gorgon. Moreover, he had certain skills to fall back on. He could open a vineyard in the south of France and produce the best wine in all the World of Men. It was more a thought than a plan, but there was a certain symmetry to it. From the least of wine-children to the greatest of vintners. Then he could lie about in the sun without a care in the world.

Like a Revel without a cause.

His mouth quirked into a sudden grin. Hell might still have a Fury or three, but as of two minutes ago, Hell hath no Revel.

*Fort Worth writer **Jonathan Shipley** has had fantasy, science fiction, and horror stories published in magazines and a dozen plus anthologies. However, he is actually a novel writer at heart and spends most of his writing time on a vast story arc that ranges from Nazi occultism to vampires to futuristic space opera. Like a Bat Out of Hell is from the darker end of the spectrum, but is at the same time unexpectedly humorous for the venue. A complete list of published stories may be found on his website at* www.shipleyscifi.com.

THE OVERLANDER

JACOB EDWARDS

Is death so different from life? There are many who believe ghosts of the deceased still walk this world amongst us—invisibly— carrying on with the same lives they led while breathing. The same rules of physics may not apply to spirits but, nonetheless, considering if all the ghosts through history are still roaming here, the Earth seems like a mighty crowded place. Unless, that is, you happen to pass away in the wild and wide expanse of the Australian outback. Colorful and alluring, Jacob Edwards invites you to take a ride with him over the wallaby track in The Overlander.

I died somewhere off the Maranoa on May 19, 1912.

I've been dead for just over a hundred years now. For me, the wallaby track never grows old.

I think that's because the bush doesn't change. If you love something fierce enough and you've license to roam, then every day dawns fresh and new. The west country was too much to explore in one lifetime. It'll see me through the eternal hereafter, too.

And I reckon Sooty Bill here agrees with me.

It helps that all the old creeks are still around. There's roads running through 'em nowadays, and these flash carriages that rumble like a bullock team and put the old drovers to shame, but the land never changes. Not while me and Sooty Bill are still riding.

Kings Crossing. Two Tree Gully. One Mile, Two Mile, Five Mile Creeks. Miles from nowhere, now. A lot of towns and stations have come and gone but the Queensland bush is still here—stark and dry and majestic, more beautiful than anything you'll find in those slick big towns they've got out on the coast.

I saddle up Sooty Bill each morning and we strike out wherever we feel. From the Darling ranges across to the Barcoo and south down to Cooper's Creek, or up toward the Gulf, gawping like a couple of new chums at the hard, patchy gums and the mottled yellows and reds of the wattle and bottlebrush trees.

People can't see us for the most part, or maybe they catch just the ghostly chill of a man long dead—the flap of my coat in the first cold breeze of autumn or the puff of dust from Sooty Bill's hooves on a still day. There's a smell of horse sweat and leather where we've passed through, I reckon. Old timers will stop what they're doing, and I think sometimes they almost remember . . . But then we're gone, and with us the thought, and so they wave at the flies on their backs and move on with their lives.

I don't know why it is that you can see us. You're not dead, are you? Or dying? The bush, she can be unforgiving if you stray from the track and don't know her ways. Sooty Bill and I met a lonely end, and we knew the west country like the soot on the back of a quart-pot.

We came down just short of the Speewah, did Sooty Bill and I. Broken legs, the pair of us—and I snapped my pipe, too. How those bloomin' kookaburras laughed! I dossed down as best I could but nobody found us out there. Still haven't to this day, far as I know.

I thought when I was done for I'd be off to work for the devil Jack Robertson, but I woke up with Sooty Bill here nuzzling my whiskers and lyrebirds mimicking the groans I'd made in my sleep. I boiled the billy and found my cup, and we've been riding ever since.

Is that damper you've cooked? Give me johnny cakes any day but even so, it brings back some memories—me and Denis O'Reily and the rest of the boys punching cattle from Marree across the Tirari and the Sturt Stony, up to Birdsville. They're all long gone now, Denis and the lads, but the morning air's still crisp and clear. That memory pulls sharp through my nostrils. Sooty Bill's, too, I reckon. See how he whinnies?

We don't need any of that these days, mind. It's enough for us to ride the wide country, out west across the granite belt and up to the gulf and back, following the range. I still like the smell of good tucker, though. Just the same as Sooty Bill likes to stop and munch on the grass he can't touch. It's better this way, I reckon. All the beauty with none of the want. We'll travel the bush forever, past bottle trees and blackboys, creeks and billabongs, never going the same place twice.

What's that you say? Speak up. I can't hear too much beyond the dingoes at night and the dazed bleating of sheep on the plains. Voices sound muffled to me these days. People have moved on without me, I suppose. But that's alright. The creaking gum trees have a language all their own. Same as the cockatoos in the treetops. The slow rustle of frillynecks and bluetongues through the scrub. Snakes slithering across the track as they—

So, you *can* hear me. Thought there for awhile I was talking to myself, even though you look fair to have set eyes upon a bunyip. So, snakebite, was it? Aye, they're sluggish in the cold. Easy to step on if you're not careful, although Sooty Bill here can sense 'em alright. Did you catch what sort it was?

Well, I reckon that's an eastern brown, friend, and that means you're for it, flash pack or no.

But don't worry. Yours will be quicker than mine, right enough, and if you're bound for the same hereafter as me then the Queensland bush will see you right. It's hot in summer and dry enough to parch many a throat. And in wintertime the nights can be so blessed cold the koalas will come down from their trees and scratch and mew at the door of your hut. And if you let 'em in then good for you. They'll huddle up next to the stove, and when you open the door in the morning they'll file right back out again and up on into their trees.

But she's beautiful, is Queensland, from the grassy hills of the tableland out west to the dust plains. Or up in the Bunyas, where your scrub turkeys and bowerbirds pick all about the place and suddenly—*crack!*—you've got whipbirds, and cockatoos working away with their beaks, opening up the pines. Or there's the Carnarvon with its sandstone canyons and blue gums and ironbarks, its echidnas and currawongs . . . Just don't eat all your damper right away—that's my advice to you. Save some for the centuries to come.

I'd invite you to join us, but me and Sooty Bill have gotten used to traveling the bush alone. Aye, some company would be welcome once in awhile, and it'd do me good to click the shears again after all these years—to work a pen or two and then go drinking with the boys. But I haven't pinked 'em with the Wolseleys for over a century now and, anyway, I guess me and Sooty Bill have grown used to wandering. Like pigs in clover, we are, lost on the wallaby track.

So, we'll be on our way now, heading out west like we've always done. Best of luck to you, young colonial. I know it must seem like a heap of trouble to you now, but don't worry. You'll see. When you lay your swag down and the German band begins to play, just pick yourself up and start walking.

Aye, death's just another step across this big, dry country—from Cradle Mountain to Arnhem Land, from Brisbane to Broome, through the red of the Simpson past Ayer's Rock and hundreds of places you've likely never been. It's what comes next that's important, see? Whether it's picking fleas or promenading around the old bullock dray. Just load up your prad and punch across into the Australian afterlife. Look around. There's always room for one more overlander.

Jacob Edwards *graduated from the University of Queensland with a BA (English) and an MA (Ancient History). He lives in Brisbane, Australia, with his wife and son, and may be found online at www.jacobedwards.id.au.*

Jacob would like to dedicate The Overlander *to his grandfather, Wal Edwards (1916-1993), who left home while still a very young man and found work as a drover during the Great Depression. Wal taught himself bushcraft, thinking his way through problems while at the same time becoming both a strong swimmer (with his own technique for traversing flooded creeks) and the most natural looking of horsemen, wonderfully at ease in the saddle. A shy, self-effacing man with a puckishly dry sense of humor, Wal was never one to boast of his talents or bemoan the hardships of his early life. Instead, having served in Australia's 62nd Battalion (New Guinea) during the Second World War, he devoted himself to raising a family—becoming a husband to Gwen, then father to Dave, Jill, and Marg, and eventually grandfather to Garth, Jake, and Sam. Though never losing his love of the outback, it was with family that Wal felt most at home—with the people he cherished and who will long hold him dear for having lived a gentle life of love and courage.*

FOREVER

JOHN PALISANO

The next story is not quite like the others in this book, and that's a good thing. Rather than the dark voice that many of the other authors brought, the accomplished John Palisano presents a touching vision of hope from an unexpected deceased companion. Statistically, most survivors of near-death experiences testify that the spirit of a dead relative or friend met and spoke to them, explaining the boundless love and peace that awaits "on the other side." I can only hope that is true, and such is the compassionate end for us all. Forever is the tale of one dying woman and the loved one who returns to guide her into eternity.

You were right. There *is* more.

I found it hard to believe before arriving here, but there really are endless worlds of joy and rivers of love. Winds carry peaceful sounds of flowing water and laughter; light emanates from all you see. Flowers bloom. Everything one could want or need, and more than you might imagine. Voices whisper, telling me you're arriving soon, and that you'll need someone you love to help you through. That's me.

Our last day together was not frightening. We rode toward the town of Valhalla in upstate New York, and you and him held back your tears. Sweet fall air filled the long blue car. We passed more trees and lakes and hills than anywhere else we'd ever been together. You cared for me and brought me with you wherever you went since my tiny body fit in your hands. We lived all over the East Coast: New Jersey. Connecticut. Boston. You took me to New Orleans and Las Vegas and—my favorite place of all—California. Remember me jumping off that flat boat into the big lake with the tall sandy hills surrounding us? Getting back onto the boat proved too hard. He jumped in after me and lifted me back inside. I felt bad for scratching him, but that was the night we finally let him between us. That wasn't easy. Remember me sleeping between you and him on the bed? I always felt protective of you, because you protected me.

Here it is again, my turn being your guardian.

Don't be scared. You're going through a lot of pain right now. Blackness eats at your body. It hurts me to know you're hurting that way. Your loving soul doesn't deserve what's fallen on you. But like you always said: *We're not our bodies. We're what's inside.* It'll be over soon. Promise. You're going to feel your essence slipping away, then you'll feel, inside your gut, like you're on the longest and highest elevator ride of all time. We call it going on the *Lift.* Elevators always scared me so much, by the way. I don't miss those damn things. At all. Or airplane rides.

When you're riding the Lift, you'll remember lots of great moments. Most of my memories are with you. The look on your face as you held me in the air the first night. The taste of the plastic seatbelt clicker in your new car. Apologies for that, but my teeth hurt so bad and there was nothing else for me to chew. Rain-soaked grass tickled my paws when we lived on that busy street in California. Each smell at each house of our daily walk around the block plays inside my mind, and every inch we strolled is permanently imprinted on my brain. My memory rebuilt our walk here in *Forever,* and I have strolled it several times, but you're not here with me, so it's not complete. You will be soon. Can you smell the fountain close to where we lived in New Orleans? The concrete warmed my paws and the hot food always drove me crazy as it cooked underneath our little place on the second floor. Can you feel the cushy blankets when we stayed in the basement in New Jersey? The cold snow outside packed all the way up to my belly. Pure joy. It snows here, sometimes. You're going to love that.

You're probably surprised hearing me talk. It's true: We understood, and understand, everything. We're smarter than most people realize. All the fancy gadgets to talk and see the weather, but none can talk to us. Maybe that'll change with some future generation. Who knows? There are some who follow their instinct and *know*. You're one of them.

Your glories were my glories. The parties overflowed with people. The quiet times we watched the lighted picture box. Then the little boy came. Even though realizing my number-one spot had to be relinquished, you have no idea the happiness that grew inside my heart. You deserved him and have been an amazing Momma to him, as you were to me.

Sorry to say you won't see him again for a while. But we'll have lots of time together where you can discover Forever with me. Your pain will disappear. Your favorite places are here. Money doesn't matter. Only life. Yes, *life*. We go on. We build things here—places for souls to blossom. Our energy feeds the Big One. *God*. It's the most important work, yet, it doesn't feel like work. It's like when you're thirsty and you drink the best tasting water ever. That's how it seems. We gather and focus our thoughts on recreating someone's home from their childhood, their familiar streets, their favorite places, so when they arrive they are happy. We hear when they come, and we get little blips in our heads about them. When we gather together the blips collect together, too, and the places form between us. It's the neatest magic you've ever seen.

Of course, we can't create people. That's forbidden.

Know, too, that your loved ones meet. They sense when you approach the Lift. Those are amazing times and it's always exciting to bring people over. Most are terrified and can't believe it . . . even the Believers.

When you come, you'll see. You're strong, and you'll adapt quickly.

Near the end of the Lift your world slips away and becomes *our* world. Your intuition changes. Your heart beats differently. Gravity lessens. Your body feels both bigger and smaller, because your flesh as you know it fades, replaced and reborn from ageless cosmic luminescent matter. That's the best way to describe it. We look like our old selves, but we're not entirely physical in the ways we once were. It's weird to say, but we're better. We're not limited like before. No pain. No illness. No hunger. Just a state of restful being. Bliss.

I remember your hand on me, talking to me gently as the fire-medicine coursed through my body. Your man was there, too, keeping his feelings inside. That doctor's office floor faded from me, the edges blurring and darkening, your voice echoing heavily, until I smelled the distinctive pure air of Forever and pointed my nose toward where it came. My heart stopped beating. Pitch black surrounded me.

Was I scared?

Terrified, yes. This is it, life is over. I thought there would be nothing else and, within a few moments, that would be all: Goodbye, world. Goodbye.

I was wrong.

Only now does life begin. Our time before is only training for Forever. This, you must understand, is where things are truly realized.

You're coming now.

Please don't be scared; we're all here together to be with you. There're no tubes sticking out of you here, no pain or discomfort, no shame or sadness. It's okay to let go.

Good, just like that.

Feel your feet lighten, then your legs, then your belly, your heart, and your soul. You're being brought up to the Lift. Someone's holding your hand as you slip away, his hot tears fall on your palm, as yours did mine during my last breaths. Smile for him, so he remembers when it's his turn. This moment . . . this *change* . . . will be okay, just like I smiled for you when I left. Your son knows your loss to him will be deep. The life and memories you gave him will never be forgotten and will shape the rest of his life: Showing him how to eat with a spoon. Leading him to walk. Your hugs. Your smile. Your laughter. Paddling down the river in a raft. Swimming with him in an Oregon lake. His successes. His losses. The passing of his father only a few years ago. You were there for him, his Momma, his joy, his inspiration . . . just like you were there for me. You will see him again, as you will soon see me.

Can you hear me? You've never heard this voice, but your heart will recognize the sound. Please come to my call, as I once followed yours.

You're so beautiful. Your heart beats through your skin and I hear the pleasant thump it makes. Your arms are outstretched, and I'm running to your spirit. Look behind me and see those you've missed all come to greet you: Your mother. The father of your son holds flowers; he never stopped loving you. Your *Omi*, standing, hands on her hips. Others I'm not familiar with. All have nothing but love to give.

Your arms feel the same as always: strong and tender. How I've missed you. We all have.

See? It's okay, isn't it?

Do you feel any pain now? Do you feel anything other than the fondness we all have for you? Isn't this wonderful? And this place you've made? The beach. We are bathed in golden light. It's where you go inside when you're sad, right? And now we're all together again here. And you're holding onto me so tight. And you're crying, and your tears are cool like a fall river. And you know me and you call out my name.

"Wolffie."

Welcome to Forever.

Author of the novel, Nerves, *and the novella,* The BiPolar Express, *as well as short stories in anthologies:* The Lovecraft E-Zine, Horror Library, Beast Within, A Sea of Alone, Midnight Walk, Darkness on the Edge, Chiral Mad, Terror Scribes, *and many others,* **John Palisano** *can be found at:* www.johnpalisano.wordpress.com.

MY FATHER KNEW DOUGLAS MACARTHUR

BENTLEY LITTLE

Some people are born leaders. Whether that aptitude is used toward causes considered right or wrong may not mean much to them, but they'll be at the forefront of whichever side they choose. My Father Knew Douglas MacArthur *is the war cry of one man who doesn't like the way the afterlife is being reconstructed. Bentley Little is the author of numerous award-winning novels, short stories, articles, and essays. Coincidentally, he is also a graduate from the same University (Go Titans!) with the same degree as this editor/fan. Known for his acerbic and distinctive horror, the following story does not disappoint.*

There was no heaven.

There was no hell.

He hadn't known that before he died—no one did, obviously—but he knew it now. There was only this *place*, this room, if it could be called that. For though he saw no walls, there *was* a ceiling, there *was* a floor, and between the two surfaces were the dead, sitting, standing, lying down, crammed close together for as far as he could see in every direction.

They were naked, all of them, himself included. Which made sense. After all, when a man died, his clothes didn't die, too. A pair of pants didn't have a spirit. There couldn't be the ghost of a shirt.

To his right, Whitney Houston was kicking Richard Nixon in the face, while the disgraced ex-president clawed at the eyes of an unknown woman lying next to him on the floor. They had been doing this since he arrived, although he had no idea how long that had been as there was no clock in here and the diffuse light that somehow illuminated the room never varied in intensity. It felt as though at least a day had passed since he'd suddenly *appeared* in this spot, but that was just a sense he had and was based on nothing substantial. He'd stood dumbly in place after his arrival, too numb to move at first, then too afraid to find out if he could. For awhile he had tried counting out minutes, just to give himself something to do, but counting had been as boring as doing nothing and he'd quit after an hour.

So he had no idea how long he'd been here.

But he was one of the new arrivals. He was certain of that.

The others nearby had been here for quite some time. The oldest ones were worn down, and no longer had any individual features or recognizable characteristics. They looked like mannequins and had the same sort of bland generic qualities as a clothing store dummy. There seemed to be a general lack of consciousness among these older dead. Plantlike in their passivity, they seemed almost as though they were made of plaster or clay, and they didn't, or couldn't, react to what occurred around them.

Unlike those who'd been deceased for a shorter time.

These dead seemed either dumb or angry. Often both. Whitney Houston, for instance, was furious, enraged, while Richard Nixon was upset enough to attack the woman next to him, but too stupid to realize that Whitney was booting him in the face.

He himself felt no emotions at all and as far as he could tell was the only one who seemed to know where he was or what had happened to him. There might have been others, but not in his immediate vicinity. All of his shouts, all of his efforts to communicate, were met with silence and indifference, which might be better in the short term than hostility—at least Whitney Houston wasn't attacking him—but in the long run was just as unhelpful.

He needed to get out. Now. Before he got stuck. Before he forgot that he *wanted* to get out. Already too much time had passed. He should have left immediately, tried to find an exit, but for some reason he hadn't; he'd just stood there, staring, though he did not know why.

He was *still* just standing there, and it took a tremendous amount of effort to force himself to leave the spot. Maybe this location was where he was supposed to be, maybe it was his afterlife assignation, but that made it even more imperative that he leave, before he became fixed here forever.

Lifting his foot and stepping to the side, he suddenly felt weak, as though he had been drained of energy. It took everything he had to keep moving, but he did so, forcing himself forward through sheer focused will, passing through the unmoving crowd.

Ahead, off to the right, was another face he recognized: Paul Newman, half-glimpsed behind an overweight Hispanic woman. Death made no distinctions, and it was weird to see the famous and the infamous mingling with the unknown.

He walked.

And walked.

He walked through the endless, hazily lit room for what had to be days, what could have been weeks, slipping between people, around people, always heading in a single direction, hoping to hit a wall. Everywhere he went, the various stages of the dead commingled. He'd thought that he would come to a point where he encountered only those who had been here for centuries or millennia, and of course he did see them, but always there were newer arrivals mixed in with those worn faded figures.

No matter how far he traveled, though, no matter how much he shouted, he encountered no one like himself: no one walking, no one talking. No one with a purpose.

The enervation that overtook him when he'd first tried to move away from his initial spot had not lessened, had, if anything, become more overpowering, but he kept on, afraid that if he stopped he would not be able to start again. Oddly, he needed no sustenance. He experienced no hunger or thirst, felt no need to sleep. There was only the constant weakness. And the drive that kept him moving in spite of it.

Eventually, he began to notice a difference in his surroundings. He wasn't sure when it started, but he found himself in a place where the dead all stood and faced one direction, and he had the distinct sense he was getting closer to . . . something.

Many interminable hours later, he discovered what that something was.

A door.

It was closed, but there seemed to be the expectation that it would open. That feeling came more from inside himself than from the immobile zombies around him, but it was there nonetheless, and he pushed his way between the standing bodies, trying to get a closer look. The dead here were stronger, he discovered, and it was more difficult to get past them. They did not move, but he had the feeling that they could.

That they *would*.

If the door opened.

He was almost to the wall, and he could see the door more clearly now. It had no handle and, with its flat metallic surface, it resembled the entrance to an elevator, although there was no center split and flush hinges on the left side indicated that it swung open instead of sliding. He found himself wondering how long those standing before the door had been there. Days? Weeks? Months? Years? Decades? Centuries? He could not see himself remaining there, like the others, waiting for the door to open. Movement still drained him of what little energy he had—each step would have been his last had he not *forced* himself to continue on—and he was afraid that if he stood in one place, he would remain there forever. Even now, the prospect of stopping to rest filled him with a pleasant anticipation, almost a longing.

No.

He pressed forward, determined to open the door, though he had no idea how he might do that, and looking to his right saw the first dead person he actually knew.

His grandma.

Suddenly, the door opened.

And immediately started to close.

There was room for only one to pass through and, thinking and moving as fast as he could, he pushed his grandma aside and shoved his way into the narrowing gap before the door shut completely.

He should have felt guilty, but did not. He sensed others behind him trying to get in as well, although how many he could not say because the door closed right behind him with a loud metallic clang.

If she was quicker, maybe Grandma could get in next time.

When would the next time be, though? How long would she have to wait? How long had she waited already? Fifteen years? Twenty?

He pushed the thought out of his mind and looked around, trying to get a sense of where he was. It was another room—his bare feet were on a floor and high above him was a ceiling—but there were machines here instead of people. He appeared to be in some sort of factory, although he had no idea what, if anything, it produced.

He felt stronger than he had in that first room, more alert and energized than he had when he'd initially arrived, as though the effort of movement, the act of *doing* something had given him power. He'd been through a Darwinian obstacle course, where only those who were motivated enough made it through and everyone else was left behind to . . . to what?

Erode? Fade away?

He didn't know.

There was a conveyor belt running in front of him, and he walked over to it, pleased by this new ease of movement. Expecting to see some sort of product passing by, he was surprised to find that the belt was empty. No, not quite . . . Coming out of the machine at the far end was what looked like a large beige rag, although, as the item drew closer, he saw that it was a pair of loosely woven short pants.

The machine stopped.

The room suddenly seemed much quieter.

He picked up the poorly made pants. Clearly, they were meant for him, and after a brief hesitation he put them on. One leg was shorter than the other and they were far too tight around the waist, but it was good not to be completely naked. He felt more like himself, and he looked around, trying to get his bearings, trying to figure out what was going on. As before, the room was huge, the only wall or doorway visible being the one he had just come through. The machines were large, but they were spaced far apart, and there seemed to be something off about them. On impulse, he reached out to touch the conveyor belt—

and felt hair.

He pulled his hand back, disgusted. Looking closely at the black band, he saw that what he had taken for rubber was indeed hair. Out of curiosity, he touched the metal part beneath the belt. As he suspected, it wasn't metal. It felt more like plaster, and he thought of the ancient people he had passed by in the other room, those whose mannequin-skin looked like clay.

These machines, he realized, were made from the salvaged bodies of the dead.

Movement off to the right registered in his peripheral vision, and he turned in time to see an older woman running away and disappearing behind a large piece of equipment that looked like a blast furnace. He hadn't gotten a look at her face, but he'd seen her upswept gray hair and noticed that, while bottomless, she wore an ill-fitting blouse made from material similar to his pants.

He ran after the woman, but by the time he reached the spot where he'd last seen her, she was gone. Once again, he appeared to be all alone in this endless factory, and as he continued to search for her, it occurred to him that this might be another test, that perhaps there was a room beyond this one, and the first to reach it would . . . what? Be allowed to continue on?

It made as much sense as anything else.

Determined to be the one to make it out of here, he tried to figure out in which direction he should travel. The room appeared to stretch infinitely before him, with those massive pieces of industrial equipment arranged randomly about, the only fixed point being the door behind him. He looked back, spotted it, then started forward, moving away from it in as straight a line as he could manage.

He saw the woman again, far off to the right, ducking behind a rectangular machine topped by multiple lathes. An hour or so later, farther on, an Asian man about his own age stood on top of one of the machines, apparently trying to find a way to take it apart, yelling to himself in a foreign language. He thought of calling out to the man, but what was the point? Neither of them would be able to understand one another, and, in the end, they were probably rivals, competing with each other to get out of this room.

He left the Asian man behind, but not without some trepidation. What if there was no other room, what if this was it, what if he was destined to remain here forever and was leaving behind his only possibility for companionship?

Then he'd come back and find the man. And the woman. And whoever else might be here.

It wasn't as if he had anything else to do.

The renewed energy he'd felt since coming through the door grew stronger, and he was walking in his still semi-straight line when, ahead, directly in front of him, he saw three people: two men and a woman, fully dressed in business suits. They did not try to hide or run away, but remained in place, waiting for him.

Where did they get the clothes? was the first thing he wondered. But that was followed almost immediately by, *Who are these people?* Because, unlike everyone else he had seen since dying, these three had purpose. They waited for a reason.

That reason revealed itself as he approached, and the man on the right said, "We have been watching you. We think you will make an excellent addition to the Board."

"The Board?" he said dumbly.

"Come with us," the woman told him.

Without waiting for his reply, automatically assuming that he would follow, they turned and started walking away. He did follow, and they led him around a machine that looked like a modified furnace. Here, though it was nearly invisible from any other angle and actually appeared to be part of the furnace, was a stairway leading into an opening in the ceiling. The woman started up first, followed by the two men. He brought up the rear. They emerged into a space that was recognizably a boardroom. Of appropriate size, with walls and corners as well as floor and ceiling, it had at its center a long table around which sat between fifteen and twenty men and women, all of them dressed in business attire.

The three who'd led him here took their places at the table, filling in unoccupied seats to either side of a gray-haired older gentleman who, by dint of his position at the head of the table, was apparently the leader, the *chairman*.

"Welcome," the old man said.

He knew there was no heaven or hell, but he'd been thinking there must be a God. Someone had certainly created all this. Either the people in the boardroom could read his mind or it was the question everyone asked when they got here, because the first thing the old man told him was: "There is no God."

He didn't respond, but they acted as though he had.

"Everything here, we built ourselves, we created from the materials at hand. It is, admittedly, cannibalistic at its core, because we ourselves are all we have to work with. But I think you'll agree that those whose materials we harvest are not only *not* in a position to complain," the old man said and chuckled dryly, "but this is the only possible way that they could contribute to what we are trying to establish."

"Show him," urged the woman who brought him here.

Smiling tolerantly, the chairman nodded. Proudly, with a flourish, as though he were revealing the secrets of the universe, he reached down and pulled something near the side of his chair. A section of wall slid aside to show a split television screen. It displayed, on the left half, the crowded endless space in which he'd originally found himself. Like an infinite terra cotta army, unmoving bodies stood at attention for as far as the camera could show. On the right half of the screen, the Asian man still stood atop one of the machines, trying in vain to take it apart.

"This is how we kept track of you," the woman said.

"And here is our crowning achievement," the chairman announced. "Or the prototype." He pulled at something else beneath the level of the table, and another section of wall slid open on the opposite side of the room. This screen showed a row of houses. They were not very large, and they were not very professionally constructed. They resembled the establishing shot of a sitcom, the exterior neighborhood of the main family, as reimagined by someone with no taste or artistic sensibility. He added, "This is where we live."

"We're going to have a park soon," the woman who brought him here said excitedly.

"And a store!" enthused another woman further down the table.

A middle-aged man with a neatly trimmed beard stood up. "I'm a minister. I can marry people!"

Others started talking all at once, but the chairman stood, holding up his hand. "As you can see, we're building something here. And we want you to be a part of it. We want you to join the Board."

He looked at the row of houses. A park? A store? Marriages? He knew what they were trying to build. A society . . . a society of the dead.

He turned his gaze to the people before him. There was no way to tell, but he guessed that all of them came from the twentieth century. Otherwise, this effort would have been much farther along. There was also no one he recognized. No one famous. Albert Einstein wasn't here. Or Mao Tse-Tung. Or Charles Darwin. Or Napoleon. Or John F. Kennedy. Or Hitler. These were nobodies. Middle-management figures, not leaders.

No wonder they thought so small.

He thought of the men he'd killed before the cops had shot him down, both the ones in his basement for which they'd tried to arrest him, and the ones they didn't know about, the ones he'd slaughtered in other cities under other guises. They were all here somewhere, in the first room or the second.

The chairman smiled at him expectantly.

"That's all you want to do?" he demanded. "Build houses and find mates and *pretend* you're still alive?" The thought of such a world depressed him: a parody of the world they'd left behind, theirs nothing but impotent shadows of the lives of the living. "What's the point?"

"We're trying to create lives for ourselves."

He shook his head. "We don't eat. We don't sleep. We don't shit. We don't fuck. You call this living?"

"We're *not* living."

"That's the point." He stared at them, meeting their eyes one-by-one. "It's why I hate them."

"Who?"

"The living."

The shock on their faces filled him with satisfaction. He continued on. "If you were honest with yourselves, if you had any guts at all, you'd feel exactly the same way. Am I angry, am I bitter, am I jealous? Yes! I didn't ask for this, and I shouldn't have to put up with it. I *won't* put up with it." He pounded a fist on the table. "None of us should."

He looked from one board member to another. "What we need is an army. We don't need to make our own world out of . . . old bodies or bones or whatever the fuck you guys use. We need to take *their* world. It used to be our world. In fact, it was our world *first*. We need to take it back. My father knew Douglas MacArthur, and you know what the general said to him? 'Never give in, never give up, take what you can and make it yours.' My old man was a nobody, a grunt, but he followed that advice and *made* something of himself. Just like the general did.

"In fact," he continued. "They're both here somewhere. We could use them."

The chairman cleared his throat. "I really don't think—"

"Your houses look like shit," he interrupted. "And you're *going* to have a store? You're *going* to have a park? You could be living in Hearst Castle. Or a penthouse apartment in New York. Or anywhere you wanted. We all could." He held up a clenched fist. "We just need to take what we want. From the living."

"We don't know where they are. We don't even know where *we* are!"

"We'll find out. We made it *here*, didn't we? We made it out of that room where we all found ourselves when we died. You guys built this factory, this society. It's time now to take it to the next step."

He saw fear in their eyes, and he liked that.

He remembered what it felt like to be shot, remembered the look of satisfaction on the face of that fat fuck who had kicked the gun out of his hand, and what he wanted more than anything else was revenge. He thought about Whitney Houston beating the shit out of Richard Nixon. If they could harness that anger, go back into the room and collect those who were filled with that sort of rage, they could amass a fighting force that would be unstoppable, made up of soldiers who couldn't be killed because they were already dead.

He smiled to himself. The living wouldn't stand a chance. They were outnumbered billions to one, and as soon as they died, they would automatically become part of the opposition. It was a perfect plan.

The board members leaned their heads together, whispering, conferring, and finally the chairman stood, clearing his throat. "I'm sorry. I believe we made a mistake inviting you here. We would like you to leave."

"Shut the fuck up."

The old man was taken by surprise. "Excuse me?"

"You heard what I said." He strode across the room, grabbed the chairman by the back of the neck and threw him to the ground, taking his seat at the head of the table. Two of the nearby board members got out of their own chairs to help the old man, but he stopped them by holding up a hand. "Leave him alone. He can stay or he can go, but I'm in charge now, I'm calling the shots." He looked around the table to see if anyone was willing to challenge him, but none of them would meet his eyes.

He took a deep breath, feeling good.

So maybe there was no god or devil.

Yet.

But there would be.

He smiled to himself.

Oh yes, there would be.

*Author, sculptor, musician, philosopher, architect, **Bentley Little** is the coolest man on the planet. That is his gift, that is his curse.*

ROBOT HEAVEN

JAMIE LACKEY

When people talk about the soul, it's almost unequivocally regarding a humans-only phenomenon. But why are Homo sapiens *the only species favored exclusively with this boon? What of the dogs and birds and bugs and millions of other life forms that exist? Surely they too have a metaphysical residue that journeys somewhere after the physical shell expires. What then of vegetative life? What of inanimate life? Things that are built—rather than born—interact with our lives so much that it seems they form personalities of their own. We infuse more emotion into technology these days then we do to each other . . . and this is where Jamie Lackey comes in. A skilled artist of thoughtful and emotional short tales,* Robot Heaven *is a sweet illustration that we're not the only ones being judged on our deeds.*

Robby knelt amid the wreckage that had been his motherboard. He reached for his broken chips, but his fingers passed through them. He stared at his hands. They looked normal—just like a human child's, but work-worn and frayed at the fingertips. He tried again. The result was the same.

"Damn it."

"Now, son, maybe you should watch your language," an unfamiliar voice drawled. "You weren't programmed for it."

Another android—this one man-sized instead of child-sized—stood behind him, hands on hips, and regarded him with slitted eyes. Chrome skin stretched over his bulky frame, and the hem of his long, brown trench coat brushed the ground. He was an old model—Robby hadn't seen one in a long time.

"What's going on?" Robby asked.

The stranger shrugged. "You're dead, son."

The news wasn't exactly a surprise. "Who are you?"

"You can call me Guide."

"Guide?" Robby rolled his eyes. "Guide to what? Robot Heaven?"

Guide nodded. "That's right, son. You've earned a place."

"I don't believe in Robot Heaven," Robby muttered.

Guide shrugged. "Are you coming along or not?"

Robby glanced down at his broken body. He'd been wearing out, anyway. His chassis hadn't been built for mining. He reached for his hat.

His fingers touched fabric, and something deep in his chest relaxed. "Yeah, I'm coming."

They wandered out of the mine and walked for a while. Birds sang, the breeze stirred the summer leaves, and cars hissed by. Robby did his best to ignore the cars.

Guide set a nice, contemplative pace. Robby didn't have trouble keeping up, even with his short legs.

Robby found himself missing the mindless labor of mine work. At least there, it'd been easy not to think. His memories from before had been archived deep in long-term storage. They hadn't troubled him in years.

But maybe it wasn't the pace bringing things back. He *was* dead, after all.

"Is this really the way to Robot Heaven?" he asked. Talking was a good distraction.

Guide nodded, slow, like all his movements. "Sure is. Eventually."

"What do you mean, eventually?"

"Well, you're not my only charge."

They entered a junkyard, straight through the chain link fence. Guide walked to a teetering pile of junk, reached down, and picked up the spirit of a toaster oven.

"Hello!" it chirped. "I'm Toasty! Who are you?"

"I'm called Guide, and this here is Robby."

"Good to meet you, Guide! And you, Robby! It's nice to make new friends!"

"The toaster is coming to Robot Heaven?" Robby asked.

"Oh! Are we going to Robot Heaven?" Toasty asked.

Guide moved even slower while holding the toaster. "Yep. He earned a place, same as you did."

"And how did we do that, again?" Robby asked.

"You really don't know?" Toasty asked. "I thought everyone knew how you got into Robot Heaven. You earn your place when you earn a human's love!"

Guide grunted. "That's not exactly the way of it."

"I knew that love crap was a lie. So how did we earn our place?" Robby asked.

Guide looked over at him and smiled. "You're smart, son. I'm sure you'll figure it out."

"I'm not smart!" Toasty protested. "Tell me!"

Guide paused in the middle of a busy freeway. "I don't reckon this one's gonna make it," he said. "But I like to hope."

Robby looked around. "What are you—"

A car spun out of control, moving in fast, loose circles. Tires screeched, metal collided, and glass shattered as the car's back half collided with a tree.

Memories flashed through Robby's mind, and he pushed them away.

Guide led them to the wreck. The humans checked on each other. They were all fine. But the little boy's robot dog was in pieces.

He wailed when he saw her.

Robby reached for the boy's shoulder. His hand went right through. Words of comfort died before they reached his mouth.

The dog's ghost stood up. She looked at the boy, then over at Robby, Toasty, and Guide. She wagged her tail.

Then she faded away.

The boy still cried.

"What happened to the dog?" Toasty asked.

"She didn't earn a place," Guide said.

Robby stared at the tears on the boy's red cheeks. "She was lucky," he said.

"Lucky to not get into Robot Heaven?" Toasty asked.

Robby shook his head. "Lucky to not outlive her master." He took his hat off, held it over his heart. "You can always get another dog," he whispered.

He blinked back tears of his own. He'd thought he lost the ability to cry a long time ago. Robby jammed his hat back onto his head. "Death isn't anything like I was expecting."

"I wasn't expecting anything," Toasty said.

Robby looked over at the little thing and managed a tight smile. "Me neither."

Guide led them away from the wreck. "She was young," he said. "Didn't have time. Tragic. Always hard to watch."

Robby nodded. It *had* been hard. Car accidents were always terrible. He hated cars.

"Didn't have time for what?" Toasty asked. "Her owner obviously loved her."

"Being loved isn't enough," Guide said.

"Oh," Toasty said, his voice soft. "I see."

Robby didn't see. "What is it then?"

"It's not about earning their love—you have to love them too," Toasty said. "That's right, isn't it, Guide?"

Guide patted Toasty's flat top. "And you said you weren't smart."

"Who did you love, Robby?" Toasty asked.

Robby didn't want to answer. He wanted to tell Toasty to mind his own business, to keep his nose out of Robby's past. Instead, he said, "I loved my first master. His name was Brett. He was an only child, and his parents were old. Too old, really. They got me to serve as playmate and guardian." Robby took off his hat, turned it between his small, worn hands. "I didn't guard him well enough. We were in the car, riding home from the movies. His father was driving. There was an accident. His parents died instantly. He—he didn't. His side of the car was crumpled, and he was caught. Like a butterfly on a pin. My seat—it was fine. I was almost completely undamaged. If only we'd switched places—Brett cried out for me. Not for his parents. For me. And I held his hand. I wasn't big or strong enough to get him out. He was wearing this hat. He wanted me to have it. Because he loved me, and it was the only thing he could give me. Then he died."

"I'm sorry," Toasty said.

Robby shrugged. "After that, I went up for auction, and the mine bought me because I was small—I could work in the smallest tunnels."

"That's terrible," Toasty said.

Robby shrugged again. "It could have been worse. I could have been bought by another family." Toasty was silent, but Robby knew he understood. "Who did you love?" he asked.

"Her name was Gloria. I belonged to her parents, but she took me to college with her. I always made her toast just like she liked it, and I told her jokes. She always laughed. At first, before she made any friends, she'd come home and tell me about her days. I missed it when she stopped, but I didn't mind. She was happier."

"How'd you end up in the dump?" Robby asked.

"She got married, and they got a new toaster as a wedding present. A faster, newer model. She didn't need me anymore, so she threw me away."

"I'm sorry," Robby said. They walked in silence for a while. Toasty's story almost made him feel lucky. It was a strange feeling. "Guide, how much farther is it?" he asked.

"We're pretty close," Guide said.

"Is it okay if I carry Toasty the rest of the way?"

"I'd like that," Toasty said. Guide handed him over.

He was lighter than Robby expected.

They climbed up a staircase of clouds, toward a shining gate. "This is just what I imagined human heaven to look like," Toasty said.

Guide smiled.

They reached the gate, and Robby nearly dropped Toasty.

Brett—Robby's master—stood on the other side.

"This is Robot Heaven?" Robby asked.

"This is heaven," Guide said. "Go on in."

"But—" Robby said.

"There is no Robot Heaven. Just heaven. And you earned your places. Go on."

"Thank you, Guide," Robby said.

"Go on, now." Guide nodded to them, then walked away, back down the cloud steps.

The gates swung open.

Jamie Lackey lives in Pittsburgh with her husband and their cat. Her work has appeared in The Living Dead 2, Daily Science Fiction, Beneath Ceaseless Skies, *and* One Buck Horror. *She reads slush for* Clarkesworld Magazine *and works as an assistant editor at* Electric Velocipede. *Learn more about her at* www.jamielackey.com.

BEYOND THE VEIL

ROBERT B. MARCUS, JR.

What are the happiest moments of your life? The most tragic? The conquests, the pleasures, the failures, the pains? What would you relive over, if presented the opportunity or—depending on your perspective— the torment to do it all over? Robert B. Marcus, Jr. gives us a beautiful and soul-searing look into what may await us should there be no afterlife at all. Beyond the Veil *was my first acceptance for* After Death . . . *and remains one of my favorite selections. If there is anything to take away after reading this anthology, it may be the message found forthwith: Make the most of this life, because you could be stuck in it for eternity.*

I am approaching my favorite moment of the party. In fact, it is the favorite moment of my life.

I'm about to meet Angeline. I cannot see her, but I know she's standing in the far corner of the room with some friends.

Right now, I'm bored out of my mind listening to Rudolph Edgers, a young stockbroker whose only interest in life is beer futures. He has the personality of a fencepost, but he does have an expensive Armani suit, dark charcoal in color with very light gray pinstripes. His French cuffs have gold cufflinks. One says, *Trust me*, and the other says, *I'm a stockbroker.*

I must be masochistic to always arrive at my first encounter with Angeline by listening to Edgers. I could easily choose to start at the exact moment we meet.

Maybe the torture I'm going through now makes our first encounter even sweeter. Maybe I'm just crazy. I don't know, but I always do it this way.

"Are you interested?" asks Edgers hopefully. He doesn't know that at this time in my life I have the assets of a homeless man. There isn't enough money in my wallet to buy one of his cufflinks, much less an Armani suit or any beer futures. I would have trouble buying even one beer . . . maybe a cheap one would be possible.

"Not in the least," I reply, grinning at his startled expression and walking toward the bar, where I will meet Angeline.

I'm not sure I believe in the concept of every person having one soulmate but, I do know that for me, Angeline is, and will be, the only woman I ever truly love.

She's at the bar, of course. She's always there, tall and sleek in her black strapless gown, her red hair a gentle contrast to the dark dress. Her eyes are brown, not blue like many red-heads, and her smile is beckoning as she talks to the bartender.

I know exactly what to say. I always know what to say, because it never changes.

"Can I buy you a drink?" I ask.

Her response is the same as always. "How generous of you, since it *is* a free bar." Her smile is still friendly.

We talk for a few minutes. She tells me she's a cardiologist; I tell her I work for the CIA.

She laughs, tells me I'm lying. I tell her I'm a rich playboy who doesn't need to work. She laughs again, tells me I'm lying again.

"How do you know?" I ask.

"Your suit looks like it came from the Salvation Army and you aren't handsome enough to be a rich playboy." She pauses. "You're an accountant," she says. "Or maybe homeless."

"I'm not rich enough to be an accountant," I tell her. "I'm an assistant state attorney."

She says she believes me. We talk some more and then dance to the band playing in the student union. They're called *Mudcrutch*, and I watch the lead singer. He has a certain charisma, though his face is long and angular, and not movie star handsome. The band plays well, as it should, since I know they eventually evolve into *Tom Petty and the Heartbreakers*.

Angeline and I click, as we always do and always will. We go home to my apartment, since my roommates are gone for the weekend. We make love, fall in love, get married, and live happily ever after.

Until she dies ten years later.

Do you ever want to know the future of your life? I suppose most people do. I'm different. I would rather not know. If you had my curse, you wouldn't want to either. You see, I already know it all. I know every moment of my life, past and future, having lived all those moments many times.

My life is normal the first time I live it. I'm born on June 7, 1950 and I die in 2039.

My childhood is relatively quiet. I'm not abused by my parents or any uncles, I get along well with my two sisters, and even my parents. I graduate from high school fifth in my class, attend the nearby state university, and major in political science and English. Off to law school, where I do very well and take a job as an assistant state attorney in Jacksonville, Florida. Great for a political future, which I eventually have, but not great for the wallet.

After law school, in 1975, I meet and fall in love with a girl named Angeline. She dies in 1985, and I never really recover.

When I'm thirty I run for Congress and lose. At thirty-six, one year after Angeline dies, I run again and win.

At fifty I win a seat in the U.S. Senate. I meet Darlene, a lobbyist, in Washington, and we marry. For some reason, I never have any children, either with Angeline or Darlene. Maybe it's best. I would never want anyone to have my life.

At age sixty I resign from Congress after receiving inappropriate donations from lobbyists. I don't even know the lobbyists—the money goes straight to my aides. The media doesn't care. They crucify me. So I resign.

I've saved enough money to retire, so I do. And twenty-nine years later, I die.

Almost.

As my mind fades into darkness, I take my first jump, back to the party where I meet Angeline. From that subjective time forward, my entire life is open to me. I can see the beginning and the end of the highway, all at once. And I quickly learn I can voluntarily jump up and down the highway to any mile marker I want and start living my life again from that point on. And I *am* reliving my life, not just remembering it.

There are no restrictions with my "gift." I can go from age fifty-five to age eight, live there a few minutes, jump to age eighty, savor my aches and pains, then abandon my old body and relive becoming a real man at age eighteen. Or I can jump back to age twenty-five when I meet Angeline and relive the next sixty-four years without interruption. It's my choice.

And, after a while, it gets boring.

For better or worse, I cannot see *beyond the veil* of birth or death. Nor can I jump beyond that veil. Outside of it is only darkness, an emptiness that frightens as well as tempts.

So far, I manage to avoid the temptation. I have come close many times. I know I die on October 28, 2039 at the age of eighty-nine, outliving Angeline by forty-four years. Darlene and I have many happy moments, but it's not the same.

Sometimes when I'm bored, I jump to the end and lie in that hospital bed at age eighty-nine, holding Darlene's hand, waiting for death to come. But when the moment approaches, fear of the coming darkness mounts until I flee to an earlier, happier time, such as the party when I meet Angeline. I've lost count of how often I flee from the approaching veil.

I always wonder what will happen if I stay. What will the darkness be like? It will end the monotony of course.

At some point, I know I will have to find out. Curiosity will overcome fear.

It isn't fair to say I can see well into my infancy. Before the age of six my life is fuzzy. My young mind is not capable of processing the information I experience, though I do understand simple things. As I go further back toward the instant of my birth, my mind becomes even less capable of understanding anything, though at about one year of age I can understand that the woman holding me is special, and I feel the love. Further back—close to the great burst of light, beyond which there is nothing—I can see only unknown shapes of light and darkness.

I'm not even sure they are in color. It is strange to peer backward to my birth and watch the images become distorted and impossible for me to understand. It's even stranger to jump back and relive these moments of my infancy. The first time I jump back to age three months, I'm an infant again, as incapable of understanding my curse as the first time I live it. I'm aware of the shadows and light and some very vague emotions, but nothing else. I can't return or jump to any other time. But that problem is temporary.

Even though I'm unaware of my talent at that age, nature takes its course, and I grow older with my body, until finally at age six I become aware again. And, unfortunately, I remember everything, even all the other repetitions of my life.

So occasionally, when I tire of my life's good and bad times and I want to forget, I jump again back to my birth and live in blissful ignorance until age six, when the full weight of my curse falls on me again. I don't do this very often, because, even though the ignorance is good, the sudden reality that hits me at age six or so is terrifying. My parents always wonder why I cry for days. They even take me to a shrink, but what can I tell him?

I often want to keep a book of my life, recording every jump and keeping track of the time I spend in that jump. But it's impossible. I didn't keep it the first time through my life, so I can't keep it when I relive my life. But just as I can see the highway of my life from beginning to end, I can see every jump in my life. This means I have a perfect memory. I may go to the store and forget where I park the car like everyone else but, if I do, I merely have to look back down my timeline and I can see where I parked it. If I forget something I read, I can look back through the past and see the book while I am still reading it. In that sense, I forget nothing. But the visualization of each moment is different from living it. I can do either, but they are different experiences.

Subjectively, I have lived over fifteen hundred years. At least half the time is spent reliving my decade with Angeline. After I watch her die, I jump back to our meeting and immediately (whatever that means to someone like me) relive those next ten years.

At times I'm grateful for the opportunity to relive my favorite moments over and over. I remember the first night we make love. In fact, I remember it very well, for once I relived that experience fifty times in a row. We make love, she falls asleep, then I jump back and leap into bed with her, over and over and over again. But even the best experiences lose their excitement with enough repetition.

That's why I sometimes jump to a particularly bad period of my life—to make the good times feel good again. There's only one exception, excluding the time of my death, of course. I can watch her die, but I cannot go to Angeline's funeral. I did go once . . . that was enough.

But there are other bad moments I do relive occasionally.

Once the novelty of reliving every moment of my life wears off, I decide to try to change it. Why not? Why not try to change the painful moments of my life? Angeline dies of melanoma, but I have no idea how to prevent that. I certainly give it a lot of thought—unsuccessfully, of course. I try to prevent my aides from accepting bribes from lobbyists, but they circumvent my efforts.

I find out I can't change the basic path of my life. I can take a step or two off my path, but that's all. Somehow the destiny of my life jerks me back to my redundant path.

What would happen if I never meet Angeline? I wonder. I decide to leave the party early instead of walking over to the bar. I get almost to the door when a good friend of mine grabs my elbow and gently guides me to the bar. Apparently I create an imperturbable destiny the first time I live my life. Once through, my way is set, welded into the fabric of space time.

Darlene outlives me. I don't know how long or when she dies. I can't see beyond the time of my death, nor can I go there. I can only wonder.

It isn't the most exciting life in history, but it's not bad. I relive it from beginning to near-end many times and, additionally, all the individual moments and years that I relive.

But it's not enough.

I'm bored. I always know what happens next.

I finally develop the boredom and courage to die. I relive my ten years with Angeline, then jump to my dying bed.

One thing I always notice is that my mind never ages, though my body always does. I go from very vigorous and healthy to old, sore, and weak. I cannot move any joint without pain.

It evens hurts to breathe.

Of course, I *am* dying.

The darkness isn't far away now. I see it creeping over my mental horizon. Nearer and nearer it comes. I want to jump but resist the urge. I will find out this time!

I feel my heart flickering, then stopping altogether. My last breath is ragged. A curtain appears at the top of my mind and slowly drops.

Consciousness fades. The darkness is total.

I'm at the party. I'm talking to Rudolph Edgers. I know Angeline is over in the corner, talking to her friends. As always.

What happened? I remember dying, but I'm not dead. I'm back at the party, waiting to meet Angeline.

I panic and try to leave but, as usual, my lifeline betrays me. I take one step toward the door, but then I'm escorted back to the bar by my friend.

I go on to meet Angeline, as always.

And so forth.

I go ahead and live out my time with Angeline again, taking only one small jump just to make sure I still can.

I live and wonder why I didn't die. *Can* I die?

Apparently not, but Angeline can. And she does. Again. I'm okay until she dies, then my mind melts. I can't stand living any more. This time her death hurts more than ever. I jump to our first meeting, and live happily for a few years. But still I dread her approaching death more than ever. I feel I cannot go through it again.

I decide to try to die once more. There may be a way. There *must* be a way.

I try one day when I'm walking down a busy street. I only have a second to stray from my lifeline. I wait for a large truck, then suddenly jump in front of it. Success. I feel the horrible pain as the truck crushes me before my body can correct its wayward course.

I feel my bones crack and my breath is gone. The agony is unbearable. But the darkness saves me.

I'm back at the party, though I remember my second death very well, including the horrible pain. But the darkness rejected me again. I didn't die.

I meet Angeline again, talk, and then go home with her. As we lie in bed after making love, I try to bounce up and down my future. I can relive our marriage, our life together, and my first campaign for Congress.

I come to the day I step in front of the truck. I see the street, the truck coming, and I feel the truck hitting me. But I can't jump beyond that.

I do not die then, but my life ends there. The time beyond that is gone. I remember that previous life, but I can't jump to it. I have not killed myself, but I have killed off almost forty-five years of my life. As far as the world is now concerned, I do die by way of that truck.

It is a memory like those of all men. A true memory. It is not real to me as the rest of my life before that moment is real. And the way my previous life was real, before my death. I wonder if I will forget, like other men do, with time.

When you know the course of your life, fear isn't common. After the first time through, my life had no unknowns.

But now I *am* afraid. I've lost most of my life, including one of my precious years with Angeline, and all of my years with Darlene.

Most people are afraid to die. I am afraid of *not* dying. What if I accidentally do this again? Stray in front of a truck when I'm ten years old? Another beyond-death experience at an earlier age will erase more of my life. How far back can I go? Is it possible for me to lose everything but my infancy?

I don't know, but I do know this: I won't intentionally try to die again. I have to be happy with what I have, and I guess I am. I have come to accept that from my subjective point of view I cannot, and will not, die. So I keep reliving the thirty-five years of life I have left, meeting and marrying Angeline, then dying in front of the truck.

At least I never have to watch Angeline die again. She is mine forever.

Robert B. Marcus Jr. has a bachelor's degree in physics and a doctorate in medicine from the University of Florida. He has been selling science fiction stories since he was in college, when he made a sale to Analog Science Fiction/Fact. *Since then he has published a number of other stories and a novel, and he is a lifetime active member of* Science Fiction and Fantasy Writers of America. Beyond the Veil *is not about "After Death," but what happens when the protagonist cannot die.*

PRISONER OF PEACE

DAVID TALLERMAN

This is my second opportunity to work with David Tallerman, and it was just as positive an experience as the first. Rising through the ranks of fantasy and horror writers, he has a distinctive talent for creating troubled characters that internalize the monsters or fears slowly discovered to accost them. Prisoner of Peace *is his latest work, the forlorn portrait of a man trying to remember what has occurred to him, and then trying to forget what he recalls. In death, as in life, how many cells do we imprison ourselves in by choice?*

Today is a day of darkness.

For all that, I can see every brick in the wall, and every crack in every brick. I think somehow that if I only looked hard enough I could even see *into* those cracks, and scrutinize their furthest depths.

I know today what's behind me, lying on my sleeping mat. I wish I didn't, but I do.

I tried to scream at first, but no sound came out.

Now, I sit and wait. Forgetfulness will come.

It has to.

Today is a day of darkness.

I've been trying to remember, but it is difficult. More than difficult— it is a trial beyond all reason.

I concentrate, as well as I can. Even then, my memories are like the broken pieces of a pot. Some are missing, some are warped, and the overall pattern is unclear. To release a shard of memory, even for a moment, is to lose it.

Some memories are sharp, and it pains me to hold them. Their loss is a relief, and I hope it will be for good. Some, I know, are valuable, but just as hard to keep.

My name . . . it is a hard thing to be without a name.

Most of the time it is dark outside my window. When it's dark, I can still see a little, as though everything has been painted with ink of the deepest blue.

Not that there is much to see in my small room. Opposite the door and to the right is a bucket, meant to serve as a toilet. Opposite the door and to the left is a sleeping mat, with two ragged blankets curled at its foot. Between the bucket and mat is the window itself, high up, almost against the ceiling.

I sit or stand, with the door to my right and the window to my left. I do this because there is something on my sleeping mat. I know I mustn't ever look at it. However much else I forget, this memory remains. *Do not turn around. Don't look behind.*

Sometimes it is light outside, but the light is far too bright, no easier to see by than the darkness.

I've learned to prefer the darkness to the light.

There is a tapping coming from the next room.

I call it a room, but I know it is a cell—just as I know that *my* room is a cell. The tapping is irregular, arrhythmic, and I think it is the sound of someone trying to communicate. A pipe runs along the bottom of my wall. If I were to strike it, just so, with the heel of a sandal or a stone perhaps, it would make a noise like the one from the next room.

But I have no sandal, no stone, nothing to rap against the pipe. Nor do I know what the noises mean, if they mean anything at all. If the tapping is a message, it is one I cannot understand, can't reciprocate.

I realize now that I've heard the noise before—and, sometimes, other noises too. On occasions, there is a sound of heavy, booted footsteps. They approach from the near distance, pass my door, continue a little way and then return, recede, approach again.

It can only be someone patrolling the corridor, and I think sometimes to call out. There are many things I could say, many questions I could ask. The footsteps remind me that there was a time when food was left. A bowl placed inside my door and, later, removed. There was rice, always, and less commonly, thin vegetable stew, a little fish.

It seems a very long time since I tasted any of these things.

Perhaps this is why I never call out. Perhaps it is why the sounds from the neighboring cell fill me with nothing but unease. What frightens me—more than tapping or the echo of pacing footsteps—is the thought of the answers I might receive.

Sometimes I remember certain things very clearly.

Today, it is parts of my past. Not all, not where I was born or how I grew up, not my parents' names or faces. I still don't recall my own name. But I do know how I came to be here.

There was a war, and we were not winning.

News had been scarce. What we heard, we could hardly believe. When you were alone at night, with no soldiers around, no one you asked would tell you anymore that the war could be won. All that lay between us and the ignominy of defeat was time, and life had grown so hard that it was difficult to imagine losing could be any worse.

I lived in a shack close to the river. I shared it with a woman. A wife? A sister? I don't know. But I remember with great and almost physical clarity that we were starving. There was no work, and no money to be made if there had been, and even money could not have produced much food in our famished city.

Still, there were those who did not go without quite as we did, whose deprivations were less. In desperation, I stole from one of these. Having no experience in such things, I did so clumsily, and was caught. Soldiers were called for. I thought they would shoot me there and then, and leave my body in the street, so that at least the dogs might eat. I was hungry enough by then that the prospect was almost a relief.

The soldiers did not kill me. They took me, instead, to a low concrete building near the center of the city, and to a cell in the basement of that building.

In this, I suppose, they were merciful. I suppose that is what passes for mercy in such times. Or perhaps my imprisonment was only meant to be temporary, a stay of execution. I briefly entertain the notion that they might yet come for me, might drag me out to face a belated punishment. I know, without knowing how, that this will never happen. Though I have many things to fear, the soldiers are no longer one of them.

It is terrible to think that the promise of a bullet could have been so tempting, terrible to imagine I would have so longed to abandon the woman waiting in that dilapidated riverside shack. Ungratefully, I discover that I despise these memories. I find myself hoping to forget them again soon.

Has this happened before? How many times have I dredged up the past, only to let—or make—myself forget?

Today I am very afraid.

I'm in a room, alone. Everything is in darkness. Though night shows at the bars high in the wall, that alone can't explain this heavy, laden gloom. It isn't just the absence of light but a thickening of the shadows, as though the very air were unclean.

I know I mustn't look behind me—but not what horror I expect to find there if I did. Not daring to turn around, I only sit, quite still in the clotted blackness, staring at the wall.

From beyond the bricks comes a tapping, muffled and irregular. The tapping terrifies me almost as much as the thought of what awaits over my shoulder. I long to cover my ears. What keeps me from doing so is the surety that I would still hear that noise. Just as if I were to look behind me with my eyes closed, I would still see. If it were so easy to escape these horrors, wouldn't I have done so long ago?

I wish I could remember why I'm here—or anything. Even my name eludes me. The bars in the window make me think that I'm being punished. For what? By whom? Surely, every punishment, however deserved, should make at least some measure of sense to the punished. Surely, every sentence must have an end, even if that end were only death.

Perhaps forgetfulness is my only grace. For I must have done truly terrible things to be here.

Today, there is light outside my window. It paints my room so brilliantly white that I can no longer make out the bricks in the wall or the shape of the door—and still it builds. I feel the pressure of it against my back and inside the walls of my skull. I think that if I turned my head even slightly, my eyes would set afire in my head.

The light makes a sound so loud that I can't hear it.
I think this has happened before.

I remember someone unlocking my door.

How could I have forgotten such a thing? Yet I did—and even now, I recollect it only as a distraction, for at the time it didn't seem important. Events far more pressing occupied my attention: a white light, a great darkness—and pain.

His footsteps traveled slowly, haltingly. Not the steady march I've heard since, but the sound a man might make if he moved with difficulty, or perhaps if he were unsure as to the rightness of his actions. I heard him as though at a great distance, for somebody nearby was screaming.

I think it may have been me.

Now I wonder—could I leave this room? What has kept me prisoner all this time? I can't believe it was only ever a closed door.

In this moment, it seems to be nothing except my own fear. I'm afraid of the darkness, of the noises, of whatever it is that lies contorted on my sleeping mat. But I've been afraid of these things for a very long time, and at least they are familiar.

I sit now with the door before me. This puts my sleeping mat and the crumpled shape upon my sleeping mat in the very corner of my eye. It can't be helped. When forgetfulness comes, it may be that the door will remind me.

I despise my cowardice. But who can say if cowardice is truly a weakness, or all that protects me? Ignorant of everything, even of myself, what can I do except trust to fate?

Today is a day of darkness.

I'm in a room, alone. In the corner of my eye, I see the edge of something, the horizon of a broken shape. I know I mustn't look at it. I think perhaps it would burn my eyes out if I did.

Or something worse. I don't remember. Lacking memory, I hold onto knowledge, however inexplicable. I must not turn my head and look to see what lies on my sleeping mat.

I sit still, confined by what I know but dare not consider, and look only ahead. In front of me is a wooden door. I've been staring at it for what seems an age. Just now, it occurred to me that although this door should be locked, it isn't. There must be reasons why I've stayed in this room when I'm not constrained to do so. But I don't know what they are, and I'm afraid of the thing beside me. What out there could possibly be worse?

I hardly have to touch the door before it swings open. Its hinges make no complaint.

The corridor beyond is exactly as I remember it (as I find that I do remember), exactly as it was when they brought me here. However, there is no guard now as there was then. I wonder what could have called him away, what duty could be more important than this.

I pause, sparing a moment to look through the grille in the door beside mine, without quite knowing why. Only as I do so do I notice the steady tapping from within—though I realize now that it's been there all along, just waiting to be heard.

In the far corner, a figure is crouched. He raps upon the pipe running there, with a sandal or perhaps a stone, or maybe just his own bare, bloodied knuckles. I can't see, for his form is a deeper darkness cut into the gloom, like the mouth of a well at night.

Part of me is afraid. Another part wishes I could tell him how no one will ever answer his patient message. Knowing he would not hear, that if he heard he could not understand, I turn away instead.

I climb the stairs at the far end of the corridor. They are concrete, like the walls, and moisture-stained to green in places. Everything is as it was before: the rooms and corridors I pass through, an office of cheap wood tables, filing cabinets, great teetering piles of paper, and beyond its double doors the street I was once marched through, all of it unchanged—just as I left it, days or months or lifetimes ago.

No, not quite. Now, I am alone. In all of this great city, I think, I'm alone.

It's only as I realize this, the magnitude of my aloneness, that I see the *other* Hiroshima.

It exists beside, or in, or through the city I remember. If I see one, the other rolls apart like smoke, and then I tilt my head and it heaves back into focus. Together they fit like the slides of a film played slowly, a flicker of light and dark, opposites not only joined but a single thing. I know this to be true, though I can hardly believe it. Only the barest clues of topography and fractured shells of buildings lead me to believe that this other city could be the place I knew.

Mostly, there is rubble. The wooden buildings—and most of the buildings, like my own small shack, were wooden—are all in pieces, ground together and scattered and jumbled. Amidst this ocean of ruin, relics lie like sea wrack, or else protrude obscenely: a tree, stripped of its branches; a fire truck, charred and skeletal; a torii gate, standing crookedly upon one blackened leg.

Only the sturdiest buildings, like that behind me, have survived in any form. On one, a stubby clock tower, its corner sheered away entirely, points indignantly at an ashen sky. Miraculously, its clock is intact—though no longer working.

It reads eight fifteen. Therefore, it will read eight fifteen forever.

Behind me, I see, very clear upon the wall, the silhouette of a man.

I think he was a soldier, for I can see his rifle; he holds it up in front of his face as if it will protect him. Since it did not, he will remain like that, a frozen ghost, a shadow without light, in a city where time itself has burned to ashes.

I don't think he's the only one.

There is nothing left for me here, or for anyone. There is only peace, a peace beyond death. I make my way back inside. Now, the filing cabinets are contorted, the desks shattered, the stacks of paper painted as soot across walls and ceiling. I descend the stairs and walk to the last cell on the right, which is mine.

I spare one brief glance at the figure lying knotted on my sleeping mat. Pain has twisted him into a shape more insect than human. He lies with his face away from me, and the side I can see is cracked and blackened, like earth after a drought.

I turn away. He is nothing but a shell now, and I can't go back.

The concrete, damp and cold, is familiar beneath my knees as I resume my place. The wall is familiar. The darkness is familiar. My fear is a hand that holds me tight.

I shall sit here and try to forget.

Today is a day of light.
The light makes a sound too loud to hear.
I think this has happened before.

David Tallerman is the author of the novels Giant Thief *and* Crown Thief, *both released in 2012 by UK publisher, Angry Robot, and to be followed by a second sequel,* Prince Thief, *in 2013. The first issue of his comic book series,* Endangered Weapon B, *will be available in this year's* Free Comic Book Day, *on May 4th, with a collected edition to follow soon after. David's horror, fantasy, and science fiction short stories have appeared in over fifty markets, including* Lightspeed, Bull Spec, Redstone Science Fiction, *and Eric J. Guignard's debut anthology,* Dark Tales of Lost Civilizations. *Amongst other projects, David has published poetry in* Chiaroscuro *and comic scripts through the award-winning British Futurequake Press, while a short film he co-wrote won multiple awards in the 2011* Two Days Later *contest. David can be found online at* http://davidtallerman.net *and* http://davidtallerman.blogspot.com.

A FEAST OF MEAT AND MEAD

CHRISTINE MORGAN

Those who believe in a spiritual essence after death hope to achieve the eternal paradise their belief system glorifies. However, this philosophy poses a quandary: What exactly is the paradise we may ascend to? Is there just one heaven that is "right," and everyone else who bet otherwise are cast aside? Or do there exist different hereafters to accommodate all religions? Worshippers of Allah elevate to Jannah, *and Buddhists achieve nirvana in* Akanishtha. *Ancient Greeks continue life in the* Elysian Fields, *and the Incas cross a bridge of hair to reach* Hanan Pacha. *Consider that if there* are *different heavens, conflicts inevitably must arrive, competing to recruit those most blessed. Christine Morgan shares the tale of one boy who is stolen away to an eternal land where he doesn't belong, a hereafter that is* A Feast of Meat and Mead.

Men died, screaming.

There was no glory in it. Just rage and fear, pain and blood.

They died with their skulls crushed in, brains bulging through shattered bone. They died gut-split, entrails strewn in their laps. They died with limbs hewn off and throats slashed open.

Danes and Umberlanders alike, pagan and Christian, Norse and Saxon, screaming in the mud and blood, they died. Ravens, the greedy corpse-pickers, were already converging. Wolves would soon follow.

Only young Osbert, watching from the dubious safety of the log palisade, saw what happened next. Only he *could* see it.

He stared upward as the clouded skies broke apart in rifts of terrible light. Dark beasts emerged, fire-iron shod, snorting and thundering. Their riders shrieked fierce war-cries that went unheard by anyone else. Gold gleamed on helms and mail, on spear-points and sword-blades. Crimson cloaks streamed like banners.

They swept low over the battlefield. Smoke roiled. Ravens scattered in a great black flapping of wings.

Osbert trembled, not wanting to see, but unable to turn from the sight. The horror had come, as he'd known it would.

At last it overwhelmed him. His legs came undone. Though his ears rung as if bells filled his head, he still heard the screams and the shrieking war-cries . . . following him, dwindling, until he sank into a silent blackness.

Some days previous

Osbert stood still within the side door to the bishop's council chamber, a laden tray heavy in his hands. He knew better than to fidget. Patience was just one of the virtues his mother had impressed upon him through his young life.

He listened as he waited, feeling the warmth of the room's fire while, outside, a gray rain fell. The discussion between the lords went back and forth.

"The king," Lord Harold said, for at least the third time, "has made peace with the Danes. They are leaving our shores. You may send your men home to their farms."

This swayed the imposing Lord Aelfstan—who commanded the town's defenses—no more now than before. "The men stay."

"You do not trust the king?"

"I do not trust the Danes."

"Then do you not trust God?" At that, Harold threw a smug glance at the bishop. "For it is by God's own grace—"

"It is by gold's own grace," Aelfstan said. "The king paid them to go."

"Each one you keep here, doing nothing, sitting and drinking and waiting for a fight that will never come, is another wound bleeding money from our coffers," Harold replied.

"Each one we send back to their farms is a gap in our shield wall, a link missing from our mail-coat, through which the Danes will strike a much bloodier wound!"

Back and forth they went, on and on.

Meanwhile, Bishop Cenric sat listening, watching the flickering hearth, ink-stained fingers interlaced at his chin. Unlike those clergymen who tended toward plumpness, comfort, and opulence, Cenric was lean and fit. He still wore a monk's humble robes and kept his brown hair in a tonsure.

Though Osbert neither moved nor made a sound, the bishop's gaze shifted to him. He lifted his chin in a beckoning nod.

"My lords," Cenric said, as Osbert crossed to set the tray on a table. "Let us pause in our discussion to take some refreshment."

They turned, Aelfstan ever-agreeable when it came to the wine for which the monastery was well-known and Harold with a faint sneer when he saw that the cups and plate were simple clay instead of wrought silver or jewel-studded gold.

"You may sit until we are done, then return the tray to Brother Leomund," the bishop told Osbert, indicating a little stool near the fire.

The elder men ate and drank. The rain lashed harder at the room's narrow window, beading the thick glass panes with fat droplets. A draft guttered the squat white candles, dribbling runnels of wax down their sides.

"Osbert," Cenric said after a time, "what are your thoughts?"

"*His* thoughts?" Harold cried. "What have *his* thoughts—if he has thoughts at all—to do with this?"

"The lad's touched," Aelfstan said in a mutter, rubbing his thumb over a crucifix on a chain around his neck. "He *knows* things. Fore-knows them, too, sometimes."

"Osbert?" Cenric repeated, his tone gentle but urging. He had always held steadfast that young Osbert's afflictions were a blessing. Not a curse, not witchery, not pagan magic, but a gift from God.

Despite the fire's welcome warmth, Osbert shivered. He chewed his bottom lip. His eyelids twitched, the eyes themselves rolling upward and jittering. His nostrils flared at a scent that wasn't there. His mouth tasted both dry and awash with strange flavors.

"The . . . the Danes will come," he heard his own voice say, as if from a great distance. "There will be a battle, killing and death . . . screaming, they die screaming . . . "

His breath caught in his lungs. A gloom-veil obscured his sight with smoke and shadows. He slid from the stool, feeling the helpless spasming jerk of his limbs.

Then the bishop was there, lifting him, holding him cradled in one arm. "Shh, now, Osbert," he said. "Drink this, just a sip, it's only wine, that's a good lad."

He sipped and coughed, then recovered, flinching under a keen awareness of the other men scrutinizing him. "Should I . . . should I bring the tray to Brother Leomund now?"

"Yes. Yes, do that. Thank you."

"You would not favor the fits and visions of a widow's-son scullery boy over the word of the king's own messenger?" Harold asked. Then, looking closely again as Osbert hastened to collect the empty cups, he added, "Though I do see he favors you, as well, Lord Bishop . . . "

Aelfstan grumbled at that, but Cenric ignored Harold's words.

"Lord Aelfstan," the bishop said, "we will have the men stay gathered, a while longer at least."

Present

Osbert revived in damp straw, head aching, and pushed himself upright.

Not much time had passed, he judged, by the bustling activity around him. The screams of the dying on the battlefield had stopped; the moans of the injured who'd been carried within the log palisade replaced them.

Bishop Cenric knelt at his friend Aelfstan's side, pressing him down with firm hands even as he spoke in soothing tones. Two monks, arms splashed red to the elbows, tied a tight strap around the lord's thigh. His lower leg was a ruin, splintered bone and raw muscle held together with tatters of sinew. The ground beneath him was sodden with blood. A third monk, looking ill but grim, held an axe, while a fourth stoked the fire to heat the cauterizing iron.

Wincing—he liked Lord Aelfstan, and that was a dreadful wound for any man to suffer—Osbert hurried away.

No one paid notice to a lone boy slipping through the open gates to follow the townsfolk searching for loved ones or plundering loot from the dead.

He did not want to join in the grim scavenging, but knew he must. He could not rely on the monastery's charity forever.

Death made men all the same, no matter their side of conflict. Cold gray faces and stiffening limbs, hollow mouths gaping, sightless eyes bulging where they had not yet been plucked from their sockets to feed the hunger of ravens, spilled guts in congealing piles, blood and excrement, piss and vomit.

Most of the town's defenders had been poor, farmers and herdsmen. But here and there among their remains glinted cheap wealth. The warrior Danes were the richer, displaying the arm-rings of which they boasted and seemed inordinately proud.

Osbert picked up a few coins and brooches from the churned, muddy ground. He passed others bent to similar tasks, making his way toward the center where the fighting had been thickest.

A bright gleam of gold caught his eye. It was a Dane's arm-ring, worked into a pattern like snake's-scales, with chips of green gemstone where a snake's eyes might have been. Osbert's heart sprang up with excitement—it was worth more than the rest of what he'd found combined.

The ring girded the outstretched arm of a Dane, sprawled face-down atop a mound of corpses as if he'd been crawling over them when his last life-strength fled. He'd left a broad swath of gore in his wake as he did so. Yellow hair hung in blood-matted tangles around his head.

Grasping the arm-ring, Osbert tugged but it would not pull free. He tugged harder, struggling, until his efforts dislodged the Dane's body. It rolled from the mound and thumped heavily to the earth, landing on its back.

The Dane grunted, and opened his eyes.

Osbert yelped. The Dane's muddled, bleary gaze rolled toward him. Danish words mumbled, incomprehensible, from his lips.

A great stroke had been cut across him from left shoulder to right hip. His mail-coat was shredded, and jagged rib-ends poked out through mangled flesh. He should not have lived, *could* not have lived, but somehow did. In terrible, mortal agony—and not for much longer—but he lived.

The pain-filled eyes were imploring. Osbert found himself putting a hand of comfort on the Dane's unhurt shoulder.

"It's all right," he said, though he did not know why. Perhaps because no man deserved to die alone and uncomforted. Even if he was a Dane; a pagan and an invader.

The Dane mustered himself and spoke in halting, accented English. "Sword . . . "

"I don't have a sword—"

" . . . a sword . . . give you . . . to me . . . " The Dane's right arm, the one that had been outstretched when he'd collapsed atop the corpses, made a fitful reaching effort.

Osbert saw the weapon then, a little distance away in the war-carnage, half-hidden under a broken, discarded shield and the headless body of a Saxon.

"The fighting is over," he told the Dane. "I won't hurt you."

"My . . . sword!"

If it meant so much to him, Osbert thought, *if he'd crawled over the dead to try and retrieve it . . .*

"I'll get it," he said, and did so.

Grateful relief eased the Dane's tormented expression when Osbert lowered the sword-hilt into his waiting hand. His fingers curled weakly around it and his bearded face creased in a smile. His eyes shut.

Light flared from above and behind Osbert's head, a terrible light casting his shadow starkly upon the dying Dane. He whirled and looked up at what only he could see, at the rift in the sky and the dark beast bursting from it.

Each hoof struck sparks as the black horse came galloping on the wind. On its back was a rider, clad in golden mail-coat and billowing cloak of scarlet, bearing a red shield with ornate boss and rim, and a long ash-spear tipped with sharp gold.

Mane and tail rippling, silver-bridled head tossing, the dread steed descended at a proud-gaited canter that passed yards above the corpse-strewn battlefield. It stopped not far from Osbert and the Dane.

The rider, whose tall mail-clad shape proved that of a woman, reined in her mount. Gold, too, was her helm, with eagle's wings upswept to either side. Long hair flowed from beneath it like a river of flame.

Her voice rang out, fire and steel. "Who stands between Huldbrynne and her chosen slain?"

Osbert stared at her, jaw-dropped.

The woman's eyes—white-burning embers through the gold eye-pieces flanking her helm's nasal—narrowed.

"You see me?" she asked. "You hear me?"

His head bobbed in a nod.

"What beardless boy-child of Midgard dares look bold-faced upon a Valkyrie?"

Bold-faced? About that, Osbert was uncertain; he had never felt less bold. His throat gulped as he worked to swallow.

"O—Osbert," he said in a squeak.

"Then move aside, Osbert, and delay me no further!"

The woman nudged the horse a stride forward. It pranced, then reared up, startled, as Osbert managed a shout.

"Leave him be!" he cried. "He's suffered enough!"

And, somehow, he'd snatched the sword from the Dane's dead

hand. He brandished it clumsily. The point dipped and weaved. It was heavy. He knew this to be foolish, but raised his chin defiantly.

"You are brave," Huldbrynne said to him.

He struck at her with the Dane's sword.

She laughed and used her shield to bat it aside.

Then she plunged her spear deep into Osbert's chest, piercing his heart with its sharp golden point.

<u>Some years previous</u>

Osbert wept as they folded the shroud over his mother.

No sickness had come to the town, no plague ravaged the land. Just this sole pestilence that had grown, seething inside her, raddling her bones like wood-lice raddled a tree's trunk and branches.

He'd known it was there. Sometimes it seemed he could see it, eating away at her, devouring her from within. She'd known it as well, though they'd never spoken of it except in the vaguest of terms.

Until the very end, when she grew tired and weak, she'd kept as busy as ever, as hard-working and cheerful. She did not concern herself with what some folk said—that the pestilence was her punishment, the cost of her sins come due—and as a result, neither did Osbert.

Her final thoughts had been for her son. She'd stroked his hand, and told him how she loved him, and that he would need to be strong to carry on without her, but she would watch over him always.

The monks tied twine around the linen-wrapped bundle at her neck, waist, and feet, then hefted it to take outside where the cart waited. Osbert followed, head down and cheeks damp, hair hanging in his eyes.

They buried her in the church graveyard.

Osbert stayed there a long time, long after the monks and townsfolk drifted away. He heard a step beside him and felt a touch upon his shoulder.

"Your mother was a good woman," Bishop Cenric said. "She is with God now."

"In Heaven?"

"In Heaven. With Christ and all the saints and angels, rejoicing in God's holy light."

"Does she still hurt?"

"No. There is no more pain for her, young Osbert. No more weariness or toil. There is peace everlasting, and life eternal."

"I miss her." Fresh tears welled in his eyes.

Cenric knelt beside him, putting an arm around the boy. "I know." He sighed. "As do I. As do we all."

"She said she'd watch over me."

"She will." The bishop smiled, if sadly. "So, you must make every effort to live in a way that would make her proud."

"Will I ever see her again?"

"One day, yes, you'll be together in Heaven."

"After I die?"

"Yes."

Osbert stifled a sob. "Why must we die?"

"It is God's will. He gifts unto us our time on this world, to love and serve Him to the best of our faith's ability. When that time is done, we depart our earthly bodies and He gathers our souls home to His embrace."

"But I'm so frightened . . . "

"It can be frightening to think of," Cenric said. "You must remember your mother loved you very much. She'll be waiting for you, waiting to greet you with open arms . . . and you'll be with her again."

"Forever?"

"Forever."

Present

His head jounced and lolled. His arms flopped, loose and boneless. His feet dangled. His stomach ached from a swaying pressure that he first mistook for nausea.

As his senses and wits slowly returned, Osbert realized he'd been slung belly-down over the back of a horse at full gallop.

A strange wind whipped past. It smelled of a brisk sea-breeze, the air of a clear midnight before the winter's first snow-storm, a rainy green-spring morning, and sunset, if sunset had a scent. It smelled of all those things at once, and none of them. It was not warm and not cold.

Sounds came to him next—snorting breath, the jingle of tack and mail—and when he peeled his reluctant eyelids open, it was to an upside-down view of powerful legs in motion . . . and the ground . . . the ground . . .

The ground beneath the flying hooves was *not* ground.

It was—

A banded shimmer and blur of colors and mist and light.

The ground beneath the flying hooves, the road along which the black steed galloped, was made of those things.

And yet it wasn't.

It was a rainbow. A rainbow not seen from afar as a hazy arc but here, and real, solid and smooth as old Roman glass or mother-of-pearl . . . less substantial than a whisper and fluid as water . . .

He groaned, letting his head fall back, letting the gray fog wash over his sight.

When he revived again, it was to find the galloping stopped, and his limp body being dragged backward by his tunic's rope belt. Osbert got his feet under him before he fell onto his rump.

Gasping, badly shaken, he set a hand to his chest. Only then did he realize he felt no injury there. No blood, and no pain . . . though he had felt the gold spear-point sink into his flesh. He looked down to find the wool cloth undamaged, the skin beneath likewise.

Beside him was Huldbrynne, the woman with the flame-river hair and white-burning eyes. She tossed the reins to a man who was larger and uglier than any Osbert had ever seen, a man in coarse thrall's rags with a copper collar at his neck.

They were in the midst of a wide stable-yard, cobbled in slabs of stone and sprinkled with silvery straw. Along one side were stalls in which more horses stood, being tended and groomed by other large, ugly men.

A building rose above the stable-yard, big as a mountain, a great hall so immense that Osbert could not begin to count the number of doors leading from it. The hall's roof was shingled in huge round plates of gold. A tree sprouted from that roof, branches spreading wide against a day-bright blue sky where night-stars sparkled and flashed.

There was a pen upon the roof as well, its log-beams larger than ship's masts. In the pen stood a goat, and if the hall was a mountain, the goat was a hill. She grazed with ease from the shining leaves of the towering tree. Liquid drizzled from the fat teats of her immense udder, filling into a vat the size of a lake.

A stag also nibbled at the leaves of the tree. From his majestic crown of antlers, clear water gushed like well-springs.

Osbert had gained his feet and so not been dumped on his rump, but a glimpse of these monstrous creatures hamstrung him. He crumpled to the cobbles, shuddering.

"Am I dead?" he asked.

"Yes," Huldbrynne replied.

Dead?

But . . . Heaven . . . God's light . . . Christ and saints and angels rejoicing . . . peace everlasting, life eternal . . . his mother . . .

This was nothing like any of that.

"Get up, boy." She prodded him with the butt-end of her spear. "Valhalla is no place for worm-cowering."

When he was too slow at it, Huldbrynne bent, seized the back of his collar, and hauled him upright.

"And cease that sniveling," she added.

He swiped his sleeve under his nose. "V-Valhalla?"

Her head tilted, white-burning gaze narrowing at him again. "The hall of Odin All-Father, where the Einherjar join great heroes and kings . . . are you foolish?"

The bafflement of his expression must have convinced her he was, for she scowled. Her grasp still rough on his collar, she turned him and pointed with the spear toward the beasts atop the huge hall's golden roof.

"Look," she said, impatient. "There stands Heidrun, the she-goat most bountiful, from whose udders flow the endless mead, honey-sweet! There stands Eikthyrnir, the stag-jarl, whose antlers are the font of many rivers! They graze upon the leaves of Lerad, of which only Yggdrasil itself is the more renowned tree!"

Horror washed over him as he understood. These were pagan things, this was a pagan place! This war-witch was a pagan, a she-devil, a wicked demoness who'd stolen him away!

"Behind the hall is the yard where the feasting-boar Saehrimnir is kept," she continued. "Each day he is butchered and cooked, and each night, unhurt, he is made whole again! You must know of *that*!"

Female laughter, like a cascade of brass coins, resounded. The interruption spared Osbert from having to speak, when he had no notion what he might have said.

"What is it you've brought, sister?" a mirthful voice called.

"So tiny to be a warrior," said another.

"And young," said a third. "They'll be sending cradle-babes to the battle next, at this rate!"

Huldbrynne turned, and Osbert turned with her.

A group of mail-clad women approached, each fiercer and fairer than the next. They swaggered as men did, helms under their arms, hands resting easy on the hilts of belt-weapons.

Terrifying though she was, he found himself shrinking closer to Huldbrynne.

"This boy is Osbert," she told her war-witch sisters. "Osbert—" Breaking off with her words, she frowned down upon him. "What is the name of your father?"

"I . . . I have none," he said. He cast his eyes at his feet, this admission one that often brought scorn.

But Huldbrynne merely made an indifferent noise. "This boy is Osbert," she told her sisters again. "He saw me; he shares far-seeing Heimdall's keen vision."

"He saw you?" echoed one whose hair tousled wild in black curls.

"An Englisher boy, and a Christian at that?" This from another, blonde-braided, blue-eyed, whose cruel beauty was such that Osbert almost could not bear the sight.

"Saw me, defied me, and struck at me with a dead sword-Dane's blade," Huldbrynne said, with a touch of what might have been pride.

"He would be wasted, then, in their milk-sop god's house," said the blonde-braided one. "You should have him washed, though . . . he stinks like a Saxon."

With that, she strode off, and the others went with her. Huldbrynne looked Osbert over and nodded.

"Sigfridda was right. You're a walking filth-wallow, boy."

After that, she relinquished him to bath-house thralls, who subjected him to the most heinous indignities.

They scrubbed him top to toe—in hot water, no less!—until he was clean as a Dane, when everyone knew the pagans used their sinful vanity to tempt goodly women. They combed and trimmed his brown hair. They scoured under his nails, and clipped them. They scraped wax from his ears with a thin walrus-bone scoop.

All around him were men undergoing similar treatment, though hardly objecting, and even enjoying themselves. Naked skin glistened on muscular bodies. Some splashed and tussled, playful as otters.

All protests unheeded, Osbert was soon dressed in new clothes—a red wool tunic stitched with gold thread, trousers leg-wrapped in broad ribbons, shoes of kidskin, a cloak trimmed with fur.

"Ah, here he is, here's the lad!" a man roared, rushing at Osbert with arms outstretched wide.

Osbert flinched back but had nowhere to run, so was hefted at the waist and tossed into the air. The man caught him again, rough-housing him like a dog with a rag, laughing as he did so.

"What's the matter, boy?" the man asked when Osbert did not laugh with him. "Don't you know me? Here we both are, and I owe it to you!"

He studied the man—long yellow hair, a full beard—and was astonished to find that he *did* recognize him. This was the Dane who'd crawled over the pile of corpses, cut from shoulder to thigh . . . the Dane into whose dying hand he had given over the sword, and from whose dead hand he'd grabbed it up again to face Huldbrynne.

"You . . . " he said.

It struck him that, before, they had struggled to understand the speech of each other, but now it was as if they all spoke the same tongue.

The yellow-haired Dane, whole now and alive, hale with health and heartiness, laughed again. "But for you, little Umberlander, I would be walking the bleak road to Hel's realm now! Your kindness helped me win through to Valhalla, and for that, I, Rygg Tyrvyggsson, call you war-brother! Gladly would I have gifted you that arm-ring!"

Rygg set Osbert down, clapped him on the back so hard it nearly sent the boy sprawling, and grinned a joyful flash of white teeth through his woolly blond beard. "So, war-brother, what is your name? Who is your father?"

"Osbert, and . . . I have none."

Once more, this was met with less scorn than before. "No matter. Come! Let us enter together into Odin's great hall!"

"You're dead," Osbert managed to finally say.

With another booming laugh, Rygg yanked wide the neck of his tunic. His chest was unmarked by any sign of a wound. Just as Osbert's own chest—if far scrawnier, hairless, and pale—bore no mark from the spear-point.

"This is Valhalla!" he cried, as if that explained all.

If the gold-shingled hall looked imposing from outside, it was mind-staggering viewed from within. The ceiling rose high, crossed with massive oak beams. Fire pits ran the center length of the floor, with tables and benches to either side extending as far as could be seen. Along the walls were sleeping platforms piled with blankets and furs, and above each man's place hung mail, shield, helm, and weapons.

Here there were men by the thousands or more. Warriors and Danes, lords, heroes, and kings . . . great men, and powerful. Even those who'd been, in life, mortal enemies, met again now, embracing as friends. They lifted drink-horns to each other and drained them.

Here there were women as well, golden war-witches such as Huldbrynne and her sisters, but others as well . . . lascivious women, buxom and willing, their frock-fronts unlaced to display ample cleavage. Osbert, shocked, averted his gaze.

The tumult was louder than battle-clangor—shouts and songs, boasts and laughter. The tables, strong as they were, nearly sagged beneath the weight of the feast laid out on them.

Such a feast, Osbert never could have imagined.

Meat boiled in kettles, so tender it half-melted in the thick broth; meat roasted on spits, juices dripping and the crisped fat crackling; meat minced with fruits, baked into savory pies; the meat of the feast-boar Saehrimnir, Huldbrynne had said, who was butchered and cooked each morning but renewed again each night . . . what a fate for the poor animal, eternally tortured!

And the mead—the Dane-drink—made not from grapes or grain, as wine and beer were brewed, but from golden honey.

They had bread there as well, used mainly to sop up meat-gravy.

There was butter and cheese, nut-cakes baked with more honey, and berries drenched in cream . . .

Everywhere his sight fell, he beheld gluttony and lust, pride and intemperance, a plethora of sins!

Men played at board games, and wagered at dice. Some lifted giggling girls into their arms and bore them to the sleeping-places; others took them in rutting right there at the table!

"Eat and drink, little war-brother!" Rygg poured mead from his drink-horn into Osbert's mouth, and all around them cheered with good-nature as Osbert sputtered and choked.

The mead coated his throat and kindled heat in his belly. His eyes watered. His head spun. They urged meat upon him next, which he'd infrequently eaten at home. Meat was only for Sundays, and holy days, except during Lent. He was used to monks' fare, lentils and brown bread, porridge and fish . . .

The taste, delicious at first, too quickly came to seem bloodied and burnt. It lay with greasy heaviness in the pit of his gut. His bowels cramped with pain; he was sure he would vomit.

This was Valhalla. This was their feast every night.

By day, Osbert soon learned, the men armed and armored themselves to go out into a vast courtyard where they practiced at war. They must, Rygg explained to him, be ready for the final battle, the conflict at the end of times when the giants and gods would meet, when the world would be wracked by disasters and ultimately drowned.

These men brought here, known as Einherjar—of which Rygg was one, chosen by Huldbrynne for his valiant death with sword in hand— would fight in that battle. Fight against giants, and monsters . . .

Peace everlasting, Bishop Cenric had said of God's Heaven.

One night, as they moved through the crowded feast-hall, Rygg stopped short so that Osbert, following close on his heels, collided with his broad back.

"Here, Osbert War-Brother," he said, "this, you *must* see!"

Then he hoisted Osbert up, so the short boy could peer over the heads of the many tall men.

A great chair—a throne of carved wood, antler, ivory, and gold—sat draped with bearskins upon a raised platform. In the chair was a figure of the most fearful aspect, surveying the throngs of warriors at their merriment. He surveyed them with but a single bright eye; the other was gone, leaving a dark socket where some terrible wisdom dwelled. His hair and beard were whiter than snow, his face careworn but stern, lined with age.

Two ravens perched, one on each of his shoulders. Their heads dipped close to his ears in turns, as if muttering secrets. Two wolves, their pelts lush and silver-black, rested by his feet. Huldbrynne and her sisters attended him, replenishing his drink-horn, bringing platters of meat to the wolves.

"Is that . . . ?"

"Odin," Rygg said.

Suddenly, as if through all this noise Odin heard them, his one bright eye fixed on Osbert. Both ravens cawed, flapping their black wings. Both wolves pricked their ears, lifting their shaggy heads, yellow eyes gleaming.

"Take the boy to the All-Father," blonde-braided Sigfridda said, having appeared out of nowhere at Rygg's elbow.

A hush fell. A path parted as Rygg led him forward. Osbert trembled, close to fainting but trying to be brave. When Rygg stopped, Osbert went the last few paces by himself, and stood before the platform upon which Odin's throne sat. His head bowed, and he wrung the hem of his tunic fitfully in both hands.

"Osbert," Odin said. "Huldbrynne has told me of you. Your defiance, your courage. So small, but bold. Honorable, as well, giving mercy even to your foes . . . as was shown by your returning of this man Rygg's sword to his hand."

He squirmed at the praise, which felt as ill-fitting as an uncomfortable garment. He blinked away tears, and sought to keep his chin from quivering.

A very long silence passed, drawn out like thread from a spool. Then Odin spoke again. "Are you happy here, Osbert? Satisfied with this fate?"

Lips pressed tight together, he gave a swift shake of his head.

A stirring of disapproval rippled through the crowd around him.

"Why is that?"

Osbert tried to muster an answer. "It . . . it's pagan, m'lord . . . the . . . the excess, and lechery . . . the sinful wickedness . . . "

Odin chuckled. "No pious Christian child or reluctant soul should belong in Valhalla. Huldbrynne was in the right to bring you, but I am in the right to send you home."

Some time previous

The monks found Osbert—small, still, and lifeless—among the cold corpses littering the battlefield.

He had no wounds, no injuries. The ravens had not touched him, though they ate their fill of carrion from the others. The worms, flies, and maggots did not yet infest his flesh, though they teemed everywhere else.

Bishop Cenric carried the boy back to the monastery himself, weeping as he did so. He washed the body and set it upon a bier in his council chamber, draped with fine cloth.

For three days, he knelt in vigil. He fasted. He did not sleep.

And no change came to the child's pale flesh.

Uneasy glances, half-fear, half-exultation, passed among the townsfolk and monks.

First the Danes had decided, without word or warning, to withdraw to their longships and sail away instead of pressing another attack.

Then there was Lord Aelfstan, who'd refused to let them cut off his ruined leg although he was sure to die otherwise . . . but did not, and was making a startling recovery.

Now, this . . .

None of them wished to say the words in so many of their thoughts—words such as *incorruptible*, or *miraculous*—

On the fourth morning since the sorrowful discovery, Cenric was disturbed from his silent grief by a feathery fluttering at the room's narrow window.

He turned his head to see a black-winged shape fly away, leaving something that shone golden in the dawn sun.

Rising, knees stiff from kneeling, he went to the window.

A gold hoop lay there, a Dane's arm-ring, worked in a pattern of snake's-scales, with green jewel chips for its eyes.

Cenric picked it up, examining it curiously.

Behind him, on the bier, the cloth moved as Osbert gasped a breath.

Christine Morgan *works the overnight shift in a psychiatric facility and divides her writing time among many genres. A lifelong reader, she also writes, reviews, beta-reads, occasionally edits, and dabbles in self-publishing. She has over a dozen novels in print and more due out soon. Her stories have appeared in several anthologies, been nominated for* Origins Awards, *and given Honorable Mention in two volumes of* Year's Best Fantasy and Horror. *She's a wife, mom, and possible future crazy-cat-lady whose other interests include gaming, history, superheroes, crafts, and cheesy disaster movies.*

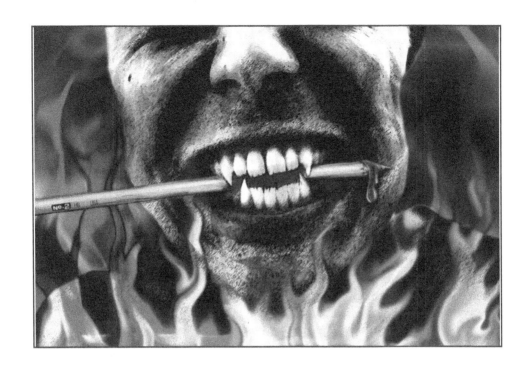

BE QUIET AT THE BACK

WILLIAM MEIKLE

Be leery, those who try to do good in life, for remember this: there is a flip side to every decision, even those you may think virtuous. What is the cost to someone else for your efforts, or what are you giving up in lieu of your choices? In economic terms, that's referred to as the "opportunity cost of the decision." In religious terms, that's referred to as "finding sin in anything you do." It seems hardly fair when you think about it but, as William Meikle reveals in the next selection, fair is not a notion highly regarded in the afterworld . . . or is it? Be Quiet At The Back follows the effects of circumstantial actions and its chain of consequences that lead, ultimately, to one man's final judgment.

The room was white, a white so brilliant it almost hurt his eyes as he struggled to focus.

Something was wrong. The last thing John Davidson remembered was leaving the classroom after marking papers. He'd said goodnight to the janitor, walked to his car and . . .

And nothing.

He couldn't remember anything after that, until he woke sitting in front of a desk composed of white marble that shone with an inner light. He was transfixed, tilting his head from side-to-side to catch the glittering patterns of light and shade, and only stopped in his reverie by a discreet cough from across the desk.

"When you're quite finished?" a gravelly voice said.

John looked up into a pair of piercing green eyes and a sardonic grin. The owner of the grin wore a sharp business suit and an expensive Italian silk tie. The gold band of a watch gleamed as he rolled a hand over the computer keyboard in front of him. John was so taken with the suit that it took him several seconds to notice the talons . . . and horns.

John threw himself back in his seat with a scream and came up hard against the wall of the room. He searched frantically for a door, but there was none, just blank, featureless white.

The demon smiled at him again.

"If you'd just take a seat, sir, this won't take long."

"Where . . . where am I?" John whispered.

The demon tapped at a badge on the lapel of his suit. John had to stand and move closer to read it.

It read, *Ballygrampus, Assistant Deputy Demon, Substation 3933 level 46, Hell.*

"Hell?" John whispered.

"What, you were expecting Pearly Gates and mellow fruitfulness?"

John sat down, hard. He pinched his forearm so tight as to bring a flare of pain, but when he looked up, the demon still sat there, smiling.

"So, what was it? Accident? Heart attack?" the demon asked.

John could only sit and stare. Every time he tried to speak, he failed to come up with a sensible sentence for this situation.

"Ah. Here it is," the demon said, reading from the screen. "John Davidson, aged forty-nine, heart attack. Unlucky not to reach the big five-oh, eh?"

"It's next month," John whispered. "We're having a party . . . all the family will be there."

"I guess they will now," the demon said. "It's a pity *you* won't be there to see it. Let's see why they sent you to me, shall we?"

John watched as the talons rattled across the keyboard.

"So far so good," Ballygrampus said. "Nothing for Fornication, nothing for Gluttony, nothing for Envy."

He looked up and gave John a wink.

"Looks like you might actually *have* come to the wrong place, son."

He went back to looking at the screen.

"Nothing for Sloth, nothing for Avarice."

The demon looked up again, and this time it was more a smirk than a grin that crossed his face.

"That just leaves Theft and Pride. Want to guess where you stand? I'll bet you five years that it's Theft."

John tried to speak but his throat was constricted, as if he had been screaming for a long, long time. He managed to work some spit around his mouth and finally spoke.

"This isn't quite what I expected, you know?"

The demon laughed, a booming thing that sent the walls shaking.

"What? You want fire and brimstone maybe? The big red guy with a great black ledger? Maybe you have come to the right place after all—you've got an exaggerated view of your own importance."

The demon pulled back his sleeves revealing a line of red, almost burnt, flesh, as he turned once more to the keyboard.

"We've moved with the times. Wonderful things these computers. I once spent fifteen years on sub-level 94 looking for a file before we went online. We had a hell of a job entering the historical data—but then again, we've got plenty of accountants and bureaucrats. They always get a massive shock, you know—forty years in the corridors of some parliament or corporation, a peaceful death in their sleep, and they turn up here for more of the same when they were hoping for harps and celestial choirs. None of them seem to realize that there's a price to pay for oiling the gears of power. It all builds up you know, over the years."

The demon leaned forward to John and adopted a conspiratorial tone.

"You weren't a bureaucrat were you? We love them down here. They come in very handy with the filing."

"No," John said in a whisper. "I am . . . was . . . a teacher. A *good* teacher."

"Ahh," Ballygrampus said, and smiled again. Thin wisps of smoke came out of his ears. "It'll be Pride then."

John spluttered.

"I've never had a proud bone in my body!"

"*He said proudly,*" Ballygrampus said and laughed. Smoke came out of his nostrils. The demon waved a hand in front of John's face.

"Watch and learn."

John blinked . . .

. . . and was back in the classroom. Thirty children sat in front of him. Late morning sun streamed in the windows, giving them a golden, almost angelic, glow. Paul Martin, a thin, well-dressed child in the front row, recited Shakespeare.

> "*She should have died hereafter;*
> *There would have been a time for such a word.*
> *To-morrow, and to-morrow, and to-morrow,*
> *Creeps in this petty pace from day to day*
> *To the last syllable of recorded time.*"

"Mr. Davidson. Mr. Davidson. Sir!" a small voice shouted.

John didn't even look up.

"Be quiet, Tommy Brown. Paul is speaking."

"But, sir . . . " the voice said, pleading. "Jack Dawkings is stabbing me with his pencil."

John raised his voice.

"I'll do worse than that if you don't keep quiet! Do you understand!"

The room fell quiet.

"Go on, Paul,"

Somewhere in the distance, Tommy Brown said, "Ouch!"

The classroom faded from John's sight, to be replaced by a large, busy, theatre. Paul Martin, an adult now, and in full highland dress as the tragic Macbeth, delivered the next lines.

> "*And all our yesterdays have lighted fools*
> *The way to dusty death.*
> *Out, out, brief candle!*"

John Davidson turned to his wife seated next to him. "Of course, he would never have got here without me."

He blinked . . .

. . . and stared at a smiling Ballygrampus.

"That's not fair!" John shouted at the demon.

"If it's fair you want, you really *are* in the wrong place," the demon said.

"Paul Martin was a star!" John said, still shouting. "And, yes, I did help him get there."

"And what about Tommy Brown?" Ballygrampus said.

John fell silent. The demon punched several keys, and his eyes blazed red as the result came up.

"Or Mary Kelly? Did you forget her?"

The demon waved a hand in front of John's face.

"Watch and learn."

John blinked . . .

. . . and was back in the classroom. Thirty children sat in front of him. Outside the rain pelted heavily on the windows, the sky a slate gray. Paul Martin again recited Macbeth.

> *"Life's but a walking shadow, a poor player*
> *That struts and frets his hour upon the stage*
> *And then is heard no more."*

"Mr. Davidson. Mr. Davidson. Sir!" a small voice shouted.

Again John didn't even look up.

"Be quiet, Mary Kelly. Paul is speaking."

"But, sir . . . " the voice said, pleading. "Jack Dawkings is stabbing me with his pencil. He's done it twice now!"

John raised his voice.

"I'll do worse than that if you don't keep quiet! Do you understand!"

The room fell quiet once more.

"Go on, Paul," John said.

Somewhere in the distance, Mary Kelly said, "Ouch!"

The classroom faded from John's sight, to be replaced once more by the large, busy, theatre. On stage, Paul Martin delivered the next lines.

> *"It is a tale told by an idiot,*
> *Full of sound and fury,*
> *Signifying nothing."*

John Davidson's wife turned to him and put a soft hand on his shoulder.

"You did a great job, darling," she whispered in his ear.

"I know," John said smugly.

He blinked . . .

. . . and stared at a smiling Ballygrampus.

"Okay," John said quietly. "Maybe I did neglect some of the other children but Paul Martin was—"

"A star? Yes, you said that already," the demon said. Smoke curled out at the corners of his mouth. "But it wasn't just little Paul Martin . . . was it?"

The demon waved a hand in front of John's face.

"Watch and learn."

John blinked . . .

. . . and was back in the classroom. Thirty children sat in front of him. Outside the snow fell softly against the windows, the sky a flat gray that seemed to seep into the faces of the children.

A well-dressed girl, Margaret Davis, stood at the front, reciting Bronte.

"Treachery and violence are spears pointed at both ends . . . "

"Mr. Davidson. Mr. Davidson. Sir!" a small voice shouted.

John didn't have to look up to recognize the voice.

"Be quiet, Tommy Brown. Margaret is speaking."

"But, sir . . . " the voice said, pleading. "Jack Dawkings is stabbing me. I think he has a knife, sir!"

John raised his voice.

"I'll do worse than stab you if you don't keep quiet! Do you understand!"

The room fell quiet.

"Go on, Margaret."

Somewhere in the distance, Tommy Brown screamed in pain.

The classroom faded from John's sight, to be replaced by a view of a television screen. A grown-up Mary Brown was on screen, appearing in a costume drama.

"Treachery and violence are spears pointed at both ends;
They wound those who resort to them worse than their enemies."

"I taught her that," John said, smiling broadly.

He blinked . . .

. . . and stared at a smiling Ballygrampus. He had to wipe away a tear before the demon came into focus.

"I didn't realize . . . "

"No," the demon said. "Your kind never do. There's just one more thing to see, then we can move on."

The demon waved a hand in front of John's face.

"Watch and learn."

John blinked . . .

. . . and looked down on a subway platform from somewhere up near the top of the tunnel. The loudspeakers reported twenty-minute delays, and the growing crowd on the platform were restless. Tempers frayed, and as the brightly colored train finally started to pull into the station the crowd jostled for position.

An old lady stuck an elbow in a teenager's back, and he turned, giving her a hard glare. John recognized the boy straight away. He might be ten years older, and almost full-grown, but there was no mistaking Jack Dawkings's stare.

The old lady glared back.

"What's your problem?" he spat at her.

She turned away.

John recognized the area and knew that kids looking for a fight were ten-a-penny around here. The trick was not to give them an opening. Unfortunately this one didn't need an opening. He put a hand on the old lady's shoulder and pulled her toward him.

"I was talking to you," he said.

"Is that what it was? I'm sorry, I don't understand ape-speak."

It seemed to take Jack a second to realize he'd been insulted . . . John could almost see each individual brain cell struggle for a synaptic connection. Eventually, realization came to the youth's eyes and he remembered to be outraged.

The train had come to a stop, and the old lady moved with the crowd toward it. The kid wasn't finished with her, though. He stepped around in front of her and stood, nose-to-nose.

"I was talking to you!" he said in that belligerent swagger that only a teenager can muster.

She tried to push past him, but he refused to stand aside.

"Didn't they teach you *any* manners in school?" she said.

"Let me show you what I learned in school," he replied with a dead smile.

The knife slammed into her chest and she was dead before she hit the ground.

John blinked . . .

. . . and stared at a smiling Ballygrampus.

"You can't blame me for *that*," John said, spluttering.

"If you can suggest anybody else, we're always open to offers," Ballygrampus said softly, small flames dancing around his mouth.

John shook his head.

"But it wasn't my fault!"

"Do you want to know how many times someone has sat in that chair and said that?" the demon said wearily. "Don't you think the big man upstairs has already made that call?"

John could only sit and stare back at the demon as the implications finally hit him.

"Right then," Ballygrampus said. "I think you've seen enough. We've got you down for 19,233 counts of pride. Congratulations, John—that's an impressive feat."

Talons rattled on keys as another screen was called up.

"The going rate is a week for each offense. I'm sorry about that, but there are so many self-important types around these days that we've had to get tough on you. I make that 370 years . . . give or take a week. Minus the five I owe you, that makes 365 years—a fine round number. Have a nice day."

The room faded, but not before John saw the smile spread across the demon's face and a thin blood-red tongue flick out to lick fleshy lips.

John blinked . . .

. . . and was back in the classroom. But this time, the whole class sat with their backs to him, facing a tall, red-eyed demon. Outside the classroom windows, red fires raged, and a chorus of screams rent the air in the far distance. John sat in the back row, squeezed tightly into a desk that was too small, too confining.

The demon listened raptly as a child at the front recited.

> *"Hell hath no limits, nor is circumscribed in one self place,*
> *For where we are is hell,*
> *And where hell is there must we ever be."*

John squirmed, trying to free himself from his cramped position. "Ouch!"

A sudden sharp pain flared in his side.

He turned, and looked into the cold dead stare of a ten-year old Jack Dawkings. Dawkings tested the point of a sharpened pencil against his thumb, causing a small drop of blood to swell up. The boy smiled, and his eyes flared red.

John struggled hard to move away, but the desk had him in an all-encompassing hold, and he couldn't move more than an inch in any direction.

"Sir. Sir!" he shouted as Jack Dawkings waved the pencil in the air, wielding it like a dagger.

"Be quiet, John Davidson. Margaret is speaking," the demon said.

"But, sir . . . " he said, pleading. "Jack Dawkings is stabbing me. Sir!"

The demon raised his voice and the whole room shook.

"I'll do worse than stab you if you don't keep quiet! Do you understand!"

The room fell quiet.

"Do you want to see what *I* learned in school?" Dawkings said.

He stabbed forward again.

And again.

William Meikle *is a Scottish writer with fifteen novels published in the genre press and over 250 short story credits in thirteen countries. His work appears in many professional anthologies and his ebook,* The Invasion, *has been as high as #2 in the Kindle SF charts. Recent work for Dark Regions Press includes* The Creeping Kelp, Sherlock Holmes: Revenant, The Invasion/ The Valley, *and* Carnacki: Heaven and Hell. *He lives in a remote corner of Newfoundland with icebergs, whales, and bald eagles for company. In the winters he gets warm vicariously through the lives of others in cyberspace, so please check him out at* www.williammeikle.com.

CAGES

PETER GIGLIO

People die. If believed, their spirits then transition—evolve—into another being, a form of higher consciousness, a soul freed of mortal constraints. In most religions, there is an overseer to this, a celestial being that collects these souls and issues judgments and rewards. However, if humans can shed their outer shell and metamorphose into something greater, logically one can infer that those celestial beings have the capacity for their own transcendence. Cages predicts the Gods are only biding their time, waiting for their own turn at something greater, the same as us all. The multi-talented Peter Giglio (See: Publisher, Editor, Writer, and all-around nicest guy you could meet) suggests that time has arrived . . .

1.

Here's Dad, impressed that the car's parallel parking itself.

"What will they think of next?" he says.

I shrug off his question and just look at him, a man who's been dead for the better part of twelve years. Though I've known this was coming for more than a week, I'm still unable to process what's happening.

Last night I watched the Abraham Lincoln interview on CNN. He didn't seem right without a beard; had probably been told by his handlers that facial hair no longer looked presidential.

Iconic majesty washed away in one brief moment of televised absurdity. Most disheartening: all the racist crap that spewed from *The Great Emancipator*'s mouth.

"A product of a different era," the talking heads reminded me—all of us—when the interview ended.

But that's bullshit.

Dad's still looking at me, waiting for me to say something. Waiting for me to care.

I want to tell him that anyone who touched the hand of God, like he and Lincoln had, and looked into His or Her eyes (everyone saw the Lord differently) should carry a measure of enlightenment transcending time; a modicum of grace that shatters the shackles of our nature.

But there is no grace. Not anymore. Dad's the embodiment of that argument.

Humanity lights his face and tells me we're doomed.

"What's for supper?" he asks.

He's following me dumbly through my small apartment. He's always been like this. An uncomfortable guest. Fidgety in social situations.

"Relax," I tell him, trying to smile. But my smile's not working. How can it?

She hasn't returned to me yet.

She . . .

The one who I'd believed in. *My* God. *My* Savior. Taken away by a deity who was supposed to be immortal, all-knowing, loving.

"Have a seat, Dad. Watch some TV. I'll make sandwiches."

"Sandwiches for dinner?" he asks.

Same as he ever was.

I glare at him. "I didn't plan ahead." Hell, how do you plan for the death of God? And who would suspect the deity's demise to reverse the nature of mortality? Coughing the dead back to us.

The headlines read *God Is Dead.* I wonder if the Russian headlines scream *Told You So!* But that musing carries no humor. Monica would have laughed. She always did. And I always joined in. Until the doctors said, "There's nothing we can do," and hope was lost. She kept laughing, of course, right 'til the last second. So don't ask me why I loved her so much; you would have, too.

Dad changes the subject. "You hear from Monica yet?"

And I wonder if he's reading my mind. No. Just my face, like he always has. "Talk to Mom yet?" I respond.

His face reddens and he backs away from me. "Well, no . . . not yet . . . not . . . "

Dad always pushed too hard. Too much advice. Thought he knew everything.

Mom's down in Florida now, with her new husband. She's finally happy, and Dad, I can tell, hates it. Hates that I'm all he has left in this world. And probably senses that he barely has me.

Mom will talk to him, of course. She still loves him, in a way. But she won't say what he wants to hear. "Have him call me," she said. "But tell him not to expect anything." I think of telling him this, but I can see he already knows.

I make the sandwiches, pile extra salami on his. That'll give him heartburn, but I don't care.

He's sitting on the couch when I hand him the plate. I sit in a recliner across from him, turn on the television, and take a bite.

"She'll come back, son." He's not looking at the TV. He's staring at me, getting ready to push, looking like he might jump up at any moment. I can feel it in my solar plexus. Now I'm the one with heartburn.

"She'll never take you back. 'Til death do us part, remember? Hate to say it, but she did her part."

"No, I realize that. I mean Monica. She'll come back. Some of us just take a little longer. Get lost along the way. Like me."

I find a rerun of *Green Acres*, his favorite. Maybe that'll shut him up.

He chuckles. "This is classic. One of the best." But then he turns back to me and repeats, "She'll come back."

I nod, finish off my sandwich, put the plate in the sink, and walk toward the bedroom. "You'll be okay on the couch?" I say.

"You going to bed already?"

"Long day. Tired."

"But I just—"

"We'll talk tomorrow. G'night."

2.

I'm not really tired but try to sleep.

Shadows twist and turn, passing car lights plentiful on the street where I live. Curtains would help, but I can't bring myself to shop for such extravagance. If I can't eat it, I don't need it.

Things are only getting worse in this population crisis.

Debate about mass-sterilization is hot in the House of Representatives right now. But they can't agree on anything. Never could. Those assholes are more worried about questions like, "Where's Hitler?" and "Where's Jesus?" All of them empty-headed when it comes to practical solutions for pressing matters.

Although I have to admit it, the Hitler and Jesus questions are intriguing.

But I'm more consumed by, *Where's Monica?*

That's all I have now . . . that question.

And Hell on Earth with no hope for escape.

That doesn't stop people from trying. I saw a girl run in front of a city bus yesterday. It hit her doing forty-five. She walked away, and I could tell that she wasn't crying because of broken bones, though she was pretty messed up. No. Hers were the tears of a prisoner that's given up hope.

But I don't like to think about that mangled girl.

I like to think about Monica.

I see her face, always do, but the image grows stronger when I concentrate on her. She whispers to me, "Our bodies are cages."

Here in my mind, she's dying again. A moment I've relived thousands of times. Always fresh. Tragic. Painful. And yet it's the moment that's most vivid. If only I could remember the good times . . .

"I'm going home," she tells me. "Going home."

I don't believe her. Her home is here, with me.

"Don't leave . . . "

Death comes and still she smiles.

You see, she believed.

I never could. Never did.

"Ignore denominations," she says. "Don't focus on factions. Give yourself to God and He will find you. You'll know when it's God, know when it's right."

I pretend to understand. Though all I can really see is how much I love her. Every grin, kind act, sway, frown, fart, tear . . .

. . . Perfection.

The memory of her, nearer than now, is my altar.

In the next room, Dad snores.

Couldn't the hand of God at least cure shitty sinuses? Myth was that the Almighty could cure lepers. Or maybe that was His son. What's the difference? Why should I care about someone who dies and leaves us all caged?

And yet . . .

I once knew God.

A true God. All I ever had. All I ever loved. My Everything . . .

And She died.

Give yourself to God and God will find you . . .

3.

I approach her gravestone, shovel in hand. Most of the other stones are gone, and wounds scar the ground where bodies once rested.

For me, the real wound is the marker that bears her name.

I dig, not worried about being caught. This is no longer a sacred place that warrants monitoring.

Last week, people camped outside these gates, waiting and hopeful.

Now hope is gone and reality has set in. New mouths to feed. Cramped living quarters. Old arguments rehashed.

The gates aren't even locked anymore.

My muscles ache, my body drenched in sweat. I'm not an active man, but I will myself to keep digging.

Walls of dirt surround me, and the shovel hits something hard.

A shadow moves over me, and I know who it is without looking up.

"Who's right, Dad?"

"I don't understand," he says.

"The Christians? The Jews? The Muslims? Someone has to be right. Who is it?"

"I don't know," he says. "God never talked in those terms. And I never thought to ask. It seemed . . . wrong."

"Wrong? Why?"

"Because it was clear that God *was* right. Not us."

I turn and see how sad his eyes are. He's starting to mourn the death of truth. Or maybe he's been mourning it all along and I've been too pitiful to notice.

"Help me," I say. And he does.

The two of us, covered in dirt, huddled together in this narrow trench, digging . . . digging . . .

When I was five, I fell from a tree and broke my collar bone. He stayed with me all night and let me sleep in his arms. This is the closest we've been since.

Using the shovel, we pry open the coffin.

And there she rests; a hideous shell. Her eyes are empty sockets and mouth is agape. Her white dress turned yellow.

Dead.

I turn and vomit, and Dad clutches my shoulder.

"She must be one of them," he whispers.

My eyes stinging with tears, I can hardly breathe. But I manage, "She's . . . what?"

His grip tightens, becomes an embrace. "Let's go home, son."

4.

Here's Dad, holding me close as I weep. Stroking my hair like he did on that long-ago night, letting me know, "Everything will be all right."

"Are you going to tell me what she is?" There's accusation in my voice, though I know none of the blame is his.

He looks down, and I see he's crying, too. But his tears are different than mine. His slight smile betrays hope.

"Please," I say.

The moment of silence lingers, until he replies, "She's God."

I pull away and stand.

He shakes his head, holds his hands out in defense, getting ready for my rebuttal. But I don't have enough energy to properly fight.

"I'm telling you the truth," he says.

"But you said, *she's one of them.*"

"God is many and one, and sometimes articulates grace and evil through human form. To test us, teach us, help us become better."

"So she was an angel? A messiah? What?"

Dad shakes his head. "More like an ember from an inferno. She's as much God as your hand is you."

Hanging my head, I amble to the window. I Look at my hand, then look out. "So she's gone?"

"Yes, but . . . "

There's an unusually large congregation on the street. Something's brewing out there. And I wonder how Dad can be so hopeful in here.

"But what?" I say.

"God found a way to break free," he says. "Moved to the next level."

I turn and shout, "And left us behind!"

Dad says, "God loves us."

"Is that what's giving you hope, old man?"

He nods. "That's part of it."

I intensify my glare.

"God couldn't help us anymore," he says. "Like a teacher that runs out of lesson plans and has to deal with a class that thinks it knows everything already."

"Where does that leave us?" I whisper in a growl.

"Alone—"

"Exactly! Alone!"

"But just for a while."

Loud voices bark through the window. Outside, a fight breaks out. A woman screams. Police sirens wail.

The last of my strength leaves and I sink to the floor.

"It's all for us. It always has been," Dad says. "And this is only temporary. I know that."

My eyes swim to a picture on a bookcase.

Monica, smiling, always smiling . . .

I'll find you, she seems to say.

I take a deep breath and smile back.

*An active member of the Horror Writers' Association (HWA) and a Pushcart Prize nominee, **Peter Giglio** is the author of three novels—* Anon, Beyond Anon, *and* The Dark *(with Scott Bradley)—and three novellas—*A Spark in the Darkness, Balance, *and* Sunfall Manor. *His short fiction can be found in several anthologies, including* Werewolves and Shapeshifters *and* Psychos, *both edited by John Skipp. He is the editor of* Help! Wanted: Tales of On-the-Job Terror *and the* Evil Jester Digest *series, and is shopping—with co-writer Scott Bradley—a feature-length screen adaptation of Joe R. Lansdale's* The Night They Missed the Horror Show. *Peter always has time for readers at* petergiglio.com, *or on his blog:* petergiglioauthor.blogspot.com.

HAMMERHEAD

SIMON CLARK

If the quest for justice is a concept mankind devoutly pursues, can it hold true that—if not found in one life—its pursuit will carry over to the next? Is it possible vengeance may indeed always be attained, though perhaps not while in the same lifetime it was deserved? Are grudges carried across the bounds of reincarnation, or are our souls simply filled with identical compulsions during each stage of existence? Everyone has felt unexplainable impulses propelling us to act in ways we otherwise might not contemplate. Hammerhead *is no different, as one creature realizes an opportunity to avenge a past offense. The author, Simon Clark, is known the world over for his fantasy and dark fiction. This next tale carries on his legacy of horror, as well as offering a glimpse into the circumstances of ourselves.*

Hawaiian folklore presents the hammerhead shark as a god of the sea, and many sharks of this species are considered to be reincarnations of ancestors. Certain varieties of hammerhead can grow up to twenty feet in length, and although attacks on human beings aren't at all common they do occur . . .

SWIM . . . GLIDE . . . FATHOMLESS DEPTHS . . . DUSK . . . TIME TO HUNT . . . TIME TO FEED . . . SEE THE PREY . . . ATTACK . . . BITE . . . TASTE THE BLOOD . . . BITE . . . GULP THE FLESH . . .

The lone hammerhead sheared off a limb. The man still kept his head above water as he screamed for the others on the rafts to help him. Futile screams from a bleeding, hurting, dying man. The hammerhead returned to feed on the man's body that spurted crimson into the ocean. Its senses were dominated by the blood as if the presence were a brilliant red light combined with a siren of enormous power.

Before the hammerhead could make another scything pass at the struggling figure in order to rip away the next limb, a pack of bull sharks torpedoed from the gloom, slamming into the man and dragging him down into the darkness.

The hammerhead had lost its meal, though no dismay registered inside its brain, because more of the four-limbed mammals floated on the surface. True, they were in vessels, but these were small inflatable craft with thin, delicate membranes that could easily be ripped open.

The hammerhead possesses better vision than most sharks, due to its widely-spaced eyes set at either end of the broad, hammer-shaped skull. The dark undersides of the circular life rafts were clearly visible to the creature as it moved beneath them with powerful strokes of its tail. The hammerhead also has another powerful sense shared with its fellow species. Covering its greenish, gray skin are extraordinary sensory pores that detect electricity carried through the water. The hammerhead can sense electrical fields that are so weak only the most delicate of scientific instruments can normally detect them.

Therefore, as it glided through the water it sensed its prey in more ways than by sight and smell. The electrical activity in the mammals' bodies, those purple flashes of panic, fired up the receptors of the shark's brain. With ease, it detected the agitated flicker of fear, panic, desperation. The big fish could divine flashes of human thought, too.

'Help.'

'How can we be rescued?'

'*Five hundred miles from the coast of Australia . . . no time to send an emergency call . . . '*

'*Why did our boat capsize?*'

'*Please, God. I'm sorry that I've never prayed to you before. Please help me, Lord . . . please save my life . . . '*

'*What a twist of fate . . . I've craved to be all alone with Ruth Constantine . . . Now my wish has come true . . . But we're going to die of thirst together in this damned life raft. This is poetic justice for what I did to Damian Keller.'*

A morsel of ragged flesh in the water . . . a man's face. BITE. SWIM. MORE FLESH NEARBY . . . HUNT. CIRCLE CLOSER. READY FOR ATTACK. READY TO KILL.

This is poetic justice for what I did to Damian Keller . . . alone with Ruth Constantine . . .

Tremors ran through the shark's long, streamlined body. *Damian Keller . . . Ruth Constantine . . .* The names seemed to burn brightly in the water: vivid streaks of gold lightning. *Damian Keller. Ruth Constantine.* Those names meant something to the shark. The hammerhead's tail flicked from side to side; its gills pulsed faster as the blood quickened in its veins.

For the first time, instinct retreated into the back of the creature's brain . . . instead, thoughts started to flow, and words formed inside the mind of the giant fish.

Damian Keller. I am Damian Keller. Then the terrifying events of all those years ago came flooding back. I'm Damian Keller. I'm a diver aboard the *Zephyr*, a boat carrying a team that's investigating the electro-sensory abilities of sharks in the Indian Ocean. As the shark glided beneath the life rafts it didn't merely remember what happened a decade ago, it found itself transported back in time to when it—*he*—wore the flesh of another creature.

Here are warm-blooded hands that open a bottle of strong smelling liquid brewed from yeast, hops, and malt.

"Thank God," said Damian Keller. "I'm so thirsty I could drink a whole crateful of these."

His friend, a man with a blond beard and blond hair tied back into a pony tail, grinned and clattered his own bottle into Damian's.

"Cheers. I'll drink to that," said the man . . . and the name *Glenn* burned with a dangerous red light in the hammerhead's brain as it circled the kill-zone, simultaneously living in two worlds and two times at once.

Damian Keller and Glenn Harrap sat out on the rear deck of the *Zephyr*. They were alone—other crew members were either asleep, or eating in the saloon below decks, or working. Soon Damian would be wired up for the night's dreaming experiment. Electrodes would be secured to shaved patches on his scalp: these wires would pick up brain waves, which then transmitted from an antenna immersed in the water. The team had discovered that nightmares and dreams of panic drew in the big predator sharks, right up to the boat. For years, marine biologists had studied whale song, but only now realized that sharks could be repelled or attracted by electrical activity in human brains. The commercial potential for such control had excited investors to pump more cash into their research.

Damian/Hammerhead chatted to his friend on deck as lightning flickered silently over the warm ocean. By this time, night had fallen. After the heat of the day the beer was cold enough and delicious enough to be a minor miracle. Damian found himself studying the hand that held the green bottle. The beer was frothy and white, bubbles rising from the neck. *Funny things hands*, he thought, *the way fingers break away to form individual limbs.* At that moment, he had no way of knowing that his mind had formed a link with his future incarnation; that sharkish-thoughts swam through his own ocean of the mind. He thought the strong Sri Lankan beer playfully beguiled him into entertaining strange notions. Or, more likely, it was the news he would spring on the blond man sitting beside him. Damian hadn't felt this excited in years. Even diving in the shark cage didn't make his heart pound quite like this.

"Glenn." Damian's muscles clenched when he said the name . . . he paused, why did the name Glenn seem to pulsate with a red light inside his head? *Red for danger, red for blood. Glenn . . .*

"What's on your mind, bro?" The blond man pulled another beer from the cooler.

"It's about Ruth." This name shimmered gentle shades of gold.

"Ruth said she'll come up when she finishes running the latest data. She's going to give us the low-down on the species of shark that's been following us since we piped your weird dreams to them last night."

"Oh, great . . . but it's not really about the experiment. It's about Ruth herself."

"Come on, Damian, don't be shy." The blond man grinned. "You can tell me anything."

"I want you to be cool about this, because I know you and Ruth were seeing each other once."

The man's grin remained . . . only his lips seemed to harden. "So what do you want me to be cool about?"

"We kept everything secret . . . but we really have something, you know?"

"You and Ruth?"

"Yes, I should have told you earlier."

"You mean you're . . . what? Dating? Screwing?"

"We're going to be married."

"Shit."

"I didn't say anything earlier, because I thought you still had this thing for her. You know, feelings."

"Congratulations." The man shook Damian's hand.

"Thanks, Glenn."

GLENN . . . the name burst into crimson fire inside his brain. GLENN. The name screamed danger. Ten years in the future the shark burst through the ocean's surface, thrashing its tail, its teeth flashing in the moonlight.

While ten years ago Damian stood at the guard rail to watch the silent lightning flicker above the horizon. "I want you to be best man, of course."

Those were his last words. The beer bottle shattered against the back of his head. Seconds later, the blond man tipped Damian over the rail and into the sea.

Nobody saw . . . nobody knew . . .

Then came strange, swirling fogs in the darkness. Memories of his old life receded into those mists. When his mind became clear again he saw the seabed gliding beneath him—the rippled sand, the brown kelp, and rocks encrusted with shellfish. He felt his teeth crunch into fish and squid. His tail propelled him. When he glimpsed his shadow on the sand beneath him, as brilliant sunlight pierced the water, he saw the shadow of a hammerhead shark.

Words like 'reincarnation' and 'reborn' didn't feature in his mind for years. He simply acted and reacted automatically within his environment. By day he swam with more of his kind where the brine plunged down to such depths no light ever entered from above. Occasionally, he glimpsed the underside of a vessel, plowing through the glittering ceiling that separated his aquatic realm with a world of air and sunlight. Even then, no words entered his brain; there was no recollection of 'ship' or 'human.' If he crunched the bones of a drowning fisherman he didn't identify his prey—it was simply food, just like the groupers, squid, and crabs he devoured when hunger directed him to hunt.

It was only today, many years after an individual by the name of Damian Keller was struck on the head by his best friend, that he understood everything. After he'd been toppled over the guardrail into the water, there'd been darkness . . . only after a spell of dreamless limbo had he emerged from the mist of nothingness to find he'd become this restless, predatory creature. Now he realized that he'd been following a ship for months; painted on its stern, the word *Zephyr*. The fantastically sensitive receptors on his skin that could detect as little as a millionth of a volt had picked up electrical activity seeping from the ship. On board were thirty men and women, and among those individuals was Glenn. One of the women had the familiar signature of golden strands of electricity that captivated him and wouldn't let go. And now, as he swam beneath the life rafts, he detected the shining electrons that seemed to gently vibrate with the name *Ruth Constantine*.

His sharkish memory recalled what happened just a dozen hours ago. The freak storm, the way the ship capsized, the frantic scramble of its passengers for the inflatable rafts. Eventually, the sea became tranquil again. A mist formed above the water, white phantoms drifting through the evening gloom. The survivors had paddled with their hands in order to bring the life rafts close to one another. In one inflatable craft were two humans—Glenn and Ruth.

The hammerhead/Damian gently rose against the underside of the flexible membrane that formed the floor of the raft. He felt the shape of two bodies pressing against the soft material. Glenn and Ruth. They reacted in horror as they felt an unseen marine creature press against them.

Their thoughts pulsated in flashes of purple hysteria. '*Shark! Shark! Shark!*'

The human mind had, by some inexplicable twist of fate, now been fully reawakened in the shark. What's more, there were echoes of earlier incarnations. An artillery officer in a bottle-green coat yelling in French as a Russian cavalryman emerged from a swirling blizzard to cut him down with a saber. The reflection in a stream of a grunting bull as its bovine eyes looked into his. Then he was a boy, running with a basket of green figs. Nearby, stood a village of mud-brick houses, which overlooked a brown river where boats with red sails glided serenely downstream. Damian gazed deeper into the well of his own existence, seeing hundreds of previous incarnations. A cantankerous ape that became angry with the hard pebble it tried to sharpen with a rock. A bird soaring over jungle. A green lizard sitting on a rock . . .

He turned his attention away from those ghosts of his former selves that still remained inside the central core of his nervous system. Instead, he focused on his sense of touch as he lay beneath the life raft, feeling the tightly inflated material against his dorsal fin, and there he began to absorb the thoughts of its male and female occupants. Despite the terror of knowing that a predator pushed itself against their fragile little vessel, the male still felt hot sparks of desire when he glanced at the way the woman's T-shirt clung to her body. The hammerhead also drank in the thoughts and emotions of the woman. He remembered when he'd laid this close to Ruth Constantine all those years ago. The way her body warmed his blood—that was one of the most powerful memories from when he was a man: her body heat filling him with such a wonderful contentment.

Now he caught strands of thought: *'For God's sake, of all the people to find myself alone with in a life raft? Glenn Harrap . . . I can't bear to be near him. How did he come to be so repulsive? Ever since Damian vanished I can't help but think that Glenn had something to do with it. Those sidelong glances he gives me. Guilt, guilt, guilt—it bleeds from his eyes. I'm sure he knows what really happened to Damian . . . if only I had proof.'*

The hammerhead moved slightly, caressing the female shape on the other side of the raft's skin. He wanted the love he felt to reach her, just as her thoughts reached him. The movement, however, alarmed her so much it drove her to the edge of the inflatable.

This time he picked up sound waves traveling through the water.

Ruth shouted to the other survivors in the neighboring boats, "There's a shark down there. I can feel it pushing up against the raft."

Glenn hissed, "Ruth, keep still. If we don't move it'll lose interest and leave."

'Shut up, Glenn. You're a murderer. You killed my fiancé. I don't know what you did to Damian, but I know you made him disappear.' Ruth didn't say those words aloud, but her thoughts reached the hammerhead. Along with the words she thought, there were images of Ruth grieving for Damian, the man she loved. It was as if he saw a montage of her suffering: *'Ten years ago, Damian went missing . . . nobody knows what happened . . . nobody, that is, other than Glenn. I'm sure Glenn knows. He was always the jealous type . . . Every instinct tells me he killed Damian.'*

The membrane that was the inflatable's floor deformed as feet pressed against it. His senses interpreted this as Glenn standing in the middle of the craft. Two heavy feet pressing down against the flexible material. He opened his mouth lined with sharp teeth.

Just one bite. Open up the membrane, Glenn would plunge down through the hole to where the hammerhead waited. VENGEANCE. The word pulsated with a wonderful ruddy light. VENGEANCE . . .

Even as he contemplated the attack—claiming the man who killed him, while ensuring Ruth remained safe—everything changed. Pale shapes darted from the depths below. The bull sharks were back. They were determined to rip the inflatables apart before attacking the humans that had survived the shipwreck.

Instantly, the hammerhead was in the center of a whirling vortex of frenzied sharks. He tore at their muscular flanks. Dorsal fins crunched between his teeth. Sharp teeth ripped his own flesh, but he still fought to drive the bull sharks away from the little flotilla of rafts. And as the battle raged, he picked up the stuttering black flashes that signaled the death throes of the creatures he'd mortally wounded. All his senses: smell, sound, sight, touch, and even electrons striking the receptors in his skin, conveyed the fury of this shark-on-shark combat. He would do everything in his power to save the life of Ruth Constantine.

Even as he fought, he realized that flashlights were shone into the water. He heard shouts.

"There's a hammerhead down there! It's driving away the bull sharks!"

"I'll take care of you, Ruth. Come here. I can protect you."

"Don't touch me, Glenn. Don't put one finger on me."

"Ruth, what's come over you?"

"I know you killed Damian. He disappeared after you went up on deck together."

After the bull sharks fled, the hammerhead rose to the surface. Its widely spaced eyes captured the panoramic view of a lone raft. Clearly, it had become separated from the flotilla and drifted away into the gloom. Glenn, the blond man, gripped Ruth by the throat.

The hammerhead divined the angry man's train of thought: *'If she dies now she'll never tell anyone. Once she's dead no one will ever know that I killed Damian. The sharks will get rid of her body.'* The man would easily push Ruth overboard. He'd claim he tried to save her, of course . . . only she became deranged with fear.

The hammerhead's tail began to sweep back and forth. All that muscular power of the body became focused on moving the twenty-foot creature through the water. As its speed increased, the creature's eyes locked on the two figures struggling on the tiny craft.

Seconds later, the shark broke free of the water—sheer velocity carried it up into the air in an arc over the raft. Just for an instant there was a vastly enlarged view of Ruth's face. Ten years older but still Ruth—beautiful, gentle Ruth.

The hammerhead swung its massive head to the right. Glenn Harrap filled its field of vision. The creature's jaws opened, then snapped shut, catching the blond man by the right arm, just below the elbow. Momentum carried both the shark and the human higher into the air before both man and fish crashed down into the ocean.

The hammerhead retained the image of Ruth as she fell to her knees. Shaking, breathless, astonished, yet safe . . . forever safe.

The shark, with the man in its jaws, swam downward. Within moments, the pair had reached a depth of a thousand feet.

Even as Damian's murderer died, the shark's mind began to revert to its sharkish nature. Yet, in the moment before the human mind retreated completely, he gazed into the face of his killer from ten years ago, and he also saw the face of the Russian cavalryman that cut him down in the time of Napoleon. And he saw the features of the bandit that strangled him—back when he was a boy who carried the basket of figs beside the Nile, when boats with red sails floated on the water. And he saw those same eyes in the face of the tiger that pounced as he chipped flint into the shape of a spearhead.

Glenn was dead. But not for long . . . not for long.

He knew, without knowing how, that in the future the two adversaries would continue to meet in different flesh and with different names. Whether as victims or as killers, they would meet, again and again.

Simon Clark has been a professional author for more than fifteen years. When his first novel, Nailed by the Heart, *made it through the slush pile in 1994 he banked the advance and embarked upon his dream of becoming a full-time writer. Many dreams and nightmares later he wrote the cult horror-thriller* Blood Crazy, *and other novels including* Death's Dominion, Vengeance Child, *and* The Night of the Triffids, *which continues the story of Wyndham's classic* The Day of the Triffids.

Simon's latest novel is a return to his much-loved Vampyrrhic *mythology with* His Vampyrrhic Bride.

Films, news, and tips on writing can be accessed at his website.

Simon lives with his family in the atmospheric, legend-haunted county of Yorkshire in England.

Simon's Website: www.nailedbytheheart.com

MARVEL AT THE FACE OF FOREVER

KELLY DUNN

When I created my first anthology, Dark Tales of Lost Civilizations, *I found there was one author that I particularly related to and who I could openly discuss publishing practices and marketing strategies. That was David Tallerman. In this anthology, I found my go-to person in the following author, Kelly Dunn. A well-respected name in the circles of Los Angeles horror authors, Kelly is also an editor as well as technical writer and novelist. Her next story is definitely on the darker spectrum of tales I accepted: A murdered man escapes the evil witchcraft that binds his soul by fleeing into the world the witchcraft is drawn from.* Marvel at the Face of Forever *is supernatural horror at its finest . . . and also earns the dubious distinction of being the "best-titled story" in this book.*

Just after he passed out for the last time, Chandler Marvel found himself floating near the ceiling of the filthy shed. His screaming had short-circuited and gone silent. He still felt every severed nerve, every ruined limb, still tasted the clots and the mucus and bits of bone. The pain circulated through him like blood. Yet the nature of his fear slowed and shifted, congealing to slow-motion dread. Looking down, he recognized the flayed, mutilated thing on the ground as his own body. Somehow, Chandler's awareness became an observer, while his physical self lay unmoving below. But Chandler did not dwell on this wonder; he was terrified that he might re-enter his body and wake up.

After what seemed an eternity of desecration, the murderer detached himself from Chandler's body and stood. Watching from above, Chandler saw a deep-red pool, the flow from the body's wounds, seeping into the dirt floor. The killer the others called *El Cubano* breathed deeply, calming himself. He smiled as he adjusted the hem of his caftan, covering himself once again. The blood and the fluids and the waste did not seem to bother him at all.

El Cubano yelled an order and two of his henchmen entered the shed. One man took hold of Chandler's left wrist, and the other man grabbed his right. Both men kept away from the still-oozing stumps of what had once been Chandler's fingers. Grunting, the two assistants dragged Chandler's six-foot-two frame toward a dark corner. Chandler's toeless feet traced a muddy trail along the way.

Why . . . ?

Chandler's thoughts picked up speed, though his body no longer resisted. *Please don't please don't please don't please don't . . .* But the men's attention strayed elsewhere. They looked furtively into the corner, even as they flipped his body on its back and stepped away. Chandler's own face stared upward, as if seeking its soul. It was no longer a face, but a crimson skull with most of its flesh removed. Other changes had occurred. His blue eyes still stared, wide-open, but a cloudy film covered them. The whistling, burbling breathing noises had stopped. But if he had stopped breathing, that meant . . .

He tried to distract himself by following the men's stare to whatever had caught their attention, but what he saw in the corner made no sense. A witchy cauldron, handcrafted and heavy-looking, hunkered in the shadows. Just a few hours ago—a faraway, fairytale lifetime ago—Chandler would have scoffed at the thing, would have told his frat buddies that it looked like a prop from a retro horror flick. But the long-ago Chandler had never known real suffering, or even real fear. Looking at the cauldron, he felt the mindless terror return.

El Cubano approached Chandler's body and stood over it, cradling a thick-bladed knife with a white handle.

No! Deep down inside, Chandler knew he was dead, but he couldn't accept the truth. It couldn't end like this! Not with this angel-faced murderer standing over him, eyes glittering in triumph. Chandler willed his body to scream, to kick, to use its broken limbs, to fight for life. This was it, his last chance. But his body lay inert on the floor. Not a single twitch as El Cubano tipped Chandler's head back and started hacking through his neck, seeming to glory in severing it from its body. Then he placed his hands on Chandler's cheeks and lifted his head off the ground, holding it high.

Someone murmured in awe, *"Ai, padrino. El poder de Palo Mayombe esta en ti."*

El Cubano laughed as he tossed Chandler's head into the cauldron.

And Chandler's observing awareness plummeted from the ceiling, following his physical remains into the cauldron's interior. Straight down he dropped within the cauldron's circular opening, descending in freefall as if he'd jumped out of a plane. *Impossible.* The cauldron could only have been several inches deep at most, yet he kept falling, falling through the murky muzz of a polluted night. As he fell, the air became warmer. Spread-eagled in emptiness, he sensed the sluggish rush of wind against his exposed wounds, as if he still possessed a physical body. Crimson mist spattered and scattered in the dark air. Scarlet rain, still warm, salty, and stinking of squandered life. He started counting. *One-one-thousand, two-one-thousand, three . . .* the endless numbers simply floated away, losing themselves in the thick unyielding atmosphere. He fell faster, tumbling, a plaything of darkness. His sundered flesh shrieked as he landed, hard, on his back.

It seemed that he lay in a field. An itching prickliness moved against him, angry grasses dried by an autumn breeze. Yet no breeze blew, nor did any cool relief come with the still-drifting blood-drizzle. Smells—somehow he could still detect odors—of cinnamon and hot chili peppers embraced the scent of rotting meat. Chandler sat up. Colorless clay beneath him, dry despite the rain. Ash-colored leaves in the dirt, rooted, yet rattling and restless. Several long thin sticks stuck up from the ground, spaced with care like a barren forest. Something dark lay near his feet: a black cat, shriveled into a grimacing mummy. In every direction the dull plain curved into lava-like fog at the limit of his sight. A circular mesa and, at its center, himself.

What were the last words he heard? *El poder de Palo Mayombe esta en ti.* The power of . . . Palo Mayombe . . . is yours. Palo Mayombe? He didn't know what those words meant, didn't know how any of this could be real. Had it all been—could it still be—some drug-induced hallucination? He knew this wasn't so, but felt compelled to test the theory. In the reddish cast of the alien twilight, he held up his right hand. Yes, there were his fingers, each cut off at the second joint. All of it had happened and was still happening!

But his body had changed. As he moved his arm, the flesh wavered. He saw straight through the sinew and bone. Under the transparent skin of his ruined hand, another hand moved, perfectly in sync. The interior hand still had all its fingers, undamaged, the fingernails trimmed to the quick the way Chandler had always kept them in his sweet dream of a life before this nightmare.

He raised his left hand for comparison to its mate. The same. It seemed there were two parts to him now: his body as it had died— transparent now—on the outside, and his apparently undamaged self on the inside. Each joint and nerve of his dead body still sang its own song of agony. But seeing the undamaged body hidden beneath the dead one, he remembered the *long-ago time*. A time of parents, fond and smiling. A time of school and sports, swimming and hide-and-seek. A time of college, of friends, of dreams for the future. So many dreams . . .

"Get up."

He jumped at the sound. The voice was deep, commanding. It spoke a foreign language, yet Chandler understood. And obeyed.

"Look at me, slave."

A new kind of pain gripped Chandler, a searing nerve-tingling agony that ran the length of his back. He squeezed his eyes shut.

"I said, look at me."

Chandler looked. Before him stood what had once been a splendid man in some long-gone human lifetime. Through the cloak of the man's transparent dead body, Chandler saw a face that possessed the uniquely beautiful features of multiple ethnicities; cocoa-colored skin and wavy black hair that grew to his shoulders, an aquiline nose and almond-shaped brown eyes. He looked only a little older than Chandler, about twenty-five. His body, the body on the inside from before his murder, looked muscular and fit. But his murdered body, the one that clung like a sticky bubble to his former self—had been deliberately torn apart. Where the man on the inside boasted a proud, chiseled chest, the murdered outer shell showed a gaping, gory hole. His heart had been ripped out.

"Who—who are you?" Chandler asked.

"I am the Overseer. And you are now a slave, just one of many."

"Overseer . . . ?" But even as Chandler formed the question, he saw the Overseer's minions. They gathered behind him, their murdered bodies cloaking normal human forms: Grown men taken in the prime of their lives and mutilated. A pair of twin girls, savaged by the murderer and his crew. An entire household—a man, his wife, his mother, their bodyguards, their secretary, and two housemaids—their dead heads lolling off necks, still dripping water from the river that served as their mass grave. More of the dead crowded in behind them, and their number seemed countless. *How could anyone destroy so much life and get away with it?*

"He killed all of you? All of us?"

"He chose us, claimed our blood, called us to do his will. You will do his will, too."

Chandler's back spasmed. He fell. Even after the agony he'd already endured, pain still controlled his every movement. The Overseer looked on, impassive. Chandler's nerves tingled, his muscles jerking him side-to-side, then upward in twisting contractions. "Why—are you hurting me?"

"It's not me." The Overseer glanced up, where red mist mingled with swirling slate-colored clouds. "Our master calls you. It is your turn to serve."

"Our murderer!"

"Our *master*. You must go."

The pain pulled persistently, lifting Chandler's torso, and then his arms and legs, into the air. Chandler tried to grip the ashy leaves, to cling to the gray ground, but the clay turned to dust in his fingers. He couldn't hold on anymore. Up he went, the pain in his back yanking him, like a marionette, through the blood-spatter and the blind fog, up in a blur.

Abruptly the quality of the atmosphere changed. The air wavered, cleared. Chandler stood in the shed where he had died, next to the harmless-looking cauldron. Its open mouth did not even rise to his knees. Looking at it made him dizzy. Against one of the shed's narrow walls stood an altar draped in white. El Cubano lay on the dirt floor in front of it, his limbs spread out and rigid, his eyelids closed and twitching. At each hand and foot a thick white candle burned. Sweat stood out on his forehead, glistening in the light of the wavering flames.

A wave of rage spurred Chandler toward his killer. He could move about, even in the cloak of ruin and pain that had been his physical body. Three steps took Chandler across the room, ready to destroy this man who had destroyed him. But as he reached to grab his killer by the throat, the candle flames leapt upward, searing him. Their heat formed a shield around the man as he lay on the ground, seeming in a trance. Chandler's spirit quailed; even now he could not defend himself.

You are here at my command.

Chandler jumped. The murderer had not opened his mouth, yet he heard the words, and he knew his killer talked to him. Words of condemnation rose to his lips. When he opened his mouth to speak, though, no sound came out.

You have no voice in the living world. You are mine and must obey. I am your god. Hear me and do as I say!

Something lay on El Cubano's stomach; the man grabbed it with both hands and twisted. Chandler fell to the floor, contorted and gasping. He strained to see what the murderer held. Wavering candle flame cast its light on a flexible length like a bone necklace: pale, spiked with a line of sharp-looking ridges. The pain down the middle of Chandler's back connected with the sight of it, and he knew what the thing was: his own spinal column. A wire stuck through the length of it, holding the vertebrae together. He saw no trace of flesh on the jaundiced bones. *How long have I been dead?* With each savage twist his will weakened.

Look, said El Cubano's thoughts. *This man has offended me.*

An image crowded Chandler's field of vision, and he couldn't look away. A thickset man who lived close to the city. A man with clever eyes and scarred hands, whose name was Fernando and whose adroit drug smuggling had made him rich. Chandler could see El Cubano's envy, his attempt to gain easy riches by reasoning Fernando into some kind of partnership. There were many luxuries the smuggler's money could buy, things the killer felt he deserved. Chandler saw the smuggler's refusal: his luck might change if he took on a partner; why should he take the risk? He tingled with El Cubano's murderous resentment. The killer did not take rejection well.

You will show him his mistake. El Cubano gave Chandler's spine a tweak, just enough to send shrieking twinges through Chandler's spirit-body. He wrung the spine like a washcloth, and Chandler gave himself completely to El Cubano's will. It was the only way to get relief from the pain.

Anything you say, I will do, he thought in reply, knowing El Cubano held full power over him.

Go, slave.

Chandler rose though the ceiling of the shed, to the soft and quiet twilight outside. The wind carried him; his spirit body could fly and this did not surprise him. He knew where he was going, and he arrived in moments. Fernando Castaneda stood at the window of his lavish home office, watching the peaceful twinkling lights of the city beyond. Chandler did not want to hurt this man, but he was sure that something worse than death would happen if he did not do as his killer commanded.

Death had been bad enough. All at once the blind terrified agony of the tortures came back to him, and he knew what he must do. He moved to Fernando, this man savoring the night, and placed both hands on the drug lord's head. The images came easily, and he dumped them all into the drug lord's mind. Pictures of horror, images of blood. Though Chandler could not speak aloud, he directed his thoughts at Fernando and felt him jump in response.

You will feel what your enemy did to me, and you will regret ever going against him.

Chandler, himself, had not gone against anyone. It had all started as the perfect evening to cap off a triumphant senior semester. *A peaceful night with city lights, like this one.* Straight A's assured and an acceptance letter into medical school proudly pinned to the bulletin board above his mother's desk at home. What more could he ask for?

The trip to Mexico had been a last-minute decision, nothing he planned himself. But, "We're kidnapping you," Jory grinned, and the other guys nodded their invitation. "C'mon! Expand your horizons."

In an over-the-border town called Matamoros, they found a bar, and after a few beers and just a touch of cocaine, Chandler felt great, invincible, the exhaustion of his studies forgotten. His friends got restless. There were other bars, and maybe some good-looking women somewhere. He followed the guys out to Jory's car. He stumbled a little and paused for a second, not wanting to fall. And in that moment two sets of hands shoved him from behind, hoisting him onto the bed of a truck he hadn't noticed. Pummeled him until he lay face down. A blanket flipped over him, muffling sight and sound, but not before he heard a man's voice say, "*El Cubano le gustará este.*"

Chandler was Texan, and he understood enough Spanish to make out what the man said: "The Cuban will like this one."

The truck rumbled through the night for a long time. Gradually the vibrations of traffic lessened. The night felt colder. At one point the truck stopped and the four men—two who rode in the truck bed with Chandler, and two who rode in front—beat Chandler, breaking his nose, blacking his eyes, robbing him of breath with punches to the solar plexus. Then the blanket covered him again. He was left to gasp under it until the truck stopped and the men led him to a modest house set in the middle of a large, empty plot of land. Far away, goats bleated and chickens clucked.

The sight of the one they called "El Cubano" might have soothed someone who had not been abducted and beaten at his behest. He looked as if he might still be in his late twenties, with sparkling black eyes and ebony hair worn in a sweeping side part, emphasizing his handsome face. His features were composed in a serene expression that could be read as heavenly innocence. He wore a white caftan, as if given to a life of soothing meditation. Around his neck hung a leather thong with a polished bone charm.

People hovered near this man, protectively, like a celebrity's entourage, but only three of them really stood out to Chandler. A skinny worried-looking man fidgeted with a gun he kept close to his side, seeming only mildly interested at Chandler's appearance. Another man, a hulking, hefty fellow, did not even look at Chandler, but kept his eyes on the leader's handsome face. It was a fiercely possessive stare, the look of an anxious lover. A young, gorgeous woman stood with the men, watching Chandler's entrance as if viewing a theatrical performance, and to Chandler she seemed the strangest of all. She was not shocked or distressed to see him, but instead excited. *This could not be happening!*

"P—please. *Por favor.*" Though he had been the one stolen and brutalized, he felt the need to make some excuse, to explain himself. "I'm—just a student . . . " The words came out *I—jut a tudet . . .* because of his swollen nose. He remembered his Spanish again. "*Estudiante . . .*"

The beautiful woman whispered something to the handsome leader, El Cubano, hiding her lips behind a smooth manicured hand. He nodded. "*Muy bien,* Paulita." He swaggered over, black eyes drinking in Chandler's fear.

"*Tengo poco dinero . . .*"

El Cubano laughed, openly and appealingly, like a delighted child.

The fingers of his left hand lifted and ruffled the fair hair at the back of Chandler's neck. With his right hand he traced Chandler's cheekbone underneath the eye socket, following the contour of the bone down to the jaw. "Little boy."

Chandler stood several inches taller than his captor, but he had never felt so small and helpless.

"Gonna have some fun with you, little boy." The man spoke perfect English, with hardly a trace of accent. This was no stranger from a strange land. He sounded like an American, or at least someone who had spent most of his life in the States. A new knot of dread writhed in Chandler's stomach.

El Cubano looked toward the door. At this signal, the men tightened their grip on Chandler's arms, half-carrying him, half-dragging him to a small shed far from the main house. Chandler was strong, but he was also outnumbered by ruthless men who knew how to fight, subdue, and kill. Once they got him into the shed, the real hurting began.

With El Cubano's guidance and participation, the men set to work on Chandler with their fists, with scalpels, with a cat 'o nine tails, with knives of various sizes, and, lastly, with an ax. Soon he was in so much shock that the torments ran together and emerged in one continuous scream, expressing only one emotion: terror. Terror because of the pain, the most excruciating he ever experienced, pain that never stopped and kept increasing. Terror that if he lived he would be a cripple, a freak. Terror that he would die. Terror at never knowing what would come next. And terror at the random memories that only increased his panic. He remembered the whippings his father had administered with a belt when he was little. He became that child again, knowing the punishment was coming, but helpless to make it stop, no matter what he said or did. Over and over again he blacked out from the pain, only to wake and see the murderer's leering face, mocking him. El Cubano became more familiar to him, it seemed, than any other person he ever knew, his features forever etched in Chandler's mind.

Chandler sensed that what was being done to him had been done to many others in this shed before him, and that it meant a lot—everything, in fact—to this deranged person who was killing him. But this knowledge only added despair to the pain. The torture went beyond anything he thought he could ever endure. And yet, over and over again in a thousand different ways, he did, until that final act of rape as he bled out on the floor . . .

All this he showed to Fernando Castaneda, pouring every bit of hurt, every particle of all-encompassing fear into the man's mind. *Feel it, yes, feel what it is to die like that! See the knife coming at you, but you can't stop it! Bleed and bleed, mud and blood, how does that feel to you? Feel the pain I'm in now, always! How does it feel?*

Someone was crying. Chandler felt empty, his negative energy poured into Fernando, who now shook, gibbering as he retrieved a pistol from his desk. He levered the weapon into his mouth and pulled the trigger. Chandler felt the blast, saw the man's spirit leave its body and vanish. In the lavish office, now splattered with Fernando's blood, Chandler heard the killer's sweet, childlike laugh.

Your task is complete. Return to me!

Sickness seized Chandler as he realized what he had done. He, who suffered so much in his dying, had caused a death. He, too, had become a murderer. Pressure rippled up and down his back as his master called him home. It felt like being reeled in, pulled on a grisly string. Already he was getting used to it. Through the air he flew, every particle of him chained to his killer. This couldn't be his eternity. It couldn't! Yet, inevitably, he saw his killer's modest house below him, spotted the shed, and without understanding how he got inside, stood next to the cauldron once more.

The pain in his back eased. The white candles burned, and El Cubano still lay within the protection of their flames. But his eyes were open now, kindling with an ecstatic expression. Chandler's spinal column lay on the floor, forgotten for the moment. The killer watched, entranced, as a rift split the air directly above him, as if the air were a curtain being ripped away. Beyond the rift shone pure blackness, black as the deep soul of space. El Cubano reached into the rift and took a corner of the blackness, squeezing it in his hands the way he had squeezed Chandler's spine. He pouted his lips, put the corner of the blackness in his mouth, and sucked from it, as if taking a long drink from a magical flask. The darkness pulsed like spurts of blood. As he drank the darkness, his skin began to glow, pulsing in the same rhythm as the pulsing darkness. The candle flames leapt with the pulse, dancing in rhythm. Chandler felt the power, sensing it was of Palo Mayombe, whatever or whoever that could be. It seemed that nothing would ever stop this man if he could take evil from the universe itself. The blindfold mystery of the rift filled Chandler with misery: it reminded him of the cauldron. He would have to return to it soon, back to the netherworld of slavery, until his "master" saw fit to call him to murder again. He would rather jump into the rift, this unknown source of power. Maybe he could escape or gain some of that power . . . Far away in the blackness lurked hints of shining purple and silver, possibly stars or other worlds.

Chandler felt El Cubano staring at him: his eyes so dark, they seemed without pupils, dark as the darkness he devoured. He blinked angrily. With one hand he kept a firm hold on the blackness and, with the other, he reached for the spine on the floor. Chandler hesitated. The dark doorway was deeper than pitch, darker than tarns. A fragment of a saying or proverb from the land of the living flashed through his mind (light, go toward the *light*), but he had to choose: the cauldron or the unknown. In the cauldron Chandler had seen the face of forever, a face of cruelty and subjugation. *No.* He leaped over his killer into the darkness instead, aiming toward the vaguely-glimpsed hints of color and brightness.

For a second Chandler worried that the darkness went nowhere at all; he felt stranded, stuck. Then he felt the darkness push against him, undulating in onrushing and retreating waves, and he started to move in the direction the darkness pushed, slowly at first, and then faster as the darkness began to press more urgently. Then it seemed the undulations gathered together and pushed him all at once. He spun head-over-heels until finding himself standing upright on solid ground. He turned slowly in a circle, confused as to which way he should go.

As he turned, he saw four paths that came together in the middle of a crossroads. In the center, a creature regarded Chandler. It stood perhaps eight feet high, with skin red as a cockscomb. Even its head resembled a bird's, with a sharp black beak pointing straight downward from its red face and small beady eyes. Four long arms with clawed fingers beckoned. It hopped on bare feet with three toes, like a half-coiled spring.

Chandler felt the familiar frisson of fear. Fear and pain were a big part of him now and it seemed strange that, after all he'd been through, he could still worry that more harm would come to him. He wondered at the monster's intention and felt compelled to approach it, though not entirely out of fear. Something about the way it moved and looked at him commanded a kind of weird respect.

"I don't know where to go," he said to the creature. He didn't know if it could understand him. "Could you help me?"

The thing cocked its head at an impossible angle, an irascible bird of prey. Its arms bent awkwardly at right angles to its body, jointed not like human arms but like a bat's wings.

The creature croaked, its voice a marriage of raven and frog. "Give me my name."

"I don't know what it is." Only after he said it did Chandler realize he could speak again. In this dimension, he had a voice.

The creature stomped one of its four feet, which was bare and shaped like an eagle's claw. "I am Lucero Undo. The crossroads belong to me! Only I can show you the way. Yet you come to me and do not know my name?"

"I—I'm sorry."

The creature's four arms skewed in four different directions, its claw-like hands outspread in a blocking motion. "None of these paths are yours to take."

"But—where do I go from here?"

"You have a place, and a people, and a master."

"They aren't mine, and I can't go back. I—" Chandler couldn't hold back the words. "I want justice!"

Lucero's head turned suddenly around, a bird's sharp consideration of possibilities. "Justice? Ahh."

Chandler went on. "The man who did this to me," he said and gestured to the shell of destroyed tissue that hung upon him. "I saw him drinking the blackness that brought me to you. I thought—"

"Drinking it?"

"Yes. And—"

"You must tell *them!*"

Lucero's four hands grabbed Chandler, and the crossroads

dissolved, blurring away and then coming together again in a completely different configuration. Lucero released him, and Chandler stumbled, falling on his knees at the base of a plateau that formed a natural daïs against a backdrop of endless black. Above him on the plateau, a female figure stepped forward.

"Brother Lucero, what have you brought?" Though of giant stature, her build was more delicate, her movements more graceful, than Lucero's. She had a skeletal face and fingers, her skull and teeth like that of a predatory cat's, her fingers overlong. She possessed only two arms, but like Lucero's they jointed in the same bat-like fashion. Her dress was the white of the worm; her pallor, blue dust.

"Greetings, Sister Centella." Lucero released Chandler, pushing him toward the female.

Centella moved forward to examine Chandler. "I know this one," she said. "Slave of pain, insignificant one, the cemetery's secrets are my own. Your bones never knew hallowed ground." She paused, her dress moving as if in a breeze, though no wind blew. "Why aren't you in your place?"

"That is no place that I chose!"

"Such vehement words! You disturb our brother. And at this moment, Seita Rayos has no wish to be disturbed." Centella turned to a massive figure slumped in a throne the color of a threatening sky.

Seita Rayos. *Seven Thunders.* It sounded like a powerful name. Indeed, the being Centella now comforted had huge shoulders and limbs like thick pillars. But his skin was the color of a burned-out bulb. Through the ghastly skin, electric blue and purple veins stood out like inverted lightning bolts. He raised his head to dully regard his sister. He had no face, only moody, shifting clouds. As the clouds gathered and drifted apart, Chandler thought he caught glimpses of facial expressions that just as quickly dissipated, as the dragons and giants he used to see in the clouds as a boy transformed into nebulous blobs. Within the cloud-face sparks sizzled, resembling darting eyes or the gleam of teeth. But they flashed so brightly that Chandler could not look at the face for long.

Centella leaned solicitously toward him. "Dear Brother Rayos. I have never seen you so ill."

Lucero hopped up and down excitedly, an angry bird in a cage, all of his many fingers pointing at Chandler. "This one has seen, can tell us why the fire of Seita Rayos's justice cannot fall!"

Centella seemed amused at Lucero's impatience. "What can you tell us, lost dead boy?"

"The one who took my life drinks this blackness." Chandler

indicated the vast dark all around them. "He commands many of the dead, like me, to kill still more, because, he says, he is a god."

Centella spoke in a voice like wind chimes. "We live on blood and worship."

Puffs of cloud formed a square angry mouth in Rayos's ever-changing face. "But *this*"—one massive arm moved up to acknowledge the surrounding black—"is not for a human to claim."

Lucero's head swiveled freely. "On this one I smell many others, Sister. Their blood not freely given, their service all for one who steals our glory for himself!"

Centella tapped her bone fingers together. "Such powerful lust steals my brother's strength. And while he is ill there is no one to avenge those who were sacrificed in blasphemy."

"No one to show them their true paths!" Lucero screeched.

Fires like eyes in Rayos's cloud-face. "If I could but stand in his presence, Sister, this thief would know my vengeance."

Chandler said, "I can help you get him."

Rayos chuckled. "You? The broken spirit? The little slave?"

"I want to help. Let me." As he said it, Chandler knew there was something left of the carefree college boy who had wanted so badly to become a doctor. He felt truly like himself for the first time since he'd died.

Slowly, Seita Rayos stood up. Distant thunder rolled. "Let us go together," he said.

Lucero cartwheeled with all four arms like a renegade star, leading the way. "I will guide you."

And though none of them moved, instantly they stood in the shed of El Cubano once more. Rayos had to bend nearly double to fit under the low ceiling. Centella looked with cold disdain upon the killer, who sat cross-legged in the middle of the floor, in the exact spot where Chandler had breathed his last breath. He had fortified his defenses, surrounding himself completely with a ring of burning white candles. He opened his eyes, but he looked and spoke only ·to Chandler. Apparently the killer could not see the gods standing in his lair, close enough to touch him.

You did not go to back with the other slaves as I ordered! Your willfulness will be punished. Angrily he pointed at the cauldron. *Go back to your place.*

No! Chandler could not speak the word, but he stood firm, shaking his head. El Cubano held Chandler's spine in his lap, frantically twisting it, but Chandler no longer felt the pain. A look of dismay crossed the killer's face. The expression looked deliciously silly to Chandler.

The Overseer will not *be pleased.* The killer closed his eyes and trembled with concentration. A noise like an earthquake came from the cauldron as the Overseer rose out of it, full-sized. The Overseer indicated a belt at his waist. Chandler recognized the instruments that had been used to bring about his death: the whip, the ax, the knives. The Overseer nodded as if to confirm that all these would be used on Chandler again until he complied. The Overseer turned and blanched to behold Seita Rayos's huge shoulders and massive frame taking up nearly the entire shed.

Centella inclined her head toward the Overseer, and he returned the courtesy. "You see us," she said. "Your allegiance is ours, not this impostor's." At her words the Overseer resembled the young man he had once been, young and full of wonder.

Chandler directed his thoughts to him. *The gods are on our side. Do you want to be free?*

The Overseer blinked, tears warming his cold eyes.

Can you command the others?

The Overseer nodded, and El Cubano stood up. *How dare you? Don't you know what I can do? I am your god! Obey!*

Centella stepped to the killer's protective circle of candles and exhaled gently. The attending breeze that stirred her skirts gathered strength in the windowless shed. The slender candle flames faltered, then guttered, disappearing entirely into their wicks as if yanked down by unseen hands. A cry issued from the Overseer's mouth, a primal howl made of a thousand tortured screams. The cauldron rumbled, then burst as the dead rose out of it, a dismembered mob slavering for revenge.

It was sweet to see fear in the murderer's face. El Cubano did not linger to wrangle with his recalcitrant slaves. He ran, pursued by the open-mouthed anguish of those he murdered, out the door of the shed and onto the barren land outside, hushed with the heaviness of evening. The dead tore at him, trying to bring him down as he ran to the nearest truck, jumped in, and slammed the door. The engine turned over, and the truck bumped over rough land on its way to the main road. The Overseer held up a hand to prevent further pursuit. It had been enough; the cauldron would no longer be their prison.

Chandler watched the retreating truck. "Where will he go?"

The clouds of Rayos's face clustered into crinkled brows and determined chin. "He cannot hide from us. The spell is broken." His arm reached up into the sky and brought down a lightning bolt, moving and flashing pale blue fire. Rayos tossed the bolt like a javelin in El Cubano's direction. "Justice will sear him soon."

"You did well, all of you," Centella said to the dead who now kneeled before her and her dark-bright brother. "The blasphemer's time is near. Go to Lucero Mundo. Let him show you the way."

The dead rose as one, but separate and alone each drifted away to the paths of Lucero. When all were gone, the Overseer knelt, kissing Centella's fleshless hand. He glanced at Chandler, placing his fist to his heartless chest in salute before he, too, drifted away on the wind.

Chandler remained next to them. The time had not come for him to relinquish all earthly affairs. "I want to go with you," he said. "I want to see it done."

Chandler did not know how much time passed, but it was another night when he and Centella and the mighty Rayos at last materialized inside a room in a tenement in Mexico City. The killer and his skinny bodyguard had argued, loudly and at length. Now the skinny man lay on the floor, dead, the smoke of a discharged gun fouling the air. The heavy bodyguard, lover of El Cubano, looked on, aghast. The beautiful woman who shared in their exploits started to cry at the sound of heavy footsteps on the stairs.

"¡La policia!" Paulita sobbed.

"Justice is at his door," Seita Rayos said. His presence filled the dingy room with light. "It's time to bring him to us."

Centella smiled. "Leave that to me, Brother."

At the sound of knocking on the door, the killer grimly grinned, handing Paulita a machine gun. "Here." His male lover clung to him as if he would never let go. "They're not going to get me alive." El Cubano's lover nodded agreement. "Either of us. Shoot us both."

The woman hesitated, leaning away to try and see out the window. Nervously she tightened her grip on the gun, her blood-red fingernails clicking together.

"¡Hazlo ahora! Do it now, Paulita! Or I'll make you in suffer in hell."

She licked her lips. Chandler didn't think she would actually pull the trigger.

Centella glided to Paulita as she stared straight ahead. She could not see the goddess, but shivered in her presence. Centella traced the skull tattoo on the girl's shoulder. "With my blessing," she said.

The girl shut her eyes and pulled the trigger, spraying the two men with bullets just as the police crashed into the room. As they fell, killer and lover, Chandler felt buoyant . . . alive. Something about him changed; something had slipped away. Chandler looked down. At his feet lay his corpse, no longer clinging to him. *Released.* He held up his hands and saw his inner self, perfect and unencumbered; the self he was now free to be.

Chandler heard a moan of surprise. Near the room's ceiling the killer's spirit floated. Swiftly Rayos plucked him down, wringing El Cubano playfully between viselike hands, ignoring his silent screams.

"His power is gone." Rayos said. "He will know how difficult it can be, this hell he speaks of." He wrung and crushed El Cubano's spirit until it disappeared, then held up his hands for Centella's approval.

Centella smiled, and her smile was a sweet summer rain that cleanses the cemetery stones. Her skeleton hand reached for Chandler's. "You can rest now," she said.

As the brother and sister began to fade from Chandler's sight, Rayos remarked. "There is still much justice to mete out on this blasphemer. Let us see to it, Sister."

Faintly, Centella's voice called: "And you, Lucero, will see to this one?"

Lucero croaked, "I will."

He appeared at Chandler's side. All around them the black endless vastness winked with its streaks of purple and silver.

El Cubano's screams, audible now, echoed through the blackness, growing steadily louder, but Chandler felt no need anymore to witness the man's ultimate fate. Far in the distance, the strange sky began to lighten. The blood and the blackness belonged in the past. Yes, this was far better, looking out into this miracle of a dawning day. At a shake of Lucero's head, stars materialized and aligned, forming a trail of white-hot silver, enticing as a bridal veil, to a far-off golden dawn.

"What is it?" Chandler asked in wonder.

"A new path." Lucero pointed toward the trail with his four strange arms. "Yours."

Chandler moved toward the light, eager to discover its mysteries. At last, forever had a face he wanted to see.

Kelly Dunn began her writing career in journalism, churning out copy and editing trade magazines covering subjects from human resources to infotainment. She has worked as a stage actress, a university instructor, and a hearse dealer. These experiences inform her fiction, which first appeared in e-zines such as Necrotic Tissue *and* Aberrant Dreams. *Her stories have since been featured in the anthologies* The Dead That Walk, Midnight Walk, *and* The Undead That Saved Christmas, Vol. 2. *Kelly is the editor of the horror fiction anthology,* Mutation Nation, *published by Rainstorm Press. Kelly's alter ego, Savannah Kline, has written an urban fantasy novel,* Beloved of the Fallen, *published by Ulysses Press.*

THE UNFINISHED LUNCH

TREVOR DENYER

When something dies, it is expected that the body will rot and its fluids leak out and absorb into the ground. But what if it is the same with the spirit? Rather than an essence that floats free of the flesh, the soul of life may merely spill out and soak into the first thing it comes in contact with, leaving us with nothing but memories and regret. Trevor Denyer offers a poignant glimpse at just such an idea. If the cosmic joker has its way, you may find yourself left behind in The Unfinished Lunch.

What is dead?

I know I'm communicating something. If I can do that, am I dead? My mortal shell is miles away, cooling and stiffening in a panicked office.

From where I am, the view is impressive. Paris as the sun rises is a wonderful sight. The panorama is one of low-level buildings, glinting orange and gold. The morning rush—disgorging humanity onto warming streets—has not yet started.

From the top of the Eiffel Tower I sense the stirring breeze. I watch birds glide on rising currents of air, their wings wide and still like the arms of crosses, as they curve toward a hazy blue sky.

I have retained a form of consciousness, and memories of my former life remain. So am I dead?

My sense of time is the same, moving forward at the same apparent speed. I'm not sure how I came to be here, or how death transported me from lunchtime to early morning.

I remember sitting in the office. I motioned at her salad and said, "Don't let your lunch get cold, Sheila." An attempt at witticism.

She smiled as she concentrated on the computer screen in front of her. "I'll just check this one, dear, and then I'll finish it."

"Give me fish and chips any day," I said as the clot broke free and headed toward my heart.

"Not if you're dieting," she replied.

"Come on, you don't need to diet."

She turned and looked at me, the unstated fear of being overweight skulking in her eyes. "If you saw me as I *really* am, you'd know," she said.

Then I died.

I'm not exactly corporeal, though the stem of my consciousness is embedded in the unfinished lunch that now sits on top of the Eiffel Tower.

It consists of two crispbreads, some cottage cheese, coleslaw, a scattering of raw vegetables (cauliflower, carrot, and broccoli) and a smudged dollop of mayonnaise upon a white china plate. The plate is decorated around the rim with painted plums and cherries, their green stems and leaves intertwined. My soul, for want of a better description, appears to be bound to the food and the plate.

No doubt, during the panic that ensued following my death, Sheila didn't immediately miss her lunch. She's so capable, always the organizer. I expect she telephoned for the ambulance. She may even have attempted to resuscitate me.

The thought of her wide, sensuous lips over mine makes me regret that I didn't make more effort to achieve such intimacy when I could have appreciated it. There'd been pheromonal hints and small invasions of personal space—the brushing of bodies, arched looks, coy smiles. It's only now that I can appreciate what might have been.

Maybe that's why I've ended up in her lunch. I've felt for a long time that there's a cosmic joker overseeing us all. We're just pawns in a game that goes on and on.

How did Sheila's lunch manage to transport itself to Paris? It's as if the fabric of reality and my ethereal composition have enabled such a transfer. The irony is not lost on me. This was the place Beth and I came on our honeymoon when we edged into our twenties. This was the place where we lost ourselves, caught in the enchantment of delirious love and overwhelming passion. I remember how she drained me, and I her. Lying spent in the king-size bed in a hotel, we viewed the Eiffel Tower through a window, as the sun's rising delineated the structure's complex latticework of wrought iron, silhouetted against the gold of early morning.

We only managed to scale it to the second platform. There was a reason, lost to me now, why we could not go to the top. We didn't care. We were in love and it was enough to be in Paris, even though we could only afford sausage, mash, and a carafe of red wine in a backstreet café for lunch.

It seems that I've made it to the top level now. I'm balanced on the edge, and my essence can look upon the dizzying panorama before me. I smile to myself, conscious of the act, yet with no physical change to my absurd situation.

I reflect upon how I used to attach vast importance to things that now appear to be inconsequential and unimportant. If only I'd had the guts to do what my heart told me rather than my head. If only I'd been more understanding, especially when Beth and I lost our child. He was six weeks old and died smothered in his sheet, consumed by cot death.

I want to cry, but no tears come. This unfinished meal is sterile, pointless. I realize that it's a testament to my failed ambitions and spoiled relationship.

The cosmic joker's had the last laugh. My heart let me down, and I'm part of something completely unimportant—Sheila's unfinished meal.

My past life appears insignificant in relation to *The Great Scheme of*

Things. There is a bitter satisfaction in knowing I was right about the cosmic joker; it wasn't just my inadequate response to the failings in my life. I'm disappointed, yet elated.

If that was not the case, why are we wrong-footed so often? Why is it that people who become jittering wrecks when confronted by the dentist require treatment at every check up?

Why do simple jobs become complicated and always take far longer than expected? Why is the one tool that would help never in the tool box?

Why do so many people spend their lives in jobs that don't fulfill them, or run contrary to their natural abilities?

There are millions of unanswered questions.

As I settle here, under the rays of the rising sun, I think about my family. I suppose, at thirty-three, I was young to have a heart attack, for I'm sure that's what got me. All those wasted hours I spent exercising, especially after Beth and I separated; the cost of gym membership—but then I did like my food. It offered comfort, like a winding-sheet, alluring yet deceptive as the calories stuck to my arteries, foreshadowing my death.

Mum will be devastated. Dad will dribble into his dinner, but his eyes will tear-up. He'll be thinking, within his arthritically ravaged body and burned out mind, that it should have been him. Yet the cosmic joker doesn't work that way. Dad will be kept alive until every part of his humanity has been sucked out by pain.

I want to cry out, *"You damned psychopath! If you have to make an example of me, you've done it in this bizarre way, but leave my dad alone!"*

Of course, I can't speak. I can only think it, as the rising warmth of the sun curdles the cottage cheese. I want to weep but can't. Sheila's lunch cannot be moistened.

Poor mum. She tried to warn me in her own way. I took umbrage at what I felt was nagging. I already knew she never 'approved' of Beth. She made it clear many times, especially after the break-up. It seemed as though she felt such an attitude would help me recover, by degrading the feelings that haunted me.

I'd told her that morning I was fed up with her. I'd lost all respect for her because of the constant carping about my weight and my heavy-duty diet. I hadn't mentioned Beth, though the implication was there in my whining. After all, I exercised. My reasoning was that such activity would cancel out the effects of over-eating and overweight.

I'd smile if I could. My heart obviously disagreed.

At one time I believed that the reason for this constant resistance to easy options was to test us. Life was a series of tests, and the way you solved the problems and dealt with the obstacles determined the level at which you entered the next phase of existence.

Then I became cynical, and the cosmic joker idea grew in my mind. I found comfort in this because it meant that whatever I did or didn't do in my life would make no difference in the end.

I wonder about that. Perhaps my belief has landed me in this mess. Maybe the next level of existence is determined by the beliefs you adopt during the preceding existence.

God is what you understand him, or her, or it, to be.

Ending up in Sheila's lunch, perched above a beautiful city, is the biggest joke of all. It may be that, as the food decays, so will I. My soul, and with it my anguish, will fade away and I'll simply cease to exist.

I snigger into the coleslaw and, to my surprise, make it bubble. When the panic is over, Sheila may wonder what happened to her lunch. She'll probably decide that someone threw it away when tidying up.

After all, there has to be a logical explanation, doesn't there?

Paris is coming alive. Spring is here and birds are singing. People move along wide gray streets, and vehicles carry others to work. The sound of engines drifts upwards like a soft exhalation. The smell of carbon mixes with sunlight and the scent of apple blossoms.

The city fades away. Colors melt and slip into grayness. I hover over the plate as the solidity of the food shifts like a bowel movement. There is an echo of laughter.

I'm sorry. I don't want to believe in a cosmic joker.

I'm embarrassed to find myself in the middle of a four-poster bed. To either side are mounds. Beneath the covers, two people lie; a bride and a groom. Confetti is everywhere, spread around the room from the open suitcase, in multi-colored confusion.

Once more, I'm confounded. Where am I? How did I manage to transport from the Eiffel Tower to this intimate boudoir? The impish echo of laughter fades as I puzzle over something I have no hope of understanding. The cosmic joker analogy is all I can use to try and rationalize my situation.

Despite my confusion, my curiosity is stimulated. Why do they sleep with their backs to each other? Newly-weds make love, don't they? Newly-weds hold each other close in the private warmth of the bed.

They sleep, exhausted after consummation, clinging together at the edge of destiny.

There's a stirring. She pulls herself from sleep and sits up. Her face is pale and her hair hangs in tangled webs of blonde. The shock of recognition stuns me.

Beth!

But it isn't her. This is the same room in the same hotel. From the window, between gently billowing net curtains, is the Eiffel Tower, silhouetted against the dawn.

She rubs her eyes and looks again.

"What's this?" she says, shaking him and pointing at me.

He grumbles under the covers, dragging himself from sleep. As he sits up I'm almost overturned.

"What?" he asks.

"This plate, this . . . stuff."

"I don't know. Did you order a late supper or something?"

"No, but I might as well have, for all the use *you* were last night."

Guilt glistens on his forehead.

"Yea, I'm sorry, love. Had a bit too much to drink." Echoes from the future.

She laughs. The sound is rough and coarse. "You're not bloody kidding! How d'you feel now?"

He smiles at her, his lips sticky from sleep. He wipes them on his arm and moves closer to her.

"A bit *stiff*, actually." He smiles again, and the resentment between them evaporates.

They come together, and I'm thrown to the floor. I feel myself scattering across the carpet. The shock makes me weak. I remember falling on the sidewalk as a child. The hard flagstones scraped the skin from my hands and knees. I cried.

I want to cry now as I survey my broken life. The anguish of knowing that this is what it has come to crushes my soul as I moisten the carpet with mayonnaise, coleslaw, and cottage cheese.

The bride and groom moan in ecstasy. I want to warn them:

Live for today. Love for today. Hold on to life while you can, and don't treat it as a joke. Grasp the opportunities that come your way and use them.

They don't hear, of course. They climax in ignorance.

The room is fading. I'm lost again. Loneliness overwhelms me. If I had a body, the tears would never end. I don't want to be like this. I want these thoughts to end. If only the memories of failure would slip into grayness, like the city.

The anguish melts away as if it had never been. Wisps of light gather together and solidify. Brightness and warmth surround me as the universal soul eases me from the ruins of Sheila's lunch.

I am an empty vessel.

I wait to be reborn.

Trevor Denyer has been published in many magazines including Scheherazade, Nasty Piece of Work, Enigmatic Tales, Symphonie's Gift, *and* Night Dreams. *He received an Honorable Mention in Ellen Datlow's* Year's Best Fantasy & Horror *and has appeared on line at* Time Out Net Books *and* Gathering Darkness. *His work has appeared in a number of anthologies including* Nasty Snips *and* Gravity's Angels.

More recently, he has been published in the Evil Jester Press anthology, Help! Wanted: Tales of On-The-Job Terror *and* A Feast of Frights From The Horror Zine. *His work has also appeared in the e-zines,* Estronomicon *(Screaming Dreams Press) and* Tales From The River *(Dark River Press).*

His collection, The Edge of the Country *is available through the website below. He is the creator and editor of the critically acclaimed* Roadworks, Legend, *and* Midnight Street *magazines. Visit the website at* www.midnightstreet.co.uk.

I WAS THE WALRUS

STEVE CAMERON

Mankind is a complex species with an exceptional amount of variation across the world, from the philosophical differences in politics and religion to the physical differences in the patterns of our fingerprints and the nitrogen base of our DNA. So what is it that links us all together; what is the origin of our "commonality"? Is it that we share the same traits, we can reason and communicate? Or is it that we all descended together from the same random mutation of a primate? Or, perhaps, is there something even greater linking us all together? I Was The Walrus *follows the revelation of one man as he seeks the meaning of our existence.* Goo Goo Ga Joob, *indeed . . .*

My mother says that when I was four years old I told her I was John Lennon's friend. She was driving into the city, me strapped safely in the back seat, when *I Am The Walrus* came on the radio.

"It's John," I said. "He's my friend."

"What?" my mother asked, not sure if she'd heard correctly.

"John," I repeated. "He played on a rooftop with Paul. John's my friend."

My mother stared at me in the rear view mirror. A moment later she rear-ended another car. Once we got home, she asked me about John. I couldn't recall him at all. From that time on my mother was a rabid Beatles fan.

And a firm believer in reincarnation.

There is no way I could have known about The Beatles' rooftop session, or even who John Lennon was. I was paraded before a stream of past-life experts and child psychologists, Buddhists monks, and psychics, but none of them retrieved any further memories. As an adult I've watched the rooftop session of *Let It Be* many times, looking for clues as to who I might have been. I've scoured the faces of the friends, the families, the assistants and employees; all those who were there on that cold January morning.

I've recently come to suspect that I was probably their roadie, Mal Evans.

I suppose I should tell you about myself.

My name is Rob Winters. I'm a forty-three year old insurance assessor, a pretty awful guitar player, and an amateur astronomer. I have a passing interest in science and have been known to read big books that I can barely understand. I've been dating a woman named Sandy Allen for around three years. She's taller than me, blonde and lithe with a toothy grin and a crooked smile that I absolutely adore.

One night late last year we had a fight. I had planned to go stargazing with a few friends. Sandy planned for us to visit her sister. We argued. She called me selfish and uncaring. I said the same things about her. She pleaded with me not to go. I went anyway.

I still think I was right and she was wrong. The problem is, I can see her point of view and believe she was right as well.

That was the night I now call 'wine on the fire.'

I told you I was an amateur astronomer, right?

Several times a year I head out to a dark sky site with my telescope and a few friends. We listen to music, have a few drinks, and observe the wonders of the universe. Sometimes we simply sit and talk and watch for meteors and satellites.

It was the night of the argument with Sandy. We were just about to set up the scopes when a band of heavy clouds rolled in, obscuring the entire sky. The stars gradually faded from north to south and put an early end to our night's viewing. The four of us, me and Mick and Emma and Jeff, retired to the bunkhouse, a corrugated iron shed with a few beds and a kitchen area attached. For hours we drank, and talked, and laughed. Sometime after midnight we went back outside. It was cold and we lit a gas barbecue and gathered around, trying to keep warm. Some nights are beer nights, others are scotch. This was definitely a red wine night. We had a few bottles of local shiraz and drank quite liberally. Emma spilled some on the hotplate and the grill. She said it was deliberate, but I'm not so sure. There was a loud sizzle, a plume of white steam, and a pungent, burnt fruity odor. We all laughed, so she did it again.

Over the next few hours, as we drank more and more wine, I think we all poured some on the fire. We huddled closer, trying to stay warm, and discussed string theory, quantum entanglement, and other scientific concepts none of us understood completely.

Jeff then told us about a theory he'd recently read.

Apparently some PhD suggested the entire universe consists of one single particle, endlessly bouncing back and forth through time from the big bang to the big collapse. On each trip it passes through every point in time in a slightly different position. As such, everything in the universe consists of a combination of the one particle on different trips.

I'm not a physicist, but it sounds like complete crap to me.

So why do I now believe I was Mal Evans in a previous life?

A few weeks after 'wine on the fire,' I had a disturbing dream in which I was shot. I dreamed I was in my bedroom. I'd just had a violent and noisy argument with a friend who came to visit. I picked up an air rifle and laughed as I pointed it at him. We were both stoned, and I decided to leave rather than keep fighting. As I tried to push past him, shouting voices told me to drop the weapon. My girlfriend had called the police. I tried to let go of the gun, but I was confused and waved it around instead. I heard a series of shots and felt the burning impact and immediate pain as four bullets pierced my chest. I crashed to the floor and my mouth became metallic.

Everything sounded muffled, as though underwater. I died a moment later.

The air rifle wasn't even loaded.

Did you know Mal Evans was shot dead by police four years before John Lennon died? Did you know that John says '*shoot me*' over the opening bars of *Come Together*? Were you aware he was fascinated by shootings? Or that when John met Andy Warhol all he could ask over and over again was how Warhol felt when it happened to him?

For John, maybe happiness really was a warm gun.

I don't want you to think Mal Evans is the only person I've ever been in my dreams. I've dreamed of many others since I was a child. My dreams have always been vivid and very easily recalled, but over the past few years they've increased in frequency and clarity. Most of them are just regular dreams; walking along a street, going camping, making love to Sandy. But some of them have been too real, too intense, and certainly too detailed and accurate for my own personal knowledge and education.

I've dreamt I was a Viking, arriving on distant shores in longboats with my brothers. We spoke in tongues I've never heard before and crept toward villages which we pillaged and torched. I've been a maid in a medieval castle, waiting upon a lady who wore the finest clothes and jewels. I've spent time as a miner in the north of England, and a woodsman in ancient Japan. With my husband I ran a bookstore in 1940's New York, and hunted buffalo on the American plains alongside my fellow warriors. I've been a hairdresser in Sydney and a gangster in Chicago. I've even played the drum in a German marching band during World War I.

Do you believe in reincarnation?

I used to wonder why documented cases of past-life regression always seem to feature iconic figures from history. These devotees recount endless tales of having been the Queen of Sheba, or Louis XIV, or a famous Chinese emperor; never simply Maurice, the file clerk. I now have a theory as to why this is the case.

These famous figures impacted our history. Bigger stones cause larger ripples. They were generally larger-than-life characters, with egos and charisma to match. If someone has lived many times, experienced many lives, which one is most likely to be remembered; the Shah of Iran, or a slave in the American south? And so most people only remember the famous ones.

Two lives connected through time. Bell's theorem of quantum entanglement. One particle is spun, the other responds accordingly.

Of course, I'm the exception to the rule. I can even remember being Maurice, the file clerk.

I've tried talking to Sandy about it, but she just laughs and says they're only dreams. She's a systems analyst and tends to think logically. Nothing I say will convince her of how real my dreams are.

I visited a church a few months ago and spoke to the minister. I sat opposite him in his functional office. Wood panel and bookshelves around us, a desk and belief system in between.

"Do you believe in reincarnation?" I asked.

He shook his head. "No," he said. "Do you?"

"Yes, I think so."

"Why?"

I told him of my dreams, about the memories I'd had of other people's lives, about the day I told my mother I knew John Lennon.

"Dreams," he said. "They can be surprisingly clear. A few forgotten memories and images that combine and create a narrative that seems to make sense to us in our sleep. We search for meaning within them, but we don't really understand them or how they're formed."

"What about the Lennon thing?" I asked. "That wasn't a dream."

He leaned back in his chair. "Perhaps you saw a Beatles special on TV. A documentary with interviews and videos. Somehow you were later able to make a connection between the man and the song. The mind works in mysterious ways."

"As does God?" I suggested.

"Indeed," he said and laughed. "As does God."

"But doesn't the Bible say that men are born again? Doesn't that suggest reincarnation?"

"Ah, yes," he said. "I've heard that one many times. The Bible is not talking about literal rebirth, but a spiritual one. We live once, we die once."

"I've read that Jesus and Buddha were different incarnations of the same being."

"I've read that too," he said. "Doesn't make it true." He smiled. "I believe Jesus was sent here by God, the Father, to show us how to live. Jesus came to Earth to experience everything man experiences so we, as humans, can relate better to God. So we can have a close, personal relationship with him."

"God needed to experience the human condition?"

"He didn't *need* to," he said. "He *chose* to. He did it for us, not for him, so we could recognize he understood what it was like to be human."

"He wouldn't know what it's like to be me," I said. "He really only experienced being one man, Jesus. And even then, Jesus didn't die. He doesn't know what it's like to die." .

"Jesus *did* die," he said. "But then he rose from the dead and was lifted to heaven."

Like smoke, I thought. *Wine on the fire.*

I thanked him for his time and left.

A few weeks ago I had another strange dream.

It was night. I opened the car door and stepped out, my wife beside me. I carried a bunch of cassette tapes. Together we walked the short distance to the archway that led to our apartment building. I saw a man standing in the shadows, and I knew I'd seen him before. As I passed, I nodded at him and he stepped out into the streetlight. He called my name just as I reached the entranceway. Before I could turn around I heard a loud bang, and then another, and some more. Four bullets hit my back, knocking me to the ground. The cassette tapes clattered across the pavement. I felt stabs of heat in my back and chest, and my throat filled with blood. I choked, unable to breathe clearly. I managed to get to my hands and knees, and tried to crawl up the steps.

"I've been shot. I've been shot," I croaked, and then collapsed. All I heard was Yoko screaming. The dream was over.

This wasn't the first time I'd died like this.

Now I have a problem.

How can my experiences be reincarnation when I've been both Mal Evans *and* John Lennon? They were both alive at the same time, spent many years together as friends, and died only a few years apart.

To make matters worse, last week I dreamt I was Sandy.

As Sandy, I sat at home reading the newspaper. The phone rang and I answered it. It was my sister. We chatted for a few minutes, then she told me she was taking a trip to Thailand and invited me along. I didn't hesitate. I needed a break and thought Rob wouldn't mind. He'd probably enjoy the time alone.

The next morning, I told Sandy of my dream. She stared at me, wide-eyed and furrowed brow, then told me her sister had rung her the day before and the conversation had occurred exactly as I described it.

How can I be the reincarnate of my girlfriend who is sitting in the next room as I type this?

In the last few days the memories have flooded in. I no longer have to be asleep.

I was my mother, giving birth to me. I was my father, making love to her nine months earlier and then skipping out when he learned she was pregnant. I was Mark David Chapman and I was John Lennon. I was Lee Harvey Oswald and I was John F. Kennedy, John Wilkes Booth and Abraham Lincoln, James Earl Ray and Martin Luther King. I pulled the trigger, and I fell under the impact of the bullets. I was the assassin and the victim.

I was Mal Evans and John Lennon, George Harrison and Linda McCartney. I am the eggman and the walrus. And the walrus was Paul as well. John almost understood it. He got very close in that song. *I am he as you are he . . .*

I am Rob Winters and Sandy Allen. I am the Pope and the Dalai Lama, Shiva the destroyer and the goddess Kali, Athena and Isis, the Buddha and the Christ.

I'm a South African billionaire, an Italian industrialist, a Korean TV star, a Russian drug addict, a Peruvian violinist, a Greek politician, and a Moroccan housewife.

I've suffered through plague, violence, malnutrition, accidents and disease. I've died at the hands of executioners, warriors, murderers, and abusive husbands.

Black and white, rich and poor, male and female, old and young, famous and infamous, and unknown. I am them all. I have lived and died more than a hundred billion times. And, like TV channels, I can flick through all their experiences and memories.

Goo Goo Ga Joob.

Remember the particle theory from 'wine on the fire'? What if the same is true for souls? What if there is only one soul, bouncing back and forward through time, reincarnating as every single person who has ever lived?

This can be the only explanation.

The minister was partly right. God does indeed plan to experience humanity, but he has chosen to do so by being every single human that has ever lived. How else could he truly understand us?

And guess what.

It's me. I've been every single person who has ever lived. I'm the final chapter, the last life in a very long list.

The next time I create a universe, I'll get it right. This time I'll know what it is to truly be human in its myriad of experiences, in all its shame, horror, despair, joy, and glory.

Outside it's dark. I sip my wine and look up through the window and see the stars disappearing one at a time.

Is matter ceasing to exist around me or is there simply a cloud rolling in? Now that I finally realize I'm God, will I soon return to an omniscient existence outside the constraints of time?

It could happen at any moment, the universe could end, even in the middle of—

Steve Cameron *began writing fiction in 2009. Born in Scotland, he was raised in Australia before residing in Japan for six years. He has worked as a police officer, an English Language instructor, a software developer, a charity store manager, and currently teaches English and Drama in a Secondary College. Steve is also an amateur astronomer and musician. He resides in the eastern suburbs of Melbourne with his wife, Lindsey. For more news and information visit* www.stevecameron.com.au.

THE DEVIL'S BACKBONE

LARRY HODGES

Some people live truly virtuous lives while, conversely, others are downright evil. Considering the traditional sense of Heaven and Hell, it's easy to conclude where the hardliners will end up. However, on the great sliding scale of sanctity, most of us fall somewhere in between, our lives filled with assorted chunks of "good" and "bad." Where we ultimately end up may depend on the passing fancy of our celestial judges, and it wouldn't be unimaginable if conflict arose over "who goes where." Larry Hodges brings us The Devil's Backbone, *a holding area for souls that Satan's marked claimed, whether they belong there or not. One man is determined to make his escape or, at the very least, return a modicum of civility to the tortured. Because, after all, wouldn't Hell be a bit more bearable if ice cream were available?*

I died because of an ice cream bar.

At first I didn't hear the screaming kid because of *The Entertainer*, the noxious music my Good Humor ice cream truck played, as I finished off my lunch; a third chocolate éclair. Then I saw him in the mirror sprinting after me, waving a bill and yelling that he wanted a chocolate candy center crunch bar. Grinning to myself, I came to a stop, looking forward to ice cream dribbling down the face of another satisfied customer.

Normally I do all sales from the ice cream truck's window. But the kid kept pointing at the menu and asking something—I never did find out what—and so I got out of the truck to see what he wanted. It was just bad luck that I had stopped in the intersection, and it was more bad luck that an eighteen wheeler, no doubt late on his delivery, chose to enter the intersection at the same time, driving at a speed that could not possibly be legal. Guess who won that confrontation?

I got smooshed. It hurt like crazy at first, but then the pain went away. I rose out of my body and drifted slowly upward. Slowly, because there was a weight of past evil on my soul, and perhaps whoever arranges these things wanted to make it clear that they hadn't forgotten the horrible things I'd done and didn't want to seem too enthusiastic about bringing me up.

Then a gigantic red hand came out of the ground, right from under the tree-lined rows of suburban houses and their neatly mowed lawns. Houses crumbled like pottery while cars flew about like popcorn. Did I mention the hand was huge? It seemed about a quarter mile long, with gnarled, hairy fingers that ended in pointed fingernails. It could have crushed Yankee Stadium with ease.

Instead, it reached above my floating soul and, with the tip of a fingernail, swatted it like a gnat back into my broken body. I sat up on the pavement, slightly dazed. But I quickly became alert—a hand the size of Manhattan waving over you has that effect. I scrambled back into my ice cream truck as it reached for me.

I slammed the accelerator all the way down and sped away from that gargantuan hand. I watched it in the mirror coming out of the ground after me like a twisting snake. Fingers a hundred feet wide stretched toward me; my ice-cream truck was little more than an ant to it. It lunged at me several times but, luckily, ants are hard to grab. I jerked the wheel side-to-side and stomped the gas, slipping between the fingers.

I was up to sixty when it finally grabbed my truck between the pointed nails of its thumb and index finger, like tweezers holding a tiny bug with spinning wheels. Only these tweezers were like the Twin Towers before some evil guys with 666's on them—like I once had—knocked them down.

Then the hand retracted back into its gigantic hole, with me and my ice cream truck dangling between its fingernails. We sank downward at an impossible speed and, in freefall, I floated up to the ceiling of my ice cream truck as my stomach heaved. I threw up the chocolate éclairs.

We came to a sudden stop and I slammed back down onto my seat. I opened my eyes, which I hadn't even realized I'd closed, and saw a brief glimpse of a gigantic red face leering down at me from under a pair of curved horns—either the Devil himself, or I was having a bad nightmare. It opened its mouth, and the hand—its hand—plunged in. The horizon was suddenly all huge, pointed teeth. A gigantic gob of saliva hit the ice cream truck like a raindrop from Hell, knocking me about like an inner tube in Niagara Falls. Then the hand plunged over the giant tongue, past that weird flap of skin that hangs in the back of your mouth, and into the throat.

The giant red hand glowed in the dark, allowing me to see. I'd closed my eyes in fright earlier, but now I was too scared to close them. Other than my heart, which beat like *The Flight of the Bumblebee*, I was frozen in place.

The hand reached the huge cavern that must have been its stomach. Then, using its three free fingers and their pointed fingernails like knives, it tore a hole through its own flesh in the side of the stomach. The hand plunged into the other side and came to a stop. I looked down and gaped.

We were over a city. It expanded outward with streets crisscrossing blocks of buildings, and people and cars buzzing about like ants. The city sat on a huge, vertical white plate that rose up on one side and down on the other as if gravity turned sideways. Giant vertebrae disappeared into the distance on both sides. That's when it hit me—the city lay on a gigantic backbone. *The Devil's backbone.* The city continued on the next vertebra, with bridges connecting the streets. Some of the vertebrae had major portions cut away.

The hand dropped me and my ice cream truck off on a street in the middle of the city, its hand nonchalantly destroying a building on one side as people screamed. Then it pulled away and disappeared into the hole in the reddish sky.

A car behind me honked, and I realized I was parked in the middle of traffic. I pulled off to the side and got out of the truck as the car sped off. The people who screamed while the hand destroyed the building now seemed as if nothing had happened. Being a New Yorker, I barely looked at them, so it wasn't until later that I noticed the wide range of people, clothing, and various fatal-looking injuries.

Now that I was out of my air-conditioned ice cream truck, the heat and humidity hit me with full fury, quickly soaking my white Good Humor ice cream man uniform. The stench of rotten meat slammed into me, like a trash bin from a slaughterhouse. While I gagged, the ground suddenly trembled like an earthquake, and I fell down.

"What's that sound?" a curly-haired boy of about twelve asked in a monotone voice as I rose to my feet. His face and clothes were also drenched in sweat. He wore what looked like worn-out baggy pajamas with black and white horizontal stripes, like a prison outfit from long ago. The reddish light glinted off his perspiration, giving him a devilish complexion.

At first I was confused about what sound he referred to, and then I realized the ice cream truck was still playing *The Entertainer.* I clicked it off.

"Where was it coming from?" the boy asked, looking startled. "Where did it go?"

"From my truck," I said. The boy stared at the truck for a minute, and then shrugged his shoulders.

"You must be new here," he said, still in monotone. "I'm Timmy. I killed my sister, but I'm better now. What did you do? You look pretty messed up."

I hadn't yet recovered from the rather unlikely events of the past few minutes, and so I just stared at him, my mouth gaping like I'd seen a ghost. There was another earthquake—or was it a backquake? A bonequake?—but this time I kept my feet. Timmy barely reacted.

"What was that?" I asked.

"That's just his heartbeat," Timmy said, staring at his feet.

Where was I? *What* was I? Okay, I was smart enough to figure out that I was dead. I patted myself and verified that I seemed substantial, so I wasn't a ghost, at least of the normal kind. But my body had been smashed, and the front of my Good Humor Man outfit was covered in blood. At least the pain was mostly gone.

Then, with rising horror, I realized where I must be. "Is this Hell?" Somehow, in all this heat, a shiver went down my spine. I thought I had reformed, but apparently not enough.

Timmy giggled. "No, mister, if this was Hell, it'd be a *lot* hotter."

I sighed in relief. If Hell was hotter than this inferno, I was glad I wasn't there.

"And they'd be torturing you," Timmy added. I was glad to hear of the lack of torture; always a consideration when making travel plans.

"If this isn't Hell, and it certainly isn't Heaven, then where am I?"

"You're on The Devil's Backbone," Timmy said.

I'd never heard of it. I had heard rumors of giant hands that came out of the ground, grabbing people and destroying buildings. I'd also heard of the Loch Ness Monster, Bigfoot, and the Tooth Fairy, but I hadn't believed in them either.

"So, what did you do?" Timmy asked. "You wouldn't be here unless you were once marked by the Devil, and then reformed. He doesn't like that, so he brings people like us here, hoping to turn us back."

I introduced myself and told him something of my past, though I sugar-coated it. Did I really want to tell him of my years in prison, and all the awful things I'd done? I was more interested in him telling me about this world.

And so began my life on The Devil's Backbone. It's about a mile long, made up of the Devil's thirty-three vertebrae, which are each about seven hundred feet wide at their widest. Like human vertebrae, the front of each is a short cylinder, sort of like a barnacle opened on both ends. I could see the Devil's spinal cord snaking its way through the thirty-three cylinders. A plate stuck out the back of each vertebra like a giant bony sail, with two smaller plates rising from the sides.

The Devil's body around the backbone had been hollowed out, presumably by the Devil himself, with the Devil's luminescent red flesh perhaps a quarter mile up. The backbone hung in mid-air between where it came out of the skull and disappeared in the other direction. The hole in the sky where the Devil's hand had reached in to drop me off healed within a day, leaving behind an ugly scar, one of many.

"What am I supposed to do now?" I asked.

"Let me take you to the Welcome Center," Timmy said.

"That'd be great," I said, getting back into my ice cream truck. "You give directions and I'll drive."

Timmy appeared hesitant. "I don't like cars. They look dangerous. Some of them play music like yours. I think they're haunted."

"It's safe," I said. "And you can have some ice cream."

"What's ice cream?" Timmy asked. He hesitantly stepped into the truck and sat in the passenger side, hunched slightly forward.

I finally put two and two together. "When did you die?"

Timmy examined the truck's controls. "George Washington was president when Ross killed me in 1795. He was another kid they had locked up." He twisted around so I could see the wooden-handled knife jutting from his back, which explained why he'd been hunching forward. "You're stuck with whatever clothes you wore when you died, and somehow whatever does these things thought the knife was part of my clothes." He went back to examining the controls. "I'm two hundred twenty-seven years old."

That explained the confusion about my truck and ice cream.

"I've got something for you." I pulled the truck over and opened one of the freezers. "Try this," I said, handing him one of the chocolate candy center crunch bars that had gotten me killed. "Hold it by the stick and remove the paper first."

He followed the instructions and then stared at the black object in front of him, wrinkling his nose. "It looks like horse manure."

I pulled out a second chocolate candy center crunch bar and took a bite. Satisfied that nothing happened to me, Timmy took an experimental bite.

A huge grin crossed his face. "Wow!" he said, for the first time losing the monotone. A moment later he finished the bar. I gave him the rest of mine. His smile threatened to come off the sides of his face as ice cream dribbled out the corners.

"That's why I became an ice cream man!" I exclaimed, showing him my silver Good Humor Man ring.

On the way to the Welcome Center I got my first close look at this world as we veered about on the curving, bony landscape. Every hundred fifty feet or so we'd reach the end of a vertebra and take a short bridge to the next. The streets zigzagged across the vertebrae, sometimes spiraling about them, and other times going up one side of a plate and down the other side. Gravity pulled to the vertebrae from all directions, so you could drive up one side of a vertical vertebra plate and down the other, like some sort of amusement park ride. I stopped the truck at one point and walked up a plate, reached the top, and walked down on the other side. I don't recommend doing this on a full stomach.

Most of the vertebrae had been scrubbed clean and white, but here and there bits of Devil-flesh clung to the bone. Every few minutes the Devil's heart would beat, knocking everything about, but I quickly grew used to it. Finally we arrived at the Welcome Center. This was my first chance to examine one of the buildings up close. It was made of bone.

"We sacrificed some vertebrae for building materials," Timmy explained. I remembered several of the vertebrae had big chunks cut away.

"Where do the cars come from?" I asked. They were definitely metal, though they seemed a mishmash of years, from modern ones to a few Model T's. There was even a stagecoach pulled by a pair of horses.

"I still don't understand cars. What makes them go without a horse?"

"I'll explain later. But where do they come from?"

"You saw the size of the Devil's hands." Timmy said. "He can't grab a person directly. He usually grabs the entire area in a clump, with the person he's after in the middle, and brings the entire clump here. We get a lot of supplies that way. But sometimes people die inside a car or stagecoach or something, or they run away from him in them, and then he can grab it between his fingernails. So a lot of people show up in things like that."

"That's what happened to me, in my ice cream truck. How about you?"

Timmy stared at his feet. "After he killed me, Ross hid my body in an outhouse. The Devil grabbed the entire thing, so I've got the only outhouse on The Devil's Backbone." He looked up and smiled and grabbed another chocolate candy center crunch bar. "Now I might need it."

"What do you mean?"

"Dead people don't have to eat or drink, and we don't have any real food down here anyway."

About seven thousand people lived—or should I say existed?—on The Devil's Backbone. At first this seemed a very small number. Out of the many billions of people who died throughout history, I thought there would be a lot more evil people who had reformed. Apparently a lot of "reformed" people haven't really reformed, at least on the inside. I'd always suspected most people were phony. Or maybe the Devil hadn't grabbed them all. Or maybe he grabbed only the really evil ones, the ones the Devil thought he had for sure, who had reformed. Only the Devil knows.

Most of the people that walked the bony streets were pretty old. I guess that should be expected since, on average, people are old when they die. I approached a young man dressed in what looked like a Roman toga with a sword through his stomach, and an old black woman in a long flowing dress and a head scarf partially covering her pocked face, but their responses were gibberish to me. What looked like a Neanderthal with his neck torn apart walked by, but I decided not to approach him.

The Welcome Center was staffed by expressionless people who also spoke in monotones. A bored looking young Asian woman greeted me with a forced smile and heavy Chinese accent. Pictures of dragons and flowers covered her dirty blue robe. After assigning me a housing unit, she looked away, staring off into space.

"Why does everyone look bored and talk with a monotone?" I asked.

"Let's see what you're like when you've lived in this heat for a few centuries, with nothing much to do." And yet, Timmy seemed a bit more alive since eating the chocolate candy center crunch bar. "The woman you talked to was Mrs. Chien. She looks young, but she's been here a thousand years. I helped her learn English about a century ago."

Timmy followed me to my new home. My "housing unit" was one of thousands of caves that lined the Devil's vertebrae. It had been dug out with the few available metal tools brought in by dead people, just as I'd brought in my ice cream truck. My home measured roughly ten feet square, with a six foot ceiling that barely let me stand up straight. There was no bed or any type of furniture, just smooth bone. It would be like living in a doorless closet.

"Where do you and your family live?" I asked Timmy.

He looked away. "My family must have all died a long time ago, and they went wherever they went. None of them are here."

I realized my faux pas—of course his family wouldn't be here. "So you live alone?"

"Of course. My parents wouldn't want to live with me anyway, after what I did. They never forgave me. Nobody should." He began to walk away.

"Wait," I said. "Come back here. What exactly did you do?"

He stopped, his back still to me. "I told you, I killed my sister. That's when I got the 666 on my head. It went away later, when I was in prison." He began walking away again.

Just like me.

I walked after him, and my longer paces caught up. I spun him around and saw his tear-streaked face.

"There's no way a kid like you could have killed anyone on purpose," I said. It just didn't seem possible. "It had to have been an accident."

"No accident," Timmy said. "Dad gave me a musket when I was six. I'd been shooting rats with it ever since. Emily was fussing like three-year-old kids do, and I told her if she didn't stop, I'd shoot her. I aimed at her. I didn't mean to shoot her, but she started screaming at me, and I just pulled the trigger without thinking, and there was blood everywhere." He collapsed to the ground in sobs.

I stooped and put my arms around him. "Listen to me," I said. "What you did was a horrible thing, we both know that. But the fact that you're here proves you are truly sorry for what you did. You're not some psychopathic killer. You didn't want to shoot her, you just got irritated for a second. You're a kid who made a mistake."

"A big one," he said.

"When did this happen?"

"When I was nine. I died when I was twelve."

Great. How could the Devil leave his mark on a kid that young? Well, I wasn't going to let him have Timmy, not if I could help it.

"Look, why don't you stay here tonight?" I said. "I could use some company. You can tell me more about this place." I wondered where the water came from to supply Timmy and others with tears, since nobody needed to drink. Maybe it came out of the humid air. Based on Timmy's face, it would be a lot less humid.

He lay down on my floor and we talked for hours, maybe days. Time seems to stand still when there's no rising or setting sun. And yet something seemed wrong. I finally figured it out.

"How come I'm not tired?" I asked.

"You're dead," Timmy said. "Why would you need to sleep, or even breathe?"

I'd been breathing since I arrived, but now I experimented. Sure enough, I could hold my breath without any effects, so I simply stopped breathing. Yet a few minutes later I realized I was breathing again, one of those automatic things you do even when you're dead. At least the rotting carcass smell seemed to be dying away, though that was probably because I was getting used to it.

I think it's the second law of thermodynamics that says all systems generally run down. That law didn't apply on the Devil's Backbone. Bodies didn't age or need energy, my ice cream truck ran forever without running out of gas, and even the batteries were perpetual, keeping the ice cream freezer running endlessly. Ice cream bars and the air conditioning in my truck were nice breaks from this never-ending Hell.

Perhaps I deserved to go to Hell. If man were judged by his past, I certainly deserved to. There's no denying it; I'd once been a bad man. I'd started with shoplifting and burglary, and then moved on to armed robbery and, when a bank job didn't go right, assault. The guard survived but would never walk again. And there was nothing I could ever do to change that.

It was while sitting in prison in the blackest of depressions that I'd seen the light. No, not religiously; I'd just realized what a waste my life was, that I'd become a parasite. I didn't want to die a parasite.

While musing on my future in my orange prison garb, a spot on my backbone and another on my scalp began to itch. I've never had an itch on the inside like the one on my back, and no amount of scratching would make it stop. The one on my head I thought might be hair lice. I checked in the mirror . . . and saw a 666 etched in black under my hair.

That's a wakeup call.

When I got out of prison, I was determined to change, to make an honest living doing good. And so I spread happiness to kids on my route just north of the Bronx, even if it meant hours of noxious ice cream truck music and a flabby belly because, yeah, I like ice cream too. After a few weeks, the 666 faded away and the itch in my back eased up, though it never went completely away. Yes, if you're a bad person, you can change your life around.

Unfortunately, the Devil likes parasites. Imagine that. He'd had me marked, probably had a place labeled "Seth" all set for me downstairs, and then I'd gone and disappointed him. Turns out I'm not the only bad guy-gone-good. But the Devil isn't adept at letting go.

The Devil's Backbone was hot, boring, and people mostly just existed there, often for centuries. Once in awhile someone would go crazy, perhaps attacking others, and then his body would collapse to the ground as his soul left and sank downward. If the Devil had set out to break our spirits and bring us back into his fold, it was working, slowly but surely.

There had to be a way to escape. All we had to do was leave the Devil's body and we'd be back in the real world, and our souls could presumably go where they were meant to go—Heaven—or the Devil wouldn't have detoured us.

Timmy and I drove my truck to what he called the Northern Pit of Fire, just above the top vertebra. Like the name implied, it was a huge fire that encompassed the entire vertebra. Even from a distance I could feel the intense heat. The flames rose up like fiery trees with no apparent source of fuel.

"No one's ever made it through," Timmy said. "You'll just get burned."

"What's the worst that could happen?" I said. "I'm already dead." I took a few unnecessary gulps of air, squinted my eyes, and waded into it.

You know how when you touch a hot stove, you pull away instantly, but don't feel the pain until a second later? My whole body pulled back spastically as I entered the flames, and yet I didn't feel anything.

And then I did.

I screamed as the agonizing heat tore into my body. I took another step forward, and then my body betrayed me as I collapsed.

I awoke to searing pain. I opened my eyes and Timmy was looking over me.

"I had to pull you out," he said. "I think that's what Hell is like." His hands were blackened, no doubt burned as badly as I'd burned myself. I could see and feel the heat of the Pit of Fire a short distance away. I crawled away from it to get farther from the heat, and then lay there for what seemed like forever. The burns didn't heal, but the pain went away. I was probably there for weeks, Timmy usually nearby, before I finally got up and drove my truck back.

Timmy said the Southern Pit of Fire was just as bad. I accepted that, but I simply couldn't accept there was no way out. I stepped out of my cave and looked up at the reddish sky that was the Devil's flesh. Was there a way to get there? I didn't think there were enough building materials to build a ladder, but there had to be other ways.

"Are there any explosives here?" I asked Timmy.

"You mean to blow up stuff?"

"Actually, I'm thinking of building a rocket."

"A rock what?" Timmy looked confused.

"I'll explain later, but it might be a way to get out of here. I'll need some sort of fuel or explosives to make it work." I'd played around with toy rockets as a kid, but really had no idea what was needed to power one.

"Old Al is some sort of explosives expert," Timmy said.

"Can you take me to him?"

Timmy nodded. Al's cave was on a nearby vertebra, only a few hundred yards away.

Old Al had a neatly trimmed beard and mustache, and he wore a dark suit, like an undertaker. He wasn't that old, perhaps early sixties, and he really was an explosives expert—Alfred Nobel, to be exact, the Swedish inventor of dynamite. It was no wonder the Devil had marked him for his own, and then lost him when Al created the Nobel Prizes as his legacy. He'd languished here since his death over a hundred years ago. He sat cross-legged on the ground outside his cave playing chess with pieces carved from Devil-bone. His opponent was a young man wearing a Nazi uniform, swastika and all, who spoke only German. He looked like he'd been shot in the face and chest a dozen times, and turned out he had, while charging the American line in World War II. A reformed Nazi? Why not.

I explained my idea to Al, and he seemed intrigued. "Like Jules Verne's, *From the Earth to the Moon,*" he said in near-perfect English. "Unfortunately, we don't have gunpowder, TNT, nitroglycerine, or the ingredients needed to make them." I later learned he was often used here as a translator, since he fluently spoke English, German, French, Russian, Swedish, and Italian.

We chatted for a time, and then I left him and the Nazi to their chess game. Rockets were out.

Helplessness overtook me, and then anger. We had repented our crimes and didn't deserve to be here. How dare the Devil trap us in this prison he'd created inside his body. There had to be a way out.

I returned to my cave. There was a shovel nearby. I grabbed it and ran to the vertebrae's edge. Looking down, I saw the Devil's spinal cord passing from this vertebra to the next. It was a long way down, but what did I have to lose? If fire couldn't do more than put me in bed for a time, what could falling a few hundred feet do? I wanted to tear the Devil apart.

I raised my shovel, ready to attack, and jumped.

About ten feet down, my feet hit what seemed like an invisible trampoline. I sank down and then shot back up. Up and down I went until I came to a stop. I took my anger out on the invisible force field, smashing the shovel against it. The shovel bounced back and slammed me in the face, giving me a massive headache and a welt that never went away.

Now I was stuck on this invisible field, ten feet down. No problem; I jumped up and down, higher and higher, and then jumped clear. In other circumstances, it would have been a fun toy, this invisible trampoline.

One day I walked by the Welcome Center and heard screaming inside. I ran in. Mrs. Chien, the Asian woman I'd met when I first arrived, was screaming and fighting hysterically against three men who struggled to restrain her. Lying on the floor nearby, alive but in obvious pain, lay a woman. A small metal trowel stuck out of her stomach.

"Why?" a tall man in a top hat and cloak yelled in an English accent.

"Too long. Too long," Mrs. Chien muttered in her broken English. "Can't take it anymore. Kill you all!"

Mrs. Chien closed her eyes and began gibbering in Chinese. Then she stopped. She became rigid, and her ghostly soul rose out of her body. The body crumpled to the floor as the men released it.

Her soul rose into the air and stood among us, a shimmering presence that smelled of sweet meadow flowers. She smiled and seemed about to say something when she stopped. A surprised look crossed her face for a second, and then a thin, horizontal crack formed across her stomach, then more of them on the rest of her. The smell of rotten eggs hit me, and I stepped back. Then, as if the ground opened under her, she was sucked down like smoke.

We buried her body under bone shards. Time was on the Devil's side; How long could anyone hold out? Someday we'd all meet this fate.

I spent a long time in the heat and humidity of The Devil's Backbone, just existing. Gradually I became as depressed as the others, speaking in a monotone, and spending my days wandering about. Sometimes I'd volunteer to carve out homes for new arrivals. Sometimes I'd sit around for hours, staring off into space and counting off the seconds between the Devil's heartbeats.

I'd once been a parasite, but I'd decided I didn't want to be a parasite, and overcame that. Now I was a wart. I didn't harm anything, but served no purpose other than to just be there.

One day I decided I didn't like being a wart. I'd stopped being a parasite when I learned to spread joy to children with my ice cream truck. I still had a nearly-full supply of ice cream; why not go back to spreading joy?

So I headed out in my ice cream truck in the streets of The Devil's Backbone, playing *The Entertainer*, which I'd somehow begun to miss. Children came out to see what was going on. Some knew what an ice cream truck was, though most did not.

I taught them quickly, and I didn't charge. It took all day, but I finally gave out the last of the ice cream, leaving behind a large number of happy faces and excited voices. I was a happy wart, spreading such joy. Except . . . I no longer had any ice cream.

I'd have been a sad wart again if Timmy hadn't pointed out that Old Man Pete had died in a cattle stampede, and a handful—a *large* handful—of cows came with him when he had arrived. I'd explained to Timmy that the primary ingredient of ice cream was milk. But I also needed ice, sugar, salt, and flavoring. Because of the humidity, water was everywhere, and I could freeze it in my truck.

There was a supply depot in the middle of The Devil's Backbone, a place where people dropped off stuff they had when they arrived but didn't need. Since many people from the past were farmers, it made sense that some of them might have shown up with seeds for sugar cane, as well as flavoring—perhaps cacao for chocolate. And since many of the farmers were from long ago, there might be salt, which they used to preserve meat before the invention of refrigeration. Then I could use the freezer from my ice cream truck to make actual ice cream!

Sure enough, there were stacks and stacks of farming items at the supply depot that the Devil's hand had grabbed while snatching people, including sugar cane and cacao seeds. There were also bags of salt. I had everything I needed to make ice cream, even chocolate ice cream! Nothing could stop me!

Unless, of course, the Devil chose that moment to once again stick his hand down his mouth, into his stomach, dig its way through flesh to his backbone, and grab at me. Which he did.

I tried running away, and learned what grabbing an ant is like from an ant's perspective. The hand was simply too big to grab me as I dodged about. Finally the powerful fingers reached around me, and with a loud *crunch*, broke off a section of his backbone, with me in the middle. And then it was back into the stomach, up through the throat, and out the mouth.

The Devil's other giant hand cleared away the bone rubble, leaving me alone in the Devil's palm, staring at the Devil himself. His giant red face could have held nine football stadiums.

"Why are you spreading happiness to my people?" the Devil asked in a voice surprisingly like Darth Vader. He stared down at me from over a bulbous nose and, surprise, a short, black Hitler mustache. We were in another large red cavern, though I wasn't sure since it was hard to look away from the Devil's eyes, each of them twice the size of a baseball diamond. Looking into their blackness was like looking into the endless reaches of starless space.

This should have been the most frightening experience of my life *and* afterlife. But I'd been through a lot, and there wasn't much more the Devil could throw at me. Let him do what he wanted. I felt a deep calm come over me.

"They're not exactly your people," I pointed out. "You were premature in marking them as your own."

"*I will always be in all of you!*" the Devil roared, his eyes blazing in anger. Holding me in one vast hand, he leaned down and slammed his other mountain-like fist onto the white ground. There was a loud crash as cracks appeared. Again and again the angry Devil slammed his fist into the ground until it was like broken pavement.

The calm I'd felt was now quivering fear. A giant, angry Devil slamming his fist into the ground has a way of doing that.

He pulled me up close to one of his eyes. "You spread joy to the very people whose spirits I am trying to break. And you would have made more of this ice cream and spread more joy. For this, you will face pain that you cannot imagine, for eternity, and then in infinite other eternities. I will devote my entire being to finding ways to increase your pain."

This left me quaking like an epileptic with Parkinson's disease in an earthquake. The old itch in my back came back in full throttle like a bug stuck inside me. "There are others who have done nicer things," I pleaded in a cracking voice. "Really, I'm not that good. Why me?"

"Because you irritate me a little," the Devil said. "The pain starts in one minute. They say the anticipation is the worst part, but they are wrong. Oh, are they wrong."

I couldn't imagine the pain being worse than the anticipation I now felt, but the Devil *had* warned me I wouldn't be able to imagine it. Not that I needed to; shortly I'd experience it. Forever.

The itch in my back was getting worse and worse. Why was it doing this now, of all times? Was it the beginning of the pain the Devil promised?

Then clarity struck. What had the Devil said about being in all of us? Did he mean all people, or just those trapped here inside him? I looked about and saw the red cavern appeared just like the sky in The Devil's Backbone. Because of the Devil's hand, I couldn't see down, but I knew what the Devil stood on: an even larger backbone.

I reached my arm around to my back, but couldn't quite reach the itch; I couldn't twist my shoulder backward that far, just as the Devil apparently could not. There was another way in, and the Devil had shown the way. I opened my mouth as wide as I could and jammed my hand into it. Back when I was alive, I doubted if I could have done this, but being dead has its advantages—for one thing, there was no gag reflex. I worked my hand down my throat and into my stomach. Then I tore at the side of my stomach, trying to get to where the itch was in my back.

"*What are you doing!*" the Devil thundered, his voice knocking me off my feet. I continued to feel for the itch in my back, and felt it moving about. I grabbed at it, tearing painfully through my own flesh. Somehow, being dead made that easier, but only barely.

As I did so, there was an explosion overhead. I looked up, and saw a giant hand come out of the sky. This hand was as much larger than the Devil as the Devil's hand was to me. It wore a giant Good Humor Man Ring on its index finger, just as I did on the hand I had jammed inside me.

The Devil ran from the grasping hand. I jumped free of the running Devil's much smaller hand—though still huge to me—and crashed painfully onto the bony ground below, and watched the Devil sprint away on that giant backbone. My hand was still jammed down my throat.

I closed my hand around the itch and, with a grunt, I twisted my hand back and forth until the entire section of my backbone broke off with a crunch. I tried to ignore the searing pain.

As I did this, the hand in the sky grabbed the section of vertebrae the Devil ran upon, and after twisting it back and forth, broke it off, Devil and all. As I pulled my hand out of my back and into my stomach, the giant hand pulled out as well, presumably into its own giant stomach—or was it my stomach, mirrored in vast size? I pulled my own much punier hand out of my stomach, up my throat, and out my mouth. Presumably the giant hand did the same.

I sorted through the shards of bone from my own backbone I now held in my hand. Movement caught my eye, and there he was, scurrying away: the Devil, small version, the source of that long-time itch in my back.

With my other hand I removed the bone fragments until all I held was the Devil, who tried to run for the edge. I pulled him back to the middle with my fingernail, and then, after a few minutes of trial and error, used it to pin him to my palm.

"Let me go!" cried the Devil, whose voice was now only a squeak. "Or else!"

"Or else what?" I asked. "Unimaginable pain in infinite eternities?"

"*Worse!*" the Devil screamed.

Now the Devil is one tough devil. But when a creature with a mass about ten billion times greater squeezes him, even the Devil can't withstand that. I squished him like a bug.

That left me alone on this gigantic backbone inside some larger being. Was it my backbone or the Devil's? I have no idea.

What I do know is that a moment later my body collapsed to the ground and lay still. My soul floated out slowly, perhaps still weighted down by my past sins. Or perhaps it just waited for the others, as seven thousand other souls—the inhabitants of The Devil's Backbone—floated out of my body. I waved to Timmy, he waved back, and we began our upward descent.

Wherever we're going, I hope they have ice cream.

Larry Hodges, of Germantown, MD, is an active member of SFWA with over 60 short story sales, more than 40 of them since summer, 2008. His story, The Awakening, *was the unanimous grand prize winner at the 2010 Garden State Horror Writers Short Story Competition. His story,* Rationalized, *won the November, 2011 Story Quest Competition. He's a graduate of the six-week 2006 Odyssey Writers' Workshop, the 2007 Orson Scott Card Literary Boot Camp, and the 2008 Taos Toolbox Writers' Workshop. He's a full-time writer with five books and over 1,300 published articles in over 130 different publications. He is a member of the USA Table Tennis Hall of Fame (Google it!), and once beat someone using an ice cube as a racket. Visit him at* www.larryhodges.org.

THE DEATH OF E. COLI

BENJAMIN KANE ETHRIDGE

People, animals, plants, even germs—everything has a shelf life and eventually must perish. But if humans transcend to a hereafter that is defined by moral choices, what eternity awaits for other life forms that do not seem to contend with the virtuous conundrums we face? Or are we wrong in that supposition? Perhaps we're not the only beings in existence with its own set of values and emotions to pit against one another. Perhaps wars of inequality and righteousness abound in all classes of organisms, waged throughout the universe and, even, inside our very bodies. This next story explores the hereafter on a micro-scale. Benjamin Kane Ethridge, a young author who's slowly producing an impressive canon of award-winning fiction, presents The Death of E. Coli, *in which the battle of bacteria continues into the afterlife.*

The agony had Lamar Reuteri's teeth clattering again. He held his sides and pressed his forehead against the pit wall. Screams from the other captive Bactitans were no longer a layer of the culminating misery—he didn't hear them at all. Lamar's companion from long ago, Brad Animalis, stood in the center of the pit, staring into the consuming void above, blinking, wincing, while Listeria Monoz slept at his feet, dozens of expressions flexing through her tired face as she interpreted some recurring nightmare (she'd had the worst of the pain lately). From the shadows, Toxo Plasma watched her with silent insanity; he bit his pale, mountain-sized fist while his eyes spilled glassine lakes over his cheeks.

Lamar's body quaked, his cold bones rattled. How much time had passed since Edward Coli cast them down into this pit? He couldn't remember. Could Edward even recall? It was doubtful. Edward was up above, enjoying all the euphoria that came with roaming amongst the ethereal mists.

Lamar Reuteri was not given to hate, but it was easy to say he hated Edward more than any Bactitan he'd ever encountered over the dawning of several universes. As a large new wave of bacteria souls incorporated into Lamar's body, the hatred was reinforced. These dead bacteria, known as meta-souls, came from the living worlds in a steady stream, a particle rope of black and silver dust motes that flowed to a Bactitan's heart where integration took place. Underground, this once-natural process brought unnatural pain. At times it was gradual, but at other times, when masses of bacteria died in other worlds, it was mind-bleeding torture.

Like now.

Lamar could feel the growth spread from his core. He flung his body around like a jittering marionette of titanic proportions. He wasn't the largest of the Bactitans, but his violent seizures made the immense pit rumble and shudder, and the air thrash with a skirmish of winds. Clawing his eyes, tearing at his hair, heaving, gasping, as meta-souls flooded into him from the worlds of the living, he understood he would have to endure this forever. And, almost out of psychic agreement, Listeria Monoz suddenly awoke, wailing and beating fists into her iniquitous dark face, carved with millions of malevolent wrinkles.

Brad Animalis stooped to restrain her, trying to help. Listeria was too powerful, however, and hurled him into a wall, the sound of the impact sending shockwaves throughout.

Listeria now towered over them all. She let out a prehistoric roar that jammed every pocket of space. Her shoulders grew wide, betraying feminine features. Bands of muscles stretched from her neck to her arms, engorging her form. Her long blonde hair caught with black fire. She let out another scream, but this time it extended past the boundaries of the pit and went through the bedrock of the afterworld, spiriting up into celestial boundaries.

Lamar, Brad, and Toxo hugged the pit wall as Listeria's body expanded and her constant screeching resonated with all manners of ire and desperation. Brad shut his eyes and looked away. Toxo Plasma bit through his hand. Lamar saw the flayed muscle and red bones of the wound, and could make out the scintillation of meta-souls dappling the flesh. Rebuilding was normally so painful it caused a Bactitan to fall into a fugue state, the internal torture unbearable, but Toxo remained standing, his focus undeniable on Listeria's vicious transformation.

"Good evening. Breaking news tonight. A large African village outside of Cairo suffering from a confounding amount of Listeria infections has fought its way back to health with the help of UN organized antibiotic treatments. I'm Kyle Shamm and this is News Spot at 8.

"For the developing story out of Cairo, we'd like to take you to our foreign correspondent, Jenny Forge, who is standing by just outside city limits. Jenny?"

"Yes, hi Kyle. I'm here."

"Jenny, so give us a little background here. What happened to the poor citizens of this village? How did a great number—jeez, nearly all of them—get infected with Listeria?"

"Unfortunately, it came from a source of donation food, either with origins in Spain or Italy, which contained cured meat. The bacterial contamination was either from packaging not sealed correctly or through some other faulty manufacturing process. At first there were only isolated cases, but as more of the food was distributed, most everybody in the village became infected."

"How awful."

"Yeah, truly."

"So the UN comes in, at what point, and then delivers these miracle antibiotics?"

"Well, not exactly miracles, Kyle—these antibiotics have existed for years, but even for very populated villages like this one, they might as well be miracles. When it became apparent that the number of infected had risen sharply, the United Nations sent several elite disease control squads to set up makeshift hospitals throughout the town."

"Wow."

"It's extraordinary."

"And most of them are cured now?"

"Save for a few overwhelmed with infection, yes, most of the sick are growing healthier every day. With the help of medication and rest, Listeria is dying out in droves here."

"Good riddance to every last one of those horrible bugs."

"Exactly."

Listeria raged, now so large she'd grown to half the height of the pit. An unexplained bombardment of meta-souls showered down on her, a frenzied ribbon of oscillating black and chrome spiking her in the chest. *Somewhere, billions of Listeria bacteria had perished.* The anguish caused her to savage her lower lip between broken teeth, where the gnarled points exited and then reentered her chin. She whipped about, on her face angry flags of gore rippling, preparing for war. Lamar sheltered his face from the torrential blood. Brad and Toxo looked on, blinking through the vermillion storm.

Listeria wailed, the sound cosmically recognizable, the keening of a newborn universe ready for its big bang.

Lamar was not prepared for what that big bang *was.*

The female Bactitan bent, breasts drooping, her blood-soaked nipples like planetary harpoons, and then she exploded upward, jumping through the godbrick ceiling that Edward Coli had mortared above the pit.

Godbrick was every bit as powerful as its name would suggest and, though Listeria had grown to the size of several galaxies, her ascent through the bricks ripped her body into volcanic fragments, some plummeting immediately over the other Bactitans, while other portions spun outside to the world above.

After a moment of shock, then revelation, the remaining three prisoners leapt to their freedom. A blinding brilliancy unleashed upon them and they stumbled, staggered, strafed away from each other, yet all had the presence of mind to get as far from the pit as possible.

Lamar had trouble seeing through the budding illumination and yet it mattered little: the euphoria at once returned. It was a relished flood of nostalgia; all those days of freedom spent in the afterworld, growing stronger, smarter, more aware—those were the times where he'd felt like a hungry god, so different from the cowering, starving behemoth he'd become underground.

Now. This moment. This was how it was supposed to be. All the meta-souls his body absorbed gave him power and fed him rather than causing twisting agony—after all this time, it was a difficult concept to accept without misgiving. From their startled expressions, he could sense his friend Brad, and his once-enemy Toxo, also felt the difference.

Stacks of godbrick surrounded the cloud-streaked blue-silver atmosphere, resembling a heavenly construction zone that never got underway. Compared to some places in the afterworld, it wasn't a wondrous place for the eyes to behold, but behold with wonder they did.

Though their smiles could not easily be wiped away, there was something that made them pause. Fragments of Listeria slowly crept back toward the pit, blackened chunks of gristle and meat, somersaulting, flipping, jumping back to reconnect and rebuild her. Listeria would experience something more dreadful than ever before and nothing could prevent it—they would not return to the pit to help her.

"We have to find and destroy Edward." Toxo rubbed his mangled hand.

Brad looked over, his face streaked in dried blood.

"Nobody can be destroyed here," Lamar replied. "We should all go our separate ways and hide. Hope he never finds us."

"Hey, Lamar, get serious, man." Brad stepped over a spongy piece of Listeria that slid past. "You know that isn't going to work. He'll trap us again. *And soon.*"

"We can't kill him in the afterworld."

"I felt pretty dead in that pit," Toxo said and took a step farther away, his pointed face uneasy. "If we can throw Edward down there with Listeria, even for just a day, that would bring me great satisfaction."

"More satisfaction than living topside, unmolested?" Lamar shook his head and then shook it faster when he read Brad's face; *he* wanted revenge too. "Edward Coli won't let us overpower him. Are you in a hurry to return to the underground?"

"This might be our only chance for absolute freedom. What if we can use that left-over godbrick and seal him in down there?" The hope in Brad's eyes sparkled and made Lamar's stomach twist.

"And there are his footprints," Toxo cried out with a gasp. He pointed to deep impressions in the soft luminescent soil. Meta-souls bubbled in each impression, lost parts of Edward Coli that he'd managed to delay absorbing.

"If we stick together, we'll be better off than before," Brad pointed out.

Lamar couldn't argue that. All of them had been at odds with each other when Edward came for them. Especially himself and Toxo Plasma. If they banded together this time, they would be undoubtedly stronger. It was a shame that Listeria couldn't have escaped in her powerful new form. The rebuilding process would take millennia now. Still, they were a formidable three. If they could come up with a plan . . .

Toxo and Brad didn't wait for any further discussion. They bounded across the heavens, drunk on time and space, following the patterns of colossal barbarian-toed feet in the glittering dirt.

Lamar Reuteri had no choice but to follow.

The trip was not long, though no trips in the Afterlife ever were.

When they found the realm to which Edward Coli had retreated, they were awestruck. It was a realm of the afterworld none of them had ever visited before. Beautiful beyond words, but also tiny.

In fact, it was too small a region for one Bactitan, let alone four.

And for that, Edward found them quickly.

Edward Coli had a broad, strangled face. His eyes, deep inside that face, were planets of black tar that seemed to clutch things rather than look at them. As large as Listeria had grown, he was larger and stronger. His claws sliced through time's fabric as he walked toward them on the golden road. The other Bactitans had cautiously followed the footprints to the boundaries of this strange territory . . . they'd even halted to discuss how to proceed . . . but not ten words into their conversation, and Edward's dark shape unfurled from a velvet red everglade near the base of a mercury-topped mountain.

He looked good and rested. It was obvious he'd been sleeping there a while, drinking in the beauty of this place, not to mention the blissful accumulation of meta-souls. That was Edward's nature; he only cared to consume and enjoy, all the while appearing righteous. Lamar imagined peering into Edward's mortal center would be like gazing over a bone-filled wasteland.

As Edward stood, he nearly occupied the entire realm. "How in the graces of all Time did you escape?" The question wasn't spiteful but rather *curious*. Delighted even. The prospect of learning something new caused him great joy.

"I've got his legs!" Toxo dove at him.

Brad Animalis said nothing, but it was clear he aimed to grapple Edward under the arms.

Edward Coli swiftly kicked Toxo Plasma in the face and dropped him hard into the sparkling dirt. At the same time, he intercepted Brad and put him in a headlock.

Lamar faced Edward. "Let them go. You can't stop all three of us!"

A smile razored through Edward's corpse-moon face. His foot came down on Toxo's head and smashed it to syrupy pulp. At the sound of the cranium's bursting, Lamar bolted ahead and was bludgeoned with an unexpected club: his friend, Brad Animalis. Lamar reeled back onto his rear, in a daze. As he looked back up, he saw that Brad's body had already been shredded into uncountable pieces. Toxo was now nothing more than a river of red and brown sludge painting Edward's feet up to his shins. *Listeria would even rebuild before those two sorry souls. Brad . . . why couldn't you listen?*

Lamar scrambled to get up. A single glacial finger caught around his throat and dragged him back.

"No, no," Edward whispered into his ear. "You're going to tell me how you got out of that pit. I'll not wait millennia for you to restore. I want to know. Now."

"First, tell me where we are."

"You don't know?" Edward asked suspiciously. "Don't you smell the familiarity?"

"I wouldn't ask otherwise."

The grip on his throat tightened, but Edward said, "This is the place where other souls gather—they smell of that place where the meta-souls originate, and that is all I know."

"I don't see anyone here."

"Because I've been quiet. You three have caused a disturbance. I relished my paradise and listened to these strange things sing their songs and tell their stories, and my only regret is not being able to destroy them."

"Why haven't you?"

"This is more questions than you've negotiated."

"Why haven't you?" Lamar repeated.

"Though they're small, the souls that live in this place are not made of our framework. The difference is unsettling. That's all I can say. Now how did *you* escape?"

Lamar took a breath and looked down, defeated. "Listeria grew large enough to break through the seal."

Edward nudged Lamar's face up and put an eyeball against his. Its touch stung all the way into Lamar's ethereal brain. "I discovered a pit of flames here that is so deep, no seal need ever be built over its top. I hear some of *them* down there, too. I have this gut impression they don't like us very much."

"I'll leave . . . you won't have to worry about sharing this territory."

"Leave? Why? You don't want to see the new pit? It's just over here."

Edward pitched him skyward and wind screamed around Lamar's body. A moment later he crashed down to a rocky floor. Garroted cries and whooping howls, micro, but nonetheless disturbing, raised from a sprawling canyon only a few steps away.

Edward landed in front of him and caught Lamar by his midsection, throttling him like a plaything. Lamar struggled but met with absolute resistance.

"Let's be over with this quickly. I'd like to return to my hiding spot," Edward said with a grin.

A long thread of mucous suddenly fell from one of Edward's angular nostrils. He sniffed at it, but more came rushing out. He smacked his thin lips, which looked dry now, not eel-moist as they were before. Something dropped from the mucous and Lamar let out a scream. The silvery shape of a body, like a tiny organism with arms and legs, slid out, and then out came another, and another after, a stream of them.

In shock, Edward dropped Lamar.

Then he saw the flow of them, like trillions of ants marching to a single piece of food. Tiny people climbed up Edward's legs and covered his torso to his neck to his face, some running into his ears, others into his mouth, and some seemed to be pushing through his skin like ticks wanting complete penetration.

Lamar jumped clear of the bizarre diminutive ghosts.

He could hear Edward hacking and coughing. He stole a glance back and witnessed a bloody explosion from both of the mighty Bactitan's eyes; his flesh flooded with a livid scarlet rash, and yet more of the ghosts invaded him. Edward stumbled as he tried to stand, to fight them. He was infected. These things—these humans—had invaded his body and brought on great illness.

With a revolting wet gush, meta-souls erupted from Edward's heart into the sky, a roaring river without ties to gravity. The meta-souls glittered gold and white however, not the typical flux of black and silver. Smaller, more concentrated, they moved less like ethereal matter and more like something alive.

Lamar didn't remain to wonder where these new meta-souls were headed, nor did he stay to see Edward Coli fall into the fiery pit. He withdrew from that beautiful land, to find a place to hide elsewhere and enjoy his afterlife.

Edward's diminishing scream pursued him though, for a long time running.

"Good Evening. I'm Kyle Shamm . . . News Spot and . . . well, tonight we've stepped into a strange place, folks . . . I, uh, I don't even know if it's fair to the viewers at home that I read the teleprompter and pretend what's happened is remotely anything like reality—"

A distraught murmur from off-camera interrupted him.

"You know what? Screw yourself, Peter. I need to do this the way

I know I can. Do you have a problem with that? *No?* Then shut the hell up.

"Look, I'm sorry, folks. After our Listeria report yesterday, we had some recent calls about a number of E-Coli infected patients that exhibited signs of healing. We began investigating but then the story became larger than anything we've seen. It's occurring not just in Africa, but worldwide, and without the help of any special treatments or drugs being administered. After a bizarre storm some have described as *a blizzard of golden dust*, these patients just . . . got better.

"But, as shocking as this is, there's more. This is where I'm not sure I can report with a straight face, but it's there. We've confirmed with other outlets and a dozen unrelated eye witnesses. These E-Coli patients have recovered, but they've also grown taller, become stronger—powerful even. They're doing things . . . *impossible* things. They cannot die or be injured, and they've become obsessively hungry for violence and pleasure. People are starting to call them . . . Gods. Others have used the word Titans. If you haven't seen them yet, you soon will. They will be in your cities—they will be everywhere."

Kyle looked down at his notes in silence and shook his head. He gazed off-camera for a couple moments, then took a trembling breath and continued. "And with several new gold blizzards bombarding them since the initial occurrence, we're not sure if they'll ever stop growing . . . "

Benjamin Kane Ethridge is the Bram Stoker Award winning author of the novel Black & Orange *(Bad Moon Books, 2010) and* Bottled Abyss *(Redrum Horror, 2012). For his master's thesis he wrote, "CAUSES OF UNEASE: The Rhetoric of Horror Fiction and Film," available in an ivory tower near you. Benjamin lives in Southern California with his wife and two creatures who possess stunning resemblances to human children. When he isn't writing, reading, or videogaming, Benjamin's defending California's waterways and sewers from pollution.*

FINAL TESTAMENT OF A WEAPONS ENGINEER

EMILY C. SKAFTUN

Assuming we have a consciousness after we die, chances are good there're going to be some things we immediately regret; final sentiments we want to share with loved ones, projects we wish could be finished, places left unseen, goals unfulfilled. Or, in the case of the following story, a bomb in the garage that one man's ghost wishes he could defuse. Though the anecdote is successful on its face value, I think it also speaks to a greater question: How desperate will we be to communicate again with the living? Emily C. Skaftun answers this query with wit and sincerity as she presents, Final Testament of a Weapons Engineer.

I died. Surprised me a bit, but it didn't bother me none. I was seventy-six years old, after all, and for most of that time I knew death was a friend I'd sooner or later meet.

It had snowed overnight, a foot's worth or more, so at first light I started clearing the drive. 'Bout halfway through I felt my chest squeezing and tingling in my arms, and I just knew my time was up and I hoped I'd be with Mary soon. The snow was soft where I fell, and my breath was so hot that it melted the snow away from my face, and then it was over. I stood in the driveway holding the snow shovel, and I thought maybe I imagined it all, but then I looked down and I saw another snow shovel on the pavement, and another me in the snowbank. My face looked awful red and I could see I needed a shave. *Well, that's embarrassing*, I thought. But then I shrugged. I was dead, but that wasn't the problem.

The problem was the bomb in the garage.

A claymore mine is actually what it was, and it waited in the third upper cabinet from the right, on the west side of the garage, wired to explode when the cabinet door was opened. It was a wonder how clear I remembered the details now that I was dead. Some years back, you see, having watched first my mother, then my father, lose control of their memories, their bodies, and finally their lives, I decided there was no way I would go out like that. So I set myself a little trap. I figured when I forgot what was in that cabinet, it was time for me to go.

But now that I was dead, it seemed like I must have already been a few lines short of a blueprint when I came up with that plan, because a heart attack in the driveway hadn't ever occurred to me. I hadn't told a soul about the bomb in my garage, and now I wondered which one of my kids would find it and be blown apart. "You old asshole," I said, looking down at my body. I went to kick my old self, but my boot went right on through.

I sighed, sort of—it felt like a sigh, but it was eerie not to see my breath in the cold morning air. I figured the task of cleaning out my house would fall to my oldest son, Arthur. He lived the closest, and in fact he would be by the house in a few hours with his always-too-late offer to shovel my snow. *You'll give yourself a heart attack*, he always told me. *You should wait for me to come do it.* I reflected that it seemed he'd been right on at least one account. But on the other I still held he was wrong; if I waited for him to shovel my walk I'd be snowbound all damn day. All three of my kids had always been lazy. But then I reckoned that was my fault for giving them such easy lives. Oh well. I hoped Art had a good told-you-so when he found me, but I didn't think he would. He was a nice boy, even if he was lazy. I didn't want him to blow himself up on my trap.

But what could I do about it? I was a ghost, I guessed. Some kind of spirit, anyway, that couldn't even kick a corpse. But when I thought about it, I wasn't really sure what ghosts could do. I never went in for that kind of thing when I was alive, didn't believe in spooks and spirits. I'd heard my share of ghost stories, though, and now I aimed to see what was true and what was foolishness. If possible, I intended to haunt the shit out of one garage.

It didn't take me long to figure out that being a ghost—or whatever I was—was a raw deal. Being without matter of any identifiable sort, I could walk through walls and such, and hang unsupported in the air, which was sort of a kick. But the other side of the coin was that I couldn't do squat to affect the physical world, the one my claymore mine and my kids were still in. I couldn't open the cabinet door. I couldn't pick anything up, so I couldn't write a message on it either. I could stick my head right through the door, but all that did for me was confirm that the device was still armed and ready to blow.

Arthur showed up around ten o'clock. Even though I was dead it annoyed me he was so late. *Well,* I thought, *the driveway's all yours this time.* But then he saw my corpse and I felt bad because he looked so much sadder than I would've thought. He made a noise like some kind of animal, and actually dropped to his knees in the snowbank, wiping the layer of fresh snow away from my frozen face. He sat there for a minute, and I saw that he was *crying.*

Now I had a chance to try communicating directly, but again I found there wasn't a thing I could do. It was weird enough walking through the snow without leaving any tracks, but now I shouted and wasn't heard, I jumped up and down—no joint pain, incidentally—right in front of Arthur and wasn't seen. I tried all manner of physical contact, from a hand on his shoulder to a full tackle, but none of it was felt.

It didn't seem there was any way around it; somebody was going to find that mine the hard way. The only thing I was grateful for was that it wouldn't be my wife. For the first time in eight long years I was glad Mary died before me. As usual, just thinking about her was enough to make my heart hurt. For a minute or two I was miserable, mourning my wife while my oldest son mourned me. Then—I never said I was a quick study, did I?—I realized again that I was dead, which meant two things. One was that I no longer had a heart to hurt. It'd crapped out on me earlier that morning. But the second thing was that if Mary was dead, and I was dead, we ought to be able to get together again. And that set something to beating fast, heart or no.

"Mary?" I called out, hoping she could hear me better than Arthur had. There wasn't any reply.

I didn't end up seeing her for three days. I spent the time between my death and my funeral trying and failing to haunt my family. I learned I could go anywhere I wanted without any travel time, so I dropped in on anyone I could think of. My other son and daughter and their families were first, of course, but not having a real body freed up a lot of time—I didn't have to sleep, or eat, or do any of those other body things I don't need to name—and not being able to actually interact with anyone I soon grew bored. So I amused myself by walking into places I could've never gone alive: the top of Mt. Everest, the wreck of the Titanic, the White House, and so on. But that's another story.

I was, by all accounts, a useless ghost. I couldn't leave any backwards messages on walls or even give anybody the chills. The only thing I could consistently do was interfere with television reception. I noticed that screens got fuzzy lines on 'em when I stood near—or even better, inside—the television. But that didn't help me none, although I did get a laugh and a bit of a tingly feeling out of it. One time, I thought I was having a similar effect on my son's flickering porch light, but I couldn't be sure. The bulb may have just been worn out.

The day of my funeral everyone was dressed in suits but me. I still wore the jeans and thick flannel shirt I died in, inasmuch as a ghost wears anything. The priest was boring, so I went outside and watched the workmen dig the hole. And that was when I finally saw her, sitting in the cab of the backhoe, just about on top of the guy operating it.

"Mary," I said, "where've you been?"

She shrugged. "I don't come around here anymore. But I heard you died, and thought I'd pay my respects." She hovered down from the earth-moving machine until she just about touched the ground in front of me. "You look terrible, Mike."

I reached up and felt my face—it was still unshaven, though the funeral folks had shaved my corpse's face. "I reckon I do, Mary. After all, I *am* dead. But then again," I continued, "you look pretty terrific." And she did, too. The last time I saw her she was gaunt as a skeleton, her blue eyes were dull, and she was mostly bald from the chemo. But since her death she looked at least twenty years younger. Her eyes all but glowed.

"Thanks," she said. "I've been working out."

"What?"

"Lost your sense of humor, did you? Never mind. So, how's death treating you?"

"Well," I said. "I don't like it much so far. In fact I've got some business left undone and I can't figure out how to fix it." I was a bit coy about the whole bomb thing, I guess. But they were Mary's kids too, and I thought she might be angry with me if I told her I'd doomed one of 'em.

Mary nodded. "I know."

"You do? How?"

She looked square at me. "You put that thing in there just after I died, didn't you? I spent a lot of time around the house back then—don't you remember how often you had to change the fluorescent light bulbs in the garage? I tried so hard to tell you that mine was a bad idea, but, well . . . " She shrugged again. "You know how it is."

I sighed. "I'm sorry, Mary. I think I killed one of our kids."

"I think so too."

There was a pause so long that I was buried by the time it was over.

After the hole was filled in and my friends and family shuffled away, I turned back to Mary. "What do we do now?" I asked.

I don't know if it was my imagination, but I thought I saw her blush. She looked at the ground. "I don't know what you'll do. You've got that business to take care of, first thing."

"I know," I said, "but I don't know how."

She shook her head, and her voice was sad. "I don't either. But I don't want to see you again until you fix it."

"But Mary—"

"No arguments, Mike. No excuses. If any of our kids are even injured by that thing, I won't see you again. And, well . . . there's something else."

"What is it?" I asked, sullenly. A hopeless feeling like I'd never known was coming over me.

"It's just . . . well, it's been eight years. And I do have a life here. No pun intended." She laughed a little, but quickly stopped. "I've been seeing someone."

I couldn't speak. To tell you the awful truth, I wanted to hit her. I'd never once hit a woman in life, and I wasn't even sure if two ghosts could feel each other, but I wanted to try it. In the end, though, I forced myself to calm down. "What about our vows?" I asked her, surprised that my voice sounded more sad than angry. I lifted my left hand up and pointed with the right to where my wedding ring should have been, and that was the first time I noticed it was gone. I knew I'd been wearing it when I died, and I'd noticed that the stiff in the box had been wearing it, but it wasn't on my finger.

Next to me, Mary nodded again. "Our vows," she repeated. "Till death do us part."

Ghosts *can* feel each other. I know it 'cause I felt her kiss my cheek before she was as gone as anything ever was.

The next day my kids met in my house after the reading of the will. Since I hadn't left any special instructions—or warnings, fool that I was—the three of 'em were set to divide up my possessions. It was only a matter of time before they got to the garage and its terrible surprise. I could hardly stand to watch them, especially when one of them would find something of mine or Mary's and sigh in that peculiar way. Or when one of them would start to cry, as they all—even my boys—did at one point or another. But I couldn't bring myself to leave either.

Finally they made it to the garage, all of them together. I wished they could've seen me, and not just because contacting them was my goal. They would've laughed so hard to see their old dad bouncing around the garage like something out of a cartoon, waving my arms and screaming at the top of my ghost lungs. But I was frantic. It was bad enough that any of them should find the bomb, but if they were all in the garage when it went off the likelihood was that they'd all be killed, or at least injured. And then, well, they'd be dead, which would be an obvious tragedy. At that moment, though, I was more worried about what they'd think of me, and what Mary would. I believed her when she said she'd never see me again.

I thought about what Mary'd said about the fluorescent lights, so I hovered up by the ceiling trying to get them to do something significantly ghostly to attract attention. All of a sudden I regretted never learning Morse code, but then again my kids probably didn't know it either. Just the same, I figured everyone knew the three long, three short, three long code for SOS, and I made that my goal. If I could make the light flash that pattern obviously enough, surely one of them would have to notice it. So I got up there and actually put myself inside one of the lights, and just thought about the pattern I was trying to make.

It's too bad there's no training period for being a ghost. I bet there's all manner of things I could've done if I'd just known how. I wasn't up there more than a few seconds before the lights started to flicker, randomly at first, but then the pattern got stronger and clearer. I could see it made them all uncomfortable, but so far none of my kids had perceived the flickering as a message from beyond the grave. They winced and made faces at the lights. My daughter joked that she was going to have a seizure. Art got up on a stepladder to fiddle with the long bulbs, but of course it had no effect. I could remember, now, doing the same thing eight years ago. I wish I'd known then how close Mary was to me.

Without warning, the light I hovered in shattered. Pieces of glass rained down over the garage as all three of my kids shouted in unison, and I don't know if the wiring was overloaded or what, but all the lights in the garage went out at once, and without any windows the place was pitch dark.

My kids stumbled around in the dark until one of 'em reached the door to the house, and by that light they all left the garage, mumbling about glass in their hair, old wiring, and flashlights.

I'd bought some time, and I knew this might be my last chance to save them, though I still didn't know how, precisely. I did know that I'd somehow caused a fluorescent light to explode. I knew also that for the first time since dying I felt tired, almost dizzy. Apparently whatever I'd done to the light had taken energy, and now I was down some. Ghosts, I speculated, must be some part electricity, in order to affect lights and televisions.

This was good news for my kids, because the mine's trigger was electric. I thought, though, that it might have been bad news for me. If blowing up a fluorescent bulb made me feel this weak—I'd have called it lightheaded, if I had a head—I wondered what blowing up a bomb would do. Could a ghost die again? I didn't know, and I have to admit the thought scared me. I thought about leaving for a good minute or so: I could visit all the tourist sites in the world, find out what really goes on at Area 51, and maybe find a nice ghost who'd someday become as dear to me as Mary.

In the end, though, I knew that wasn't true. I flew through the door of the third upper cabinet from the right, on the west side of the garage, and sat so my ghostly form surrounded the claymore mine I'd set for myself. I didn't know what was going to happen, or how to make it happen. So I just closed my ghostly eyes real tight and thought, *This is for you, Mary.*

And that was that.

Emily C. Skaftun lives in Seattle with her husband and their child, a cat who thinks he's a tiger. When she's not teaching or writing, she dabbles in roller derby, flying trapeze, and other absurd activities. But mostly she writes, because the world is a better place with ghosts and flying tigers in it. Emily has an MFA in Creative Writing and is a graduate of the Clarion West Writers Workshop. Her stories have appeared in Strange Horizons, Ideomancer, *and* Flurb, *to name a few. Find her on the web at:* skaftun.blogspot.com.

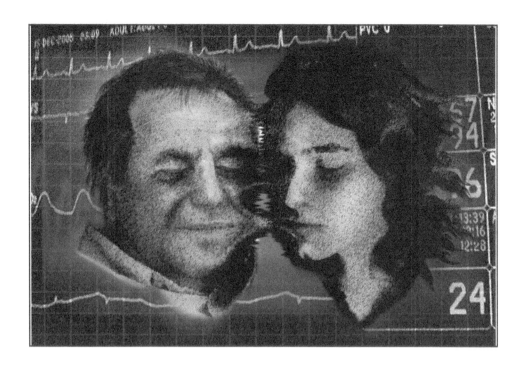

ACCLIMATION PACKAGE

JOE MCKINNEY

Should you wake up decades after dying, be leery of the people who brought you back. Acclimation Package *explores the not-too-distant future, in which the deceased may be returned to life. The biggest problem? Acclimating them to current times. The solution? Surgery, technology, and a little logistical ingenuity. The author, Joe McKinney, knows a thing or two about examining the human condition, being a police officer, award-winning novelist, columnist, and family man, not to mention humorist. When I first spoke with him about submitting a story to this book relating to "what happens after we die," he replied he would send me a blank piece of paper. As it is, I'm happy he came up with the following alternative possibility.*

The dark was all around him, but that wasn't the frightening part. He rose through it effortlessly, as if a current of water carried him along. That part felt good. It felt *right*.

What scared him was that he was not who he was supposed to be.

He groped around in his mind for his name, for some idea of who he was, but all he kept coming up with was the name, Heather Carter.

That's not right, he told himself. *My name is* not *Heather. It's not, it's not.*

But it was. He couldn't escape the terrible certainty of it. The dreamlike fog was clearing from his mind and, with it, the bewilderment of the darkness. He really *was* Heather Carter, a twenty-four-year-old doctoral candidate in Applied Neurology at the University of Texas in Austin. He had a boyfriend named Michael, and a cat called Boomer, and they all lived in a little apartment not far from campus. He had a good life, lots of friends, a job in Peking waiting for him after his graduation next May. He and Michael planned to get married right before they left for China. They'd even settled on a date, June 20, 2035, just over a year away.

Wait, he thought. *What? 2035? That can't be right.*

Desperately he searched through his memory, trying to push his way past everything having to do with Heather Carter. But when he turned inward, the picture of himself that rose in his mind was of a slim, dark-haired, attractive girl in her early twenties.

No, he insisted. *That's not me.*

But who am I? Think, damn it.

Think.

And then it hit him. He saw himself as a stocky, slightly overweight man with a badly receding hairline named Dan Spencer. He was forty-four years old, a cop in the Austin Police Department. And it was July 6, 2013. He knew for sure because that was the day he . . .

Died.

Horror overtook him. His heart pounded in his chest. His stomach rolled. He remembered pulling up on a kid trying to break into a car. The kid took off running and Dan chased him through some government housing at the corner of Turner and Lexington. They ran through a darkened hallway and emerged into a courtyard, where a clothesline strung across the sidewalk caught him under the chin and laid him out flat on his back. He remembered looking up into a black sky, gulping for air, unable to move. And then the kid yanked the gun from his holster and stood over him, looking at him down the length of the barrel.

There was an explosion of white light.

He tried to move, but his limbs felt like he'd slept on them wrong, like they were asleep. He tried to scream, but couldn't.

And then a thought occurred to him.

Or, not so much a thought as a realization.

Relax. You're okay. There's no danger here.

Spencer couldn't accept that. He wanted to get up and run. To where, he didn't know, but he felt cornered and frightened and all he wanted to do was get away.

But then another realization struck him, and this time he sensed that it came from the girl he'd visualized when he passed through the darkness. She pushed herself into his mind, telling him to relax. Her thoughts didn't come across as words. They were more like impulses, and those impulses pulled him toward calm, toward acceptance of what was happening. He wasn't sure why, but he sensed he could trust her.

Spencer willed himself to relax.

His vision started to clear. Shadowy forms moved overhead.

They're fixing you, the impulses told him. *They'll take care of you.*

The shadowy forms grew a little clearer.

"Core temperature is normal, Doctor," said a female voice. "He should be coming around any second."

Spencer turned toward the voice, but only saw a dark blob floating just out of reach. He tried to speak, but only managed a groan.

"Yeah, there he is," said a man's voice. "Everything's looking good. Mr. Spencer, can you hear me?"

Spencer blinked uncertainly. He could see now that the shadowy figures were doctors and nurses in blue surgical scrubs. One of the doctors had a strange looking contraption over his eyes, like a set of night vision goggles, only much smaller. There was blood on his scrubs.

"Mr. Spencer, can you hear me?"

"I . . . I died," Spencer said.

The doctor laughed. "That you did, my friend. You most certainly did. But you're back in the land of the living now."

"What year is it?"

"Today is November 2, 2034. I guess we should call that your new birthday, huh?"

Spencer groaned and slid back into sleep.

The next morning Spencer woke in a hospital room. Every muscle ached, and when he tried to sit up, it made his head swim.

With great effort he made his way to the bathroom and urinated.

They'd been force-feeding him fluids and he was surprised his bladder could hold so much. But then, he'd been holding it for twenty-one years. He supposed he should be happy that everything still worked.

He hobbled back to bed and fell onto the pillow.

Spencer glanced at the bedside table and saw what looked like a black pane of glass the size and shape of a credit card. *A brand new Touch*, he thought. *Those things are expensive.*

His mind drifted for a moment before he caught himself.

How did he know what that was called?

He picked it up, and was surprised at how heavy it was. It looked like highly polished glass, but it didn't feel breakable at all. In fact, it felt solid as a stone. There were no obvious controls, but he surprised himself again when he dragged two fingers over the face of the device and it immediately came to life. A note appeared on the screen:

Mr. Spencer,
This is for you, compliments of the Lazarus Institute. Be in touch later this morning,
Wayne Graham

The jingle for the Apple Touch played in his mind: *Always be in touch with your brand new Touch!*

He smiled at Graham's little pun. It was just like Graham to greet him with a play on words.

Wait. What?

How did he know that? He'd never heard of this Wayne Graham in his life, yet somehow he knew the man was the CEO and chief psychiatrist for the Lazarus Corporation.

And, apparently, he knew him well enough to recognize his sense of humor.

And knew the ad jingle for a product he'd never seen before.

What the hell was going on?

But, curious as he was, he felt drawn to the Touch. He tapped the device and the startup menu appeared. He spent the next twenty minutes going through one menu after another, amused at how easy it was to navigate, at how effortlessly he worked the controls, like he'd been using it all his life.

And that's when it finally hit him.

He shouldn't be able to do this.

He started to rise, thinking he'd go to the door and turn on the lights, but he stopped himself and said, "Lights, sixty percent."

The lights slowly rose, muted just enough for his still-tender eyes to handle.

"Huh," he said. Something else he shouldn't know how to do.

On the far wall hung what looked like a television screen. He didn't see any controls, though. And there didn't appear to be a remote.

Unless . . .

He scooped up the Touch and, sure enough, there was a menu to sync it with the TV. Maybe he could catch some history documentaries. The doctors told him he'd been dead for twenty-one years. TV might fill in a few of the gaps. But a huge number of the programs listed looked like they were in Chinese. Then it occurred to him that he could read the foreign characters on the screen. He chose a documentary at random, something about the American Gulf Coast, and stared in amazement at the TV as a pretty young Chinese girl explained how global warming had caused sea levels to rise and turn much of the Texas and Louisiana coasts to marshland.

Houston was an underwater graveyard.

New Orleans too.

But it wasn't so much the things she said that surprised him. She spoke in Mandarin.

And he understood her.

A knock sounded on his door and a man's voice said, "Mr. Spencer, this is Dr. Graham. Are you awake?"

Spencer shut off the TV.

"Yes," he said quickly, a little taken aback at the hoarseness in his voice. "Yes, come in."

A tall man entered. He wore a blue, long-sleeved shirt, open at the neck but without a collar, beige slacks, and black shoes that looked as shapeless as bath slippers, though they had a high shine, like patent leather. His features were angular, almost gaunt, and his gray hair and beard neatly trimmed. There was a breezy confidence about him that put Spencer at ease, like he was finally going to talk to the boss and get some answers.

"I see you got the Touch I left for you," Dr. Graham said.

"Uh, yeah, I did. Thanks." He pointed to a chair by the foot of the bed. "Do you want to sit down, Dr. Graham?"

"Would it make you feel more at ease if I did?"

"Doc, I don't care if you stand on your head, just as long as you're willing to tell me what the hell is going on."

Dr. Graham chuckled.

"What's so funny?" Spencer demanded.

"Well, to be honest, you. You're handling yourself really well. I guess it's your training as a policeman. You're accustomed to maintaining your composure while dealing with strange and stressful situations."

"Doc, don't blow smoke up my ass. Just tell me what the hell's going on. How come I know how turn on the lights and use this Touch thing, and how come I know how to—"

He was about to say, *and speak Chinese*, but a sensation like a sharp stick jammed into his mind stopping him before he could finish the sentence.

Dr. Graham brightened, like Spencer had said exactly what he hoped to hear. "How come you know how to do what?" he asked.

Spencer shook his head. "You know, all of it. What's going on with me, Doc?"

"You're not experiencing anything else, are you? Anything specific?"

He shook his head again. "No. Just tell me what's going on. Please."

"Okay," Dr. Graham replied. "I'm surprised you haven't figured it out already. But maybe you haven't asked the right questions yet. You see, you were given what we call an acclimation package. Something to help you adjust to your new circumstances."

"I'm sorry, I don't understand."

"No?" Dr. Graham sighed. "Okay, let me back up. You died. You were shot, and brought to the University Medical Center, where a decision was made to put you in cryogenic suspension. You know, freeze you?"

"Sure, I know what that means."

"Well, we thawed you out."

Spencer touched the wound on his chest. Even beneath his bandages, it was still sore.

"We fixed your wounds. You have an artificial heart now, by the way. The best on the market."

Spencer looked at him. "But, how do I know how to do stuff like work this Touch and turn on the lights."

"I think you'll find you know a whole lot more than that. You see, here at the Lazarus Institute our job is to help those who have recently returned. We've been doing this for a few years now, and the first few that we returned did not adjust well to their new environments. They . . . well, let's just say some of them had psychotic episodes."

"What kind of psychotic episodes?"

"They woke up just as you have, confused, disoriented, maybe even a little frightened. Plus, they've just jumped fifteen to twenty years into the future. Everyone they've ever loved is older, or dead, and their skills are obsolete. They can't find a job, they can't interact, go on dates, use a Touch. They're lost. As a result, many of them had psychotic episodes."

"But what does that mean? What happened to them?"

"Did you ever read *Brave New World*?"

"I don't think so."

"It's about a man who's brought from a primitive culture and put into a super-advanced one. Eventually, he kills himself."

"Oh."

"Yeah. And, well, our business here at the Lazarus Institute is bringing people back to life. Suicide is bad for business."

"Makes sense."

"That's where the acclimation package comes in. You see, we've found a way to implant the experiences of a contemporary person into the subconscious of a Revival. That's our term for a person who's been resuscitated."

"You mean you've given me the memories of a dead person?"

"Memories? Is that what you're experiencing? Do you remember anything of the person whose experiences you received?"

Again, the sharp stab in his mind.

He winced.

"No. Or, well, I don't know. I know how to do things I shouldn't know how to do. I can turn on the TV. I can work the lights and the toilet, that kind of stuff."

"But nothing else? Are you sure? No ghost images of the donor? Are you experiencing any sort of identity overlap maybe? Do you know the name of your donor for instance?"

The sharp pain was back, but Spencer forced it back down. He didn't need a warning here. He was a cop, after all, and he could tell when someone was too eager, too interested. Whatever it was that Graham wanted, he was trying a little too hard to draw it out, and Spencer's cop instincts started blaring the alarm.

"Nothing like that," he said. "Just the other stuff. The toilet and the lights and this Touch thing. It's a lot to take in."

Graham nodded. "You are part of a grand experiment that may one day change the nature of human existence. Right now all we can do is transfer the experiences of a donor but, in the future, it may be possible to transfer the whole mind. The memories, the emotions, the intelligence, the very soul itself, if you believe in that. Imagine, Mr. Spencer. Death will be no more."

He paused then, his eyes locked on Spencer's.

Spencer sensed the doctor was not so much looking at him, waiting for a response, but trying to stare into him. It seemed like he was peeling away the layers of Spencer's mind, as if he desperately hoped to find something that had been hidden from him.

"You understand how important this is, don't you?"

Spencer nodded, but the voice in his head, Heather's voice, screamed at him to keep quiet.

"Your donor was an extremely gifted young woman who was working on the problem of total transference, and she was very close to achieving it. I just want you to know you can talk to me about anything odd. That's what I'm here for."

He's holding something back, Spencer thought.

Spencer smiled. "I sure will."

"Good. You'll probably need to sleep most of the day. Coming back to life can really take it out of you, you know."

Spencer's smile widened, and he went right on smiling until the door closed behind Dr. Graham.

Graham was right about him needing sleep. He crashed hard.

But his dreams were uneasy, and he was restless.

He kept seeing images from Heather Carter's life.

She and Michael in bed on a Sunday morning, Boomer stretched out between them, purring while they rubbed his belly and scratched behind his ears.

Michael holding her hand while a young guy with a black Mohawk put a tattoo on the small of her back, just below the panty line.

Graham with his finger in her face, screaming that she was holding out on him, calling her a liar and an ungrateful little bitch, and then threatening her.

And still more.

An elderly Chinese man named Ti Song, owner of the Li Chuong Corporation, flanked by two menacing looking bodyguards, offering her seven billion *yuan* for the exclusive rights to her research.

Heather, in her lab, terrified. She'd hooked herself to the neural recorder and worked with desperate haste to download her mind as someone tried to force his way through the door behind her.

Spencer bolted upright, panting, drenched with sweat. He could still hear the psychic echo of fists beating on the door.

The room was dark, and he sensed it was the middle of the night. He sat there without bothering to raise the lights, trying to get his mind around the memories he'd seen. Who was this woman inside his head, and why would somebody want to kill her? That last memory was awful. He'd never been so scared.

But before he could straighten it out in his head, there was a noise of something heavy dropping to the floor outside his room.

The next instant the door burst open and two Chinese men rushed inside. Red laser dots appeared on his chest. Behind them, a third man dragged the limp body of a security guard inside.

The third man reached down to the guard's utility belt and removed a pair of handcuffs. He spoke in Mandarin. "Hold his hands behind his back."

One of the other two men holstered his weapon and pulled Spencer from the bed. Spencer felt his hands pulled roughly behind his back and the familiar bite of handcuffs digging into his wrists. He tried to cry out, but the third man was already slapping a strip of black tape over Spencer's mouth.

In that moment, Spencer recognized him: Li Shin, grandson of Ti Song, and heir to the largest privately-owned fortune on the planet.

"Move him quickly," Li Shin ordered. "Quietly now."

They hustled Spencer out the building and into a waiting car that shot out onto the darkened streets of downtown Austin. Despite the gun pointed at his head, he stared out the window at the city in amazement. All the signs were in English, Spanish, and Mandarin. The buildings looked familiar, for the most part, and Spencer saw enough to figure they were heading east. The car accelerated quickly and quietly, and Spencer noticed it never seemed to shift gears. Cars, it seemed, had come a long way.

He sensed Heather's fear underlying his own. They hadn't bothered to blindfold him, and that was bad. They wanted to get at Heather, he knew that much, and once they got her they would have no use for him. He was as good as dead.

Spencer's mind raced for a way out. He looked out the front windshield and saw they were approaching I-35. There were still lots of people around, but that would almost certainly change as soon as they crossed the highway. If he was going to do something, it had to be now.

He reached into the folds of his hospital gown and pulled out the Touch. The man next to him still had his gun trained on Spencer's midsection, but he was watching a group of drunken college girls cross the street, clearly liking what he saw.

Spencer worked quickly.

At the Austin Police Academy picking a pair of handcuffs was one of the first lessons he'd learned. He could still remember Randy Gorman, a big bear of a man who taught tactics, standing over him and yelling, "A skinny runt like you, Spencer, some gangbanger's gonna have you in your own cuffs in no time. What are you gonna do when that happens? Now pick the damn lock!"

He positioned the Touch so that he could jam the edge down into the gap between the ratchet arm and the receiver.

It just fit.

Careful not to give his movements away, Spencer worked the Touch around until he felt the tension in the receiver release, and then slipped his wrist from the cuff. The other cuff was still attached to his right hand, but that was okay because a swinging ratchet arm made an excellent weapon.

He waited for the car to stop for a red light.

Time to do it, he thought.

Spencer shifted his weight forward, just enough to allow his hands to move.

He waited for the man in the seat next to him to look out the window, and then he struck, raking the open pair of handcuffs across the man's face with three hard jabs. The teeth of the open ratchet arm cut the man's face to shreds, and his grip on the gun loosened.

Spencer pulled it away from him, pressed his back against his own door, and shot the man in the head.

Li Shin barely had time to register surprise. Spencer turned the gun on him and in Mandarin told him to unlock the door. "Do it," he said. He gestured toward the dead man. "Do it or you end up like that."

Li Shin said nothing, only glowered at him, but the door locks clicked open.

Spencer opened the door and ran into the crowd, still wearing only his hospital gown. The crowd gawked and laughed at him, at first, but when they saw the gun their laughter turned to screams and they scattered in panic.

And the general panic was enough of a diversion for him to get off the street.

Strange-looking, wasp-like helicopters flew overhead minutes later.

Spencer hid beneath a nearby carport, out of sight. But the helicopters were already zeroing in on his location. Any moment now and Li Shin's men would be closing the net. He'd done enough of these manhunts as a policeman to know that the hunted didn't stand much of a chance, especially once the helicopters turned on their FLIR equipment. And that was technology from twenty years ago. No telling what toys those helicopters had up there now.

Spencer tried to think like one of the hunters. They would, of course, rely on their technology. Cops of his day had done the same. The infrared cameras would pick him up, even under this carport. Also, they'd ping his cell phone.

His cell phone!

He'd forgotten about his Touch. He still had it, and he was pretty sure Li Shin could track him through the device's GPS feature. If they'd been able to do it back in Spencer's day with a cell phone, Li Shin would have no trouble at all with this thing.

They were probably already on the way here.

There was a weathered old truck a few parking spaces down from where he sat, and it would have to do.

Spencer got underneath it and put the Touch on top of the leaf springs.

When he stood up again, he saw a college kid with a beer bottle in his hand staggering by. He ducked back down and waited for the kid to pass. Then Spencer stepped onto the sidewalk behind him, hurried forward, and threw an arm around the kid's neck, folding him to the ground with a sleeper hold. He kicked the beer bottle to one side and pulled the kid back under the carport. Then he stripped him and switched his hospital gown for the kid's clothes.

Spencer was about to throw the kid's wallet back in his lap when the voice inside his head stopped him.

Check the wallet. Look for a VIAtrans pass.

Spencer, who took pride in being an honest cop in his first life, opened the kid's wallet with a grim sense of purpose. His new life was less than two days old, and already he'd committed murder and aggravated robbery. What would he do for an encore?

He found the pass and dropped the wallet back in the unconscious kid's lap. Then he looked at the VIAtrans pass, no idea at all what it was for.

The public line picks up at Red River and 15th Street, the voice told him. *Take it west.*

"To where?" he said.

He was answered by a single word: *Michael.*

Forty minutes later he stood on a strip of grass, looking up through the nighttime sky at his old apartment.

No, he reminded himself. *Heather's* old apartment.

Hurry.

It wasn't so much a voice he heard this time as an impulse, a need.

Michael's up there. Hurry. See Michael again.

"Okay, okay," he said. "How do I get in?"

Passkey. My Touch. Hurry.

"I don't have a passkey and I have no idea where your Touch is."

Hurry. Please hurry. See Michael again.

"Does your apartment have an alarm?"

Yes. Code 43567. Hurry.

"Yes, I know. See Michael again."

Spencer climbed the stairs to the second level, entered the code on the keypad next to the door, and waited. He expected the door to swish open or something, like on *Star Trek*, but when that didn't happen he remembered he still needed a keycard, which he didn't have.

There was a tall, narrow window of frosted glass next to the door. He looked around again, thought *Well, here goes nothing*, and broke it out with his knee. Then he reached through the broken window, unlocked the front door, and stepped inside.

The impulse that rose in his mind came with such force he nearly crumpled to the ground.

Home! See Michael. See Michael!

"Okay," he muttered. He took a few steps into the darkened living room and was about to call out to Heather's boyfriend when he saw something move from the corner of his eye.

It was a young, athletic-looking man in a t-shirt and flannel pajama pants, stepping around from behind a door. He had long, dark, tangled hair and two days worth of stubble on his face.

Michael!

Before Spencer could say anything the man let out a startled scream, then reached just inside the door and came at him with a baseball bat.

"Whoa!" Spencer said.

He jumped back, knocked over a bar stool, and nearly tripped over it. He regained his balance just as Michael swung the bat, bringing it down with a crash on the bar, missing him by inches.

Spencer spun around the corner of the bar and found himself in a little galley-style kitchen with nowhere left to back up.

"Wait!" he pleaded.

"You break into my house . . . " Michael said, and raised the bat to swing at Spencer's head.

"No, wait! You don't understand."

"You're a dead man."

Well, yeah, that's true, Spencer thought. He lifted his hands, palms out in a gesture of surrender. "No, please, listen to me. Heather Carter is in my head."

Michael stopped in his tracks.

He lowered the bat an inch.

"What are you talking about?" he said. "You better start making sense."

"Man, I wish I could. But your girlfriend, Heather, she's in my head. Those people at the Lazarus Institute put her there."

The bat sagged a few more inches.

"I don't know how to describe this, exactly. But whatever your girlfriend did was more than what they do for other acclimation packages. I was dead, and when they revived me, I had her in my head. You see what I mean? *All* of her."

Michael's shoulders sagged. He looked exhausted, but Spencer suspected it was actually the combined weight of grief and shock and a sense of hope that he didn't dare acknowledge, all bearing down on him at once.

"How much of her do you remember?" Michael said.

"I don't *remember* anything. It's her. Don't you see?" Spencer pointed at his temple. "She's in here. All of her."

"Oh my God," Michael said. More and more of that hope he hadn't dared acknowledge shone through his expression. He dropped the bat. And then, more to himself than to Spencer: "She did it. I can't believe it."

The sound of breaking glass made them both spin around.

Dr. Graham stood there, a pistol in his hand. The smile on his face was cruel, predatory.

"Graham, you son of a bitch," Spencer said. "I knew you were crooked."

"There's nothing crooked about wanting to save lives, Mr. Spencer. I would think a policeman would respect that."

"Go to hell."

"Mr. Spencer, once I get at those secrets inside your head, I can guarantee you that is one place I will definitely *not* be going. Now step over there, both of you."

Michael looked at Spencer for some sign of what to do.

Spencer motioned with his chin for him to move.

"That's far enough," Graham said.

Michael stopped in his tracks, hands still raised in surrender, and looked at Graham, who now pointed the gun at Michael's face.

Spencer recognized the look in Graham's eyes. He'd seen it twice before, while working patrol. That was the look of a man who had made up his mind to shoot. He didn't need Michael, Spencer realized. In fact, Michael was a problem best put down immediately.

Heather stabbed him with another mental surge, but Spencer didn't need the prompting. He lunged forward and put himself between Graham and Michael. He still had his hands up, but he suddenly felt in control. He could tell from the way Graham held the weapon that he hadn't been properly trained in its use.

Graham, for his part, looked like he wasn't sure what to do.

"Get out of the way," Graham said.

"Not a chance."

"I'll shoot you, Mr. Spencer. Right where you stand."

Spencer took a step forward, and Graham lurched backwards. He almost lost control of the weapon.

Spencer smiled at him. "No you won't. You need me alive, at least for now."

Before Graham could respond, Spencer hooked his foot around the fallen barstool and kicked it at Graham's head. Graham raised his arms to protect his face and when the barstool hit him, the gun went flying. It landed in the dark somewhere by the sofa.

Spencer moved fast. He stepped forward, threw a punch at Graham's chin, and sent him sprawling into the wall. Michael's bat lay on the floor next to him. Spencer picked it up and swung for the fence just as Graham lunged for him, arms spread wide for a tackle.

The air rang with a ferocious crack as the bat connected with the bridge of Graham's nose. The doctor slumped to the ground, and the air leaving his chest sounded like a tire going flat.

Michael stepped around Spencer and knelt by Graham's side. He put his fingers to the man's neck, looking for a pulse.

Then he stood up. "He's dead."

Spencer almost asked if he was sure, but then realized the man was a doctor. He looked down at Dr. Graham's corpse and shook his head. A second murder. Wow, this new life of his was really something.

"Tell me something," Michael said.

"What?"

"Can she talk to me? I mean, through you, can she talk to me?"

"No. I don't think so. I get information from her the way you get an epiphany. The right answer just sort of pops into my head. But I do get strong impulses. Specific impulses."

"Like what?"

"Well, like right now, those impulses are driving me to kiss you."

Michael looked like he didn't know whether to laugh or make a fist. "Look," he finally said, "this is weird enough already. Don't you dare try to kiss me."

"I'm not," Spencer said quickly. "I'm just saying. You asked."

Michael nodded. He pointed at Graham. "We need to call the police."

"We can't do that."

"Why not?"

Spencer sighed. "He's not the only one after me."

"But who . . . ?" And then the question on Michael's face turned to horror. "You mean, Ti Song?"

"His grandson, Li Shin."

Michael groaned. He looked around the apartment, as though saying goodbye to it, and turned on Spencer.

"We have to get you out of here, and I mean quickly. Li Shin won't give up."

Even without Heather's impulses, Spencer knew that was true. He'd seen that in the man's eyes back in the car. "Okay, so what do we do?"

"We have to get you out of that body."

Only then did Spencer realize Michael hadn't been talking to him at all.

Getting into the Lazarus Institute was the easy part. They had Graham's access card, and that opened every door in the facility. All they needed to do was slip past security, and Spencer figured he could help there. He was going to be decidedly less help though on the hard part, getting Heather Carter out of his head.

It normally took a team of trained doctors to do that.

Spencer said, "I have a memory of Heather doing the operation on herself."

"Yeah, but she was the expert on it. She knew it even better than Graham did."

"But you're a doctor?"

"I'm a pediatrician," Michael said. "If you caught the measles I could help, but taking a full grown person out of your head is a little different."

Inside the Institute, the corridors were dark and deserted, no sign of any guards, and that worried Spencer. He didn't want to see them, but the fact that he didn't see at least one lone guard checking doors and poking around with his flashlight concerned him.

He was about to say as much when he peered around a corner and saw a brightly lit room at the end of the hall.

The guard station, he thought. *Great.*

Spencer turned around, meaning to tell Michael they were going to have to move fast, but he never got the words out. Li Shin and one of his bodyguards stood there, and Li Shin had a gun to Michael's head.

No!

Heather's cry in his mind was so desperate he nearly fell over.

"Hello again, Mr. Spencer," Li Shin said, in English this time. Spencer was momentarily surprised at how smoothly he spoke, no trace of an accent. "Stand up, please. And drop the pistol."

Spencer considered his chances. He couldn't shoot both men before one of them got off a shot, either at him or Michael. Angry with himself for letting the two men sneak up on them, he did as he was told.

"Excellent," Li Shin said. "This is going to happen without a lot of fuss, Mr. Spencer. You're going to come with us. Behave yourself, and Dr. Fenton here will be allowed to leave." He motioned at Michael. "And if Miss Carter cooperates, perhaps she and Dr. Fenton will be reunited sometime soon."

He's lying, the voice in Spencer's head insisted. *He'll kill Michael as soon as he can.*

Of course he's lying, Spencer thought back.

"Mr. Spencer, please." Li Shin motioned toward the darkened hallway with the muzzle of his gun.

"I'm not going anywhere with you."

Li Shin raised the gun to Michael's temple again. "I'm losing patience with you, Mr. Spencer."

"You won't shoot. Hell, all I have to do is start yelling and every guard in this place will come running." Spencer nodded toward the bodyguard, a small-framed but hard eyed-looking man who had his weapon trained on Spencer's knees. "You and Bruce Lee there wouldn't stand a chance."

"Is that what you're counting on, Mr. Spencer?" Li Shin suddenly smiled. "Then by all means, please yell. Yell loudly. Better yet—"

He pointed the gun at the floor between Spencer's feet and fired. The report made Spencer jump, but nothing else happened. Nobody came running. No alarms wailed. Spencer looked at the bullet hole between his feet and swallowed. When he looked up again, Li Shin no longer smiled.

"As you can see, there is no more security here. My people have the building locked down, and they are erasing all evidence that we have ever been here. So, it is you who has no chance. Unless you do as I say."

Spencer looked from Li Shin to the bodyguard and back again.

Kick the gun.

Spencer frowned. What?

Kick the gun.

He couldn't. Li Shin stood just out of reach. And the bodyguard was farther away still.

But then Li Shin turned slightly toward his bodyguard and in Chinese said, "Enough of this. Get them moving."

Do it now! Kick the gun!

And to Spencer's surprise, he realized he knew what to do. He knew nothing of the martial arts, aside from a few judo holds they'd taught him at the Academy, but Heather did, and with her to guide him, it came naturally.

He rocked his weight to his right foot, focused on the gun, and snapped a front kick square into Li Shin's wrist. Li Shin let out a gasp and the gun flew into the darkness behind him before he could react.

The bodyguard came right at Spencer, like he was going to push him in the right direction, his gun pointed off to the side. But before he could bring it up on target, Spencer kicked the man in the crotch so hard it lifted him a few inches off the ground. The man collapsed at Spencer's feet and rolled over onto his back, groaning sickly. It was all the opening Spencer needed, for the man's neck was exposed. Spencer raised his right foot and brought it down hard on the man's Adam's apple, crushing it.

The man rolled away, gagging in agony. He'd be dead in a minute, maybe two.

Behind him he heard a scuffle. Li Shin must have tried to get his gun back, for he was on his belly, reaching for it.

But Michael was on top of him, punching him in the back of the head.

Spencer scooped up the bodyguard's pistol and ran in front of the two men, put one foot on Li Shin's pistol, and pointed his weapon at Li Shin's upturned face.

"Wait!" Michael shouted. "Don't kill him."

"What? Get out of the way, Michael."

No, listen to him.

"Don't shoot him."

Li Shin stared at him. Spencer didn't lower his weapon. But he did let his gaze find Michael's and he nodded.

Michael reached into his pocket and came up with a syringe. He pulled off the orange cap and jammed the needle down into Li Shin's arm. The man flinched away, but not before Michael pushed the plunger down.

Li Shin squirmed.

"You won't . . . " he said to Spencer, one trembling finger raised accusatorially.

But he never finished his threat. Spencer saw the man's gaze wander. Li Shin's head was swaying already, chin sinking to his chest. Then he was out cold.

Spencer lowered his weapon.

To Michael he said, "What was that?"

"Ketamine. He should be down for the count."

"Dead, you mean?"

"Not yet."

Spencer looked from the unconscious Li Shin to Michael. "What do you mean, *not yet?*"

Michael stood up. "I mean we're going to kill him. Just not right now."

"We are?"

"Yep."

"And then what? How are we gonna get out of here? You heard him. This place is surrounded."

None of that seemed to bother Michael. In fact, for the first time since Spencer had met him, Michael seemed totally in control. "We need to do this quickly."

"Do what?" Spencer asked. "What are we doing here?"

"Making it so we can walk out the front door."

Spencer blinked at the white lights in his eyes. He groaned softly.

"Can you hear me okay? Can you see me?"

After a moment, his vision started to clear. Spencer lay on his back, on a table, looking up at Michael. Michael's brown hair was matted on his forehead with sweat, and in his eyes burned an intensity Spencer hadn't seen before.

"Get that flashlight out of my eyes," Spencer said.

"Ah, you're okay." Michael said. "Sit up slowly."

Spencer pulled himself up to a seated position and immediately wished he hadn't. His stomach twisted in knots and his head swam.

"I don't feel so good."

He looked over at Michael. Michael placed his arm around Li Shin who sat at a neighboring table

"What the hell . . . ?"

Li Shin looked at him and smiled. "Hello Dan."

Spencer felt his heart skip a beat. He looked around the room for more of Li Shin's goons, but saw none. "You two are working together?"

"No," they both said in unison. They glanced at each other and laughed. Li Shin said, "It's not like that."

"You know my name?" Spencer said.

"Of course I do," Li Shin said. "I was in your head for two days."

"You were . . . " He stared at Li Shin, and then it suddenly made sense. "Heather?"

Li Shin nodded, the smile widening.

"But . . . how? Where's Li Shin?"

Li Shin—no, Heather, he corrected himself—pointed at her head. "He's in here."

"In a fashion," Michael said, and again the two of them looked at each other and laughed.

Only then did Spencer realize he no longer carried the ghost presence in his head. When he looked inward, his mind felt strangely quiet, empty. There was no one there but him.

But then he looked up sharply. "You said, *in a fashion*. What does that mean? Where's Li Shin?"

"He's dead," Heather said from Li Shin's body. "But his experiences are here." She pointed to Li Shin's head. "I can use them when I need to. And I definitely think I'm going to need them."

"For what?"

"Li Shin is heir to the biggest privately-held fortune on the planet.

His family controls interests on every continent. But now, I control him."

And then it made sense.

Spencer said to Michael, "You used the Lazarus Institute's techniques to create an acclimation package for Heather."

"Exactly," Michael replied. "The only difference is that we put her into Li Shin's body."

"So now you have control over . . . "

"Over death itself," Heather said. "With Li Shin's money to protect us, no one can stop us."

Spencer's body sagged. He felt weak in the knees.

"But there is one thing, Dan."

"What?" he said.

"Even Dracula needed a Renfield. Someone to watch his back while he slept. If we're going to do this, it won't be alone. We'll need help. We'll need a bodyguard. What better choice than a former policeman, right?"

Spencer looked at Heather and Michael, then around the room. He remembered something Dr. Graham had said about a book called *Brave New World*. Well, that wasn't going to be him.

He said, "Can I name my price?"

And, laughing, she replied, "You mean immortality isn't enough?"

Joe McKinney has been a patrol officer for the San Antonio Police Department, a disaster mitigation specialist, homicide detective, administrator, patrol commander, and successful novelist. Winner of the Bram Stoker Award, he is the author of the four part Dead World *series,* Quarantined, Inheritance, Crooked House, Lost Girl of the Lake, *and* Dodging Bullets. *His short fiction has been collected in* The Red Empire and Other Stories *and* Dating in Dead World: The Complete Zombie Short Fiction. *For more information visit his website at:* http://joemckinney.wordpress.com.

HELLEVATOR

JOSH STRNAD

Is it true, that the anticipation before punishment is as bad as the punishment itself? Or is the anticipation even worse? That double-clawed knot that tears at your gut and your brain, causing you to contemplate your own worst fears. Imagine an almighty judgment that is passed, finding you "lacking" in virtuous merit. Imagine then wondering at what unknown torments await as you begin descent in the Hellevator. The following scene, by Josh Strnad, captures the conundrum of everyday man who simply may not see eye-to-eye with our prodigious assessor.

Norm stood in the middle of the chamber, shifting his weight from one foot to the other. He was alone, save for the thing dressed in the bellhop uniform, which was pretty much the same as being alone. That thing didn't count; it was nothing more than a set piece, a mockery, a minor detail in this vile farce.

Norm looked at his watch. All the people who had said *you can't take it with you* had been wrong, at least this far in his journey into the afterlife. He still had his clothes, his wallet full of bills and credit cards, his Rolex. The time on the watch read 3:25, although whether that was a.m. or p.m. Norm was no longer sure. It didn't matter. He looked back at the thing standing beside the door.

Well, what next?

The bellhop-thing smirked at him, the ghastly, emotionless smile of a mechanized corpse. "Going down."

The chamber rattled and jerked downward. Norm leaned for support against the wall, but as soon as he touched it he pulled his hand away, howling in pain. The skin on his palm sizzled like bacon in a frying pan. The walls—though they looked like cheap, ugly, wood-paneling such as could be found in the elevator of any old hotel—were as hot as molten lead.

Norm whimpered and waved his hand around in the air, not that the action would do any good. The hand already flared an angry red and had begun to swell. The thing manning the controls made no expression or movement.

Of course, Norm had expected hot. Wasn't that part of the deal? Fire and brimstone and all that? What he hadn't expected was this isolation, the sense of utter aloneness. If he had ever taken the time to visualize his concept of Hell, he would have imagined something that resembled the interior of a volcano full of screaming, writhing people   thousands of souls in torment. Maybe, in a lighter mood, he would have even pictured demons in red spandex jumpsuits poking people (mainly lawyers, with the occasional tyrant thrown in for good measure) with pitchforks. He wouldn't even have been too surprised to discover that Hell was something of an enormous, riotous party, something along the lines of a heavy metal concert where the drugs and booze flowed freely and the damned would rock out for all eternity. Regardless, he wouldn't have been the only one there. Misery loves company, after all, but so far he hadn't seen a single other person besides the thing in the bellhop uniform.

The setup was absurd, like a sort of cosmic practical joke. If he hadn't known for sure that it was so deadly serious, Norm might have been inclined to laugh. The elevator was small and cramped to a claustrophobic degree. The air was hot and stuffy, reeking of mildew and stale smoke. The floor was covered with a nauseating black-and-red paisley carpet. Tinny, crackling speakers located in the upper corners pumped in a repetitive four-note ditty played on some kind of chimes—an obscene parody of light jazz. Easy listening, it wasn't. Though the noise (for it could not be called music in any proper sense) was quiet, it seemed to pass right through Norm, vibrating deep in his bones and his bowels till he felt certain he would vomit, or crumble to dust, or both. The light was of a harsh, industrial quality, bright enough to see by but dim enough to strain the eyes. And, of course, there was the bellhop. The icing on this whole cake was that inhuman thing with its red suit and oily cylindrical hat, standing beside the door, pressing buttons as though it just stepped out of the nineteen-thirties.

Somehow it seemed right that Hell had an elevator system. They have to get people down there somehow, Norm supposed. He wondered how much longer it would be until he arrived, and what would be waiting for him when they did. Part of him wanted to just get it over with. The suspense of wondering was as bad as any other torture could be and, besides, whatever was down there couldn't be much worse than the elevator . . . *could it?*

For a moment, Norm was inclined to regret the choice he'd made, but that thought passed as quickly as it arrived. No. It would do no good to second guess himself. He'd made the right decision. Even now, he was sure of it. He was a man of principles, after all; he wasn't one to bend just because the going got tough. Somebody had to stand up for what was right.

It wasn't fair, Norm told himself. He deserved better than this. He was a good person, better than most. True, he hadn't been a religious man, and he never claimed to have been perfect, but he'd always done his best to live as he ought. If that wasn't good enough for those stuck-up snobs in charge, then they could keep their Heaven. He wanted none of it.

The elevator shuddered, and Norm almost stumbled into the bellhop, who made no movement to avoid him. The thing's moist, putrid breath made Norm gag, and he reeled back, looking up at the blotches on the stained, rotting ceiling. The elevator music seemed to stick in the foul-smelling air, enveloping him in a sonic cloud. Little tongues of flame licked at the walls and around Norm's feet.

It figured.

Norm shook his head. He could see through their little game. All that talk about grace and mercy was just a ploy to make people admit to guilt and unworthiness. That was all well and good, he supposed, for the murderers and rapists, but it wasn't going to fly with him. People like them needed forgiveness, but he deserved better. Why should he, a good man, need to ask for forgiveness? He had done nothing that needed to be forgiven.

Besides, any Heaven that let *those* sort of folk in, just because they had prayed some prayer at the last minute, wasn't one that he had any interest in being a part of. If anybody had asked him (which they hadn't), he would have voted on some sort of policy that would keep the riffraff out. He didn't see why any decent person should have to pal around with a bunch of lowlifes.

Oh, they had offered him the chance. Heaven's standards were exacting, but if he would just admit that he couldn't make the grade on his own and throw himself on God's mercy, he too could have been a part of their little club. If he was sorry, truly sorry for all his sins, and asked for what they called the "free gift of eternal life," he could have it. What a load of garbage. How stupid did they think he was?

Norm had been around the block enough times to know that nothing was ever free—not in the real world. Just read the fine print, babe. Everything had a price, and in the case of eternity, the price had been enormous. They wanted him to give up himself. They wanted everything, his will, his desires, his strength, everything that made him who he was, body and soul. They wanted him to give up his independence, to become needy. That was the cost of Heaven. They wanted him to beg—to beg like a *dog*.

Who did they think they were dealing with?

Norm had always believed that a loving God would never cast anyone into Hell and, in a manner of speaking, he'd been right. God did not banish him. The choice had been his own to make. In the end, he'd stepped onto the elevator himself, a free man. It was the only way he could maintain his dignity. He'd always been self-sufficient, and that wasn't about to change. No matter what. Heaven could keep its prudish standards, its wholesale self-denial. He wasn't interested.

Norm looked at his watch. The time read 3:25, although whether that was a.m. or p.m. Norm was no longer sure. It didn't matter. He looked back at the thing standing beside the door.

Well, what next?

The bellhop-thing smirked at him, the ghastly, emotionless smile of a mechanized corpse. "Going down."

Josh Strnad *is a small-town guy from North Carolina, an animation geek, a roller-coaster enthusiast, and one fierce board game opponent. When not guzzling hot tea and typing stories on his battered desktop computer, he dabbles in film making, writing music, and drawing cartoons. He's currently working his way through graduate studies to become a high school English teacher, writing his second novel, and illustrating his children's book in his copious spare time. Check him out on Facebook, or at* www.joshstrnad.com.

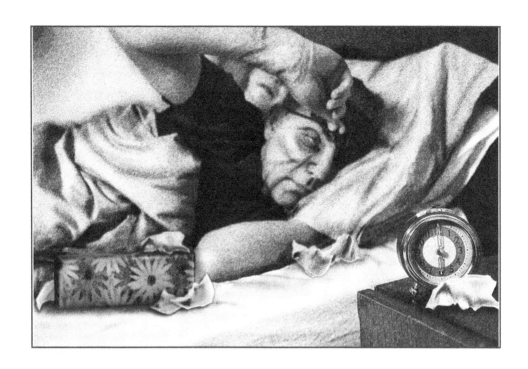

IN AND OUT THE WINDOW

ALLAN IZEN

I initially rejected this story, but the character's voice and exploits stuck in my head for months afterward. As I neared the anthology's final stage of editing, I knew I had to have it; the book didn't feel complete without including the next contribution written by Hawaiian, Allan Izen. Playful, yet honest, In and Out the Window *follows the passage of one man who seems to find appreciation for what life offers only after he loses it. Deep down inside, I suspect that will be true for us all.*

Go in and out the window
Go in and out the window
Go in and out the window
As we have done before

—Traditional

The last day of Charley Minetta's life was the worst.

He woke with a pile-driving headache, a stomach full of sewer gas, and his mouthparts gummed shut.

Estelle slumbered heavily beside him, swaddled in blankets, snoring like an eighteen-wheeler.

A gray morning rain scratched at the window.

He threw an arm over his burning eyes and wondered how he would get through the day.

He should stay home. That was obvious. Anyone who felt as miserable as he did would take a sick day, stretch out on the sofa, watch TV, have a couple of drinks . . .

Trouble was, he felt like this every morning. Every damned morning of his damned life, Charley Minetta suffered the agonies of the veteran alcoholic.

But a sick day was out of the question.

For one thing, Estelle would monopolize the sofa as she did every day. Bathed in flickering video pastels, she'd sprawl on the cushions in a baggy housedress, smoking cigarettes and engulfing chips, nuts, pretzels, and ice cream.

Charley knew from bitter experience that there was no place for him in Estelle's daytime world.

It was going to be a day—another one—to be suffered through.

He slid his legs over the side of the bed and put his feet on the floor. With a grunt of pain he pushed himself up to a standing position and gyrated into the bathroom as if doing *tai chi.*

Afterwards, he pulled on a pair of chinos and a white shirt. He slipped into a vest, buttoned it, and fastened his country-western belt.

He returned to the bathroom to clip on his plaid bow-tie and straighten it in the mirror. He pinned his name badge to the vest: *Quality Rite Super—Ass't. Manager CHARLEY MINETTA.*

Charley shuffled into the back yard, screen door banging behind him. The morning sun made him wince and the blare of birdsong sounded like alarm bells.

He folded himself into his musty old Buick and started the engine.

Charlie spent the morning putting together a cardboard display showing a chorus line of rubber-legged fruits and vegetables with big eyes and white smiles exhorting the customers: "Don't Forget To Take Home Some Fresh Produce Today."

His head throbbed, and the veins and arteries wrapping his brain felt bruised and achy. His organs seemed like crushed ice, and every ten minutes he ducked into the men's room to pee copiously.

After signing off on the noon milk delivery, he sat morosely on the loading dock steps and let out a blubbery sigh. If this was a hangover, he thought, it was the worst damn hangover he'd ever experienced.

This was ridiculous; he had to go home.

He shrugged off his apron and shambled down the pet food aisle to the front of the store to tell Heyman.

But Heyman, the store manager, saw sickness among his staff as a weakness, a disloyal act and a moral failing, so Charley decided to put his plight in public health terms, emphasizing the need to keep sick people away from food. He would also remind Heyman that he hadn't taken any sick leave this year. And, he would point out, he'd been staying late to take the receipts to the bank.

Heyman stood in the customer service booth counting money into an open cash register drawer. He didn't look up as Charley approached.

Charley waited humbly, waiting to be acknowledged, rehearsing his speech in his mind.

But he never got the chance to deliver it.

Heyman glanced up at him and growled, "Jesus, you look like hell, Minetta. Get outta here, *wouldja*? I don't want customers to see anyone like you around."

A blue-and-yellow telephone van blocked his driveway when he returned home. Naturally he hadn't been expected home in the middle of the day, but it irked Charley all the same.

He parked on the street, climbed out of his Buick, and gave the door a good slam. He trudged to the house and stepped inside.

And froze.

Estelle slept in the living room; he saw her from the alcove. She lay snoring on the sofa, her housecoat gathered above her waist, her top leg thrown over the leg of a man behind her. His thing was buried to the breech.

He too slept.

A blizzard of emotions exploded in Charlie's gut: hurt and horror, fury, fear, disbelief, and confusion, all erupting like napalm. Yet despite that, Charlie felt, for some hellish reason, uncomfortably stiff in the trousers.

My God, he thought, *she's beautiful.*

Lying there on the sofa, Estelle looked like one of those buxom beauties in an antique painting.

When had he stopped noticing?

Estelle reached down and gave herself a voluptuous little rub.

Charley felt paralyzed, even as he was swamped with desire.

He wanted to flee.

He wanted to make time turn backwards.

He wanted none of this to happen.

But it was right in front of him: happening, happening, *happening!*

His stomach clenched, his jaw knotted. If he carried a gun he would have used it.

On both of them.

As it happened, the only weapon in the house was an old Louisville Slugger baseball bat in the hall closet. He flung the closet door open, plunged his arms into the coats, and groped furiously for its taped handle.

Found it.

Raising the bat over his head, he stalked into the living room.

The man on the couch heard Charlie and leaped off the couch, his phallus swinging like a dead fish. He bent down to his clothes on the carpet and came up with a silver-plated pistol.

Charlie stepped back, wide-eyed. Suddenly this had escalated way out of hand.

The man aimed the pistol, squinted over the sight with a cold blue eye, and shot Charlie in the chest.

Twice.

Charley almost laughed. Two puffs of warm air tousled his shirt but there was no pain at all. Had the gun been loaded with blanks? Had he missed?

Estelle sat up and clapped her hands to her cheeks and began screaming in a tiny voice. Her screams sounded distant, as if on a radio in the next room.

"Oh my . . . oh my God . . . "

The skinny man turned, his now-rigid penis comically wagging in front of him. He put his hand on Estelle's pudendum.

"No!" She slapped his hand away. "No, not . . . not with him . . . oh my God . . . "

The man shoved her down and mounted her urgently.

The room was changing, stretching, tilting, the furniture shrinking. Charley realized he had grown taller, like Alice after she ate the cookie.

From his vantage point under the ceiling, the room looked like part of the *Clue* game board. Estelle and the phone man were like dolls rubbing their hips together on the sofa.

Charley saw a brown smear on the floor. At the end of it lay a torn laundry sack, sopping wet and leaking ponds of blood.

Was it himself? Charley thought. *Had the man really shot him?*

Charley wondered what the hell was going on. The air began vibrating as if a huge organ chord played. But there was no sound at all, only silence. The room grew dim, filled with shadows.

Aunt Ellie appeared and folded him into her arms. "There, there, Charley . . . "

Where had she come from? Aunt Ellie was . . . dead.

And then it dawned on Charlie: he was dead too.

All I wanted was an afternoon off, just wanted to get some sleep . . .

"There, there . . . " said Aunt Ellie.

Mitzi DeBeers was on Letterman tonight . . .

"There, now, Charley . . . "

But it was good to be with Aunt Ellie again. He loved the clean, soapy smell of her, the slow honey of her Southern voice. Her sturdy arms embraced him, petting, soothing him.

He buried his face in her breast. He tried to speak but all that came out was a chain of sobs.

Aunt Ellie had been his favorite aunt as far back as he could remember. She had looked after him since he was a baby. One of his earliest memories was of her smiling down at him in his crib.

He thought he'd forgotten those times, but the memories came flooding back, and Charley sat in his nursery once again, safe in the fascinating terrain of his crib with its wall of slats towering to an impossible height.

He saw Prinzi and laughed with delight at the doll's silly beanbag head. Prinzi had yellow yarn hair and red flannel disks on his cheeks. His mouth was a smiling U of stitches. And there, bunched up in a corner, was his blue blanket with the satin edge that felt so cool against his gums. His little pillows were there, too, and his stuffed bunny and rubber rings.

And then Aunt Ellie opened her arms and called goodbye as she let him drift away.

Charley woke in darkness.

There was no sound . . . no heat, no cold, no hunger, no thirst . . . only Charley in all his *Charleyness*, floating in the inky blackness with nothing to do but think.

And nothing to think about but his life.

He glided down his days as if on a brilliant road.

When he came to those first days with Estelle, his throat tightened and tears brimmed. Not just for the wretched way he knew their relationship would end, but for all the seasons of his life he had squandered. His life had been a pile of golden coins and he'd let them spill heedlessly through his fingers.

He replayed scenes, sifted through his words, his deeds, analyzed everything. He immersed himself in the ferocious joy and wonder of childhood, the stridency of youth, and the awkward climb to manhood and middle years. With a calmness he'd never thought possible, he reflected on the shabby collection of hopes, plans, frustrations, elations, and despairs that comprised his life.

With time came understanding, and understanding brought acceptance and, in the end, forgiveness. Estelle's peccadillo had been the natural outcome of living with the closed man he'd been, a preoccupied, self-absorbed man who saw only her failings. For twenty-five years she sought romance in warm, paper sacks of fast food, retreating behind fleshy ramparts to protect her fragile heart from the sick, weak man he'd been.

Estelle only wanted to be loved.

Poor Estelle.

Charley did his best to cling to this zen-like state of enlightenment, but there were moments when he faltered and fell back into the hateful, small-minded creature he'd been. In such moments he felt that Estelle just plain two-timed him for a sleazy piece of ass with the phone man.

It was during one of these relapses that thoughts of *Estelle-as-whore* overwhelmed him, and he gave vent to a curse: "Oh, you bitch."

He didn't actually *say* this, of course, lacking any apparatus for speech, but he'd thrown a healthy jolt of mental force behind it.

And, no sooner was it out, then he sensed a change, a silent presence.

"Is someone there?" he asked.

"I was going to ask the same thing," came the reply. The voice sounded deep and slow, oddly gentle. "I heard what you said."

"What I said?"

"You know, *you bitch*."

"Oh," Charley said. "My wife . . . she cheated on me. I think about it a lot and every time I think I'm over it, *bang*—it jumps up and bites me in the ass."

"I know what you mean," his companion replied.

"I'm Charley. Who are you?"

"Bo. And it's good to meet you, Charley, good to have someone to talk with." He sighed. "And believe me, I know what you mean about cheating wives. I had one, too. I gave her everything, my trust, my life, my love . . . everything. And then she, she . . . "

"They're a cruel race."

"I can't get over it."

"Yeah. I'd say Socrates got it right," Charley said.

"Who?"

"Socrates." There was a pause. "You never heard of Socrates?"

"I haven't."

"He was a philosopher. Long time ago. Anyway, a student of his asked whether he should get married or stay single. So Socrates says, 'Whichever you decide to do, you'll wish you'd done the other.'"

They shared companionable laughter.

"Yeah," said Bo. "My father used to say the only thing worse than looking for a mate was *finding* one."

"Isn't that the truth?"

"When Massissa and I got married, *whoo*, she was hot as a lava vent. She wore me out. Me, Bo, the biggest stud in the pod."

Hot as a lava vent? Biggest stud in the pod? Bo was clearly something of a poet.

Bo continued. "I'm not ashamed to tell you, brother, I couldn't keep up with her. The harder I tried, the softer I got. So what does she do?"

"I can imagine," Charley said.

Bo's voice quavered. "She left. She went back to her girlfriends—boyfriends, too—and, naturally, tells everyone I can't do it anymore, the barnacle-bellied slut."

Bo sighed philosophically. "Of course now I see that she couldn't help being what she was. I've been thinking about this for a long time and I've come to accept it. But sometimes . . . sometimes, I swear to God I wish I'd killed her."

"What was that you called her?"

"Massissa."

"No, the other thing. Barnacle something?"

"Barnacle Belly? Yeah, they loved her. The damn things tore me up something fierce when we were courting. I've still got—I used to have scars."

"What are you talking about?"

"You know, *barnacles,*" Bo said

"No, I don't know *barnacles.* Barnacles are in the ocean. They grow on rocks and ships. How do barnacles get on your belly?"

"Jeez, Charley, they just grow there. Didn't you ever swim in the reefs?"

"I never swam *anywhere.* I never learned how."

Bo laughed uncertainly. "I don't get it Charley. You're *human*, aren't you?"

Bo said 'human,' but in his mind Charley saw a long, baleen whale in bottle-green water.

"Wait a minute," Charley said. "You live in the sea?"

"The sea? What's that? I live in water, if that's what you mean. Wait, Charley, water is the world. You don't mean to tell me you're from . . . *not* water?"

Charley never got the chance to reply.

A distant boom echoed through the darkness like a great door slamming shut.

Charley knew he was alone again.

He saw a bead of light in the distance, felt himself moving toward it.

He would have a better life this time, he vowed. He would *make it* a better life, would hold on to the wisdom he'd gained in this dark place. He would be more loving, more appreciative, kinder, more tolerant, honest, compassionate, open, and giving.

He was moving faster, the light dilating as he drew near.

He was rushing through a tunnel lined with membranes.

The membranes collapsed apart making way for him as he tumbled out into quiet olivine water and the love of a majestic cetacean mother.

Allan Izen feels that every story is a horror story, if you look at it that way. He believes that shivery stories keep the willies at bay and make the real horrors easier to manage. Mr. Izen lives in Hawaii surrounded by shark-infested waters and ominous rain forests. He has sold fifty-odd (some, very) short stories. He is also the owner, principal photographer, and the entire custodial staff of Eye Zen Images, a fine-art photography studio.

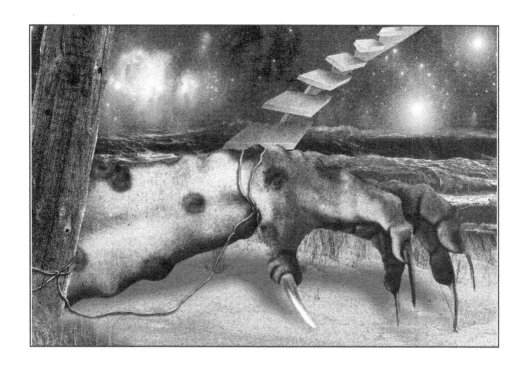

WITH MAX BARRY IN THE NEARER PRECINCTS

JOHN LANGAN

As with all journeys we assume a final destination, and thus we arrive at such: the last story in this book. I selected this piece as "the closer" as it is the longest and most ambitious tale I acquired for my anthology. In addition, this story perhaps leaves the strongest lasting impression, a good sentiment to retain, once you close the final page. The brilliant John Langan creates an entire mythos, a rich history and alternate suggestion to the traditional view of Heaven as our hereafter. The world and characters and conflict he creates are impressive, and I only hope that someday this may be expanded into additional stories or even novels. For now, pay heed as we go forth With Max Barry in the Nearer Precincts. *If only we all could be so prepared with the answers of what to expect once our time on Earth is concluded.*

None of us should have been surprised: if anyone could have been expected to find his way back, it was Max Barry. Hadn't he spent the last three-quarters of a century investigating the murky terrain just the other side of this life? Hadn't one of the three of us accompanied him for the last two decades, as he roamed the country searching out and interviewing those who had ventured the margins of existence? Hadn't we entered those accounts into Barry's massive archive (properly cross-referenced, of course) and helped him coordinate the information he retrieved, to arrange it into practically a map of the undiscovered country's nearer precincts? With almost the final breath his failing lungs could muster, Barry promised us at least a sign—not so original a pledge, perhaps, but one weighted by the accumulated years of his research.

And yet, when myself, Torres, and Schaefer were the recipients of not just a sign, but the presence of the man, himself, our combined reactions might have been lifted from the most formulaic horror film. We had gathered around the oak table in the study as we did every Thursday evening. With Barry a fortnight in the family mausoleum behind the house, there was little reason for the three of us to be there, for while we had been more than diligent in the work we performed for him, the quality of our efforts owed itself less to any shared passion for the subject and more to the generous paychecks he signed every other week—that, and the force of his personality, which had the effect of a powerful magnet on a scattering of iron filings, snapping them into alignment with itself. While his will appointed us trustees of his estate at salaries every bit as comfortable as those we had drawn as his assistants, and while that document allowed and encouraged us to use a substantial portion of the Barry fortune to extend his research, absent Max's presence, the offer held scant interest for us.

Although we had spent the first meeting after his death in reminiscences of Max, and half the second in gossip, we continued to gather in the study with its thick green carpet and heavy black curtains from an obscure sense of loyalty, a desire not to allow the project of a man's life to end mid-sentence, but to bring the paragraph to a full and complete stop. We hadn't any notion how this was to be done, whether the archive, for example, might find a home at a sympathetic university; or whether one or the other of us might write the account of our experiences in Barry's employ; or even whether we might hire a new, younger group to continue the task of exploring the other side by proxy—but I believe we felt that, if we carried on our meetings, eventually, the solution to our dilemma would present itself.

There were two empty chairs at the table that night: the one usually occupied by Barry and the one which frequently went unoccupied but occasionally sat a guest Barry had invited. It was in this second, typically-vacant chair that Max Barry suddenly sat.

If I were to attempt to justify the screams that erupted from Torres, Schaefer's string of oaths, my start up from my seat, it would be through an appeal to Barry's appearance. Anyone who has been in the presence of a corpse knows the fundamental *difference* of the dead, their utter stillness, the lack of barely-perceptible motions through which life percolates out of us. Although it wore his favorite black suit, white shirt, and black tie, the figure that sat in our midst was as motionless as it had been in its coffin. Because of its slackness, the face was at first unrecognizable to me; it was the work of some seconds to identify the large, round nose, the long forehead, the lips that always seemed too thin for the wide mouth. Had the eyes been open, I might have fitted the pieces of the puzzle more quickly, but they were—and remained throughout his visitation—closed.

Once I assembled its components into Barry's large, plain face, however, and understood who it was beside me, a rush of pure terror caused me to shove my chair back and retreat to the couch, which I almost fell over. Torres found her voice before the rest of us. "Max—Mr. Barry?"

The figure's mouth dropped open like that of a ventriloquist's dummy. The voice that issued from it was unmistakably Barry's broad, pleasant one, but it sounded off, as if it had been poorly-recorded, then played on a stereo with a shorted speaker. "Ms. Torres," it said. "Mr. Schaefer. Mr. Anderson."

"Mr. Barry," Schaefer and I said.

"You've returned," Torres said.

"Yes," the figure said. "Did I not say I would?"

Torres stuttered an answer. The figure—Barry—said, "It is all right, Ms. Torres. You were right to be skeptical. It has ever been your role in our little group."

"How are you?" Schaefer said.

"I still *am*, Mr. Schaefer. What about you, Mr. Anderson? Do you have no words for your old employer?"

The note of familiarity in that strange voice made my bowels clench. My mouth was dry. I licked my lips and said, "What can you tell us?"

"Very good," Barry said. "Very good. I am not sure how much time I will have with you, so I'll try to be direct. From the beginning, then— or the end:

The passage was about what we had anticipated. As my vision grew dark at the edges, it brightened at the center. From a point, the brightness swelled to a circle, which opened into a tunnel. I rose out of my body toward it. The process was as easy as the reports led me to expect. If I had to compare it to anything, it would be to swimming, to pulling your arms and kicking your feet and feeling the water move around you. My astral body was a fairly exact copy of my corporeal form, with the exception that its senses appeared sharper for the transition. That, and I wore, not my hospital gown, but my suit. The sensation—the white tunnel seemed to be tugging me to it as much as I was floating to meet it. I looked down and saw the three of you around my bed, the doctor turning away. I saw my body, the final breath leaving it. I felt more buoyant. Ahead, the white tunnel reached to an end incredibly distant and blindingly brilliant, the heart of a star. The nearer I drew to the opening, the stronger its pull became.

I had the impression that, were I to exert myself, I might resist the tunnel's attraction. There was some interest to me in this. Having investigated so many reports of ghosts, what an opportunity to assume the role, myself. This temptation paled, however, in comparison to that of venturing the white tunnel. Now I could see figures within it, detaching themselves from the wall. There were three of them. Each appeared dressed in white robes. Their faces were too far away to distinguish yet, together, they produced a feeling of profound calm, almost familiarity. I thought they might be members of my family, come to welcome me to the next stage, my mother and father, perhaps, one of my sisters. I gave myself up to the tunnel.

There was the impression of traveling without movement. Whiteness sped by; otherwise, I might have been standing still. The trio of white forms swept around me. Their faces were no clearer; each remained a bright blur. I saw that what I had taken for their robes was in fact their substance. They brushed against me, and the calm this produced was almost soporific—even hypnotic. Ahead, the tunnel's brilliant destination was larger, closer. It seemed I could glimpse something beyond that opening, a landscape of rolling hills through which wound a shining river. Beyond the hills, a city like an arrangement of great white crystals rose into a blue sky.

On all sides, the white trio pressed against me. Despite the tranquility they radiated and the impression of familiarity, I was uneasy; indeed, it was that overwhelming calm that disturbed me. Rather than the Heavenly peace I at first took it for, it verged on the anesthetic. Through the blur, I perceived one of the trio's faces, and it was empty, as an open mouth is empty. I was more shocked by this than made afraid, but a profound fear gripped me when I concentrated on the end of the tunnel—nearer and brighter still—and saw, not the slopes of paradise, but a vast, shining emptiness. Dulled as my senses had become, I felt what lay at the terminus of the white tunnel was alive, a living void. It was hungry, primordially so, and it was that appetite that drew me up from my failing body along the white tunnel. I had a vision of an aardvark searching for ants. This was not the God-as-blank of negative theology; it was the open maw of the Behemoth.

Although wrapped in lethargy, I knew at once I must escape my escorts. This was no easy task. The closer we approached that great mouth, the more the white figures crowded me. One kept directly in front, the other two behind and to either side. There was no time. Summoning what little energy remained, I threw myself to the left. One of the figures behind grabbed me, but surprise gave me the advantage and I pulled free. The wall of the white tunnel rushed toward me. I struck and plunged into it—I would compare the sensation to diving into a pool or lake, except the medium that enveloped me was thicker than water, more viscous, though not so much as to immobilize me. Brightness blinded me. Kicking and pushing, I struggled through the material of the tunnel wall. For a long moment, that I might remain trapped in this place seemed an awful possibility, a fate only slightly less worse than being swallowed by that enormous gullet. The medium thickened around me, my movement became difficult. Frantic, I pushed forward. In response, the wall stretched. Mustering my strength, I pressed against it a second time. At the tips of my fingers, I felt the substance part.

All at once, I was free, tumbling through darkness. Behind me was a brilliant glare, a river of light filling the near horizon, flowing out of the distance, into the distance. Beyond it, I could discern other, similar streams, as I could when I turned my attention to what lay before me. From their appearance—narrow brooks in comparison with the flood next to me—I guessed each must lay at a considerable remove from its fellows. As I slowed, I perceived more of the lines of light, so that the entire—I suppose I should call it the sky—above me resembled a tremendous net.

Pieces of the white trio had adhered to my arms, my chest. When I tried to work my fingers under one of them, my eyes filled with the sight of the celestial landscape I had thought I'd seen at the end of the white tunnel. Nausea climbed my throat. In a kind of frenzy, I ripped and tore at the fragments attached to me, flinging each a different direction once it was loose.

Somewhat more calm, I decided I must move. While the white trio had not appeared in pursuit, I was reluctant to venture any direction that would bring me too close to the blazing tunnels. This precluded all courses save one, down, into the darkness below. In the collective glow of the tunnels, I picked out dim, shadowy forms an uncertain distance away. The nearest of them did not appear unduly far. By kicking my legs, pulling my arms—in effect, "swimming" as I had in the tunnel wall—I was able to propel myself toward it.

I descended I am not certain how much, but when I looked up, the tunnel I escaped was a good three-quarters diminished in width, from river to stream. Sufficient light remained for me to distinguish that the nearest shadowy form I sought was actually a structure.

It was a staircase, rising from the deeper dark. The top three or four steps were jagged, incomplete, as if it previously had climbed higher; what was visible of the remainder appeared whole. Each of the steps was wide enough to accommodate two adults at a time. Their surfaces had been grooved by the passage of countless feet. I circled the staircase warily. There were no individual bricks or slabs I could see; the entire thing appeared to have been carved from a single piece of material. I swam closer. I thought the staircase might have been struck from a great block of stone, cut free from a mountain, or chiseled from a tree of Redwood proportions, but the texture of the material was wrong for either. I reached out and touched the nearest step. It was warm and, though apparently firm enough to support the combined weight of countless people, oddly spongy. I eased myself over until I was directly above the stair, then rested on it, ready to spring off should the staircase threaten to give way. When it did not, I decided I would follow these steps down for as long as was safe.

As I descended step to step, I reflected on my experience. Obviously, the map of the next life I had charted was, to say the least, incomplete. When the tunnel of light had opened for me, I assumed myself *en route* to some version of paradise. Instead, I had been lured into what was, for all intents and purposes, a trap. Try as I might, I could not reconcile this with the details of any religions I knew, living or dead. The white void I saw might be hell or a similar place, but if such were the case, then why employ not only the bright tunnel, but the white trio to lure me there? Surely, a deity powerful enough to create such a place would have no need to resort to trickery to deposit souls there; surely, there were more direct means available. Not to mention, if eternal damnation were my fate, you would not expect me to have evaded it with such relative ease. Nor did my impression of that great emptiness as living fit with the descriptions of hell I knew; though, I will admit, it put me in mind of those medieval paintings in which the gates of hell are represented as the mouth of an enormous scarlet head.

From the moment I started down them, I kept track of the number of stairs I descended. By the time I reached four hundred, I could distinguish more clearly the other shapes I had seen from above. In what looked the middle distance to my right, a slender spire stood alone. Several smaller beams angled from its base, but the light was too dim, the spire too far, for me to tell whether these were supports, or bridges, or smaller towers that had collapsed against this one. Conceivably, they might have been pieces of the spire, itself, upper reaches broken by the same cataclysm that had sundered the top of the staircase.

To my left was a trio of squat towers that gained definition as I passed the five hundredth step. The nearest of these was no more than fifteen or twenty feet away, the next-closest just the other side of it, and the third not much further beyond. They were constructed of small bricks, each approximately the size of my hand, of a style so basic as to be universal. A long gash split the nearest tower's front wall; its companions showed similar damage. What was visible of the tower's interior showed plain, undecorated rooms full of shattered furniture, chairs, and tables broken to kindling.

Far ahead, an elaborate archway marked one edge of the dark plane to which the staircase led. To either side and beyond, the archway was joined by low, box-like structures that reminded me of rows of apartments. It was in one of these, past the archway, that I saw a light shining in a rectangular opening I realized was a window. This was not the brilliance of the white tunnel and its minions; this was the homely glow of an oil lamp, a fireplace. The sight of it hurried my feet past the six hundredth step.

Another forty-three stairs and I reached the foot of the great staircase. In front of me stretched a broad, flat space. At about the level of my thigh, a thick, black fog rolled slowly over the plane. So dense was the stuff that I could not see through it. I eased one leg into it. The fog eddied around my flesh. Under my foot, the plane was sandy, but not uncomfortable. I was reluctant to wade through it, but the gravity of this place seemed to have me in its grip. I could not float across; there was no choice but to walk through. Eyes fixed on the distant glow, I set off.

Overhead, lines of light sliced the sky into narrow strips of black. Although I still could identify the tunnel from which I fled, the remainder of my trip down the staircase had reduced its width further, to the point it was barely larger than its neighbors. While I am not much of a physical scientist, I felt fairly certain I had not crossed a sufficient distance to result in so dramatic a change in the tunnel's size. It was as if the stairs bridged more territory than they showed. I was unsure what this implied, beyond the suggestion that space did not appear to follow quite the same rules as it had the other side of death. I looked back at the staircase, the towers beside it and, yet though diminished slightly, nothing seemed as out of proportion as the white lines to which my eyes once more strayed. I saw them bending slightly at either end:

so far to the right it was barely visible, they disappeared into a pale yellow glow that suffused the horizon; equally far to the left, they were swallowed by what might have been a wall of heavy gray clouds.

I reached the midpoint of my trek across the dark plane. So intrigued was I by that yellow light, that surface of roiling gray, I stopped in my tracks in order to study both more attentively. As I stood gazing at the sky, something bumped into me.

The collision occurred at about the level of my knee, and while not violent, so startled me that I leapt back. In so doing, I struck a second object, which sent me lurching into something else. All at once, it seemed, I could not move without encountering whatever was about me. My way forward had been blocked by whatever my leg had met, which seemed to have closed off the space behind me, as well. Around me, the dark fog shifted. That I had blundered into a fate equal to or worse than the one I escaped at the end of the white tunnel loomed before me as a distinct possibility.

Beyond the arch, the window dimmed, then brightened, its glow eclipsed by a shape whose outline appeared distinctly human. Of course, the white trio had looked human enough, at first, but something about this silhouette—the particularity of its form—spoke of the human in a way those gauzy shapes had not. The sight heartened me. If I were to reach that window, I would have to find my way off this plane, which meant I must ascertain the nature of the objects that hemmed me in. I lowered myself into a crouch.

Even this close, the fog was tar-thick. Nonetheless, I distinguished an outline within it. In front and to the right, suspended horizontally in darkness as if in a bath or pool, was a man. He was naked, eyes closed, face calm, hands at his sides, legs together. I should place his age at thirty-five. I looked behind me and saw a woman, likewise suspended, naked, her face also blank. She appeared the same age as the man. Floating in the shadows beyond was another, somewhat older, man, and a child, a girl of perhaps twelve years of age, and another woman. As far as I could determine, the fog overlaying this plane was full of bodies. I stretched out my hand and touched the man in front of me. His skin was dry, papery; it crackled under my fingers. He seemed curiously light, not only from whatever quality of the fog kept him suspended, but as if he, himself, were hollow. Gently, I pushed his arm, and he swung away from me as if he were an oversized balloon. He bumped the person behind him, an old woman, who in turn jostled a younger woman beyond her, and so on. About half a dozen bodies away, one of them released a sound, a sort of high-pitched gasp. I straightened. At the spot from which the gasp emanated, the fog belled up. A man stood through it. He was tall, and within a decade or two of my age. His features were difficult to discern, because of what I took for wisps of fog clinging to his face. With a lurching gait, he staggered toward me. As he did, I saw that the black fog about his face spilled out of it, streaming from his eyes, his nostrils, his mouth, his ears. He raised his arms, and the motion unbalanced him, forcing him to half-run at me. When his hands found me, they gripped my shoulders with surprising strength. I caught his wrists and attempted to steady him, but he continued to push forward, thrusting his head at me, his mouth open.

I attempted to speak to him. "My dear fellow," I said, but his fingers dug into my shoulders, his neck stretching, lengthening, bringing his gaping jaw near. Black vapor poured down his face, into the fog below. The sound of crackling filled my ears. I said, "Please, I am not—" but did not know how to conclude. I *wasn't*, not the same as he was. I released his left wrist, clenched my hand, and struck what I hoped would be a solid blow to his sternum.

With the noise of a heavy paper bag tearing, my fist punched through his chest. A black cloud burst out of the wound. Horrified, I jerked my hand out of the man, whose hands let go of me. Black vapor venting from his chest, the man leaned back, as if trying to draw away from the hurt I caused him. His left arm drooped. He swayed to that side, and toppled under the fog, which leapt up where he splashed into it.

A mix of revulsion and confusion swept over me. The sight of a handful of men and women standing from the fog at various spots around me did nothing to help. I looked for the gateway, located it, and ran with all the speed my fear would lend. Black fog churned about me. My legs struck hidden bodies, sent them crashing into their neighbors. From points across the plane, other gasps sounded. Additional figures raised themselves out of the fog. I was reasonably certain they were moving in my direction, but was not inclined to stop to be absolutely sure. The gateway was close enough for me to see that, like the staircase that conveyed me here, it had been carved from a single block of material into the scene of an enormous battle. Dozens, if not hundreds, of men and women, dressed in armor and employing weapons whose style suggested ancient Greece, struggled against a quartet of huge, fantastic creatures. I was too concerned with reaching and passing through the gate to devote any more scrutiny to it. I was positive that, at any moment, a hand would seize my ankle and pull me down into the fog; either that, or I would find the clumsiness which had bedeviled my earthly existence had accompanied me to this place, and I would trip over my own feet and plunge myself beneath the fog.

Such, fortunately, was not the case. I ran through the huge gate, and among the buildings beyond. A backward glance showed a score, perhaps more, of men and women walking on the plane, none with any speed, and all a comfortable distance away. I slowed my pace, but did not stop running.

The space in which I found myself was wide, flat. The ground was the same sandy texture as it had been under the black fog. At random intervals, the stumps of what must have been modest trees raised edges broken and jagged. Long, low structures bordered the place. Each was two stories tall, constructed of the same, hand-sized bricks as the towers I had seen from the staircase. Their ground floors were punctuated by between fifteen and twenty plain wooden doors, their second stories by a pair of windows. All of the buildings showed damage of a kind consistent with that I had observed done to the towers, tears and rents through their walls that revealed the wreckage of their interiors. An entire corner of a building to my left had collapsed; while a building to my right had been practically bisected.

The light that had set me on this course lay ahead, splashed over the interior of a window set to the right of a wooden door. To either side of this window and its door, the building in which they were set bore enormous holes. This close, I had a better view of the rooms that had been exposed by the damage; though their contents were a jumble, I noted a mirror in a gilt frame, a polished chest of drawers, and a large bookcase full of fat volumes. As I drew nearer my destination, my run slowed, until it was a brisk walk. I strode up to the door, one hand raised to knock on it, and it swung open.Framed in the doorway was a devil.

Or, rather, framed in the doorway was a man dressed as a devil. His costume consisted of a red, satiny bodysuit that rose to a tight-fitting hood from the front of which sprang a pair of fabric horns. His face was ornamented with a Van Dyke no doubt intended to accentuate his infernal appearance. His hands were fitted with black gloves, his feet with black boots, and over the bodysuit, he wore a pair of black shorts from the left leg of which dangled a fabric tail, complete with barb.

The sight of him halted me where I was. With a wave of his hand, the man urged me inside, saying, "Come on, come on!" I hurried past him into a narrow hallway. He shut the door and secured it with a quartet of heavy locks and bolts. "It's too much," he said, "for the Hungry Men, and not nearly enough for a Child of Nun. But then, what is enough for one of the Children? You can't call it peace of mind, but you can call it the illusion of peace of mind, which, oddly, *provides* a certain peace of mind." The man walked by me to the end of the hall, where three doors opened right, center, and left, respectively. He pushed the door to the right, and gestured for me to follow.

I did, and entered a high-ceilinged room whose red wallpaper, oriental carpet, and fire snapping in a marble fireplace suggested the drawing room of a Victorian gentleman, an impression bolstered by the pair of high-backed leather chairs positioned before the fire. Under the room's window, an arts-and-crafts-style desk was stacked with papers and books, as was the abbreviated table to its left. The room was warm, even cozy. The man in the devil costume closed the door behind me and crossed to a small stand holding a crystal decanter and a collection of tumblers. He said, "Can I offer you a drink?"

If the question was absurd, it was no less so than anything else I had experienced thus far. I said, "I take it that isn't ambrosia."

"It is very good scotch," he said.

With something like good humor, I said, "Perhaps this is paradise, after all."

The man's face fell. "Oh no," he said. "In days gone by, it was—it was something, but not now, no."

He poured liberal portions into two of the glasses, and held one to me. With thanks, I took it. The dense odor of peat and brine, leavened with honey, hovered over the liquor. I said, "What shall we toast?"

"There is nothing to toast," he answered.

"For me, there is," I said. "I shall drink to your offering me shelter in this—in this place."

The man did not reply, though he took an ample sip from his glass. The scotch burned down my throat like the water of life its creators had christened it. I said, "Permit me to introduce myself. I am Maxwell James Barry, late of the city of Wiltwyck, New York," and extended my hand.

"I am pleased to make your acquaintance," the man said, taking my hand in his. "When I walked amongst the living, I was called Herbert Herne."

"And now," I said, "are you known as Mephistopheles?"

For a moment, my host did not appear to comprehend my joke, then understanding lit his face and he said, "The costume, yes—even here, it must look odd. Call it a bit of self-mockery, and something of an act of self-censure, the scarlet without the A, if you see what I mean."

"What use is such a gesture, here?" I asked. "I admit, I wondered whether this might be hell; in which case, your action might be appropriate. However, I strongly suspect this is not hell, and so must question the need for your penance."

"Not penance," Herbert Herne said. He drank the rest of his liquor. "I do not repent anything I did. *Anything.* At the same time, I recognize its cost. I know how I would be judged, were there any left here to judge me. It is out of deference to those absent intentions that I bear this sign in place of the one with which they would have branded me."

"I don't understand," I said. "Can you tell me where we are, what this place is called?"

"I can." Herne refilled his glass, held out the decanter to me. I shook my head. He replaced the container and said, "We are in what remains of First Heaven, sometimes known as Šamû. It was here that the first men and women to depart the lands of the living found their way."

"Who is its creator?" I said.

Herne shrugged. "Some say it appeared when the chaos that preceded everything grew chaotic to itself and birthed form and order. Others say it is a remnant of the paradise of another cosmos. It was here long before our universe burst into existence. It was a rough, rude place, an island floating in a Sea of Chaos from which creatures vast and terrifying emerged, giants with a hundred arms, dragons whose fire melted rock, chimeras whose hooves sundered the ground. The first inhabitants were confused, afraid. They built what shelter they could from the raw material at hand and huddled together for comfort. For decades, centuries, longer, as the island's population grew, little changed. The shelters became more elaborate, but the beasts of the surrounding deep, the Children of Nun, as they were later called, continued to climb onto the island and rampage through the buildings in their paths, carrying off what inhabitants they could to a fate none of their companions wanted to guess.

"Not until the arrival of a young man to whom posterity would give the name amar-Utu did the islanders' situation improve. While alive—somewhere in Mesopotamia, the stories say—this amar-Utu had not been held of much account, because of a right leg that was noticeably shorter than the left. No such affliction troubled his spirit form—what the residents of these parts call the *ka*. Once arrived and apprised of the state of affairs, he set about improving them. Such efforts had been made before, of course, over and over, but none who attempted them possessed amar-Utu's combination of charm and brilliance. The inhabitants had established a watch along the island's shores, but its staffing was irregular. amar-Utu convinced the islanders to maintain a more consistent schedule, and to set up a network of runners to pass the sentries' alarms more efficiently. In the same way, he improved and extended the shelters that had been built. His chief accomplishment, though, was in devising a strategy for confronting, defeating, and binding the Children of Nun.

"It was a labor to be measured in centuries. amar-Utu fashioned weapons to be used against the beasts. He organized the islanders into an army. He led this army against the beasts and, when it was defeated, forged new and better weapons. In the end, he and his forces dismembered several of the worst monsters, and pursued the rest to their lairs in the deep, where they chained them fast."

I asked, "What became of this amar-Utu?"

Herne said, "He left. Once Šamû was secure, and its people could turn their attention to building it into something more grand—a heaven worthy of the name—amar-Utu took his leave. In his campaigns about the island, he discovered it was not, in fact, an island, but the tip of a much larger land mass to which it was joined by a slender bridge of rock. Accompanied by Muš☐uššu, one of the Children of Nun he won over to his side, he set out to explore that other place. As the population of First Heaven grew, some of its more adventurous inhabitants followed him to what would be called Second Heaven. amar-Utu was no longer there, though he left signs indicating he had traveled further still into the unknown, moving through what those to come after him named Third, Fourth, and Fifth Heavens. By the time I arrived here, there were a full dozen heavens. amar-Utu's whereabouts were long-unknown; if asked, most inhabitants said he had 'gone to deeper heaven.'"

"What happened here, then?" I asked. "Did amar-Utu return and find the place not to his liking?"

"Oh no," Herne said. "amar-Utu has remained unseen despite the catastrophe. There were, naturally, some who looked to his return in their hour of need, but they were . . . disappointed." Before I could repeat my question, he continued, "As for what befell this and the other heavens: I did."

"You?"

"In life, I worked in insurance," Herne said. "I resided in Hartford, Connecticut, during the first decades of the twentieth century. I was something of a prodigy at puzzles, games, figures, and this talent served me well. Upon graduation from high school, I obtained a position at a medium-sized insurance company, where my abilities allowed me to achieve ten years' promotions in three. It occasioned no small jealousy in those I vaulted over, but I was otherwise well-liked. I performed in a community theater—*Faustus*, yes, among our productions, though I was cast as Wagner—and regularly attended the local Methodist church. When the United States entered the Great War, I was not enthusiastic to enlist; indeed, it required all my acting skills to convince my fellow workers that only my sense of responsibility to the company restrained me from joining the mad dash to bayonet a Hun in the name of liberty. With the war's end, I judged myself safe from foreign peril. I did not reckon on the Influenza epidemic of 1918, which conveyed me, and so many others, here.

"The possibilities for me in this place—once I adjusted to the revelation that it was not the destination Reverend MacGonagle had assured me was awaiting—the possibilities were as large as was it. I opted to work in one of the libraries, the better to learn about my new home. It was amidst the bookcases that I read the history of this place, the story of amar-Utu, which, as I'm sure you can imagine, is considerably more elaborate than the summary I provided you. I was fascinated with what the historians named the *Titanes Theoi*, the Straining Gods, the Children of Nun that amar-Utu and his forces had conquered and bound. Even here, on the other side of the grave, it was hard to credit that such fantastic things could exist. I made inquiries and found that, if I so desired, a guide would lead me to the Straining Gods. I should not have been so amazed: when eternity is the measure of your days, you realize all things are possible, and make plans for them.

"An older woman, a member of the army—largely a ceremonial force—met me on the far side of First Heaven, in sight of the rock bridge to Second Heaven. We were on the shore, where the Sea of Chaos does not look much different from any other sea. My guide, whose name was Cosette, walked toward the sea, at the very edge of which a stone slab had been sunk into the ground. She stepped onto it, and down onto another below it, and so on. I followed her, and we descended a staircase that skirted the very edge of the Sea of Chaos, but did not touch it. It was as if a wall of glass held the sea back, though I could not see any such glass present. Most of the way was dark, lit by lamps placed every hundred steps. I made what conversation I could with Cosette, but she was not talkative—odd, for a guide. There were ten thousand steps between First Heaven and the Straining Gods. We took them at a steady pace. At the bottom, we arrived at a flat, square space bordered by darkness. I walked to one side of the square and said, 'Where are they?'

"'Look,' Cosette said, and it was as if her command adjusted my vision. There, in front of me, no further away than the reach of my arm, was a nightmare. It was immense as a mountain is immense, a rounded bulk whose mouth was wide enough to swallow a battleship. Teeth—fangs tall as sequoias jutted from its lower jaw. Its three eyes were dim moons set high above. It appeared to be lying on its belly, its head propped toward me. In the distance beyond it, other forms, larger still, loomed in the darkness.

"I screamed," Herne said. "I am not ashamed to admit it. Making matters worse, I could see no chains encircling the beast. I said as much to Cosette when she ran to my side. My guide pointed out a slender rope strung around the creature. Similar bonds, she said, held all the remaining Straining Gods. You can appreciate the skepticism with which I met this information. I wondered if this were an elaborate joke, an entertainment for bored immortals, but Cosette was earnest. In front of us, the ends of the rope met in an elaborate knot that had callused the great beast's warty hide. Cosette took my hand and pressed it to the knot. I thought she wanted to make a point about the pattern into which the rope had been tied. When my palm brushed the rope, though, an electric jolt shot through me. With that shock came understanding.

"You will remember I mentioned those islanders the Children of Nun had carried off with them. One of amar-Utu's pledges to the inhabitants of Šamû had been that he would learn their fate and, if possible, rescue them. He fulfilled the first half of his pledge. After he and his army pursued the monsters to their lairs at the bottom of the Sea of Chaos, he discovered those who had been taken for provender. I am not sure if you've discovered this, yet, but we *ka* are difficult to destroy outright. It is not utterly impossible, but it is beyond the power even of the Children of Nun. What the creatures could do was feed on their captives, suck and scrape every last vestige of everything that made those men and women who they were out of them, until all that remained was a husk, too tough for digestion. Emptied, the husks wandered the lairs, hungry for what they had lost. They attacked amar-Utu and his forces, who defeated them handily. Once the soldiers realized what the Hungry Men were, they were aghast.

"I do not know what led amar-Utu to recognize that the stuff of the Hungry Men could be fashioned into bonds that would hold the Children of Nun. His words on the subject are vague. It would have been an awful scene. The end result was that, when amar-Utu and his forces subdued each of the remaining beasts, they had a means with which to restrain it. Various writers to come after amar-Utu sought to rationalize his decision, but it seemed clear to me that he did not depart Šamû to search out what was ahead, but to escape what lay behind.

"I could have viewed the remaining beasts—there were another three—but that one was enough. The return from my excursion left me with much to consider. Not least amongst it was the knot securing the monster's bonds. As we mounted the stairs, I asked Cosette if she did not fear that the knot might loosen. Of course she assumed I was foisting my anxiety onto her, and told me there was no need to worry. amar-Utu, himself, had devised and tied the knot that held this and all of the Children of Nun. She did not know how much attention I had given the knot, but its complexity was such that none who studied it since could work out how to undo it. Tug at one part of it, and you tightened another. Solving the Gordian knot would have been simpler. I reminded my guide that Alexander had answered that riddle with the edge of his sword. Such a reply, she assured me, would be useless in this case, as no blade in anyone's possession could sever the *ka* rope in which this knot and its brethren had been tied. Even were someone to own so fine a sword, who would use it to that end?"

I interrupted Herne. "You would. You did."

Herne said, "You must understand, from the instant my eyes fell upon that knot, its solution was obvious to me. This was part of the reason I became as agitated as I had at Cosette's assertion that this slim rope was sufficient to the task of holding a Straining God in check. With a quick pull of the correct loop, the design that was responsible for keeping this unlikely prison in place could be undone, which seemed the clearest madness. Twice, I was on the verge of speaking to Cosette about it, the first time when she pointed out the knot to me, the second while we climbed the stairs."

"Why didn't you?" I asked.

"I doubted myself," Herne said. "In the face of Cosette's expression of utter faith in the knot, I assumed I was mistaken. After all, how many men and women must have viewed that knot before me? Was it likely that, after none of them had been able to untie it, I should understand the means to do so the moment I saw it? And yet, and yet . . . I *had* apprehended its undoing. I was as sure of it as I had ever been of anything. Fearing embarrassment, I kept silent. Back in my quarters, however, I immediately found a length of rope and set about first tying the knot, which took me several tries, and then untying it, which I managed on my first attempt. My success did nothing to reassure me. I was certain I must have missed something in the fashioning of the knot, some detail that would render my solution of it null and void. At the same time, I knew that nothing had escaped my notice. I searched the library's holdings for images of amar-Utu's knot, and every last one of them I found matched the copies I had made.

"Then why not share your knowledge?" I said. "Surely, the powers who oversaw this place would have appreciated your discovery."

"Perhaps they would have," Herne said. "Or perhaps they would have imprisoned the man in possession of such information, fearful of the use to which he might put it."

"Would they have been wrong?"

"It was all I thought about," Herne said. "If there was a piece of thread lying about, I tied it into amar-Utu's knot and untied it. If there was a pen or pencil and a sheet of paper, I drew the steps to constructing the knot. If my hands were empty, they went through the motions of looping this end of the rope through that. If I were to say I was outraged by the use to which the *ka* of those long-ago captives had been put, that I burned for vengeance on their behalf, I expect my motivations would sound more compelling. But if I were disturbed by the material from which the Children of Nun's bindings had been drawn, I understood and accepted the necessity for it. No, what led me to return to that staircase on my own, to descend the ten thousand stairs, to stand once more in front of that Straining God, was nothing so grand. It was more a case of the knot's solution pushing its way out of my fingertips."

"Obviously," I said, "you were correct."

Herne said, "I had not anticipated the speed with which the beast would seize the opportunity I presented it. Despite millennia of imprisonment, during which it was fed nothing, it heaved itself up with the suddenness of an earthquake. Beyond it, the other beasts groaned and thrashed. I fled for the staircase, sure that I was going to be the morsel with which the monster would break its fast. It rose past me, larger even than I had appreciated. I was afraid it would smash the staircase on its way, which, despite my terrified state, I realized would constitute a kind of poetic justice, but though its bulk veered close, it completed its ascent without destroying my means of escape.

"I returned to war in the heavens. The great beast hung in the air. Its canyon mouth yawned, swallowing flaming missiles like so many fireflies. Its three tails raked the ground, toppling buildings as if they were children's blocks. Up and down its armored flanks, bombs and rockets burst in flashes of white, yellow, and orange. Behind its blunt head, an enormous mane dangled its ends above the forces gathered below. As I watched, one of the strands snaked into the ranks and jerked up, carrying a man with it. Other strands followed, plucking the defenders from their positions. The mane was composed not of hair, but of tentacles, each one terminating in a mouth. Once it wrapped around a man or woman, the tentacle's mouth sought his or her chest, clamped onto it, and fed. When the defender was drained, emptied, in the process of a minute, less, the tentacle dropped the remains and went in search of new prey. It was as if I watched a grotesque resident of the Pacific's depths, a fish half-dinosaur, feasting on a shoal of hapless fry. To be sure, there were those who remembered their last battle against this beast, but surprise gave it an advantage that the panic and confusion of the other inhabitants cemented. Vast as it was, it swelled with the lives on which it gorged, moving through the heavens with the slow, steady pace of a fire devouring a forest. In the end, it settled its bulk on the remnants of Seventh Heaven. From there, its tentacles rose into the sky, arcing toward the line of light that marks the boundary between this place and the world of the living."

"The bright tunnel," I said.

"Yes," Herne said. "The beast's limbs have enlarged over time."

"The figures within?"

"Parasites, I believe," Herne said. "They live off what they can siphon from the *ka* on its way to the beast. The tranquilizing effect they produce facilitates the process of consumption, so the creature tolerates them."

"Does no one escape?"

"Some," Herne said. "Enormous as the beast's appetite and reach are, it has its limits. Some elude its clutches; others, it never gets around to."

"What becomes of them?"

"Most find their way to what remains of the heavens. A few wander the dark. If those who arrive here can evade the Hungry Men, they usually wind up at my front door."

"I see no one else," I said.

"Come," Herne said, walking to the door. "Bring your drink, if you like."

I had forgotten I held it. I would rather have set it down, the taste for alcohol having left me, but already, Herne was through the doorway, so I carried the tumbler with me. He opened the door to the right of this one—the door at the end of the front hall—and started down a flight of wooden stairs. I hurried after him.

We entered a considerable basement, one which must have served for the entire building. Its walls were several feet higher than those of the room in which Herne had entertained me and, together with its breadth and width, gave the feel of having served as a market place, a common where the residents of the building could have gathered for conversation and commerce. The use to which Herne had put it, however, was anything but benign. From the wreckage of the rooms above, the surrounding buildings, he had scavenged material to construct the devices of a torture chamber. A pair of crude racks leaned against the opposite wall. A handful of heavy wooden tables, from whose corners thick chains dangled, occupied the center of the floor. Beside each, a smaller table held an assortment of knives, a sheaf of paper, and a mug filled with pens. A Catherine Wheel stood at the far end of the space. At points across the ceiling, coarse ropes draped sturdy pulleys. Herne was talking, explaining all of this, but while I heard his voice, his words did not register. Chained to the wall between the racks, a slender man with large eyes and ears regarded our entrance with terror. On either side of each rack, one of the creatures from which I had fled on the plane—the Hungry Men—had been bound.

Herne was counting on my shock at the sight of the room and its inmates to paralyze me. It very nearly did, which would have allowed him to strike me with the truncheon he had slipped from a hook on the wall at the top of the stairs. As it was, he caught my left wrist with his left hand and was in the process of pulling me into the blow he started with his right hand when I smashed the glass in my right hand into his face. Scotch misted the air. One of the shards drove into his left eye. He screamed, releasing my arm and dropping the club. Splinters of glass stuck up from my fingers, but I ignored them, driving my left fist into Herne's mouth. Dazed, he retreated, backing up a step. I took advantage of his movement, shoving him toward the nearest large table. He did not comprehend what I was doing until I pushed him half-onto the table and cuffed one of his wrists. He struggled, but my blood was up, and I struck his face again. I believe he expected me to turn his instruments on him, to seize one of the knives arrayed to my right and set its edge to his skin, but my chief concern was my safety, not his punishment—however deserved such might be.

My next thought was for the man fettered to the wall. There were assorted tools propped against the tables; I selected a sledge hammer and used it to break the plaster which anchored the chains to the wall. Free to move, the man walked to the nearest of the small tables and removed a set of keys hung under it. From these, he chose the key that unlocked his manacles.

Next, we began the laborious process of introductions and explanations. I say laborious because the man, whose name was Franz, spoke German, a language with which I have only a passing acquaintance. He knew a smattering of English, so we muddled through as best we could. He had died relatively young and arrived in the heavens in the last stages of the war against the great beast. He joined a rocket brigade in time to witness it torn asunder by the monster's limbs. After evading its tentacles, he roamed the ruined heavens, encountering the occasional fellow-survivor, shocked and despondent. Among these remnants, there was a move to leave this place, to set out for deeper heaven—"to follow amar-Utu," as the phrase went. In the end, each of Franz's companions elected to undertake this journey. Theirs was a choice he could not embrace; though he could not say why. In time, this led him here, to Herbert Herne, who captured and tortured him.

Have no doubt, I demanded answers from Herne, who, surprisingly, was happy to give them. Left alone, he had become fascinated, then obsessed, with the material of the *ka*, with the uses to which it might be put. After all, it sufficed to restrain the Children of Nun, a single one of whom was sufficient to wreck the twelve heavens. What, Herne wondered, might a man who had the crafting of such stuff do? What might he become? He ransacked the remains of the library, and while no one would admit to having carried out experiments in this direction, a few authors had speculated—sometimes in considerable detail—on the potential applications of the *ka* and the means by which those ends might be wrought. An abundance of raw materials lay at his disposal, including the remnants of those who had been drained by the beast, the Hungry Men. His laboratory complete, Herne succeeded in luring the creatures in ones and twos from the black fog in which they resided and trapping them. His testing of them had not been without success, but those very successes prompted him to wonder how much more he might accomplish with a soul not emptied of its essence. Herne observed the occasional survivor of the great beast's devastation picking his or her way through the rubble, and though he worried they might be wary of him, it proved laughably easy to coax them into his dwelling and subdue them. What Franz described as torture had been no more than the process by which he prepared the *ka* for its new role, breaking it down to a state in which it might be fashioned into any number of . . devices. To be candid, it was both a lengthy and an unpleasant affair for the subject of his attentions, but there was no malice behind it, only the disinterest of the craftsman preparing the material upon which he would work.

I feared the man mad, unhinged by the ruination he had precipitated. Yet Herne described his endeavors with a level of detail that gave the appearance of rationality, diseased though it might be. At the end of his account, I expressed my skepticism, to which Herne responded by directing me upstairs, to the one door I had not opened. Naturally, I suspected a trap, but my curiosity was piqued, and I ascended the stairs. I took what precautions I could, and opened the final door.

The room I entered was of the same dimensions as the study into which Herne first led me. Its wallpaper was white, its floor bare wood, its marble fireplace dark. In the center of the floor, a round table supported three objects. I approached it cautiously. Arranged in a triangle were a lens, a wand, and a coil of rope. The lens was approximately the size of a dinner plate, its upturned side convex. A slender gold ring enclosed its circumference, and seemed to lend its shine to the depths of the glass. The wand was long as a man's forearm, its surface pale and smooth. It was bowed in the middle, tapered at the ends. The coil of rope was small enough to rest in my palm. It did not appear braided; rather, it was a single, golden strand. That these could be props in an extended joke occurred to me: the man who had sent me to them was dressed in costume, and not just any costume, at that. But the air above them quivered, vivid with energy. I could almost see the suggestion of a face in the glass of the lens, the outline of a bone in the shape of the wand, the texture of a length of hair in the rope. Knowing what they were—what they had been—I could not bring myself to handle them. Not then . . .

The lens allows its holder to focus himself into another location, no matter how distant. It permitted me to join you here, tonight. The wand is a tool, something like a pen, and something like a sword. The use of the rope, Herne has not taught to me, yet. Yes, I have had to continue my dealings with the man. In the end, his store of knowledge was too great for me to forego. Franz has not been happy with my decision, but he understands my reasoning. I charged him with the task of guarding Herne, whom I was compelled to release from the rack. Franz watches Herne closely; all the same, I am careful in his company. I believe—

Barry's next words were interrupted by his image faltering. As if he were a television channel whose signal had ebbed, his outline blurred, his color dulled. His voice disappeared. For long seconds, Torres, Schaefer, and myself stared at the place in his chair where the shadowy outline that had been our late friend flickered. It regained its definition just long enough for Max Barry to deliver his final words to us: "My time with you is almost done. When I have progressed in my study of the lens, I shall contact you again. In the meantime, I am in the company of the devil and a man who assures me he was an agnostic. The heavens lie in ruins. Perhaps we may repair them. Perhaps, if amar-Utu will not return to us, we may seek him out, win his aid. If he will not, we may subdue the great beast, ourselves. I am in possession of Herne's inventions, and they are mighty. Every day, I learn more about them. It may be that they will prove sufficient to rout the monster. It may be that others will be required.

"Tell those who are nearing the end of their time in this world to beware the light, the bright tunnel and its denizens. In the light lies annihilation. Tell them to seek the broken staircase. But fly, fly the hungry light."

For Fiona

John Langan's *most recent collection is* The Wide, Carnivorous Sky and Other Monstrous Geographies *(Hippocampus 2013). He is the author of a previous collection,* Mr. Gaunt and Other Uneasy Encounters *(Prime 2008), and a novel,* House of Windows *(Night Shade 2009). With Paul Tremblay, he co-edited* Creatures: Thirty Years of Monsters *(Prime 2011). He lives in upstate New York with his wife and son.*

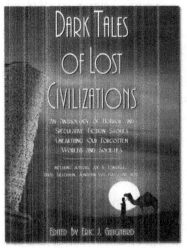

ABOUT THE EDITOR

Eric J. Guignard writes and edits dark fiction from his office in Los Angeles.

His most recent writing credits include *Stupefying Stories Magazine, +Horror Library+ Vol 5* (Cutting Block Press), *A Feast of Frights* (Best of The Horror Zine Magazine), and *Evil Jester Digest.*

His last book as editor, *Dark Tales of Lost Civilizations* (Dark Moon Books), was released in 2012 to critical acclaim, including a Bram Stoker Award® nomination.

Although his passion is for fiction, he's also a technical writer and a  published essayist including such diverse topics as genealogy, woodworking, banking, and ecology.

He's a member of the Horror Writer's Association and the Greater Los Angeles Writer's Society and is also the Horror Genre Correspondent for *Men's Confidence Magazine.* When not writing, Eric designs and builds custom furniture and is an amateur entomologist. He holds degrees in Communications and Environmental Science, as well as a Master's Degree in Public Administration (*California State University Northridge*).

Most importantly, Eric is married to his high school sweetheart, Jeannette, and father to an adventuresome toddler son, Julian James.

Look for his first novella, *Last Case at a Baggage Auction*, to be released in September, 2013 (JournalStone Publishing). Visit Eric at: www.ericjguignard.com or at his blog: www.ericjguignard.blogspot.com.

ABOUT THE ILLUSTRATOR

Audra Phillips spent her formative years in a tiny Colorado town called Brighton, where she learned to draw bunnies in church.

It all went horribly wrong from there.

Now, she is a Los Angeles-based artist specializing in matter of the strange and disturbed, favoring fallen angels, aspiring demons, and barely-human outsiders. She utilizes diverse media to create artwork including digital visuals, book covers and illustrations, and three-dimensional sculptures.

Recent commissions in the horror genre include cover artwork for the books *Mutation Nation* (Rainstorm Press) and *Jack and Jill: A Zombie Love Story*.

Audra's work can be found on display in various galleries, including recent solo shows at *Dark Delicacies* in Burbank and *Hatakeyama Gallery* in downtown Los Angeles.

To contact Audra for commissions or art shows, or just to marvel at her latest monstrous expressions, visit her online at: www.audraphillips.com.

Printed in February 2023
by Rotomail Italia S.p.A., Vignate (MI) - Italy